A DETACHED

RAIDER

Also by Ana Night

A DETACHED

RAIDER

THE BLACK RAIDERS

ANA NIGHT

A Detached Raider

ISBN: 978-1-97701-049-0

Digital ISBN: 978-1-38617-295-6

ASIN: B077G51M5N

Second edition, April 2020

To Eric, thank you for not only putting up with me and all those 'spatial relationships,' but also for your immense help and guidance. I wouldn't be where I am right now, and this book wouldn't be what it has become, if it wasn't for you.

Thank you, Lindsey, for reminding me why I started this book in the first place and for sharing my love for Cade and his craziness. I'm not sure when or even *if* I would've returned to this book if it hadn't been for you.

To my family who, even if they don't always understand, support and believe in me no matter what. Thank you.

Chapter One

Cade

"WOULD THE defendant please rise." The emphatic voice of the judge resonated through the courtroom, his eyes narrowing on the man in the navy-blue suit, now standing in front of him. "Mr. Tully, do you have anything to say before the sentence is entered into the record?"

"No, Your Honor," the defendant replied in a deflated voice. He knew exactly what was coming for him; nothing he could say would change it. Nothing would change what he'd done.

"Very well, Mr. Tully. Please remain standing." The judge looked up, scanning the room before, at last, settling his gaze on Tully.

"Elias Tully, for the murders of Janice Spencer, Jared Doyle, and Mary Coulson you will serve three life sentences. Furthermore, you will serve 20 years for the attempted murder of Detective Michael Hobbs, all of which are to run consecutively. You will now be taken to Chesapeake Detention Facility, where you will be held without the possibility of parole," he said evenly as he kept his sharp gaze on the defendant. The sound of the gavel banging bounced off the walls of the courtroom.

"Bailiffs, remove the prisoner."

The judge took a final glance around the room before pausing and giving a nod to which he received three in return, then he retired to his chambers.

"Bastard got what he deserved." A strong, Southern-accented voice sounded from the seat next to where Detective Cade Lawson slumped down in his chair.

Cade turned his head to grin at Detective Lara Samuels, the petite, strongly tempered woman who was sporting a wide smile that, frankly, freaked Cade out a tiny bit—not that he would ever admit to that—while she waved enthusiastically at the man being escorted out of the room in shackles.

"Don't we have the death penalty?" was asked in a gruff voice belonging to the very same Detective Michael Hobbs whom Tully had tried to kill.

Lara turned to the man sitting on the other side of Cade and sent him a wicked smile before saying, "Yeah, Pumpkin, we do. But that bastard's gonna rot in prison till the day he dies. In my book, that's worse than bein' put out of your misery, don't you think? He's gonna rot in a four by four cell, probably going to be someone's bitch and if not, there's always the showers. You know, if we didn't have the laws we do, gettin' what he deserves would be hanging him in a tree by his family jewels. Maybe burn him at the stake."

She gave a one-shouldered shrug when she finished. Then she simply got up, leaving her coworkers staring after her with odd expressions on their faces as she exited the room.

"Remind me not to ever piss her off. Shit, man. She's crazy. How do you do it?" The tiredness and exhaustion were clear in Mike's voice and with a look at his pale face and slumped shoulders, it was quite obvious he hadn't been sleeping and was probably in a lot of pain, too.

"What? Survive her?" Cade asked with a cheeky smile.

"Survive her? You spend all your free time with her. Forget what I said. You're the crazy one," Mike huffed out with a poor resemblance of a laugh.

"Gee thanks." Cade pulled a face at Mike, a smile breaking through when he managed to draw out another laugh from his friend.

"Come on Hobbs, let's get the hell outta here. You look like you're about to fall on your face, and you know I'll just laugh at you if you do," Cade said. He winked at Mike as he stood and offered a hand to help him up.

"Screw you, Lawson," Mike retaliated in an almost pathetic voice. He took his hand and let Cade pull him out of his chair. Cade let out a chuckle before putting his shoulder under the other man's arm and, more or less, towed him out of the courtroom.

"You wish," Cade said in a mock serious voice, getting a snort combined with an eye roll in return. They both wore smiles on their faces as they made their way to the parking garage. Hobbs stayed quiet, making it possible for all those thoughts Cade held down during the court session to spring free and fill his mind.

Mike had almost died. The bullet Tully put in him traveled almost to his heart. Had Lara found them just a minute later, he might not have made it. Elias Tully was an accountant who'd suddenly killed one of his coworkers. Before they managed to get to him, he'd killed another coworker and her boyfriend. They still didn't know why, and it was driving him nuts. You didn't just go all murderous without a reason.

So even with Mike surviving and recuperating it'd been a hell of a few months. What with Lara going bat-shit crazy, cursing everyone up and down, and threatening to put Tully six feet under at least five times a day for bestowing her all that extra paperwork when he'd put her partner in the hospital. Cade knew her well enough to know paperwork had nothing to do with her wanting to put Tully down.

Mike had been home for one week now—well, home as in forced to move in with Lara and her daughter until he'd be able to care for himself. Lara wasn't one to take no for an answer. In three more weeks, Mike would be in his own apartment and in another three after that, he'd be back at the station, too.

"To the station?" Cade asked after they were both situated in his car.

"To the station," Mike confirmed with a swirl of his finger. After buckling in, he leaned his head back and closed his eyes.

"You doing okay, Mikey?" Cade asked after taking a right turn out of the parking garage.

Though Cade liked having Lara as his partner again, he really just wanted things to go back to normal. Or as normal as they could get.

"Fine. Think I'm just getting old," Mike replied with a pout on his lips and his eyelashes batting away—obviously looking for flatter of some sort.

Cade snorted.

"You're thirty-five," Cade exclaimed with an affronted puff of air.

"Don't say it out loud, dumbass," Mike grumbled.

Cade snorted as he turned onto the highway and sped up. "What? If I say it, it comes true? Isn't that the other way around; you say it and it doesn't come true, like wishes?"

"Shut up. I don't know what I'm saying, I'm heavily sedated, thanks to Lara."

"She didn't give you a choice, did she?"

Well, that wasn't actually a question, since there could only be one answer to that and they both knew it.

"She can make the devil do her bidding," Mike said with such obvious belief that Cade couldn't help the laughter bursting from him.

"Wouldn't surprise me if she did," Cade said with a small shake of his head, a smile on his face and gratitude filling him, not only for Mike surviving and recovering, but for having Mike and Lara in his life and not to forget Morgan, Lara's daughter. They may not be his family by blood, but they sure as hell were by everything else. He was still smiling when he drove into Baltimore Police Department's parking garage.

When Cade and Mike stepped out of the elevator on the floor of the homicide division, they were met by hoots and claps.

"Good luck, mate," Cade said to Mike.

Cade shook his head, albeit with a smile on his lips, slapped Mike on the back and left him to get torn apart by the gathering horde of wild animals aka their coworkers. It was Mike's first time back since the murder attempt and Tully was just sentenced, so it was to be expected that their fellow detectives would be overjoyed to see him. Or perhaps they were just glad to have a legitimate reason to be obnoxious.

Cade walked through the open door to his, Lara, and Mike's combined office and after discarding his jacket and gun, dumped himself in his chair with a tired sigh. He leaned back and closed his eyes, enjoying the peace and calm since he was alone for once. It didn't last more than half an hour.

"Darlin', when is the last time you slept? You look worse than Mikey, which kinda says it all, don' it?" Lara said first thing when she walked into their office and found Cade slumped over his desk, several chocolate wrappers lying around him.

Cade groaned as he lifted his head slightly to look accusingly up at her. His head felt heavy from the headache he was sporting after too many days with too little sleep. He needed coffee—bad, and lots of chocolate. Chocolate could fix everything; that's what his grandma told him when he was five and he'd lived by it ever since. It was the second religion he'd ever been introduced to and the only one he ever indulged.

"I don't remember what sleep is," he answered in a rough voice, plagued by what little sleep he'd just gotten.

Lara cocked an eyebrow at him before opening her mouth to say something just to be cut off.

"Lawson!" The captain's voice boomed through the office. He probably hadn't even gotten out of his own chair to call for him. Bastard.

"Good luck, darlin'," Lara drawled and winked at him before twirling her chair around and diving back into her work.

"Bite me," he mumbled to her back.

"I heard that, and don't think I won't," Lara yelled after him, making him fight a smile.

Yeah, they were bantering like a bunch of high school kids and he liked it. He liked it a lot. It took some of the seriousness out of their occupation. Besides, it felt like it used to be around his siblings and cousins.

He mentally shook his head to clear any of that sort of thoughts from entering his mind and knocked twice on Captain Morris' open door.

"Sir?"

"Close the door, Lawson," the captain said without taking his eyes away from the papers he was shuffling around on his desk.

Cade did as he was told and sat down in one of the plush chairs on the other side of the captain's desk. He looked around at the pictures of smiling people while he waited for the captain to begin. A few formal photos mixed with a variety of Morris' kids and wife decorated the otherwise plain walls. Cade had met the wife, Susan, on an occasion or two. She'd been a street cop for years until she got pregnant with their first girl and then she'd chosen to be a housewife. That was as much as Cade really knew about her. They had four girls, all taking after their beautiful mother. Morris was going to have a hell of a good time running guys off with his AK-47. Yeah, no petty rifle for this Kentuckian.

"You heard 'bout the Executioner?" Morris finally asked, looking up at Cade over his reading glasses.

"The serial down in Fairfax?" Cade asked, a frown settling between his brows.

Shit, the whole department had heard about the serial killer who seemed to concentrate on rapists and pedophiles. Some even—discreetly, of course—cheered him on. Himself included.

"Yep. Except he ain't down in Virginia no more," Captain Morris said pointedly, an eyebrow cocked.

"He's in Baltimore?" Cade asked in a low voice after swallowing the lump in his throat. This wasn't good.

"Well, his latest victim sure is," the captain grumbled, not sounding pleased with the news himself. "We're joining forces with Fairfax PD?"

Working with others in this line of work almost always ended badly, one way or the other, which Cade found incredibly stupid and just plain unnecessary. They were trying to solve murders and catch killers, for Christ's sake. At least it wasn't the feds. Now that wouldn't have gone over very well.

"Sure are, and I've taken the liberty of offering you up on a silver platter," Morris said with what Cade thought to be a pleased smile but it was pretty hard to see with the full beard the man was sporting.

"Captain," Cade said. "You're downright evil."

Cade crossed his arms and scowled at him, which Morris ignored. Honestly, it was why Cade liked the man so much; he didn't take shit from anyone. But he stood up for his guys, always. Cade knew he could count on him no matter what, not that it stopped either of them from busting each other's balls.

"I sure like to think so. Now, get your witty ass out of my office and down to the crime scene. The detective from Fairfax who's working the case will meet you there, and he should have the case files with him. The rest you can get from Claire," Morris said. He returned to the papers on his desk, clearly dismissing Cade, who grumbled to himself all the way to the office where he sat down in his chair and, with a loud sigh, laid his head on the desk, on top of the pile of paperwork he was yet to get done.

"That bad, huh?"

He took in a deep breath before lifting his head to put his more than likely, bloodshot eyes on the red-haired devil who was, as usual, grinning down at him. He scrunched his nose up at her.

"Don't you have some paperwork to do, Lara?"

She snorted and sent him a glare before lifting herself up on his desk gracefully. You couldn't tell she'd just turned forty-two. She leaned forward, resting her elbows on her thighs.

"What's wrong, darlin'?"

She was using her soothing-mom-voice on him.

"The captain just offered me up on a silver platter to FCPD," he whined, genuinely not caring how pathetic he sounded. He was damn tired. He'd already pulled an all-nighter what with court this morning.

Lara wrinkled her nose in distaste. "Seriously?"

"Those were his words," Cade said with a pout, making his eyes big to use his best puppy dog expression on her. Unfortunately, she'd developed immunity sometime in the three years they'd worked together. She was one of the few, right up there with his grandma and youngest sister. Lara was actually a lot like both of them. Fiercely protective, but neither of them was the hugging type. They were the kick-your-fucking-ass-if-you-whine kinda girls.

"Good luck with that, darlin'," Lara said and patted him on the top of his head before getting off his desk and walking over to her own.

Cade let out another sigh before standing and pulling his jacket from the back of his chair. He only stopped at Claire, the Captain's assistant's desk to get the address before making his way to the elevator. He was betting today was going to be a fucking blast.

Cole

After ducking under the yellow tape and having to show his badge at least three times, Detective Cole Banks walked through what looked like a much-loved home of four—if the pictures on the walls were any indication—with those annoying blue shoe covers on, giving away his position with the squeaky noises they made, and finally, he stepped through the doorway into the main bedroom.

The two forensic scientists—one spraying luminol over the floor and the other dusting the headboard on the bed for fingerprints—both looked up when they heard him enter.

"Detective," the one crouching on the floor said as the other offered a nod of his head before returning to his dusting.

Cole greeted them and then took his time to look around the room. The body had already been taken away since it was several hours ago when the police were called out. He got his phone call the second someone found a connection between this murder and the case he was working on.

Blood was coloring the otherwise white cotton sheets, some of it having dripped down the sides, pooling on the floor. The drab, gray curtains were pulled closed, the closet untouched, as usual. The white dresser opposite the bed had been opened to take out four ties. They would only find the victim's prints and DNA in there, though. The killer was a smart-ass who, unfortunately, knew what he was doing.

Nothing Cole hadn't seen before. Nothing new at least. The only thing that might work in his favor was that the perp had moved his business elsewhere and therefore might mess up this time around. Otherwise, they weren't going to catch the guy via DNA. But something caused him to leave his comfort zone. Something Cole needed to find and exploit.

After taking a last glance around the room, he made his way back outside where he surveyed the law enforcement officers present. He spotted two guys in uniform who didn't seem to be doing anything but stand to the side while everyone else was working. He started toward them.

"Officers," he said when he was within hearing range.

The two cops turned to look at Cole with surprise showing in the young one's eyes and suspicion in the older ones. Both of them took a good, long look at him while waiting for him to introduce himself. Cole held his ground and raised an inquiring eyebrow at them. His badge was visible at his waistband, and they had to at least have noticed his car's plates showing it was from Virginia. The older one, with what seemed to have been blonde hair once upon a time but was now almost completely white, cleared his throat and took a step closer to Cole.

"I'm Officer Ted Blanchard and my trainee here is Officer Gerard Ford," the cop said and gestured to the man to his right. Ford smiled up at Cole, his young face devoid of the strain and dark memories covering the much older cop's face. He couldn't have been able to drink legally for more than a year or two. Hell. He shouldn't judge. He'd only been seventeen when he'd joined the Marine Corps. His father had been only too happy to finally be rid of him. That went for both of them.

"Detective Banks. Fairfax County PD," Cole said as he shook Blanchard's hand. The older man's handshake was firm. He liked that about him.

"Fairfax? So this *is* that serial killer then?" Ford asked.

Ford was definitely wet behind the ears and as eager as a puppy being shown its leash. Cole didn't recall ever being like that himself. The only deaths he saw were brutal ones.

"I wouldn't be here if it wasn't."

Cole didn't elaborate on it, which seemed to subdue Ford a bit. Thankfully. Cole gestured toward the house and the crime scene, asking, "You were first on scene, right? You mind walking me through it?"

"Sure. The call came in at 7:24 this morning. The wife's the one who found him. We were first on the scene at 7:29. Found the wife sitting on the floor by the bed," Officer Blanchard said before going on to tell him what he already knew.

"The victim was lying naked in the bed, tied to the bedposts with ties around ankles and wrists. One gunshot wound to the lower torso. He was cold when we got here," Blanchard finished just as a silver-gray sedan pulled up to the curb and a grimace crossed Ford's face as he noticed the car.

"Lawson's here. Better hope he didn't bring the She-Devil with him."

Cole raised an eyebrow at him before returning his gaze to the car. It was an older model, but it looked like she was kept quite well.

"She's scary, man," Ford said. "You should stay outta her way. Shit, if we hadn't been with her at the time Hobbs was found, I'm sure she would've taken the bastard who hurt him apart. I think she knows more cuss words than the criminals she puts behind bars, too. She's one tough lady, that one."

Ford's awe and apparently, reasoned fear, was evident in his voice but Cole ceased to pay attention as soon as the driver's door opened. The man steeping out made Cole's eyes widen. His sturdy jawline was covered in two-day-old stubble, his light complexion making it look darker while his ruffled blonde hair was falling over his eyes, making it impossible for Cole to see what color they were. His nose was straight and below it lay luscious lips. Lips he shouldn't be thinking about, much less keep looking at.

Cole tore his eyes away with as much finesse as he could muster. He redirected his gaze to the dark gray suit jacket that was hanging open, making it possible to get a good look at the brown leather holster only just showing the silver handle of the man's gun. He moved his gaze from the gun to the light blue, almost white dress shirt. The top buttons were left unfastened. No tie. He looked to be five-eleven pushing six feet tall. He was lean but seemed to be in good shape. And even though he looked like he hadn't slept for several days, he had a calm and serene air around him. An easy smile on his face.

"Ted. Gerry," the man said with a nod and a smile in their direction as he walked up to Cole. "I take it you're the detective from FCPD?"

Up close, Cole noted that the other detective's eyes were a piercing dark blue still partly covered by his unruly hair.

"Cole Banks," he said and held out his hand for the other man to shake.

"Cade Lawson," the man said in a tranquil voice as his hand enveloped Cole's. The fact that Cole found himself not wanting to let go made him drop the other man's hand almost immediately. Lawson raised a brow at him but thankfully turned to Blanchard and Ford.

"Who got the call?" Lawson asked.

"Tanner. He's at the station with the wife," Ford answered.

Lawson nodded and said his goodbyes to the officers before gesturing Cole toward the house. They were almost at the bedroom when Lawson asked, "So, what've we got?"

"Chris Henway. Thirty-four. Married. Father of two. Wife found him this morning," Cole said.

"Do we know where the wife was and why she came home at, what, seven in the morning?" Lawson asked while looking around and taking in the crime scene.

"Not yet."

"Well, that's one explanation I'm looking forward to."

Cole nodded his agreement shortly. He took an extra look around, hoping to see something he might've missed before, but he didn't feel optimistic about it.

"You sure this is your guy?" Lawson suddenly asked.

Are you fucking kidding me?

The look on his face must've said it all as Lawson stammered out, "I wasn't saying... I didn't mean..." Cade shook his head and ran a hand through his hair before asking, "Your guy only targets pedophiles and such, right?"

"So far," Cole's voice sounded strict and a bit too hard to his own ears. He didn't like being questioned.

"Okay. So, was this guy a pedophile?"

They always were.

"Looks that way," Cole said.

He started toward the exit, wanting to interrogate the wife as soon as possible. It'd already been hours and memories often faded fast.

"It *looks* that way?"

Shit, was this guy going to second guess every damn word he said?

"Yes," Cole ground out between clenched teeth. Why was he letting this little shit get to him? He gave himself a mental slap on the head and let out a breath to calm down just when the bastard made a noise that sounded suspiciously like a snort. Cole turned on his heels to glare down at the man who was squinting up at him.

"Do we have a problem, Detective Lawson?"

"Sure, we have a problem, if you're not gonna do your damned job."

Cole took a step closer, cocking his head to the side. "And what exactly is it you think I'm not doing?"

"How about looking for evidence instead of playing Mr. Know-it-all?" Lawson crossed his arms over his chest and tried to stare Cole down; he was in tough luck being three inches shorter than Cole. He would've laughed if anger wasn't surging through his veins. Who the fuck did this guy think he was? Who the fuck was Lawson to judge him?

Cole used his size to back the other man against the wall. Lawson glared up at him. Cole put a hand on either side of Lawson's head and leaned in close to say in a low voice, "Why don't you stay the fuck out of my way and when I'm done here you can go back to being Mr. By-the-book."

The little bastard had balls. He kept his chin high and his eyes burrowed into Cole's as he said, "Do your job, and I'll do mine."

He hated being attracted to Lawson. He knew it made him come off rougher than usual. He liked that the guy had spirit, but he needed to keep him at arm's length.

"Stay out of my way."

Cole kept staring into Lawson's eyes, willing the other man into submission like he would a dog. It didn't take long before Cade's eyes closed. Cole couldn't help following the movement which led him to Lawson's mouth as he bit down on his lush bottom lip. Cole jerked away when he felt a stirring in his body.

"Let's go," Cole commanded and watched in astonishment as the other man opened his sparkling blue eyes and smiled up at him before practically bouncing out the door.

What. The. Fuck?

He felt completely baffled as he followed Lawson out of the house and onto the lawn where the other man stopped and looked over his shoulder at Cole.

"Do you know the way to the station? Or you can just follow me. Where's your car?"

He just stared at Lawson who frowned up at him before turning back around to look for Cole's car. It didn't take long for him to find it.

"The Chevy's yours? What year is it?"

"Sixty-nine." He was surprised he got the words out.

"Wow. She's a real beauty."

"Thanks."

"Just follow me," Lawson said with a smile before turning and starting toward his car. Cole hated he now knew exactly what the man smelled like; a subtle scent of cologne—lavender or something—and coffee.

Cole shook his head and headed toward his baby. She was all sleek lines, smooth leather, and horsepower. She drove like a dream. The only way he could possibly love her more was if she sprouted wings. God, he missed flying.

He got in, closing the door after himself, and just sat there for a moment, breathing. When Lawson pulled out, he started the car and followed. He spent the entire ride trying not to think about the other detective. He wasn't near successful.

He let out a sigh of relief when Lawson took a turn into a parking garage. He followed, parking right next to him, and got out to follow him to an elevator located in the corner of the parking garage. Lawson pushed the button and they stood there, waiting in silence as it slowly descended.

After the short trip up to the third floor, Lawson turned and walked backwards out of the elevator, throwing his arms wide. "Welcome to the Homicide Investigation Division Headquarters of Baltimore PD or as us locals like to call it; the *hit*-quarters."

With a grin, Lawson turned around and waved him along. Cole spied a kitchen and the toilets to his left before following Lawson to the right down a short corridor which led into a bigger room. Desks were situated to the right and there were two offices to the left. The room was almost empty except for them and one guy sitting at a desk, typing on his keyboard like crazy. Lawson headed straight for him.

"Tanner."

"I was wonderin' when you'd show up," the guy said as he swiveled in his chair, turning to face them. His brown hair was gelled back from his face, his dark brown eyes framed in by his black glasses. He had a light tan which stood out against his white shirt. His jaw was clean-shaven, laugh lines showing as he grinned up at Lawson before turning his attention to Cole. He looked Cole over from top to bottom, assessing him.

"Shawn, this is Detective Cole Banks. Banks, meet Detective Shawn Tanner." Lawson gestured between them as Tanner got out of his chair to shake Cole's hand.

"Nice to meet you."

"You, too," Cole said while shaking his hand, the ring on Tanner's finger cold against his skin and Cole almost cursed out loud when nothing happened like it did with Lawson. This guy was his fucking type and he felt nothing?

"So?" Lawson asked, making Cole tamp down on his inward cursing of himself and put his focus back on Tanner.

"Well, it was pretty clear to me, ya know? My parents live down in Fairfax and they didn't stop talkin' 'bout this guy last time I was there, and we've all heard 'bout 'the serial down in Fairfax', but I wouldn't't've called if I wasn't sure. I first made a call to someone I know in SVU and the vic is on the Sex Offender Registry."

"On what charges?" Cole asked.

"Statutory rape. I've got the case files for ya and I was just 'bout to look up the victim."

"Great. Thanks. Can you have it ready for us when we're done?" Lawson asked.

Tanner nodded. "Yeah. You going to interview the wife?"

"We are. See ya in a bit, Tanner," Lawson said with a wave of his hand before he bounced out of the room. So, that might be a bit of an exaggeration, but Cole could just imagine the man skipping down the halls. He just had that way about him. Crazy all around.

"Anything else, detective?" Tanner asked, looking over his shoulder when Cole didn't leave.

"Your contact in SVU?" he prompted with the raise of an eyebrow.

"Ah. Detective Callie Thompson."

With a dip of his chin, Cole turned and made his way toward Lawson who was waiting for him with his arms crossed and a questioning brow raised. Cole stopped in front of the man, clenching his jaw as he fought the urge to let his eyes roam over his body. He needed to quench this attraction.

"You ready?"

Cole grumbled an answer which only made Lawson grin at him before he turned around and led them out of the room. Cole's eyes dropped to the ass in front of him and he nearly let a groan escape. Quench it. Crush it. Whatever. He needed to do it and fast, otherwise, this case was going to drive him even more crazy than he already was.

Chapter Two

Cole

"MRS. HENWAY. Please, tell us what happened this morning," Lawson said, while Cole planted himself in the far corner from them both to be able to observe her—and, he belatedly admitted to himself, to observe Lawson as well—and leaned back against the wall with his arms crossed. He kept his expression neutral as he watched Lawson try to get some answers out of the sobbing woman. There was just something about Lawson that seemed to make people trust him. Everyone but himself, of course.

Cole turned his focus on Mrs. Henway who was answering Lawson's questions with a shaky voice. She wore clothes from the station, her own taken by the BPD Crime Lab to be processed because she'd gotten blood on it.

"I don't know what time I was there. It was after seven, but you can check with the nine-one-one call, right?"

Lawson gave a confirming nod and she continued.

"I went into the kitchen first, put my purse and keys on the counter. Then I went into the bedroom—" she sniffed, tears filling her eyes. Lawson pushed a box of Kleenex toward her which she took with a small smile. Her hands were shaking, and she didn't get to pull out a tissue before she started sobbing.

"He wasn't supposed to be there. He wasn't supposed to be there," she said.

"Where was he supposed to be?" When she didn't seem to hear him, Lawson put a hand over hers, drawing her attention back to him. "Where was he supposed to be, Natalia?"

"I…" she shook her head, closing her eyes briefly before going on. Something definitely wasn't right. She hadn't said it as he wasn't supposed to be there like he shouldn't be dead, but more like he wasn't supposed to be there because she made sure he wasn't.

"The kids and I were at my sister's place. Chris had to work twelve-hour shifts, three days in a row and he usually doesn't like to have anyone disturb him when he's home. That's why we always stay with my sister; so he can get some sleep."

"Alright. You're doing good, Natalia. Do you mind writing down your sister's number and address for us?"

She took the pen and paper Lawson gave her and quickly scribbled down on it. They would have to check her alibi with her sister. There was still something that wasn't quite right, though.

"Was the front door open when you got there?" Cole asked.

"No, I used my keys to unlock it. I remember that."

Lawson patted her hand, an understanding smile on his face. Lawson's eyes caught Cole's. He pushed off the wall and placed himself behind Lawson's chair to be able to meet Mrs. Henway's gaze and to keep those fucking blue eyes off him.

"Why did you come home this morning?" Cole asked.

She seemed taken aback by his question for a few seconds, then she let out a breath and more or less collapsed in her chair. She was watching her owns hands, her voice low when she finally spoke.

"I was stupid, you know? I just wanted them to have a home. I married him after two months. That was six months ago. He seemed to love me, to love the kids and it gave them a home and with his job, a steady income."

"What happened?"

"I found out about Tommy."

Cole cocked his head to the side with a frown. "Who's Tommy?"

He had an inkling who Tommy was, and it wasn't a good one. Mrs. Henway looked more heartbroken now than before.

"He's someone Chris hurt. I got a letter from him. That poor boy. He was so brave."

"How so?"

"He wrote me the most honest and kindest letter. He told me about Chris' record. I read what Chris did to that boy. It scared the hell out of me. I was there to pack our things. I was going to leave him."

"We're going to need that letter," Cole said.

She nodded and agreed to deliver it.

"I'm sorry to say this, but you need to take your kids to a doctor. They need to get checked for… we need to make sure he didn't touch them or hurt them in any way," Cade said.

Her tears started again but this time it was out of fear and not of relief as Cole reckoned the earlier ones must have been.

"I just wanted them to have a home," she whispered.

"A house isn't a home. A home is where the people you love are. People who would never hurt you," Cole said in a rough voice. He'd learned that the hard way. But, fuck, was it ever the truth.

They left her with a uniform to make sure she got home to her sister alright and as soon as the door to the interrogations room closed behind them, Lawson turned a glare on him.

"You didn't need to say that. She's in a rough place already. She just realized that her husband—who she found murdered—might have molested her kids. Have some respect."

"She doesn't deserve my respect," Cole said and turned around. He walked back to Tanner's desk, Lawson following close behind him. He could feel Lawson glare at his back the whole way.

"The rape victim wouldn't happen to be a Tommy would it?" Cole asked, startling Tanner who'd been staring at something on his screen. He quickly recovered and turned a smile their way.

"Sure is. Thomas Carlisle Lowe. Twenty-four. He was fostered by the Henways for a few years when he was a kid. He has an apartment with a Sandra Levine by Patterson Park—I've got the address for ya—and he works in a construction firm as an electrician. I already called and he's on a job. I wrote the address down. It's 'round here somewhere," Tanner said as he flipped through the case files lying on his desk. He picked up a file, turned it upside down and started shaking it until a yellow legal pad fell out. "Tricky little bastards. Always hidin' around."

Cade huffed, snatching the paper from him and then turning on his heels to walk toward the elevator. He didn't bother waiting for Cole.

"Uh oh, you're in trouble," Tanner sang.

"Shampoo, really?"

Tanner looked surprised that he'd recognized the song. But with as many times as he'd had to endure it, it was now seared into his memory.

"You know them?"

"I have goddaughters," Cole muttered. He was only biding his time before he needed to catch up with Lawson. With the way his body continued to react to the man, he didn't want to spend too much time close to him.

"They're a 90's duo," Tanner said and tried to hide a smile but failed.

"They were in St. Trinian's and that's from 2007."

Tanner's smile went from almost hidden to full-blown with teeth showing.

"You've got to be kidding me," Tanner said, shaking his head. "You watch girly movies?"

Cole couldn't help himself as he clamped a hand down on Tanner's shoulder, squeezing tightly and bending down to say in a soft voice, "I do. I also know a lot of different ways to make someone disappear if they decide to tell people about it."

He enjoyed watching the smile on Tanner's face dim. Obviously, the guy didn't know he was kidding. Which was just as well. He'd gladly take a ripping about his knowledge of *girly movies* because if his goddaughters asked him to watch them with him, he'd happily wear a dress and a tiara while doing it. But he didn't like to mix his private life with his work.

He left Tanner, feeling just a bit better and took the elevator down to the parking garage. He found Lawson leaning against the Camaro with a sour look on his face. Either the guy didn't want to spend money on gas, or he knew Cole hated not being the one driving. Cole cursed himself. Internally of course. No need to let the bastard know he got on his nerves. Lawson was finally silent, but something told Cole that that was going to bite him in the ass at some point. Lawson was probably plotting his demise or something. It was the *or something* which made him curse himself. Why did he have to be attracted to this guy?

He admitted to himself the whole sulky thing Lawson had going on was cute. Which made him question his sanity, because he didn't do cute.

He unlocked the car and got in. Lawson put his seatbelt on, crossed his arms over his chest and turned to look out the window. Cole resigned himself to enjoying their silent ride as he drove to the construction site.

He barely managed to put the car into park before Lawson was out the door and trotting toward the building. Cole let out a sigh before getting out and following him. A brand new twelve story building stood tall in front of him. It didn't look like much more needed to get done on the outside.

When he caught up to Lawson, he was just inside the front door of the building, talking to a man wearing a white hard hat. The man pointed them to where a man was crouched down in a corner, fiddling with a lot of wires and then hurried to get back to work. Lawson indicated for Cole to follow.

"Thomas Lowe?"

Brown eyes darted up and widened when they landed on them. The young man put down the tools and wires he'd been holding and slowly straightened. He looked like a deer caught in the headlights.

"I'm Detective Lawson, that's Detective Banks. We need to talk to you about Chris Henway."

The guy visibly paled. But if it was because Henway was the one who'd molested him or because he was the guy he'd just killed, well, that's what they were there to find out.

"Not here. I can't—Not here," the kid stammered out.

"Alright. Is there somewhere we can talk?"

Thomas nodded and led them toward a door opposite the one they'd entered through. They followed him down a hallway and into a smaller room with a door, which Cole closed behind them. There was a table, a fridge, and a few chairs scattered around. Probably the worker's breakroom Lawson and Lowe sat down. Cole decided to remain standing, his back against the wall.

"What can I help you with?"

"Chris Henway was murdered last night," Lawson said.

Lowe stared at them with his big brown eyes. He seemed dumbfounded by Lawson's words. Cole cleared his throat, getting Lowe's attention.

"Where were you last night between midnight and 8 am?"

Lowe frowned at him but didn't hesitate to answer. "At home. In bed, and yes, my girlfriend can confirm that."

"Do you know where she is at the moment?"

"She's at work."

"We're gonna need you to write down her work address. She'll need to confirm your alibi." Lawson pushed his writing pad and a pencil across the table. Lowe took the pencil and started writing with shaking hands. When he was done, he slid it back and, after a quick glance, Lawson ripped the page off and stuffed it into his pocket.

"You were in foster care at the Henway's, correct?" Cole asked, already knowing the answer.

A shadow passed over Lowe's eyes. "Yeah."

"Please, tell us what happened."

Lowe closed his eyes tightly, his fingers grasping the tabletop in a hard grip, turning them white. He looked like he might pass out.

"I was nine when I got to the Henway's. Chris was twenty-one and off to college, so he didn't come home until I'd been with his parents for five months and had turned ten. It started the day he returned after graduating. I remember his eyes that night; the way they darkened when he looked at me. The way he... He came to my room that night and he kept on coming until I turned twelve. No one noticed for two years. He changed me. He made me afraid of my own shadow. No one even cared to ask me if I was alright.

"His aunt found out. Aunt Chrissy. She lived in Europe for a few years, but then she moved back. She caught him one night as he was... you know what. She was raped when she was younger, so she went ballistic. She's the only reason the case made it to court. She was the only one on my side. He got two years. He was out after fifteen months and now he can just keep on doing whatever he wants. Like nothing happened."

He knew the kid was telling the truth but that didn't mean he hadn't killed Henway. From the looks of it, it would make sense if the kid was the killer. Them living this close to each other when neither were from this state was one hell of a coincidence and he didn't believe in coincidences.

"Have you been in contact with Chris Henway's wife?" Cole asked.

"Yes."

"What kind of contact?"

"I had an envelope delivered to her." Lowe shrugged, trying to look unaffected, but they could both see straight through him. The kid was scared. But of what, he didn't know.

"Where?"

"Where she works."

Jesus, did they have to pull everything out of the kid now?

Lawson looked up from his writing pad. "What was in the envelope?"

"A letter and Henway's pages from the Sex Offender Registry," Thomas said.

"When was this?"

Apparently, Lawson had more patience than Cole.

"Two weeks ago."

"Then what happened?"

"She called and wanted to meet."

"Did you?"

The kid shook his head, his bangs falling into his eyes. "No. I told her she could go to SVU or the police station or whatever. She's his wife; surely she can get his record pulled."

He didn't sound too sure, though.

"Have you otherwise been in contact with her or Chris Henway?"

Thomas shook his head vigorously. "No. No, I haven't been in contact with him. Are you… Are you sure he's dead?"

Cole raised a brow at Lowe and said, "Yes. Very sure."

Thomas stared at them with wide eyes for a full twenty seconds before he collapsed in on himself, folding over and heaving for breath.

"Give us a minute," Lawson said to Cole. His eyes were hard as they bore into Cole's. He nodded and left them to it. He hated when people got emotional anyway. The things people complained about, cried over, were nothing when you'd been to war.

Cade

As soon as Cole closed the door behind himself, the tears started to fall. He just kept an eye on Tommy as he let it all loose. It was heartbreaking to watch but at least he knew the kid was safe from Chris Henway.

"It's okay to be relieved. He hurt you and now he's gone," Cade said.

"He's ruined so much," Tommy gasped out between breaths.

"I know. But he can't hurt you anymore."

Big brown eyes met his, a speck of hope shining in them. "Is he really gone?"

Cade knew that feeling all too well.

"Yes," Cade reassured him.

"Thank you," Tommy whispered.

"It's alright, kid."

"I know this might sound horrible, but when you find out who did it, I want to thank that person. There are a lot of people safer because of them."

"Don't worry. I know what you mean."

He wouldn't be sharing this with Banks. It was between him and Tommy, and the murderer when they found him. Because he didn't believe for a second this boy was a killer. He was hiding something, sure, but he hadn't killed anyone.

Tommy looked torn between relief and concern as he met Cade's gaze. "Are Natalia and the kids okay?"

"They're alright."

The kid let out a sigh, relief stark on his face. Tommy's hands were shaking as he ran his fingers through his hair. Cade was starting to worry about him. "Do you need us to take you home?"

"No, I... I think I'll stay and work. It'll help clear my head."

"Still. It's a lot to take in."

Tommy's deep brown sorrowful eyes met his.

"Here," Cade said and laid one of his business cards on the table in front of Tommy. "Call if you need anything."

Tommy nodded his head, folding his fingers around the card.

"Come down to the police station tomorrow so you can give a written statement. The address is on my card."

"Okay."

Cade felt bad leaving him just then, but he knew he couldn't stay. He had a murderer to find. He walked outside to find the car running and Banks waiting for him, looking like someone had taken a piss on him. He got in, buckled up and took out his phone. He typed Lowe's girlfriend's work address into his phone's GPS and put it on the phone mount on the dashboard.

Banks made a point of ignoring him as he drove. Not that he truly cared; it gave him an opportunity to study the other man. His brows furrowed and his jaw clenched like he was concentrating really hard or pondering over something. His green eyes were ever vigilant, scanning the road and observing everything around them covertly. Cade didn't doubt the man knew he was being watched. He wasn't the kind of man you could sneak up on. Didn't mean Cade wouldn't try. He was named after a rebel for a reason. He tended to want to do the opposite of what was probably safe for him. He wanted to break down Banks' defenses. As dangerous as it was. It just appealed to him on a whole other level.

Cade shook his head slightly, knowing full well he was being watched in return. He couldn't be caught off guard with this man. Banks would see him as a weakness and for some reason, Cade didn't want to let him down. He didn't want to be seen as weak to this man. Cade let his gaze wander over Bank's jawline and found himself appreciating the stubble covering it. He shouldn't be attracted to this man. But damn, was that a feat. He was hot, in his own dark, dangerous, and rugged way. Like the way Banks' eyes would darken whenever he looked at Cade. There were a lot of secrets in those eyes and Cade wanted to uncover every last one.

Cole

The address they'd gotten was for a clothing store. Looked like something fancy and expensive. He got out of the car, Lawson right behind him. He'd tried hard to ignore the man as he'd been driving. Not that he'd succeeded when he'd found he was being watched closely in return.

They walked into the store. It was bigger than he'd thought it would be. A blonde-haired girl wearing a store uniform walked toward the checkout counter in front of them, her arms loaded with clothes and she had a young woman in tow. Her nametag said Sandra, so Cole steered toward her. She came to a halt when she noticed them approaching.

"Sandra Levine?" Cole asked.

They both showed their badges to her. She put down the clothes, called on a coworker to take over her customer and moved out from behind the counter. She gestured for them to follow her a few feet away before she turned a too sweet smile on them.

"What can I do for you, officers?"

"Detectives. Can you tell us where you were between Tuesday night the twenty-third and Wednesday, the twenty-fourth?" Cole asked.

"Um. I was at work from nine a.m. to nine p.m. and then I went straight home and to bed at around 11 pm with my boyfriend," she said.

That was quite a late work day. They would have to look into that.

"Is this about Chris Henway? I saw it on the news," she said.

So, Lowe hadn't called her? He kept his facial expression neutral and noticed Lawson doing the same. Lawson glanced at him before answering her.

"It's concerning his murder."

"Murder?"

He cocked an eyebrow at her and watched as realization dawned on her face.

"You think—Jesus. Tommy didn't do anything. He wouldn't hurt a fly. A month ago, he found someone trying to hurt a cat and he saved her, took her to the vet and nursed her back to health. She rarely leaves his side when he's home. He even catches the spiders to let them outside instead of killing them and he's afraid of them."

"So, because he's afraid of spiders, you don't think he could have killed the man who molested him?" Cole asked.

She narrowed her eyes at him, propping her hands on her hips. Defiance radiated from her. "He didn't do it. Besides, he was with me. He couldn't have done it."

"We're going to need a written statement of that."

"Fine," she said.

Lawson pulled out a card from the inner pocket in his jacket and held it out for her to take. "Come down to the station as soon as you're available. The address is on the card."

She snatched the card from him and begrudgingly agreed. She was quick to get back to work and he had no problem with leaving the store. Once they were outside, Lawson walked up beside him and asked, "Did that seem like she was trying to convince herself of Tommy's innocence?"

"I think she's trying to cover her own ass. She hates that cat," Cole said.

"That's sweet, right? That he saved it."

Cole thought the unimpressed expression on his face was answer enough to that.

"Either way, it seems Tommy's a real little Doctor Dolittle," Lawson quipped.

He turned a blank stare at him. Lawson's mouth dropped open as he blinked at him with his big, blue eyes, conveying his surprise. Cole tried to ignore him, but he couldn't stand those bloody eyes on him.

"What?"

"Seriously? Haven't you seen Doctor Dolittle? Not even the one with Eddie Murphy?"

"I don't particularly care for comedies," Cole said with a frown.

"Well, what *do* you care for?"

"You shutting up."

"You've got a problem, then."

He stared down Lawson. The dumbass was still grinning at him, his eyes crinkling at the corners and, God help him, a fucking dimple showing.

"I don't shut up," Lawson said. Then he threw Cole a wink before walking on, leaving Cole standing there with his mouth gaping like an idiot.

How could he be attracted to this… this… hell, he didn't even have a word for him. He snorted, shaking himself out of his stupor. Christ.

Chapter Three

Cade

AFTER HAVING returned from questioning Miss Levine, they bought some lunch from a vendor not far from the Police station. Even though he'd assured Banks the food was delicious, he still looked at it like it might jump up and eat him. Cade watched the man with amusement as he tentatively bit into the tasty goodness. It wasn't long before a moan escaped, and he stuffed more into his mouth.

"Told ya," he said.

Banks hummed affirmatively.

They ate as they walked, both finishing before they made it back to the station. They stepped into their office to find Lara in her chair with her head resting on her arms on her desk.

"Is she... sleeping?" Banks asked in a low voice.

Cade snorted, earning a raised eyebrow and a disapproving glare from Banks.

"Not a fat chance," he told the man before turning toward Lara and yelling, "Hey She-Devil, you asleep?"

"Not a fat chance, darlin'," she answered without moving.

Cade took a step back, clutching his chest dramatically. "I must have spent too much time with you. You're picking up on my wording."

"Fuck you. I want my partner back. He rubs my feet and brings me coffee."

"He's scared of you," Cade deadpanned.

"He ought to be. If he hadn't been about to kick the bucket by the time I found him, I'd have shot him myself. Stupid ass," Lara grumbled before finally lifting her head.

Her eyes grew wide as she caught sight of Banks, then, when she raised a brow at Cade, they grew mischievous. A smile spread across her face.

"Who's the hotshot?"

Banks straightened and clasped his hands behind his back. One hand around the other wrist. His feet shoulder-width apart.

"Detective Cole Banks, Fairfax County PD, ma'am," Banks said. He looked like he'd cut himself short before he recited his badge number as well. Or saluted her.

He actually made it sound as if… hm, well, it was possible. He did seem the type. He had that dangerous, lethal, commanding air about him. Cade's new partner was likely a veteran. He should've noticed before then, but, he admitted to himself, he'd gotten distracted by green eyes and one hell of an attitude, and that body of Cole's certainly hadn't helped either.

"Your new partner, then," Lara said to Cade with one of her signature grins in place. He flipped her off. Lara knew him and therefore she also knew better than most that Mr. Dark-handsome-and-silent was just his type. Or as he would say; just the type he wasn't going to get near. For everyone's sake.

Cade turned to Banks and gestured toward Lara as he made the introductions. "New partner, meet temporary, and former partner, Lara Samuels, also known as She-Devil. I'm sure Gerry told you about her."

Lara rolled her eyes when he winked at her. Secretly, he was pretty sure she was more than content with her reputation as a hard-ass bitch. She wasn't a marine for nothing. Or a drill instructor. Damn but that woman could yell and curse, probably worse than any other good old sailor.

"So, if you weren't sleeping, what were you doing?" Cole asked Lara.

Lara smiled at him and tapped her temple. "Trying to connect dots."

They all had their own way of doing things. Back when he'd been a rookie detective and just partnered up with Lara, he'd tried her technique only to fall asleep within minutes. Safe to say, Lara hadn't been impressed and as lucky as he was, she'd left him alone, giving their coworkers plenty of opportunities to draw dicks on his face. He'd had his revenge, though. They'd never seen it coming. The homicide department and its detectives would never be as sparkling or doused in glitter as that fateful day.

"That yours?" Banks said and gestured to the whiteboard in the corner. When Lara nodded, Banks planted himself in front of it and stood there for some time, taking in everything he saw on it, before he turned back to Lara. "Did you try the foster kids?"

"The foster kids? Yes, I did. They both have solid alibis."

Cole turned back to the whiteboard, looking as if he was searching for something. He tapped a finger against one of the documents. "They were removed? Why?"

"Because he used to beat them up," Lara said.

Cade sat down in his chair, watching them intently. Sparring with Lara could get intense, but he got a feeling Banks could keep up.

"What about the bio kids? You think he didn't beat them, too?"

Banks leaned back against the wall, his attention solely on Lara as hers was on him, which was the only reason Cade cocked his head to the side and didn't bother hiding that he was ogling Banks, when the man crossed his arms over his chest, showing off his muscles through his thin T-shirt.

"I'm not sure. Nothing ever happened with them," Lara said.

"Social Services let them stay with a man they knew beat up kids?"

"Don't look at me like that. I'm not the one who fucked up."

Banks had the good sense to look apologetic. "I know. But someone did."

Cole turned his head like something just occurred to him, his brows meeting in consideration. "Or maybe they didn't."

Lara straightened in her seat, her head cocked to the side and her eyes narrowed on Banks. "What are you saying?"

"Where are the bio kids?"

"I haven't been able to locate any of them. I have nothing on them after high school."

"They just disappeared?" Cole asked.

"More or less." Lara shrugged.

"Quite disconcerting, isn't it? They aren't taken away from the home when they should be, and as soon as they leave high school they go missing?"

"None of them applied to any colleges and I haven't been able to find anything in their names. It's all one big nothing," Lara said. She picked up a folder from her desk and handed it to Banks who opened it and looked through the documents inside it.

"Interesting," he groused.

"You mean annoying," Lara said.

"That, too."

Banks didn't smile at Lara per se, but there was an amused gleam in his eyes. It made something burn hot through Cade's veins. He tried to shove it deep down.

"You know if you need—"

"In case you forgot, *Hotshot*, we've got our own case to solve. Maybe you should get on that before you start taking over my coworker's cases," Cade said. He didn't try to hide the irritation lacing his words. Banks glared at him. He put down the folder and turned on his heel, leaving Lara and Cade alone in the office.

Lara arched a brow at him. "You jealous, honey? You want your partner all to yourself?"

Cade rolled his eyes. Lara sported a knowing smile. It annoyed the shit out of him. Sometimes, he thought she might actually be able to read minds.

"Bite me," he said.

"You should be so lucky."

Curses flew out of his mouth before he could stop them, and he promptly turned around and trudged after his annoying partner.

Cole

When Lawson joined him in the parking garage, he still didn't know what he'd done to upset the man. He was just going to offer Samuels the number for someone who'd worked loads of cases like hers. Lawson looked slightly embarrassed as he got into the car. Served him right.

"Where to?" Cole asked.

"Let's see if Mrs. Henway's sister can spare us a moment to confirm her alibi."

Cole nodded and started the car, pulling out of the parking spot and with Lawson's directions, he drove them toward Johns Hopkins Hospital.

When they exited the elevator on the third floor of the cancer center, he strode right up to the front desk, holding up his badge to the nurse sitting there. "We're looking for a nurse. Camille Stevens."

The nurse squinted her eyes at him for a few seconds before she turned to one of the other nurses standing behind the desk crossing things off on her clipboard.

"Didn't Camille just take her break?"

The other nurse looked up from the clipboard, smiling when she saw them.

"Yes. She also said you guys might come by sometime and to tell you that she's in the Juice and Java Bar on the first floor if you came while she was gone," the nurse said.

"Thank you."

"You're welcome. Oh, and she likes to sit at a table in the right corner."

They took the elevator down, the serenity of the place keeping them both quiet. They followed the signs on the wall to the bar, which was only half filled with people quietly eating sandwiches and drinking coffee.

A dark-haired woman sat in the far right corner, the salad in front of her untouched. She looked up as they neared and gestured for them to sit down. There was no need for an introduction. They both sat down and stayed quiet, waiting for her to talk.

"I knew something was wrong. That man… I never liked him, but there was something else. I just had this feeling that there was something dark in him," she said.

Camille seemed lost in thought for a few moments before she said, "I tried to tell her. To get her to see reason, but she wouldn't listen."

"It's not your fault. We all make our own decisions. She made hers," Lawson said.

"Yes, and now her kids are the ones who have to live with it. They are the ones who have to pay for what she did. What she didn't do."

Her distress had Cole on edge. He hated getting this involved with people.

"My partner already told her to get them checked out, but I don't believe he touched them. In my experience, sexual predators are very specific with what they want, and your nephew and niece were too young for his taste," Cole said.

Camille scowled up at him. "Is that supposed to make me feel better?"

"What my partner is trying to say, is that there is a possibility he didn't touch them. Until you know otherwise, hang on to that," Lawson said.

Cole took out his writing pad. Better get this over with.

"Please, tell us what happened," he said.

Camille looked up, meeting his eyes. "She called me a week ago. She said she and the kids would be coming over and that there was something she needed to tell me."

She paused, glancing down at her hands.

"Go on."

"She came by before picking up the kids from school, and she told me she was leaving Chris because she found out what kind of monster he was. He was

38

still at home and she was afraid to go get their things while he was there, so we picked up the kids and they stayed the night as we originally planned. We didn't sleep that night. We just laid in my bed, holding each other while she cried."

"When did she leave?" Cole asked.

"She left at seven in the morning. I remember because she closed the front door just as my alarm went off. It takes about twenty minutes, maybe a little longer, to get there. I told her I would go with her, but she convinced me to stay with the kids instead."

"Your sister mentioned a letter?"

Her eyes softened.

"From that poor kid, yeah," she said.

"Did you ever meet or speak with him?"

"No."

"Do you know if your sister did?"

"No. If she did, she never told me about it."

"Alright. Thank you for your time, Miss Stevens," Cole said.

"If there is anything else I can do, please let me know. Oh, and I'll make sure you get the letter and my statement as fast as possible," Camille said.

Lawson shook her hand, a sympathetic smile on his lips.

"Thank you."

Cole could feel Lawson's eyes on him the whole way to the car. He glanced over his shoulder, meeting Lawson's curious gaze Neither said anything until they made it to the car.

"You ain't real good with feelings, are you?" Lawson asked.

"I have no idea what you're talking about," Cole grumbled.

"Yeah, you do. But, sure, let's go back to ignoring each other, 'cause that worked wonders before."

Cole felt like he'd taken the silence between them before for granted because Lawson didn't stop yapping the whole way back. He felt a desperate need to slam his head against a wall. Repeatedly.

Cade

He was turning out the last lights at the homicide department. They'd returned about an hour before from Mrs. Henway's sister to get some paperwork done before they went home for the night. Mrs. Henway's alibi was solid, not that he doubted for a second that she hadn't killed her husband. Banks looked skeptical throughout the whole thing, though. Or perhaps that was just his face.

They entered the elevator together and Banks pushed the button for the garage. Cade looked forward to going home to his bed. Which reminded him he didn't know where Banks was going.

"Hey, where are you staying?"

"I'll find a hotel," Banks grumbled.

On a police budget? Yeah, that wasn't gonna happen.

"If you want, I've got a spare bedroom with a connected bathroom. Just in case you want a nice bed, clean sheets, and a shower that actually works instead of some rundown motel."

Why the fuck did I just do that? Fuck! Sometimes his mouth worked faster than his brain. Right then, he wanted to slap himself.

"Thanks," Banks said with a nod. "I'd appreciate that."

Why the fuck would he accept?

"You're welcome."

Face meet palm. He was going to have a serious case of blue balls.

"Do you want the address?"

"I'll just follow you."

They split up once they exited the elevator. He backed out of his parking spot and waited for Banks to do the same. He felt like he was taking a date home to meet his parents for the first time. It really irked him, especially since he'd never actually done that. He'd never been with anyone he'd wanted to introduce to his parents. He wasn't sure what they would've thought about Banks. He was quite the enigma. Who the hell was he kidding? They would've loved him.

The thought caused a lump to form in his throat. He turned the music up, singing along the rest of the drive while he kept an eye on Banks in the rearview mirror.

He parked his car in his driveway, making sure to leave Banks enough space to park behind him. He turned off the car and breathed in a few gulps of air. He got out just in time to see his elderly neighbor hauling several bags of groceries up her driveway. She was a small woman, only reaching up to below his shoulder.

"Mrs. Jones. Let me help you with that."

He hurried over and grabbed two of the bags from her.

"Thank you, dear."

She smiled up at him, but her attention was quickly directed over his shoulder.

"Oh, that is one fine piece of meat you've got yourself there, sweetheart."

She wagged her eyebrows at him, making him roll his eyes.

"You are one naughty old lady, Mrs. Jones."

"Well, I gotta keep up with you dear," she said.

"Not a lot to keep up with, is there?"

He winced when he heard the resignation in his own voice.

"Well, it has been some time since you brought someone home." She looked over his shoulder, her eyes going wide and he just knew she was checking out Banks.

Nosy hag. But she was right. He wasn't much for one-night stands and it'd been quite a while since he'd last had a boyfriend. His work always seemed to get in the way... or something.

"That one is my work partner," Cole said, pointing with his thumb over his shoulder.

"Sleeping with your partner? Kinky."

How was she eighty and someone's great-grandmother?

"Um. No, I'm not."

The thought, though, was quite exhilarating. The images it provided his starved brain were with vivid details. He blinked to try and erase the pictures of Banks pounding into him, touching him, kissing him. It didn't work very well. He held back a groan when Banks joined them.

"Banks. This is my neighbor, Mrs. Jones."

"Cole Banks. It's a pleasure meeting you, Mrs. Jones."

"Oh, the pleasure is all mine," she said before turning to Cade with mischievous eyes. "Do you share?"

"I think it's time for you to go inside, Mrs. Jones. Wouldn't want you to catch a cold," Cade said.

"It's sixty degrees," Banks said. Cade glared at him a few seconds before he turned back to Mrs. Jones with a sweet smile on his face.

"Isn't the Horton Saga on about now?"

"I don't watch that boring ass show. Now *The Kardashians* though. Kim is a mean bitch. She reminds me of my sister."

"She reminds me of you," Cade said in a stage whisper.

Banks was looking at him with a horrified expression, but Mrs. Jones just laughed and pinched his cheek all grandmotherly.

"Let me know if you two need something in the middle," she said. She wagged her eyebrows suggestively. The images that provided made him gag.

"Oh, dear god, no."

Mrs. Jones smiled and patted his cheek. His butt cheek. He sputtered something inarticulate and jumped away from her, almost falling over from the weight of the bags in his hands. Two big, steady hands caught him. One held him up around the waist, the other on his arm, taking the weight of one of the bags.

Mrs. Jones tsked at him. "Such a prude. No wonder you never get laid."

She turned around to head inside, waving over her shoulder.

"Crazy old wench," he yelled after her. He stayed where he was, enjoying Banks' hands on him way too much.

"You love me," Mrs. Jones yelled over her shoulder.

"To pieces; if she isn't careful," Cade said under his breath.

"You alright to stand on your own?" Banks asked.

"Yes."

No.

He felt the loss immediately when Banks let go of him. Though, it was mostly because he got the full weight of the grocery bags back. Or so he told himself.

"Just wait here," he said to Banks.

He walked into the house. Knowing the place inside and out, he continued straight into the kitchen. He put the bags on the kitchen counter before turning to Mrs. Jones with raised eyebrows. She obviously wanted to say something, and he doubted it was PG rated.

"If you don't tap that, kid, something is wrong with you, or your equipment." She pointedly looked down, making him cover his crotch with his hands.

"I'm pretty sure there's something wrong with *him*. Not me," Cade grumbled.

"What about all the other guys you've been with?"

"I'm gonna leave now so I don't have to put 'old lady slugger' on my résumé."

He leaned down so she could press a kiss to his cheek. Not his ass this time, though. That would've been gross. That privilege was reserved for boyfriends.

"Thank you for the help."

"You're welcome. Please let me know if you need anything. I can get your groceries for you," he said. She just turned eighty, so he couldn't help but worry she would fall and hurt herself.

"You have enough going on. Catching killers and all. Besides, I'm pretty handy and I can take care of myself."

They agreed to disagree. He left her with a smile on his face though.

Banks followed him back to his house where he unlocked the door and gestured for Banks to proceed him inside. The row houses were just built when he'd bought his. Though they were modern; with a garage, high tech equipment, and more than one bathroom, the exterior of the buildings remained in the same style as the older buildings in the neighborhood. It was what he liked so much about it.

"She's something else," Banks said.

If only he knew. She hadn't changed one bit in the seven years he'd lived next to her. She might be foul-mouthed, but she was brilliant and rather amazing.

"Yeah. I believe they call it *certifiably insane* nowadays," Cade said.

He dropped his keys into the bowl on the sideboard. They both shucked their jackets and put their shoes on the shoe rack and then Cade led Banks into his living room. His stomach growled, reminding him they hadn't had dinner yet.

"You want something to eat? I've got lasagna in the fridge or I've got some of those famous microwave meals in the freezer."

"Lasagna will do fine, thank you," Cole said.

Cade dug out the lasagna from the fridge. He put their food into the microwave and found water and beers in the fridge, which he put on the coffee table along with the cutlery, deciding they would just be eating there. When the timer beeped, he hurried back to take out the steaming food and placed it on the table.

"There you go, Lasagna a la Cade. Which, more or less, mean someone else made it and I just warmed it. Which also makes you lucky, since I'm a really bad cook," Cade said.

They dug in, both famished from a long workday. Mrs. Jones really knew how to make a great lasagna. Banks looked like it might actually hurt whenever he had to speak and the only way to ensure he didn't have to speak, was by stuffing food into his mouth. Cade decided to let the man be while they ate. Though when they finished, he was determined to get something out of him.

"So. Where are you from?"

Banks looked at him with suspicious eyes. "Why?"

"It was just a question. You know, to get to know you better?"

"I don't mix work with my personal life," Banks said.

Like he had one.

"Right."

Something wasn't right. No one was that closed off without a reason, and, unfortunately, that just made him want to figure Banks out even more.

Cade stood up, brushing himself off. "Why don't I show you the guest bedroom, then."

If he was so keen on being an asshole, he could be one without Cade present. Besides, he missed his pillow.

"That's the bathroom," he said as they walked by it. He stopped in front of the last door before the stairs and opened it, gesturing for Banks to step inside.

"There you go. There are fresh towels in the bathroom and the sheets are all clean."

His sister wouldn't mind if he lent out her room. Technically, it wasn't hers, but he'd bought a house with the extra space so he'd always have room for her. Then, that quickly became a room for Lara's daughter as well. He was sure neither of them would mind sharing with a hottie like Banks. Not like *share* share with him. *Aaand* there went his mind into the gutter, again.

"Thank you," Banks said.

"Sure thing, partner." He winked at Banks, grinning when the other man rolled his eyes at him. "See ya tomorrow."

"Goodnight Lawson."

He took the stairs two at a time; not at all trying to put some space between them. It was bloody lucky the guest bedroom was downstairs; he didn't think he'd survive having to sleep closer to Banks. Not when his dick seemed to like him so much or, you know, the fact that his mouth had a life of its own. Yeah. His mouth and his dick; just two other things he couldn't control around Banks. Fucking A.

He went straight to his ensuite bathroom, closing and locking the door before taking off his clothes and throwing them into the laundry basket. He turned on the water, waiting for it to get warm before he stepped under the spray. He quickly washed his hair before soaping-in his body.

Though his dick seemed adamant on some attention; he ignored it. There was no way he could rub one out without thinking of Banks, and that was a complication he didn't need. He dropped his head against the tile, the water cascading down his back. He tapped his forehead against the wall.

He just needed to keep it together for as long as they were forced to work together. He could do that. No biggie.

Chapter Four

Cade

THE SMELL of fresh brewed coffee woke him up. He was still half asleep as he made his way to the kitchen and apparently someone had moved the wall separating the kitchen and the living room. He heard the smacking sound before he felt the impact. He grabbed onto the wall he'd just walked into in an attempt to not fall flat on his ass. He let out a grunt, more of surprise than pain, though his forehead and nose were throbbing a bit.

"What are you doing?"

Cade squinted to his right where an already clothed and fresh-looking Banks stood with an almost smile on his irritatingly handsome face.

"Hugging the wall, what do you think?"

Banks said nothing, just raised a brown eyebrow, studying Cade with those unnerving, dark eyes of his.

"Why the hell did you move it anyway?" Cade asked, pushing away from the wall. Since Banks didn't move and he was standing in the doorway, he had to squeeze past him, their bodies brushing against each other. That certainly woke a part of him up.

"I didn't," Banks said, amusement in his voice.

Cade gave him a nasty look over his shoulder as he moved into the kitchen. He grabbed a coffee mug and poured himself a cup. He took a sip and fought to hold back an appreciative moan. Why did Banks have to look so hot and make such good coffee? It just wasn't fair. He took another sip. No, not fair at all.

Banks leaned back against the counter, watching him with those attentive green eyes. It made him twitchy and unable to enjoy the coffee which was something that never happened to him; no one could make him not enjoy coffee.

Or chocolate. Banks better not make him unable to enjoy his chocolate. He mumbled something under his breath, not sure exactly what, and then he downed the rest of the coffee.

He went back upstairs to shave and put on some clean clothes. He felt marginally better as he made his way down the stairs. Banks stood waiting for him and they went to the front door together. They got on their jackets and shoes in silence. He was surprised he didn't fall over when he put his shoes on. He certainly felt like he would. He did have a hard time falling asleep last night. Emphasis on hard.

He patted himself down, not finding what he was looking for. He moved the things on the sideboard, looking under them with a frown. Where the hell was his keys?

He crouched down to look under the sideboard. He let out a huff as he closed his fingers around the keys and pulled them out. He got up on his feet and started dusting himself off.

"Are you always like this?"

The tone of Banks' voice made him freeze up. He glanced up at him, keeping his expression emotionless. "Like what?"

"Disorganized. Confused. Easily distracted."

That made him straighten up, his arms crossing over his chest and his eyes narrowing. "What the hell are you trying to say?"

"I just want to know what I'm in for," Banks said.

The snide tone in Banks' voice made Cade step closer to him as the blood in his veins began to boil. How dared he? He got up into Banks' face.

"You're in for an ass-kicking if you don't back off."

Banks let out a sound that could've been a snort before he stepped back to let his gaze wander over Cade's physique, his eyes intense. Cade felt his body stiffen. All of it. *Shit.*

"That's never gonna happen."

"Fuck you, Banks," he hissed and turned around to hide his arousal from the other man. He grabbed his badge from the sideboard and opened the door, waiting impatiently for Banks to step through it. After slamming and locking the door, they went to their respective cars. Cade slammed the door to his car, told himself he did not have anger management issues and turned the key. The car spluttered a few times before it died with a pitiful sound.

"No. No-no-no. Come on, baby."

He turned the key repeatedly and when it still didn't start, he let out a groan and dropped his forehead against the steering wheel. It just *had* to happen right now. He smacked his head against the wheel a few times before he got out of the car.

Banks was leaned back against his own car, the look on his face not exactly one of surprise. He must've really set the bar low for himself if Banks was expecting something like that.

"Need a ride?"

Cade decided to just glare at the man as he walked past him and opened the passenger side door of the car and got in. Banks slid into the driver's seat.

"Happen often?"

"No."

Fate must've just decided to deal him a shitty hand around Banks. Way to kick him while he was down. Maybe if he got laid, he wouldn't be so receptive to the other detective. Or perhaps it wouldn't change a thing. That thought was disconcerting, to say the least.

Lara wasn't there when they got to the homicide department, which meant she was out looking for clues and probably wouldn't be back for hours, leaving him alone with Banks.

An hour later, he'd escaped to the kitchen where he was making himself an extra-large coffee. He took a big sip of the coffee before heading back toward the office. He had to take a little detour when Claire called his name. He leaned a hip against her desk and smiled down at her.

"These just came for you," she said, holding up two files.

"Thank you, Miss Claire."

He took the files and skimmed through them. They were Tommy Lowe and his girlfriend's statements. As far as he could tell, there were no changes from their stories yesterday. He closed the files and made his way back to the office where he dropped the files onto Banks' desk.

"Here."

Banks glanced up, his dark eyes meeting Cade's as Cade sat down behind his desk. Then Banks grabbed the first file, reading through it slowly while occasionally glancing up at Cade with a frown. When Banks was done reading, he sat back in his chair, his gaze on Cade. Not that he saw Banks watching him. He didn't need to; he just felt it. His pulse picked up, his skin crawled, and the hair at the back of his neck stood on end. It unnerved him to no end.

Half an hour went by before he couldn't take it anymore. He cursed under his breath, calling Banks something inappropriate, hoping he'd hear it. When Banks looked at him like he was a disobedient child, he got out of his chair and grabbed his gun, then his jacket, putting it on with harsh movements.

"Where are you going?" Cole asked.

"To the morgue."

"Why?"

"To piss off the coroner, since apparently, it's all I'm good for," he snapped.

He stomped to the elevator, pressing the button hard a few too many times. He hated not being in control of his emotions like this. Banks riled him up like no one else. It drove him insane. He let out an irritated groan when Banks stepped into the elevator after him. He'd planned on stealing one of the unmarked cars, but since Mr. I'm-better-than-everyone-else decided to come along, he'd just ride with him. Saving gas and all that.

They'd only been driving for a minute or so when Banks asked, "Why are you moping?"

Cade grunted, crossing his arms. "I'm not."

"Really?"

He turned angry eyes on Banks, but Banks didn't see it as he was busy driving and keeping his eyes on the road. Right then, he sort of wished looks could kill or at least burn.

"Yes, really."

"Alright then," Banks said.

They both kept quiet for the rest of the ride. He didn't even have to guide Banks there. Go figure, the guy knew the way to the morgue. The Chief Medical Examiner's Office was located just two miles from the station, in a big ass building on West Baltimore Street.

A young girl sat behind the front desk, her fingers skating quickly over the keyboard of the laptop in front of her. She didn't notice them as they neared.

Cade pulled on one of her curls gently to get her attention. "Hi, Sasha."

She looked up, a smile spreading on her face when she saw him. She was only fifteen, but it never seemed like she minded being in such close quarters with dead people. The chief medical examiner was her father, so she'd probably been there more times than even Cade.

"Hi, Cade," she said.

He leaned against the desk. "Shouldn't you be in school?"

"Teacher conference. We got the day off," Sasha said with a shrug. She cocked her head to the side, looking behind him. He looked over his shoulder. Banks stood with his arms crossed over his impressive chest, an assessing look in his green eyes.

"Oh, right. Sasha, this is my new partner, Cole Banks."

Sasha gave Banks a smile and stood, leaning over the desk to shake his hand. Banks took her hand a lot gentler than he'd thought he would.

Sasha motioned toward Cade.

"Good luck with that," she said to Cole, tongue in cheek.

"I have a feeling I might need it," Banks grunted.

"You can go on in. He should be writing reports. Pretty much everyone else is out."

Cade gave her his most dazzling smile, to which she faked a swoon. He thanked her before moving toward the morgue, Banks following him silently.

"Doc," Cade said as they walked through the door to the examination room.

Glancing up from their latest victim with a wooden toothpick hanging out of one corner of his mouth, the stocky man looking like he fit more in a boxing ring than in the morgue, smiled when his twinkling eyes landed on Cade.

"Lawson. Good timin', I was just 'bout to call ya."

"Oh, I bet you were," Cade said while giving him a knowing once-over and wagging his eyebrows.

"I'm married. Quite happily so. You know, since she doesn't really mind that I like to chop up dead people."

"She sounds like a real gem," Cade said.

"You've tasted her food, so you know damned well she is."

A throat clearing behind him made him glance over his shoulder at Banks. The man had his arms crossed and an impatient look on his face. He couldn't help if his lips twitched a bit.

"Banks, this is the chief medical examiner, Michael Barnes. Doc, this is Detective Cole Banks, Fairfax PD. Funny enough, I'm the one on loan to him."

"Yeah, because it'd be real shocking if someone wanted to be rid of you."

"Who'd not want a piece of this?" Cade gestured at his body with both hands. Doc let his eyes roam, but no interest showed in his expression, just as he'd known it wouldn't. Banks, though, averted his eyes and seemed to find something interesting to look at on the wall.

"So. What've we got, Doc?" Cade asked.

"Just about what you would expect if you've read the files on the other victims."

Doc led them toward the body of Chris Henway. It was almost impossible to recognize him as the man they'd seen in pictures. His skin was almost white, everything looking dull and dead. He was opened up by an incision from the tips of each shoulder to the sternum and then further down to the navel which the incision was made around and then down to the pubic bone.

"He's got contusions 'round ankles and wrists from the ties he was bound with," Doc said while lifting Henway's arm for them to see the red and blue marks around his wrist.

"Cause of death is blood loss caused by a shot penetrating the right side of the liver. The bullet nicked the inferior vena cava causing the blood loss."

"Do sink beneath your level of intelligence and explain that to us mere mortals, please."

A cheeky smile found its way to Doc's lips. "Damn. Thought you were gonna say morons."

Cade flipped him off and was about to retaliate when Banks cold, serious voice cut him off.

"Please continue, Doctor," Banks said, his voice hard.

"Yes, of course," Doc said in a tone making Cade believe that if he hadn't been there, the doctor would have apologized and possibly called Banks *sir* as well.

"As I said, the bullet nicked the inferior vena cava which is one of the large veins in the body carrying blood from the lower half of the body into the right atrium of the heart. The wound wouldn't have killed him instantly because it was to a vein and not an artery. It took some time for him to bleed out. I already sent the bullet to the crime lab."

"Time of death?" Banks asked while looking down at what remained of Chris Henway. A cold, pale, piece of dead meat on an equally cold slab. It made chills run down Cade's spine. Always had. He was all for the figuring out and arresting parts, but the dead people part? Not so much. He'd only been present at one of Doc's autopsies and suffice it to say, it hadn't ended well for him. Doc got one hell of a laugh out of it, but Cade managed to sprain a wrist when he hit the floor.

"Approximately six thirty the morning he was found. By my estimation, he would've been shot somewhere between two and two thirty in the morning."

"He bled out slowly?"

Doc nodded.

The bastard got what he deserved. Not that he would voice that thought. Banks would probably try to have him fired for it.

"Lacerations and tearing in the rectum are consistent with rape with a foreign object. No traces of lubrication or latex. I also found small amounts of what seem to be gunshot residue and gun oil in the victim's mouth. He most likely had a gun barrel down his throat before he was killed," Doc said with an expectant and curious look at Banks.

"Probably a part of the ritual," Banks mumbled, his jaw clenching and his eye squinting as he looked intently at Chris Henway's mouth.

Cade waited to see if Banks had any questions, but when it didn't seem likely, he turned to Barnes.

"Thanks, Doc," he said.

"No worries. I'll have my report finished and on your desk by the end of the day," Doc said as he took off his gloves. He shook both their hands before they headed toward the exit.

They walked out of the building just as a group of five assistant medical examiners walked in. They all greeted Cade heartily as they passed them. They were all young, reminding him of Thomas Lowe. He didn't even want to imagine what Henway had done to the kid.

"I think it's sorta fitting that Henway's the one lying on a cold slab right now. Though I'm pretty sure that's not how he planned on spending his weekend," Cade said.

"Do you have to make a joke out of everything?"

Though Cade wouldn't bet anything on whether that was actually a question or not, he still answered. "No, I don't *have* to."

"Then don't," Banks said.

He should probably let it go, but there was something about this man that just got his blood boiling, granted, sometimes in a much, much different way than now.

"No."

"No?" Banks asked with an annoyed and yet surprised expression on his face. Guess he wasn't used to people telling him no. Well, he was in for it then.

Banks put a fist on his hip while leaning a bit down, getting closer than what was possibly a good idea, as he asked again. "No?"

"No. I won't just do whatever the hell you tell me to, Banks. I'm my own person and I won't change who I am just to make you feel better, brace your ego, or whatever floats your fucking boat. I know how I come off to some people and if you wanna go stoic, dark, and serious, then that's fine. Despite what you might think, Banks, I actually take my job seriously and I'm good at it. Joking and having whatever fun I can while working is just my way to cope with all the shit we see all the god damned time. I've seen what it can do to people. Fuck, just look at you." Cade knew he'd gone too far, but as far as he was concerned, if what you could say was the truth, then you'd better say it. "When is the last time you took time off? When is the last time you enjoyed yourself and had some fun? Shit, do you even remember what that is?"

Cade felt bad for laying it out like that and right in the guy's face, too. But he couldn't help but feel the relief of having said it. He knew a man on the edge when he saw him, and one such man was standing right in front of him, pupils blown wide, body frozen and tense as he just stared down at Cade and then something flashed in his eyes. What, he didn't know, but it was the first time Cade saw anything resembling emotion besides disapproval and irritation from the man.

For a moment, he actually thought he may have gotten through to Banks, but then the man just stared him down. Again. Fucking hell. When he couldn't take those searing green eyes any longer, he turned on his heel and stalked toward the car with a loud sigh.

Cole

Cade wouldn't meet his eyes and refused to talk to him as well. This guy was like a fucking kid. He didn't know how Cade could get on his nerves so much. It annoyed the shit out of him. Why was Cade the one acting offended? Cade was the one who'd just spat a lot of shit in Cole's face, not the other way around. Cole decided to just ignore him back. Cade would have to step up and be an adult for once and either apologize or talk to him.

As soon as he turned off the engine in the parking garage of the police station, Cade was out of the car, headed for the elevator. He groaned before getting out of the car to follow him. He caught up to him and made it inside the elevator just before the doors closed. Cade sent him a dirty look before turning away from him. They'd only just made it out of the elevator when a booming voice called their names. Cade let out a deep groan before trudging into the captain's office, Cole right on his heels. Morris was standing in front of his desk, arms crossed as he waited for them.

"Sir?"

"Please tell me you have something for me," Morris said.

"Not much I'm afraid."

"Shit."

Shit was right.

"We just saw the coroner and he gave us a time of death," Cade said.

"Start talking, then. I need to know if there's something I can divulge to the press."

He felt for the man. He must've been swept up in one hell of a media storm. When he'd talked to Morris over the phone when they'd connected Chris Henway's murder to his case, Morris said he'd take care of the media as long as Cole showed up and worked with one of his own detectives.

They both relayed what they knew to Morris. Which wasn't a hell of a lot. Cole was probably more used to that than Cade was, seeing as the man couldn't keep his irritation at bay. He didn't keep still for more than a few seconds. He was practically bouncing.

"Alright. Do what you can. I'll try to keep the media off your backs," Morris said.

"Thank you, sir," Cole said with a nod.

Morris returned his nod. Cole turned to leave and only just caught sight of the tail of Cade's jacket as the man hurried out of the room. Something wasn't right, he was sure of it. He wouldn't ask about it, though. He didn't care if something was wrong unless it was about the case.

"Samuels," Cole said when he followed Cade into their office. Samuels looked up from her computer screen and smiled at them.

"Hi, boys. You been playing nice?"

Cade grunted and dropped into his chair, turning it away from them as he flipped through the pages of a case file that'd been laying on his desk.

"Where've you been?" Samuels asked.

"The morgue."

"Oh."

He caught her brief glance at Cade. There was something there. He'd find out what, eventually. He sat down in his own chair and turned toward Samuels. "How's your case coming along?"

She gave him a grim smile and tucked a red curl behind her ear when it fell loose as she leaned forward. "I found one of the bio kids. He was stupid enough to pay the motel room he was staying in with his father's credit card."

"You think he killed his father?" Cole asked.

She nodded. "He broke down when I arrested him; said he'd been through hell because of his father. I think there's more to the story than simple homicide."

Cole felt his heart speed up and his hands turned clammy, yet that didn't stop him from asking. "You think he sold them?"

"That sure is a possibility I'll be looking at," Samuels said.

"If it comes to that, then I know a guy," Cole offered.

"So do I," she said with a wink.

"Until then, I have some experience with cases like that, if you'd like to—"

"Can you focus on *our* case for once?" Cade hissed.

They both turned to look at a petulant Cade who was out of his chair, his arms crossed over his chest. When Cole didn't answer, Cade cursed at him before storming out of their office. Cole couldn't stop his eyes from dropping to the guy's ass. He averted his gaze, acutely aware of Samuel's eyes on him. Instead, he turned big eyes on her.

"What the hell is wrong with that man?"

She smirked, something flashing in her eyes so fast he wasn't sure what it was.

"Honestly? A lot. But I think the word you're looking for is jealousy."

Cole blanked for a few seconds. "He's jealous because I'm helping you? Because… you're his former partner?"

Samuels quirked an eyebrow, her eyes gleaming with something he didn't dare try to interpret.

"You want to know why he's acting out? He's scared of you."

"No, he's not," Cole grunted. That little spitfire of a man was not scared of him. Not one bit. Which was one of the things that set him off.

"Oh yeah. He's scared of what you represent, of what you make him feel," she said.

What the hell did that mean?

"Good luck, Hotshot."

She got up and patted him on the shoulder before walking past him and out of the office. If he was being honest with himself, he might actually need some luck. There was just something about Cade that set him off again and again. He wasn't sure if it was just pure luck that the other man hadn't noticed exactly the way he set him off. He found it almost impossible to hide his attraction to Cade, but luckily, the man seemed oblivious to it. He should've been better at hiding it after all those years in the military. Yet, his team had been mostly isolated, and they didn't keep secrets from each other. But this was entirely different. This man wasn't his brother. You didn't want to fuck your brother. There was no way he'd willingly let Cade know of his feelings.

He put himself in front of Samuels' whiteboard and stood there, letting his eyes run over everything for a while. Then he pulled his phone out of his pocket, pushing speed dial.

"Dom. I've got a case you might want to look into," he said when his friend picked up.

As he listened to his friend, his brother, and former superior officer talking on the other end, he glanced out of the office. He saw Samuels leaning in to speak quietly with Cade who threw his arms up in frustration, his cheeks reddening and his eyes blazing under his blonde curls. Samuels shook her head. Cade rubbed the back of his neck before glancing up, his eyes meeting Cole's. There was something buried deep in those eyes. Something he couldn't quite discern.

"So, what's with this case?"

He broke the eye contact, turning his back on Cade and trying to concentrate on Dom's words.

"What?"

"I said, what's with this case? And what the hell is going on with you?"

"Nothing." He glanced in Cade's direction, finding him leaning on his elbows on one of the other detective's desks, his ass right in Cole's line of sight. He bit his lip to hold back a groan. "I'm just a bit distracted."

"Good distracted or bad distracted?"

He could hear the grin in Dom's voice.

"Don't worry about it," he grumbled, tearing his eyes away from Cade. Again. "About that case; I think it might have to do with our discharge."

Chapter Five

Cole

HE WATCHED with amusement as Cade slurped down his second coffee of the morning. It was quite obvious he wasn't a morning person. The whole walking into walls, tripping over himself, and trying to keep his eyes closed as much as possible was a dead giveaway, but it was the things he mumbled under his breath that first made it clear that he was practically sleepwalking the first two hours of the day. There was no way the eloquent detective would be saying the things that came out of his mouth in the morning if he was actually awake. Or, at least he hoped that was the case.

Late last night, Cade had mumbled an apology, his cheeks reddening. He didn't know why he found that so attractive, but he did. After that, Cade had hurried upstairs, not giving him time to respond.

After taking a shower and getting dressed that morning, he'd put over a fresh pot of coffee and two minutes later, Cade was in the kitchen, walking blindly toward the coffee maker. He hadn't tried to vanquish any walls, though. Which was lucky seeing as it was more than likely Cade would end up on the losing end of that debacle. The man was making it a difficult task to keep his attraction to him under wraps. Everything Cade did or said seemed to turn sexual in Cole's mind.

Just then, Cade let out a groan before he bent down to pick up a spoon he'd just dropped on the floor, presenting a clear view of his backside. Cole bit his lip, but he didn't look away. He could appreciate what he saw, even if he couldn't touch. Cade's pants hugged him just right, the fabric taut over his ass. He hadn't tucked in his T-shirt, so it was riding up, showing a mouthwatering amount of skin.

Cole averted his gaze only when Cade had already straightened and turned around. Not that Cade seemed to notice. The doofus popped the spoon he'd just picked up into his mouth, grimaced, and spat it out again.

"Ugh. Gross. Why did I do that?"

He had no idea what was wrong with this man. He didn't even want to think about what was wrong with himself because he actually liked Cade.

Cade dropped the spoon into the sink and bent under the faucet to wash his mouth. He gargled, sounding like he was trying to drown himself and spat out the water. After drying off his mouth in his shirt, he turned around and looked up at Cole with an incredulous expression.

"You're smiling," Cade said.

He tried not to choke on the air he drew into his lungs. "Excuse me?"

"You were smiling, or I suspect, quietly laughing at me," Cade said. His nose scrunched up and Cole found it hard to hold back another smile.

"See? You're doing it again."

"You're ridiculous."

Cade grunted something unintelligible under his breath, all the while scowling up at Cole like it might set him on fire. Cole leaned back against the kitchen counter, a cup of coffee in hand, and watched Cade try to find another spoon to use with his breakfast.

His phone rang and when he saw who was calling, he put his coffee down and started toward the front door. He found himself smiling again when Cade didn't even notice, still searching through cupboards and drawers. He stepped outside to answer his phone.

"Dom," he said.

"He's in the shower."

That made him snort out a laugh.

"Franklin. What the hell are you doing using Dom's phone?"

"Well, he was being fucking cryptic after your call yesterday, so I thought I'd go straight to the source."

"I'm not telling you shit," Cole said. Fuck. He couldn't tell Franklin. Not before they actually had something.

"That just tells me it has something to do with me, sugar."

Cole held back a curse and instead said, "Not everything is about you."

"Isn't it? Wait, did I not get that memo?"

"Franklin. Shut up or I'm gonna come over there and kick your ass."

"Good. That means we'd actually get to see you more than once a year," Franklin snapped.

Before he got to say something snide in return, he heard another voice over the phone. "Put the phone down or I'mma shoot you in the ass."

Dom sounded serious, and even though he knew Dom wouldn't hurt Franklin too much, he knew as well that his threat was valid.

"Better do as he says, Franklin."

"You two are no fun," Franklin muttered.

Cole didn't doubt the man was pouting. Many were fooled by his impulsive and exuberant personality, but underneath that veneer was a very deadly man. He was just better at hiding it than most.

He heard Dom say, "Take a hike," and then Franklin replying with, "Bitch, I might."

Cole snorted to himself, only then realizing just how much he'd missed the crazy bastard.

"How is he?" Cole asked.

Dom sighed. He imagined Dom was rubbing the bridge of his nose as well. He did that when he got frustrated. He'd done it a lot during their marine days.

"I don't know. He's good at hiding it," Dom said.

"He still thinks we blame him?"

He'd never blamed Franklin for anything that'd happened. Not one thing. None of them had.

"No. Just the lieutenant," Dom said.

"Fucking asshole."

"Yeah, well. That's that."

Cole rubbed the back of his neck, dropping his chin to his chest. He took a deep breath then asked, "Did you find something?"

"Not yet. I'll call when I do."

"I might have something, though. You know the kid Samuels arrested yesterday? After I talked to you, I watched her interrogation. He confessed to killing his father, then he clammed up completely. She couldn't get anything out of him after that."

"Huh. Sounds intriguing."

The sound of the door opening made Cole glance over his shoulder. Cade stepped out onto the front porch, his eyes questioning as he watched Cole, but he stayed where he was, giving him his space.

"Listen. I've gotta go. But I think you should look into it," Cole said to Dom.

"Alright. Take care, brother."

"You, too. Tell the family I said hi."

"Will do."

He hung up and put his phone in his pocket as he walked toward Cade who was looking up at him with doe eyes. He may seem innocent with his fair looks and big blue eyes, and that fucking adorable dimple, but there was no doubt Cade was anything but innocent.

"Hey. You mind dropping me off at the State's Attorney's Office?" Cade asked.

Cole hadn't offered, but he could probably fix Cade's car with ease. Evidently, he liked torturing himself as he kept putting himself in close quarters with Cade.

"Sure."

Cade

After taking the elevator to the ninth floor, Cade walked through the doors to the State's Attorney's Office and descended straight into chaos. He stopped at what looked to be a secretary's desk. A woman with her hair pinned up, her clothes looking freshly pressed, and glasses perked on her nose, had a phone pressed to her ear, held by her shoulder as she rifled through a big stack of papers.

"Excuse me. I'm looking for Detective Thompson?"

The woman didn't so much as glance up at him, she just pointed to her left and continued to go through her papers. He went the way she'd pointed and found a big open office with *Special Victim's Unit* in big letters on a plaque next to the open door. He proceeded through the door, finding a blonde woman seated behind the desk nearest the door. A badge and a gun in a hip holster were on her desk. He walked up to her.

"Hi. I'm looking for Detective Thompson?"

She looked up, and when she noticed the badge in his waistband, she smiled. He smiled right back.

"Hi. You must be Cade. Please, call me Callie," she said.

She stood up and they shook hands.

"Hey, Callie. You ready to go through this with me?"

She bobbed her head and glanced around the room with a swift turn of her head. "Sure. Let's get out of here before I go stir crazy. Wanna get a coffee while we look through your files?"

"Sure. I know a nice place down the street," he said.

"Let's go, then."

He followed her through the building, looking at all the people milling around.

"You guys working on something big?"

"Someone is always working on something big. They're all perfectionists, so at least the chaos is organized."

The coffee shop was just two streets over and they made their way there with fast strides. Once they entered the shop, Cade found them a table in the back as Callie went to order them some coffee and came back with that and a batch of cookies. Cade smiled sheepishly up at her as she gave him a knowing grin and pushed the plate toward him. It was chocolate chip cookies. There was no resisting that temptation.

They spent some time enjoying their cookies and coffee before getting to the case.

"Your victim; Henway. I had to do some digging to find him in the system. He wasn't registered as a sex offender in Baltimore. He can't legally be around anyone underage, yet he was living with two kids and in a family-friendly neighborhood," Callie said.

That made him frown. "Our suspect, Henway's victim, sent Henway's wife a copy of his profile on the sex offender registry."

"Either he's good at digging, had a copy at the ready, or there's something he's not telling you."

"He's most likely had it since Henway was sentenced, but my partner will probably go with the 'something he's not telling us' option."

"Ah. So, he's the kind of guy you need to prove your worth to. You know, it doesn't seem like that bad a thing. I'm only guessing, but you seem like the type where people have to prove unworthy before they lose your trust."

Cade nodded. "I used to be. But you know, experience has taught me to be cautious even though I always try to see the best in people."

"I think I might like you," she said.

"I'm not sure if *that* is a good thing or not." A smile bloomed on his face as he said it.

"Me neither," Callie said with a laugh.

They sat in comfortable silence for a while, both just sipping their coffees and stuffing themselves with more cookies. When the last cookie was devoured, Cade leaned back in his chair, watching Callie as she sat in her own thoughts. Her eyes were unfocused as she fiddled with the sleeve of her shirt. She glanced up at him, then leaned forward, asking, "The Executioner. Do you know why they call him that?"

Cade shook his head. "I only heard the office-chatter about him before I got the case. You been following the case?"

"Yep. The first three victims either got a much lower sentence than they should have or had a mistrial so some fancy reporter thought the 'Executioner' fit just right since the judge and jury failed in the trials and he ended what they began. I like it. I mean, it's pretty awesome for a serial killer name. It does have a double entendre and one of them is legal. Well, they're both legal, in some states," she said.

"Judge, jury, and executioner, and an actual executioner at that," Cade said.

"Exactly."

He put his elbows on the table, resting his chin in his hands, and leaned forward. "He rapes his victims with a foreign object. What's your take on that?"

She cocked her head to the side, eyebrows rising. "Foreign object? You've considered him being impotent, right?"

"Yeah. We're even considering *he* might be a *she*."

That caused her lips to quirk into a smile. "Interesting. Why, if I may ask?"

"Because of the cleanliness. The method. Because of the lack of a struggle," Cade said.

Callie leaned back in her chair, cocking her head to the side as she squinted at him. "How does a lack of struggle fit with the perp being a woman?"

"It fits because a woman would expect a struggle and prepare for it. Make sure there wouldn't be one."

"You saying a man wouldn't expect a struggle?" she asked.

Cade shook his head. "No. But this guy wants to hurt his victims and the guys he picks aren't exactly small. If it is a guy, I'm certain he would enjoy beating his victims into submission first. But a woman, or at least a smaller man would have to be more careful."

Callie bobbed her head in agreement and said, "That sounds plausible."

"Why do you think he rapes them?"

"Well. He could be retaliating," Callie said.

"Huh. So, it's not actually about the victims? I mean—"

She waved him off. "I know what you mean, and I think you're right. Of course, it's about the victims, but only to the extent that they fit the profile of the… well, it could be his first victim, it could be who he wanted to have killed, or who he plans on killing in the end."

"You going profiler on me?"

She shook her head but didn't try to hide the smile teasing her lips.

"If you want my professional opinion; you're looking for a person who's been abused by someone close to them, think family close, and someone who wants to retaliate, not only against the abuser but also against other abusers," she said.

"So, that matches with, what, around eighty percent of all abuse victims?"

"Got your statistics right there, detective. Eight out of ten abuse victims know their abuser," Callie said.

"A lot of them are family members too, right?"

She gave a curt nod, her eyes flashing with emotion. Anger? Pain? She must've seen a lot. He wouldn't survive a day in her shoes. His victims were dead, hers were alive but more likely than not, they felt dead inside.

"Easy access and they already trust them seeing as they're family. I've seen it one too many times."

"How do you do this?"

"How do *you* do *your* job?" She shot back at him.

"I nail those fuckers."

Her lips quirked into a smile, her eyes gleaming with humor. "Me, too."

"How much do I owe you?"

"Not a thing," she said and pointed a finger at him. "Don't even try to argue with me."

"Alright then. Free coffee and cookies for me," Cade said.

They got up and made their way through the coffee shop. He held the door for her, making sure she needed to brush against him to get out and slipped a ten dollar bill into her jacket pocket. He could appreciate a woman being independent, but he was the one who'd asked her to meet. He also knew she wouldn't take his money if he tried to give it to her.

"Thanks for the help, Callie," he said.

"You're welcome, for what little I could help with. Call me if there's anything else, okay?"

He nodded and watched as she turned and walked back toward the State's Attorney's Office. He had to take a cab to the station. He needed to get his car fixed, and soon. Carpooling with Cole proved to be a challenge.

He used the car ride to reflect on everything he'd talked about with Callie. He came to the conclusion that he was glad to work homicides. When the car came to a stop, he pulled out his wallet and paid the cabbie. He stepped out onto the street in front of the police station. Not long after, he walked into his office to find Cole behind his desk, a blue folder in his hands. Hearing him enter, Cole looked up over the folder, then put it down and straightened in his chair.

"What did she say?" Cole asked.

"She thinks our perp is someone who was abused as a kid." Cade shrugged off his jacket, draped it over his chair and turned to face Cole as he leaned back against his desk. "By someone close to him or her, and they are now retaliating against others who abuse someone close to them."

"Tell me something I don't know," Cole muttered.

He'd figured as much. He let out a sigh as he dropped down into his chair.

"How can someone not leave anything behind?" Cade mused.

"I'd say someone who watches CSI, but this is too much, this is someone who *knows* exactly how not to get caught. Someone who's used a lot of time perfecting their routine."

"You're thinking a cop, aren't you?"

"It's very likely, actually," Cole said.

Cade leaned back in his chair as he gave Cole a once over, letting his gaze wander all over his impressive physique. He cocked an eyebrow at Cole.

"You've killed before, right?" Cade asked.

Cole gave him an incredulous look but didn't answer.

"Did you enjoy it?" Cade pressed on, sure he wouldn't be able to hold back the laugh that was threatening to break free.

Cole stared at him for a few seconds before catching on. He let out a low laugh that made Cade smile and try desperately to push down the feelings fluttering around in his stomach. There was something special about making that stoic man smile, let alone laugh.

"Oh, and she also said that Henway's file in the SOR was buried pretty deep," Cade said.

"Then how did Tommy get it?"

"Now, that is the million-dollar question, isn't it?"

Their gazes met as silence ensued. He couldn't help himself as he got lost in eyes hardened by the things they'd seen. Those green depths of shielded emotions tended to leave him speechless. There was a gleam of something that hadn't been there before. He was sure of it. Cole cleared his throat, effectively breaking their staring contest.

"The ballistics came through. Though they're still working on the rest," Cole said.

Cade didn't even know if the guy was gay. Or bi. Or anything at all. He hadn't caught him looking at any women, but he hadn't looked at any men either. Except for Tanner. Actually, he was pretty sure Cole did check out Tanner, but it could also be his mind playing tricks on him.

"Yeah? That was fast," Cade said.

"The bullet and gun matches. Glock 22 and 9 mm rounds. The grooves on the bullet match the other ones."

"So, the most used gun in law enforcement and one of the most common types of bullets. Yeah, that definitely narrowed it down for us," Cade said, sarcasm lacing his words. He narrowed his eyes at Cole when a thought struck him. "How come the FBI isn't all over this case?"

It'd actually been bugging him for a while now. A serial killer like this was right up the feds' alley, what with all the publicity the case was getting. Well, normally, the feds needed to be invited, but they should've at least gotten a call from them.

"Back when we were on victim number four, we called them in. They sent someone to help create a profile, but it did nothing to help the case. They couldn't tell me anything I didn't already know."

Cole rolled his chair so he was in front of Cade, their eyes meeting and holding for only a second.

"Even if we hadn't sent them packing, I'm sure they would've gone anyway. Their input didn't help, and they didn't want their good name sullied because we couldn't close the case," Cole said.

That sounded about right. Politics.

"Bastards."

"Did Mrs. Henway drop off the letter from Lowe yet?" Cole asked.

"Let me check."

Cade stood and straightened his back, a groan escaping him when it popped. He caught Cole looking at him, but the guy quickly glanced away, pretending to be occupied by something on his computer. Strange. He shook his head at himself and went to the kitchen to pour a cup of coffee. After that, he stopped at Claire's desk.

"Hello, Miss Claire."

The slightly older lady looked up at him from under the black-rimmed glasses that made her eyes look big and adorable. He held out the mug to her. She took it with a pleased sigh.

"What can I do for you, Lawson?"

He smiled down at her while she took a sip, moaning when she found it just as she liked it. Thank god for Nespresso.

"You are a godsend," Claire said.

"I aim to please, milady," Cade said and threw in a wink that made her blush.

"Did you get anything in from Mrs. Henway yet?"

"Not here, no. But let me call the desk sergeant," Claire said.

She picked up her corded telephone and pressed a button before holding it up to her ear. He waited patiently as she chatted over the phone for a minute or two.

"He's sending it up right now," she said.

"Thank you. What would I ever do without you?"

"Gotten off your pesky ass and asked the sergeant yourself," Lara said as she walked past them, not even bothering to glance in their direction as she spoke.

"Talk about pesky, aye?" Cade said.

"She's just mad 'cause she doesn't have anyone to bring her coffee." Claire lifted her mug in a salute and Cade sent her a kiss before walking after Lara.

Lara was already in their office, but from the looks of it, she left some bodies in her wake. Cade grinned at Tanner who stood with his hand raised and his mouth gaping. He promptly shut it when he saw Cade.

"Why does she have to be so mean?" Tanner said.

Cade laughed at the whining man. Poor fellow. He must've taken the brunt of her bad mood. It wasn't often it happened, but she *was* known for her harsh words. He thought she may actually be exerting some restraint considering the lack of gunshot victims. He grinned as he walked through the door. Lara sat behind her desk, a deadly gleam in her eyes.

"So, what's up your ass?" he asked.

"Nothing nice, that's for sure," Lara quipped.

Cade caught the disturbed look on Cole's face. His grin widened. He sat down and waited patiently.

"What happened?" Cole asked, caution filling his voice.

"I was trying to have the sex talk with my daughter," Lara said.

"Oh shit."

Cole looked like the words just tumbled right out of his mouth before he could catch them. He had a grimace on his face as Lara turned her stern gaze on his.

"*Oh shit* is right. You know what she told me when I started talking about condoms?"

They both kept quiet. Cole out of trepidation. Cade out of anticipation.

"'Mom, you don't need condoms, or lube, if you're fucking a *girl.*' She said that to me."

"So, she's…?" Cole flapped his hand, making Lara grimace as well. This was probably where he should save his partner.

"Bisexual. Don't worry Lara, she asked me about it all."

"Disconcerting. Very disconcerting," Cole said.

Cade flipped him off.

"Why would she ask *you?*"

That was sort of offensive, wasn't it? He blew out an offended puff of air and crossed his arms over his chest. "What the hell is wrong with asking me?"

"Because it's *you*," Lara said.

Cade looked from Lara to Cole, who raised a brow at him.

"She makes a solid argument there," Cole said.

"Bitches. Both of you."

He planted his ass against Lara's desk, making her look up at him with a distraught look in her eyes. He knew her well enough to guess what she was about to say.

"Why didn't she come to me?"

"You're not gonna like my answer to that. Are you sure you wanna hear it?"

She gave a curt nod of her head, her curls bouncing. Cade drew in a breath.

"She didn't want to make you worry. She thought you had enough on your plate as it was," Cade said.

"I'm her mother. I'll always have enough time for her," Lara said, her voice quivering.

"She knows that."

He knew Morgan knew. The problem was Morgan was overprotective when it came to her mother. That went the other way as well. Those two were so much alike, he was sure they wouldn't ever see it themselves.

"You know; I'm just trying to keep her from kicking your ex-husband's ass. She's fierce, your girl."

The truth was, he was having a hard enough time trying to keep himself from beating some sense into Robert and he sure as shit wasn't going to hold Morgan back if she wanted to throw a few punches. That asshole more than deserved it.

"I know." Lara sighed.

"She takes after her momma."

Just then, Claire popped her head into their office, waving the folder she held in her hand.

"Express delivery to the best-mannered detective in this whole building," she said while glaring over her shoulder at anyone within distance. He may or may not have had a smug grin on his face as he walked toward her.

"There's a note for you," Claire said as she put the folder in his hand. She winked, making a big smile spread across his face before she turned and trotted out of the room.

"What did you bribe her with?" Cole asked.

Cade turned to see Cole looking at him funny.

"What?"

"She said you were the 'best-mannered detective in the whole building.'"

"Oh, shut up."

Cade felt heat trickle up his neck. He averted his eyes and bowed his head in an attempt to hide it, but he could still feel Cole's eyes on him. He glanced up fleetingly, meeting green eyes. Cole was standing so close. He fought the urge to reach out and touch. He wanted his hands on Cole and he felt a crazy need for Cole's hands on him. All he had to do was lift his hand and he'd be touching Cole. Instead, he tried to concentrate on unfolding the note.

"It's from Camille Stevens," he said.

He read the note and a relieved breath whooshed out between his lips. "The kids didn't show any signs of abuse."

"That doesn't mean he didn't abuse someone else," Lara said.

"Once a child molester," Cole added, not having to finish his sentence.

"Well, let's see what Tommy told Mrs. Henway," Cade said. He pulled out the paper from the folder, unfolded it and straightened out the creases. Then he read out loud.

Hello Natalia

I hope you can forgive me for this, but I couldn't just stand by and let someone else get hurt. I suspect you don't know this, but if you do, then I have to admit I will never understand how someone can put their children in danger such as this. My name is Tommy Lowe. I was in foster care at the Henways when I was nine. Your husband abused me. He made me do things. Sexual things, and I only have the courage to write to you now because I fear for your children. I don't know what else to say, except that your husband is a monster and he ruined the life of a little boy. I don't wish that on anyone else.
I understand you may not believe, or want to believe me, which is why I've put his papers in this letter. He was sentenced to two years for statutory rape. He's a sick and dangerous man.
Please understand that I am only doing this because I want to see you and your children safe and happy.

With all sincerity,
Tommy

"Wow," Lara said.

Cade nodded somberly. The poor sod probably hadn't experienced love a day in his life and yet he did something like that to protect others. He pulled out the papers, reading through them first then holding them out so he could look at them.

"Let me have a look at that," Lara said, holding out a hand toward him. Cade gave them to her. She looked them over, holding them this and that way.

"It looks like it's a copy of the original. There are lines that look like they are from creases, put this paper is new and fine," she said.

He knew that. He also knew that the ink was rather new. He knew a lot of things he couldn't share with them.

"He's probably had the original for a long time. Let's find out how long and maybe we can narrow down when Henway's record was hidden," Cole said.

"Let's go," Cade said.

Cole

As soon as they got into the car, Cade turned on the radio and found a station with eighties hits. There were a lot of good eighties songs, so Cole didn't mind. Normally, he didn't let anyone touch his radio. Or his car. Or him. But fuck, did he want Cade to touch him. The thought, the urge, was driving him insane. He'd never wanted someone that much, and he had his doubts about it being a good thing.

He pulled into the parking lot in front of Lowe's building. After parking the car, he followed Cade inside and up the stairs. When they reached Lowe's door, Cade hesitated before knocking. There was some shuffling and then the door opened to show a ruffled Tommy Lowe. He looked like he hadn't slept or eaten in days.

"Mr. Lowe. May we come in?"

Tommy let out a sigh but waved them inside. He led them to the living room where they all sat down, Cade and Cole on one couch and Tommy on another.

"What can I do for you, detectives?"

"We have the letter you sent to Mrs. Henway. We have some questions about it we'd like to ask you," Cole said.

"Alright."

"The papers you have on him, how did you get them?"

"My lawyer gave them to me back when the trial ended," Tommy said, confusion on his face.

"Would your lawyer be able to attest to that?" Cade asked, leaning his forearms on his legs.

"Yeah. I can give you his name and number if you'd like?"

"That would be very helpful," Cade said.

Tommy rose from his seat and left for a few moments to come back with a stack of papers. He handed them over to Cade.

"This is the original papers. The ones my lawyer gave me. I sent Natalia a copy," Tommy said.

The look on Tommy's face was so earnest and pained, Cole was forced to take a deep breath to calm himself down. He didn't know what the hell to believe about this guy. He was hiding something; he was sure of that. But if it was murdering tendencies, he hadn't figured out yet.

"Did he hurt the kids?" Tommy asked.

Though they didn't have right or reason to give out that information, Cade did so anyway.

"No," Cade said.

Tears pooled in the kid's eyes, but he looked away from them. He turned his body away, but they still heard his whispered words. "He followed me here. I thought I was safe. Free. I was wrong."

"How so?" Cole asked.

"Why do you think he moved here of all places? He was planning something." Tommy turned around, a somber look on his pale face. "I know how that sounds. But can you imagine how much he must've hated me after I sent him to jail? A man like him would never let that go."

That made alarms ring inside his head. That gave both Lowe and Henway motive.

"You think he was coming after you to get revenge?" Cade asked.

"I know I might sound paranoid. But why else would he be here?"

That was a question he wanted an answer to himself. It wasn't their job to find out; their job was to catch a serial killer. But he couldn't help but feel there was so much more to this.

"We don't know as of yet," Cole answered.

Cade pushed up from the couch.

"Thank you for your time, Mr. Lowe," Cade said.

Tommy followed them to the door. Cole stepped out and waited for Cade who was saying something to Tommy he couldn't hear. Tommy bobbed his head and Cade squeezed his shoulder before turning and walking through the door.

Neither of them spoke until they reached the parking lot. Once they were walking across it, toward the car, Cole asked, "What do you think?"

"I think he may be right," Cade said.

They got into the car and Cole waited until they'd both closed their doors before he spoke. "Right about what?"

"That Henway may have been gunning for him."

"He could also have been trying to make a new life for himself," Cole said.

"Do you honestly believe that?"

Their eyes met.

"No."

The fact Tommy wasn't in handcuffs or being escorted to the station said enough.

"I think Henway had his record hidden so he could move close to Tommy," Cade said.

Cole turned the key, starting the car, and pulled out of the parking space. He glanced at Cade, finding the man's gaze on him as well.

"Let's see if we can find out who hid them and why," Cole said.

Cade

They hadn't found a damned thing about those papers. He was dead on his feet when he dropped down on his couch after having disposed of their takeout trays. Ten victims. Nine were men and one was a woman. All different ages. Three different ethnicities. Two cities. What they all had in common was that they'd molested someone close to them. It was all they had to go on and so far, they had nothing.

"How long have you been on this case?"

"Almost two years," Cole said from behind him as he returned from the kitchen with two cold beers.

"It's a hell of a long time without any leads."

"Tell me about it," Cole said before plopping down on the couch with a sigh. He ran a hand through his short, dark hair, a frustrated and tired look on his face.

"Sorry," Cade mumbled.

Most of the time, they solved the cases months or maybe even a year after they got it, and, of course, some never got solved, but sitting with the same case for so many years and the murders just keep piling up? It must've been hell.

Cole opened both their beers and held one out for Cade. They both took a swig.

"The first two murders took place before my time. I was transferred in after those. They were my partner's cases. He moved out of homicide before the last murder in Fairfax," Cole said. "You know, this guy, he just doesn't leave anything substantial behind. No message, no trophies taken, no nothing."

There was a lot of frustration behind that statement, yet Cade thought he may have caught onto some self-doubt as well.

"Yeah. This guy isn't playing with us. He genuinely doesn't want to get caught," Cade said.

He hadn't dealt with a lot of serial killers, but more often than not, that sort of guys liked to play with the ones trying to catch them. They enjoyed the cat and mouse game because they thought they were invincible. Thought they were smarter.

Deciding to change the subject, Cade asked, "You were in the army, right?"

Cole stiffened for no more than a second before he managed to school his features and posture, but Cade noticed.

"Marine Corps," Cole said shortly.

"Did you work in a team or something?"

He had the deepest respect for soldiers, but he didn't claim to know anything about their structure or culture.

"It's called a squad," Cole said, his tone harsh.

"Oh."

Cade glanced down at his hands, clasping them together so he wouldn't fidget under the man's sharp gaze. What was it with this man? He never fidgeted. He got restless when he'd been on his ass for too long, but he never fucking fidgeted.

"Sorry. It's just a…" Cole sighed.

Cole met Cade's gaze and he found an apology in Cole's eyes.

"Sore subject?" Cade finished for him.

"Yeah," Cole said.

"It's okay. I'm sorry. I pry a lot. I'm nosy as hell."

"Really? I hadn't noticed," Cole said with the ghost of a smile on his lips.

"Oh yeah. Wait. Was that sarcastic?"

He did what he could to look affronted instead of surprised and felt warmth spread through his body at the widening of Cole's smile when Cade crinkled his nose as if he smelled something bad.

"So. We're gonna be pretty much up each other's asses for a while, and not the good kind of up the ass, so how about a safe word?" Cade suggested.

That got a reaction out of Cole. "Asses? Safeword? What the hell, Lawson?"

"Not that kind of safe word, pervert."

"You're the one talking about being up each other's asses," Cole said.

Cade tried not to grin and put on his serious face before saying, "A you're-getting-too-close-so-back-off safe word."

Cole was looking at him with suspicion present in his eyes. "Hm. And what word would you suggest?"

He sat back and tapped his chin with a finger, pretending to be mulling it over. He didn't need to think about it. The opportunity was too great to waste.

"How about...*fuck me*?"

"Fuck me?"

"Aw. Now that you ask so nicely," Cade said. He was trying hard to hold back a laugh but the scandalized expression on Cole's face made him burst into laughter.

"One of us is gonna be dead by the end of this partnership, and it's not gonna be me," Cole said.

Cole shook his head at him and, he wasn't sure, but he thought there was an eye roll in there, too.

"Buzzkill."

Chapter Six

Cade

THE TECHS were swamped so Cole had called in a favor from one of his old team members and that was about as much as he'd divulged. Cade hadn't pressed on, something telling him it would be a very bad idea. His partner had a temper, and that temper had an explosive effect on his body.

Even though it was Sunday, they'd only been off the clock for about an hour. They'd worked through the weekend in the hopes of finding some clue, but so far, they were without luck. He felt bummed but he'd noticed Cole favoring his shoulders throughout the day, which was why he'd cornered the man and forced him to endure a massage the second they'd finished their dinner. Not that Cole actually put up much of a fight.

Cole was tense under his hands, but if it was only because of Cade touching him or from being too fucking aware and on the god damned edge all the time, Cade didn't know. Not until his fingers connected with the knots of tension between Cole's shoulder blades. He almost let out a sigh of relief. Almost.

"No wonder you're such an uptight asshole. Looks like that stick up your ass goes all the way to your thick neck," Cade joked.

Cole snorted but didn't move away from Cade's hands, so he kept going, kept kneading the muscles under his fingers into compliance. Cole let out a moan that went straight to Cade's dick. He didn't stop—evidently finding his masochistic streak.

When Cole's shoulders slumped, he thought that might be a good time to stop. Not just because he was fighting a futile war against his libido, but because he was afraid to overdo the massage.

"Good boy," Cade said in a patronizing voice while patting Cole on the top of his head like a dog. It was surprisingly easy to picture Cole as a dog. The picture that came to mind was of an all-black German shepherd with those captivating green eyes that turned nearly all black under strong emotion, shining with intelligence and Cade knew, buried deep down, a splash of mischief and humor resided. Shepherds are intelligent and dangerous—the reason they're often used in the K-9 units. Of course, if Cole were a shepherd, that's exactly where he would be. Busting criminals, even as a dog. The whole idea made Cade go from a snicker to a hard-repressed laugh.

"When I get up from here, I'll knock you on your ass, Lawson," Cole said.

The threat wasn't really believable since Cole was too relaxed from the massage and was slumping further down in the couch.

"You can try," Cade said, earning a condescending snort from Cole.

Yeah, it was pretty obvious who'd win that fight. Even if the guy wasn't three, almost four inches taller and a lot sturdier than himself, Cade wouldn't have tried. He didn't like fighting. Not one bit. Not that he would ever run from a fight. That's where brains came before brawn, well, words at least, and if there was anything he excelled at, it was words. The only one he hadn't been able to smooth talk was Cole. Cole both confused and intrigued him to no end. He was enthralled with the man. So complex, yet so simple. It was annoying as hell.

He leaned over the back of the couch to grab their empty plates from the coffee table. Dinner had consisted of take-out and beer. Again. Not the best meal but certainly not the worst he'd had during a difficult investigation.

He walked back into the living room from the kitchen where he'd put their plates in the dishwasher when the attack came. Okay, so a foot tripping him was maybe a bit much to call an attack, but still. He executed a perfect forwards roll, complete with a girly squeal. He barely made it to his feet before the marine was on him again. Cole's movements were clean and calculated. It didn't take much for Cole to immobilize Cade. Granted, he didn't exactly fight back. Cade blew an annoying strand of his hair out of his face. Cole had his arms pulled behind his back, so Cade had to glance over his shoulder to see him.

"It's not fair. I hate violence. 'S why I became a cop."

Well, a part of it anyway. He'd seen violence up close. Cold, organized violence. Yep. He so didn't like violence. Pushing those thoughts and memories deep into the back of his mind, he put on his well-known puppy-dog face, pouting lip and all; doing his best to shift Cole's attention to where he wanted it and get him to slacken his hold. As soon as he felt Cole's fingers loosen, he made his move. Unfortunately for him, Cole was faster and disturbingly, prepared for it. Cade found himself plastered chest to chest with Cole, his back against the wall and his hands seized behind his back in Cole's iron grip.

He blinked up at Cole. He couldn't help himself what with Cole so close and his lips looking so exquisite. Right then, he didn't care about the risk he was taking. Before he could think it over and possibly dismiss the idea altogether, he pressed his lips to Cole's.

He pulled back when Cole kept still and unresponsive. Only his hands moved; releasing Cade's wrists and falling limp at his sides.

"Well, shit," Cade breathed when he saw those enchanting green eyes of Cole's flooded by confusion and what looked an awful lot like trepidation. Cole stood there, mouth slightly agape and stared at him.

"Sorry," Cade said, swallowing hard against the lump forming in his throat. He stepped around Cole and made his way into the kitchen.

What the fuck was I thinking? That Mr. dark, handsome, and silent would jump into my arms? Much less, jump my bones? Stupid. Stupid. Stupid.

Yeah, this is so gonna help the tension between us at work.

"Oh shit."

Work. Now they had to work together while having this disastrous kiss—and not just Cade's fantasies, Cade's lust for the other man—between them. Fuck. Why was he always doing shit like this? Acting before thinking. Again.

Resting his elbows on the countertop he put his head in his hands. Okay, in all fairness it could've gone worse. Except there was still time for that to play out.

"Cade," Cole's soft voice sounded from behind him, a bit breathless, but no anger or horror as he would've predicted. On the off-chance Cole might not punch him in the face, he slowly lifted his head and turned around. With a silent prayer, he met Cole's gaze.

Cole

When Cade turned around and glanced up, looking like a deer caught in the headlights, scared, frustrated, Cole wanted nothing but to put his arms around him and make him feel safe.

Damn! Where the hell did that come from?

The second Cade's lips had touched his, he'd found himself flabbergasted. Surprised as hell too. He hadn't seen it coming, and he always did. It'd left him frozen in surprise and agitated with himself, which he was sure must've shown on his face. He didn't want Cade to think it was because of him; he didn't deserve that.

"I'm sorry. I…" Cade glanced down at his feet, color filling his cheeks.

Cole waited for Cade to look at him, and when he did, he squared his shoulders and looked Cole straight in the eye, those deep blue eyes blazing and unwavering.

"Actually, I'm not. So, whatever you've got to say, get on with it."

Cole didn't know what possessed him to do it. Maybe it was the hope shining in eyes that always seemed to have a gleam of mischief in them? Maybe it was the desire coursing through his body? Sexual frustration? Whatever it was, it made Cole take those few steps, reach out to put his hand around the back of Cade's neck, pull him closer, and press his mouth against Cade's.

After a few seconds of hesitation Cade was clinging to him, arms around Cole's waist and his hands bunching the back of Cole's shirt. Everything telling him he shouldn't do this, that *they* shouldn't do this, disappeared with the feel of Cade's soft lips, feathering across his own, Cade's tongue sliding across his lower lip and the hard body pressing against him. He tried to suppress a moan unsuccessfully.

Cade moaned in return, sparking something inside Cole and the next thing he knew, he'd pushed the other man up against the counter, pressing hard against him and holding him there. Cade didn't seem to mind as he rubbed against Cole. The kiss deepened and became rougher; tongues battling, teeth clashing, grips bruising.

"Cole," Cade whimpered, pulling at the clothes separating their bodies. Cade grasped the hem of Cole's shirt and he let him pull it over his head. He watched as Cade took a small step back and let his eyes travel down Cole's chest.

Cole let out a hiss and closed his eyes when Cade ran his nails down his chest and over his nipples. He bit his lip, his fingers tightening on Cade's hip. He brought their groins together, thrusting desperately against Cade as he pulled him in for another kiss. He licked at Cade's lips, needing more.

When Cole opened his eyes, he connected with dark, hooded eyes. An expectant shiver ran down his spine.

"Fuck me. Please," Cade said.

Those words, coming from that man, caused another bout of desire to ripple through his whole body.

"Bed," he ordered in a hoarse voice he barely recognized.

Cade nodded and started pulling him out of the kitchen. They only made it up the stairs before Cole needed to have that wicked mouth again. He drove his tongue into Cade's mouth, fighting for control of the kiss. Cade wasn't having it, though, and Cole soon found himself pressed against the wall. Cade worked his way down Cole's chest with kisses, strokes of tongue, and a bite that made both Cole and his dick jump. Cade soothed it over with his tongue before moving further down until he was on his knees in front of Cole, pulling at his belt.

Cade looked up and kept his eyes on Cole's as he popped open the button on his pants and pulled the zipper down. He reached into Cole's pants and wrapped a hand around Cole's erection.

"Fuck," Cole groaned when Cade's hot, wet mouth surrounded his cock.

He wound his fingers into Cade's hair, not wanting to hold him, just wanting to feel those soft strands between his fingers. He watched as Cade took him to the back of his throat again and again. He felt his orgasm draw near. He didn't think either of them was going to last long.

"I'm gonna come if you keep going," he said and tugged on Cade's hair to get him to back off. Cade sat back on his heels and looked up at him with a smirk, his eyes sparkling through the dark lust and his lips swollen and red.

"That's the idea," Cade said, wagging his eyebrows.

Cole groaned, gritting his teeth as he tried to control himself. He pulled Cade up, the man flailing at the sudden movement. Cade grabbed at Cole's shoulders to steady himself.

"Not yet," Cole growled and slanted his lips over Cade's, his tongue demanding access to Cade's mouth. Cade opened up with a soft moan.

He led Cade backwards toward the bedroom, not breaking the kiss even when they stumbled over something that gave a hollow thump as it toppled over. By the time they landed on the bed, Cade under him, they were both naked and Cole was so hard he ached. Cade arched up into him, the friction making him hiss out a breath.

"Top drawer," Cade said in a husky voice.

Cole gave him another deep kiss before moving off the bed. Rifling through the drawer, he came up with a condom and a bottle of lube. When he looked up, Cade had rolled over onto his stomach glancing over his shoulder at Cole. That was out of the way then. Not that he really minded having Cade face to face, but...this was just easier.

He flicked open the cap of the bottle and squeezed lube over his fingers. He kissed down Cade's back as he pressed a finger into his tight heat. He watched as he pumped his finger in and out of Cade, barely keeping himself in check. He wanted Cade so fucking much it almost scared him.

He added a finger and twisted them so he could rub against Cade's prostate. Cade squirmed under his hands, pushing himself back onto Cole's fingers with a desperate sound. He held his breath as he added a third finger. Cade was so fucking tight.

"No more," Cade gasped. "I need you to fuck me. Now."

"You sure?"

"I can handle it."

Cade looked over his shoulder at him, his pupils blown wide. Cole got on his knees behind Cade. He pushed against the tight ring of muscles, stilling when Cade tensed and only continued when Cade pushed back against him. Once he was past, the muscles starting to give, he stilled again to let Cade adjust around his cock.

Cade let out a loud breath as he started to relax. Cole leaned forward, biting down on the exposed flesh between Cade's neck and shoulder and pushed in the rest of the way. He held himself up with a hand on Cade's back, cursing as he tried not to blow his load at the sweet, tight, hotness that was Cade.

"Babe, need you to move," Cade said as he pushed back against Cole, moaning as he did.

Cole slid out slowly to slam back in fast and hard.

"Fuck," Cade hissed, arching his back as he clenched his hands in the sheets and then dropped his head forward while he panted. He waited for Cade to move, and he did, pushing himself back on Cole's cock. He was enjoying the sensual sight playing out in front of him when Cade barked out, "Fuck me already."

Cole chuckled. "Bossy little shit, aren't you?"

"Fuck, yeah. Now fuck me."

Cole could do nothing but comply.

He fucked him hard, his hips slamming into Cade with every thrust. He reveled in the sounds Cade made, the ones he knew he caused. Having Cade's lithe body squirming beneath him was mind-blowing. Cade, rising to his hands, let out a breathy moan at the different angle Cole's cock drove into him.

Letting his hands wander from around Cade's hips, Cole closed his eyes at the feel of soft skin over hard muscle under his fingers. He reached out and grabbed Cade's chin, turning his head enough to capture his lips in a searing hot kiss. Cade gasped into his mouth every time he hit the right spot inside him.

He moved his hand to Cade's chest, lifting him to his knees and pressing Cade's back against his chest. Cade reached back, his fingers grasping for purchase, trying to hold onto Cole as their sweat-slicked bodies slapped together. It wasn't long before Cade was moaning with each of his hard thrusts. Cole lost his rhythm, noises escaping through his parted lips.

"I'm… I'm gonna… *Fuuuck,*" Cade moaned.

His body clamped down around Cole's cock, jolting him into climaxing with him. Pleasure shot through him, making him gasp for breath. He rode out both their orgasms, only stopping when Cade whimpered. He shut his eyes, pressing his forehead against Cade's back. That was something else. He hadn't even touched Cade's dick.

"One of those guys, huh?" Cole asked once he got his breathing under control.

"Mmm," Cade mumbled with his face still pressed down against the mattress.

"You breathing?" he asked with a smile in his voice.

"Haven't breathed since you kissed me," Cade said.

Cole couldn't help his grin as he pressed a kiss to Cade's shoulder. He pulled out carefully and threw the condom in the trash can next to the bed. Cade groaned as he tried to turn around but couldn't. Cole smiled and moved back to let Cade turn around, then he crawled back up Cade's body and bent down to kiss him. When he pulled back, Cade followed. He pressed a kiss to Cade's lips, his own stretching into a smile.

"I like kissing you," he said against Cade's lips.

He opened his eyes to find Cade's gaze burrowing into his.

"Oh really?"

"Yeah. It makes you shut up."

Cade snorted before falling back on the bed. "There are easier ways to shut me up."

"Putting my dick in your mouth works too," Cole said.

"You should do both more often, then."

Now *that* was a brilliant idea.

Cole got up and went to the bathroom. He grabbed a washcloth from the towel rail and held it under warm water. He cleaned himself off before readying the washcloth for Cade. When he walked back into the bedroom, Cade was still in the exact same spot; sprawled out in the middle of the bed. He cleaned off Cade who hissed at the contact, his eyes shooting open. A smile spread on Cole's lips as he took in the blissed-out expression on Cade's face. He liked that he was the one who put it there. He liked it more than he probably should.

After going to the bathroom to throw the washcloth in the laundry basket, he crawled back into bed, lying down next to Cade. Cade rolled onto his stomach. He was so silent, Cole thought he might've fallen asleep. He couldn't help himself with all that bare, delicious skin on display. He just had to touch. Cade was all flushed and he found it sexy as hell. He ran his fingers down Cade's shoulder to his back. Cade shivered under his touch.

"What was that look you gave me when I first kissed you?" Cade asked.

"What?"

He pulled his eyes away from Cade's back to concentrate on what Cade was saying. "Oh. That wasn't... I was giving myself hell for not seeing that one coming."

Cade snorted out a laugh. He rolled over, closing the distance between them.

"Have you met me? I'm not exactly the kinda guy you see coming," Cade said, laughter still in his voice. He laid his head on Cole's chest and closed his eyes.

There was a smart reply on the tip of his tongue, but he let it go with a breathy laugh, his eyes never leaving Cade's face as he blinked against the sleep creeping up on him.

"I'm gonna fall asleep. Wake me when you're ready for another round," Cade said around a yawn and burrowed closer to Cole. Cade pushed a leg between both of Cole's, something he never allowed, but at that moment he just didn't care. Cade felt too damned good pressed against him.

"Don't think you've had enough?"

He ran a hand through Cade's disheveled curls. Cade cracked an eye open, looking up at him with a smile grazing his lips. "Of you? Never."

Chapter Seven

Cole

FRANKLIN LOOKED *worse. How could he be the one alive when he was the one who looked like death? He didn't know. There was no explanation. There was no reasoning. Not in war. He couldn't keep looking. He didn't want to see. Didn't want to know. If he didn't, it might not be true.*

The sky had been pitch-black when he'd landed the plane only an hour earlier. Now orange and pink were starting to tint the sky. He'd known they'd be coming from two different directions. He'd been watching through the scope of Franklin's Barret M82 sniper rifle as Tank and Stanton arrived first, drawing his attention away from his own surroundings for a mere second.

It was all it took; a second. They all knew that.

His face had been pressed into the mud by one of the enemy soldiers when he'd heard Dom in his ear requesting assistance. He'd managed to throw the man off himself and rolled around to his back. He'd received a punch to his face for that, but he'd barely felt the pain because of all the adrenaline pumping through his veins. The fucker—who'd probably broken his cheekbone with that punch—was on him again and this time he'd pulled a knife. Cole had growled before smacking a fist into the bastard's ugly face while he'd used his other hand to reach down and pull his gun. A second. All it took was a second and the guy was dead, a hole through his skull, and Cole had picked up the rifle again and was back to providing cover for his brothers.

Now, he was standing in the cargo bay of his beloved Lockheed C-130 Hercules airplane—named Meg after the Disney character, because his brothers were childish assholes— where he took in the fact that one of those brothers was dead. It was his worst nightmare come true. He'd finally found his family and now one member was gone. The agonizing pain was worse than any bullet wound he'd acquired over the years. It was worse than the time he'd been too close to one of Mad Dog's bombs.

He was broken out of his reverie by his lieutenants softly spoken, "Go."

He jerked his head up, tearing his eyes away from Derek's bloodied body and looked at Lieutenant Stanton who was standing at the edge of the open ramp, his assault rifle in hand and a deadly look in his eyes. Even though Cole considered all the Raider's his brothers, he couldn't imagine what Stanton was going through, because right there, in front of them, laid Stanton's dead brother.

"Now! That's an order," Stanton yelled when no one moved. He turned to Cole, his voice pleading. "Gunner. Get our brothers home safely and don't come back."

Even as Cole's body was wired to follow the order, his mind couldn't—wouldn't—allow him to move a muscle. He wouldn't be taking all his brothers home safely. One was… Derek was gone. He knew, if he did as he was told, it was two and not one brother he lost. If he hadn't already.

It fucking hurt. More than anything he'd ever felt in his entire life. More than when his mom died, more than when his father took his own pain and sorrow out on Cole. More than when he took his anger out on Cole. The only thing comparing was his lieutenant leaving. He was leaving his team, their team. Their family. And he was putting everything on Cole as he did it.

He closed his eyes. A tear ran down his cheek, blending with the blood and paint covering his face. He was losing everything all over again. He steeled himself. This was it. This was what his father talked about all those times when he hadn't been strong enough. Not this time.

He opened his eyes, gave the Lieutenant a nod of his head and turned on his heels. He made his way to the cockpit. His cockpit. And as he pushed buttons, flicked switches, and turned on the engines, he felt his heart freeze and did nothing to stop it.

Cole woke with a jolt, gasping for breath as he jerked upright. Fucking nightmares. Fucking flashbacks. He drew in breath after breath, relaxing his body and putting his hands back down on the bed when he realized he'd clenched them into fists and held them up in front of his face.

Cade roused next to him and rolled over, latching himself to Cole's body. Cole's gaze went from a spot on the wall to the mop of blond hair in his lap.

"Mm. What time is it?" Cade asked in a gravelly voice.

Cole turned his head and squinted to see the illuminated numbers on the alarm clock on the nightstand.

"Zero five hundred."

"What?" Cade mumbled, sitting up and rubbing his eyes, confusion clear on his face.

"It's five," Cole said with a frown. Shouldn't he know what that meant?

"Too early," Cade grumbled and flopped back on the bed, throwing an arm over his eyes.

Cole took a moment to just stare at the man lying next to him. His blond curls were in disarray. His chest was bare, the blanket barely covering him from the waist down. He couldn't believe he'd been inside that man just a few hours before. He shook his head and moved to get up. He knew he wasn't going to sleep more. No reason to keep Cade awake, too. He'd never gotten a lot of flashbacks, but the nightmares were almost impossible to get rid of. That happened when you'd seen the shit he had.

"Oh no, you don't," Cade said.

Cade was up in a flash, his hands landing on Cole's chest, pushing him back down on the bed. Surprise made him unable to do anything as Cade straddled his hips. He slid a hand into Cade's hair, the other wrapping around Cade's thigh, the ability to think eluding him at the sight before him.

"You woke me at shit o'clock, now you get to pay the prize," Cade said and leaned down to press his lips against Cole's in a sweet, sensual kiss. If that was Cade's version of 'paying the price', he'd pay right up.

The nightmare had shaken him, but he was thankful that it hadn't been a full-blown flashback. Otherwise, Cade wouldn't be able to kiss him and grind down on him as he was right then. With every kiss, with every touch, the darkness disappeared a tiny bit at a time.

With a grunt, he let himself be taken over by his desire. He dug his fingers into Cade's ass, pulling him closer, trying to chase away the remnants of the nightmare.

"Condom," Cade gasped out.

Cole wrenched his right hand out of Cade's mop of hair and searched blindly for the drawer while his tongue ravaged Cade's sweet mouth. Cade laughed when Cole put too much force into pulling the drawer open, sending the damned thing crashing to the floor in his haste. Leaning over the side of the bed, he fished up a condom and the bottle of lube. Cade took it from him with a wicked smile playing on his lips. He ripped the condom open and slowly rolled it down Cole's length. Cole let out a hiss at the touch, fighting to keep his orgasm at bay.

Cade rubbed lube over his fingers before reaching behind himself. A small gasp escaped his lips. Cade didn't use much time preparing himself before he squeezed more lube over his fingers and wrapped them around Cole's dick. He pumped his hand up and down, getting the lube spread out.

Cade then grabbed Cole's dick, squeezing tightly as he held himself over it. Cade took him inside in an agonizingly slow pace and the smile on his lips was downright sinister when he rose up just as slowly. Cole let him play, afraid if he took over he wouldn't be able to control himself. He watched Cade pleasure himself instead. It was one hell of a sight.

He bit his lip. Fuck. He could come just from looking at Cade. He let his eyes roam all over Cade until his gaze was caught by two almost completely black eyes; only a small ring of blue around his wide-blown pupils could be seen. Those dark eyes were filled with lust and mischief as Cade cocked his head to the side, slowing down his movements.

"Am I gonna have to do it all myself?"

"Cade," he warned. A hiss escaped his lips when Cade clenched around him. He grasped at Cade's hips, his fingers digging into overheated skin.

"Come on, baby. I won't break," Cade said.

Cade stilled on top of him, making him choke back a whimper. He looked up from where they were joined to find Cade's scrutinizing eyes on him.

"Is that what you're worried about?" Cade asked. The smile spreading on Cade's face was downright sinister. Cade leaned down, putting his mouth next to Cole's ear, his breath on Cole's sensitive skin causing a shiver to run through him. "Don't worry, I've had bigger guys than you."

Oh, he was not getting away with that. Cole growled and rolled them so Cade was underneath him. Cade let out a breathy laugh which turned into a throaty moan when Cole grabbed his hips and rammed into him. He closed a hand around Cade's pulsing erection and started frantically pumping his hand in time with his thrusts.

When he felt his orgasm close in, he changed his thrusts to long and slow, dragging a mewl out of Cade who squirmed and writhed under him.

"Fuck," Cole gasped when Cade's nails dug into his back.

"Please, please, please," Cade chanted as he writhed, digging his nails further into Cole's skin.

Cole growled and caught Cade's wrists in a vise-like grip, trapping them in his hands above Cade's head. The little bastard liked that, arching his back and trying desperately to drive himself back on Cole's cock. Cade let out a string of curses. Cole had a wicked smile on his lips as he bent down and shut him up with his lips and tongue. He continued with the slow thrusts, enjoying the feeling of being inside Cade.

Cade looked up at him with earnest eyes as a whimper escaped him. That pushed him to the fucking brink. He released Cade's hands to brace himself with the palm of his left hand on the mattress while reaching down with the other to wrap it around Cade's dick. Cade arched up into his touch, a curse falling from his lips. Cole caught all other sounds leaving him with his mouth.

Pleasure shot up his spine just as he felt Cade come over his hand. He watched as Cade came undone, his head thrown back, and his mouth open as ecstasy rocked through him. He kept thrusting into Cade, stroking Cade's dick, until they were both completely spent.

"Shit, that was good," Cade gasped.

"Just good?"

"Bitch," Cade growled.

Cole let out a low laugh before slipping out of Cade's slick heat and putting most of his weight on the other man as he laid his head on Cade's chest, not able to move any further. His body was sated, his mind blissfully blank, and his heart felt lighter than usual. All because of the crazy bastard beneath him. He wasn't entirely sure, but there was a big chance his back was all messed up and he couldn't have cared less.

"You scratched me," Cole mumbled.

Cade's chest rumbled under his head as the man laughed. A mischievous grin met him when he glanced up at Cade. His blue eyes sparkled in the light that flittered into the room from the window.

"Want me to give you a matching set of bite marks, too?"

Cole

Before they left for work, he couldn't help himself as he pressed Cade against his car and devoured his mouth. He'd never done anything like that before, but it felt good. He concluded that Cade must be driving him insane. He wasn't sure if that was such a bad thing.

"Not banging your partner, my ass," Mrs. Jones yelled from her front porch. Cole looked up to see her standing in a pink bathrobe, her arms crossed and a newspaper in hand. She grinned at him, looking like she approved.

"He's not a prude," he yelled back.

Cade gasped and smacked him on the arm, grumbling something unintelligible under his breath. Cade pushed at Cole's chest, making him take a step back.

"I know. The walls aren't as thick as you might think. I get quite the show when you forget the blinds, too," Mrs. Jones said.

Cade turned beet red and hurriedly got into the car, slamming the door hard behind him and dropping his head into his hands. Mrs. Jones' laughter filled the air for a moment before she yelled, "Cute, isn't he?"

"Good day, Mrs. Jones."

Cole got into the car, turning his head to watch Cade. He was sitting stock still, only moving after a few moments to look at Cole with his big eyes.

"She did not just say that," Cade whispered, looking miserable.

"Oh, but she did."

Cade blinked his blue eyes at him. "Please kill me," he whimpered.

Cole was sporting a grin the whole way to the station. He hadn't felt so... light, in a long time. He felt like he could breathe easier around Cade, and then sometimes he felt like he was going crazy, if not with lust, then with anger or irritation at Cade. It confused him more than he'd like to admit.

Cade went in search of coffee first thing when they arrived at the homicide department and Cole continued to their office. He stopped short in the doorway. A young girl sat behind his desk.

"Can I help you?" she asked without looking up from whatever she was doing on his computer, probably checking her Twitter or whatever the hell teenage girls did online.

"I believe that's my line. You *are* sitting at my desk."

Her lips quirked up, but she kept her gaze on the screen as she said, "Hm. I guess that makes you Hotshot, then."

"Excuse me?"

He moved into the room, planting himself in front of his desk. The girl finally looked up, her green eyes lightening up as she smiled widely at him.

"Hi. I'm Morgan."

Cole shook her hand, finding himself amused and pleasantly surprised. Those twinkling eyes of hers held a splash of mischief yet seemed to analyze everything in their path. Seemed like he'd been deemed worthy of her attention.

"Cole Banks. Does your mother know you're here?"

Slight surprise showed on Morgan's face, but it was quickly turned into a smile and a nod of approval. *Well, praise the Lord, the kid might actually like me. That's not strange at all.*

"Yeah, she does. How?" Morgan asked, narrowing her eyes at him.

"Obviously, you don't have your mother's eyes." Lara's were light blue with a ring of orange around the pupils. "But you behave a lot like her from what I've just seen. You've definitely got her I-can-see-right-through-your-bullshit look," he said with a wink. "Besides, you scrunch up your nose the same way. I reckon you're very much like your mom."

"Well, alright then. I'll definitely take that over anything any day."

For a teenager, she seemed a bit overjoyed being told she resembled her mother.

"Not much for your father?" Cole asked on a hunch.

Morgan crossed her arms over her chest and let out an indignant huff. "He's a cowardly bitch."

Hunch confirmed.

"You'd better be talking 'bout your father," Cade said from behind Cole, making him flinch before getting his reflexes back under control so he wouldn't drop the man to the floor.

"Uncle Cade," Morgan shrieked.

She jumped out of Cole's chair and leaped at Cade who enveloped her in a big hug and swung her around with a big dopey smile on his face. He nearly didn't recognize the look in Cade's astonishing blue eyes, it was that long since he'd seen anything close to it. Love. Devotion. Protectiveness. What did that say about him? About what he'd become? He almost couldn't recognize love when it was right in front of him, that's how far he was divided from his emotions. In his efforts to keep out the bad, he'd thrown away the good as well. Some of it, at least. But, was love worth it? Was it worth the pain? The betrayal?

"How are you doing, pretty lady?" Cade asked after letting her down and pressing a kiss to her forehead.

"Fantastic. I like your new partner. He says I'm a lot like my mom," she beamed, pride obvious on her face and in her eyes.

Cade turned his smile on Cole, kicking it up a few notches. Damn, that smile just did something to Cole. He didn't think he'd ever seen anything quite like Cade's smiles.

Hold on. Did she just say she likes me?

"Hey mom, Uncle Cade's new partner seems cool," Morgan called out just as Lara entered their office.

Yeah, she actually did. Well, that was sort of discomforting.

Lara smiled at Cole and then turned to her daughter who'd already started talking about something else. Something about a hawk and wanting to learn archery. Deciding to ignore them—it's not like he understood what the hell they were talking about anyway—he turned to Cade.

"Did you get coffee?"

Cade looked confused for a moment before the question sank in.

"Oh. Yeah, I got coffee. Black, right?" Cade asked, not seeming to require an answer, as he picked up the coffee he'd put on Hobbs' desk before Morgan jumped him and shoved one of the mugs into Cole's hand.

"Thanks," he mumbled down into his coffee mug, keeping his eyes discreetly on Cade as he dropped down into his chair and booted up his computer. He didn't know what was going on. Cade had him tangled in his web somehow. At the moment, the only thing he was sure of, was that he liked fucking Cade. He wasn't sure why, but he liked making him smile as well. Of course, there was the man's body, too. Holy hell. He hadn't thought Cade would have such an athletic build. He had a runner's body; well-defined but still slim.

"Guess what I just found," Cade said.

Cole tore his eyes away from Cade's body and cleared his throat before he could get any words out. "What?"

He winced at how raspy his voice sounded, but Cade just grinned at him and pointed to his computer screen, seemingly oblivious to Cole's slip up. Thankfully, there weren't anyone else around to catch him ogling Cade.

"Sweet little Sandra Dee isn't so lousy with virginity after all," Cade gushed.

"What?"

"It's *Grease*. Really? You don't know *Grease*? What the hell is wrong with you?"

Cole hid a smile behind his coffee mug before he took a sip.

Cade shook his head, looking offended, and turned his screen around so Cole could see it. He recognized the girl in the picture as Sandra Levine, Lowe's girlfriend. She was draped over some guy in the middle of a dancefloor. Cade tapped the right corner of the screen, drawing his gaze there.

The date was the day of Chris Henway's murder, at ten minutes past two in the morning. Just about the time Henway was shot. That could only mean one thing.

"She wasn't home at 9 pm," Cade said.

"Tommy Lowe's alibi doesn't stick."

"Nope," Cade said, popping the p.

"You think he's our guy?"

Cade shook his head. "No. It would've been incredibly stupid of the kid to lead us on a wild goose chase to cover his real intent to kill Henway. It also doesn't make sense for him to kill the others in another state if they were to be a cover for his only important victim, and then draw attention to the final victim by having to switch cities to kill him. Oh, and not to mention that he warned the wife about him."

Cade was right. Unless, of course, Henway screwed it up for Tommy by doing something like move out of town.

"Did Henway live in Fairfax at any point?"

"I don't think so." Cade swiveled his chair around to check on his computer, pulling up Henway's file. A few seconds later he shook his head. "No. He's lived in San Francisco but nowhere near Fairfax."

"Guess we can scratch that theory then. Which still doesn't clear Lowe."

"The only thing that can really clear him is a solid alibi."

"Let's just hope he actually has one." Cole got out of his chair, grabbing his jacket from the back of it. "Let's go have a chat with Lowe."

Cade

"Looks like our lucky day," he said as they exited the car. He gestured toward the beat-up, blue Toyota in the parking lot. The license plate matched Lowe's. He wasn't working then. Cade hadn't thought he would be, which was why they'd gone here first.

Cade pushed the door to the complex open, holding it when he spotted a woman on her way out of the building. Blonde hair, green eyes, and a sneer met him as he looked down at Sandra Levine. When she recognized him, she narrowed her eyes, hissing as she pushed past him. He turned to follow her with his eyes for a moment, then he glanced up at Cole.

"You know. I'm thinking I got the Doctor Dolittle part right, because, I don't know what the hell that was, but it sure as shit wasn't human."

Cole just looked at him with a deadpan expression on his face. He had his work cut out for him where Cole was concerned. Making the man smile and laugh was quickly becoming one of his priorities.

Stopping at Lowe's door, he raised his hand to knock but before his fist could connect with the wood, it opened and Tommy came to a skidding halt in front of them.

"Detectives," he said.

Wherever he'd been going, he hadn't bothered with clean clothes. Or shaving. Or combing his hair. The kid was a wreck. Cade had an inkling Sandra Dee may have had a hand in that.

"May we come in?"

"Sure."

Tommy gestured for them to follow him into the living room. They took a seat on the couch while Tommy offered to make them some coffee. Cole declined but Cade said yes, if only to give the kid some time to collect himself before Cole had at him. When Tommy returned from the kitchen, he put a steaming mug down in front of Cade and sat down.

"Did you find out who killed him?"

"Where were you the night of Chris Henway's murder?" Cole asked.

Tommy blanked for a moment. "What? I already told you—"

"You lied."

Tommy's eyes looked like they were about to pop out of his head.

"You gave us a false alibi. Do you even understand the consequences of that?"

Tommy shook his head. "I don't know what you're talking about."

"You deliberately told us your girlfriend could vouch for you, which she can't because you know damned well she wasn't home until three a.m., which also means that you've made her an accomplice to hindering the police in a murder investigation or essentially an accomplice to murder," Cole said.

"I don't—"

Cade and Tommy both jumped when Cole slammed his fist down on the tabletop, rattling their coffee cups.

"You lied to us and because of that lie you're our number one suspect. Do you get that? Do you get that you're being considered a murderer? That because of you, we might not find the one who actually killed him? Now. Where were you the night of Chris Henway's murder?"

Tommy was breathing rapidly, looking down at his clasped hands, tears rolling down his cheeks as he choked out, "I'm sorry. I'm sorry."

"It's okay," Cade said, sending Cole a warning glare when he looked like he was going to object. Christ, couldn't he see the kid was close to having an anxiety attack?

He let Tommy take his time to get his breathing under control before he encouraged him to answer Cole's question. "Tell us what happened that night."

"Sandra was out, and I was supposed to be home. I told her I was gonna be home that night, but I… I went out. I needed to know. I had to try. For her, you know? I couldn't let her be stuck with me if I were… if I were… gay." He said the last part so low Cade almost didn't catch it. But he did, and he found himself surprisingly speechless.

"So, you didn't tell us, because?" Cole prompted.

"Because I still don't know."

"Can anyone confirm where you were?" Cade asked.

Tommy nodded. "There were cameras in the club. I remember trying not to freak out about it."

"What's the name of the club?"

"Glitter."

Cade scribbled down on his pad, then paused and glanced up at Tommy. "You hook up with anyone while you were there?"

The pink tinting Tommy's cheeks and neck was answer in itself. Still, he gave an embarrassed nod.

"Did you get his name?"

"Do you really have to—"

"Thomas."

Tommy let out a defeated sigh, then rubbed his hands together nervously. He gnawed a bit on his lip before answering. "Liam. He works at the club. Bartending. It's all I've got."

"We'll need a description with that."

Fifteen minutes later they were standing outside the club. It was located by the Inner Harbor section of downtown Baltimore. It was a big two-story building and if he wasn't much mistaken it hadn't been a gay club named *Glitter,* of all things, a few months ago.

"It's too early for the club to be open. We should try to find out who the owner is and give him a call to get Liam's credentials," Cole said.

Cade turned his back to the door, grinning up at Cole. "Or, we could just go inside." He pushed the door handle down behind him. The door slid open.

Cole shook his head and brushed against him as he walked first through the door.

"Hello? Police. Is anybody here?"

Silence was all that met them.

"Let's split up and see if we can find someone here," Cole said.

He nodded in agreement and started down a hallway opposite the way Cole was headed. The walls were painted a dark red and black doors adorned each side of the hall. If he had to guess, he'd say this was probably a private section of the club. Something told him not to call out. Chills ran down his spine. Something was definitely wrong here.

"Will you look at that," a deep voice sounded from behind Cade. He didn't have to look to know who'd snuck up on him. The hairs rising at the back of his neck said enough.

"Slay," Cade said.

He turned around to find dark eyes roaming over him. The man was big and sturdy, his dark hair pulled back in a ponytail. He was dressed in black leather and motorcycle boots. Cade knew what the man looked like beneath those clothes, though he sure as shit wished he didn't.

"Didn't take you as the gay-clubbing type," Cade said. At least not while it was light out.

Slay grinned at him. "I'm not."

"Then what are you doing in a place like this?"

"Working."

"Really? Working? You want me to believe that?"

"Yes. We own this place."

"The Destroyers own Glitter?" Cade asked with an astonished look on his face. Well, hell. A motorcycle club owning a gay bar? He would've laughed if it weren't for the big, dangerous biker glaring down at him.

"What are you doing here, detective?"

"I'm looking for Liam." He didn't doubt Slay knew exactly who he was talking about.

"Torell? What'd he do?"

"You know I can't share that with you," Cade said.

"Oh, but I remember you sharing plenty with me, detective," Slay said with a lascivious smile on his lips as he let his lusty eyes take in Cade from top to bottom.

Cade fought a shudder.

"Lawson."

Cade looked over Slay's shoulder to find Cole glaring at him, though he also found concern in his eyes. The man was a marine, and a homicide detective; he recognized a threat when he saw it.

"Got yourself a new partner, huh? Maybe he'll last longer than the last one."

Slay was baiting him, but he ignored it and instead asked, "Torell?"

"Don't know where he is, but he ain't here," Slay answered with an indifferent shrug. Cade wasn't about to ask him for the papers he knew Slay kept with Torell's information. He just needed to get out of there.

"I'll see you around, detective," Slay said, backing away.

Cade didn't wait, he just hurried the hell out of there, knowing Cole would follow. He pushed through the front door, stopping to take in a much-needed breath.

"Lawson. What the hell?"

He ignored him and walked toward the car.

"What the hell was that? What was he talking about?"

"I'm not corrupt if that's what you think," Cade said, his voice low.

"Then what the…Wait. You let that guy fuck you?"

Cade heard the surprise but all he seemed to latch on to was the judgment in Cole's voice. His blood ran cold and his whole body started thrumming. He couldn't stop his mind from connecting Cole's question to another guy, another time.

"So what? I let you fuck me," Cade sneered, his anger and anxiety taking over.

"What the fuck?"

Cole grabbed Cade's wrist to stop him, but Cade twisted around and slammed the heel of his hand into Cole's chest. Cole let go, though it was most likely out of surprise and not pain. Seeing the shock on Cole's face, he couldn't help but sneer.

"What? You think because I don't like violence it means I can't defend myself?"

Cole barked out, "What the hell is this about?"

"Fuck off, Banks," Cade said, pivoted on his heels and started toward the car on the other side of the street.

Just as he reached it, he was spun around and pinned against the side of the car. He struggled, but Cole pressed his body against his, rendering him immobile. He knew how to get out of the hold, but the fight was slowly seeping out of him.

"What is this about?"

The look in Cole's eyes made Cade shut his own tightly and drop his head back. Bloody hell. He'd done it again.

"I'm sorry," Cade croaked.

"No."

Cade opened his eyes to stare at Cole. Warm, soothing fingers trailed down his jaw, making a sigh escape him.

"Don't be sorry. This has nothing to do with him or me, does it?"

"No."

They stood there for a moment, Cole holding him gently, a hand brushing through Cade's hair and the other on the small of Cade's back.

"Survivors guilt?" Cole asked.

A surprised puff of air left Cade, then he narrowed his eyes. "How the hell...?"

"They always get this special look in their eyes," Cole said, his voice hoarse.

"Who?"

"Most of my team."

"Who died?"

The silence stretched for so long Cade thought he might not answer, but he did, closing his eyes and leaning his forehead against Cade's.

"The only one who really deserved to live."

"It's always them," Cade said. He swallowed the lump of grief and regret clogging his throat.

Cole nuzzled his face into Cade's neck. Cade slid his fingers into Cole's hair, holding onto it tightly to keep Cole against him a bit longer.

They rode in silence after Cole made a call to get Torell's address. They were doing that more often than not; driving in silence. It was starting to look like a habit. He really hated it. He leaned back in his seat, watching Cole out of the corner of his eye, his brain finally functioning again.

"You didn't get survivors guilt from a look in my eyes," Cade said.

"No. But it's still there."

He drew in a breath and leaned forward to turn on the radio, finding a channel that played eighties tunes. He kept an eye on Cole as he started singing along, but save for a quick glance in his direction, Cole didn't react.

Cole parked it at the address they'd been given and they both got out of the car. When Cole came around to Cade's side of the car, Cade turned to him with a puzzled expression.

"He's a bartender, right?"

"Yes," Cole said.

"How does a bartender afford something like that?"

He gestured toward the two-story house in front of them. It was white with a black roof, a big front door, and an even bigger walkway. Then there was the garage and the car in front of it.

Cole didn't answer, so he walked up to the front door and rang the bell. The man opening the door could only be the man Tommy had described earlier. He was a bit more on the scruffy side than Cade thought he'd be, but otherwise, the green eyes, the wavy brown hair, the sprinkle of stubble covering his chin and even the muscular chest was on point. He could even see the perfect v-cut the guy had, seeing as he was only wearing sweatpants.

"Can I help you?"

Cole held up his badge. Cade was too busy looking the guy over, not having any trouble imagining him with Tommy. He looked like the kind of guy who would protect someone like Tommy.

"Detectives Lawson and Banks. We're looking for Liam Torell."

"You found him," the guy said.

"We would like to have a few words with you," Cole said.

"Come on in."

He opened the door for them and led them into the living room where he gestured toward the couch.

"Please, take a seat. I'll just go grab a shirt."

When Torell returned, he was wearing a blue T-shirt. He sat down opposite them, crossing his ankles and his arms.

"Where were you last Wednesday night?" Cole asked.

"Glitter. The nightclub where I work. I was covering for Chase that night."

"Something happen to make you remember that night specifically?"

Liam squinted at Cole, uncrossing his arms and leaning forward. "What is this about?"

"Were you with someone that night?" Cole asked.

"You mean intimately? Yeah," Liam said.

So far, so good. If Liam confirmed Tommy's story, the kid would officially be off the suspect list. Tommy had been through more than enough in his young life and he wanted the kid to be able to move on.

"Give us the rundown of the night," Cole said.

"The club is popular, so we get a bit more patrons on the weekdays than most others. This guy walked in about twelve, and he seemed like the ordinary closet case. You know; trying to look inconspicuous but failing hard. We started talking and one thing led to another."

"His name?"

"Thomas. I don't know any more than that. We didn't get to exchange numbers, unfortunately. He's a sweet little thing, I'll tell ya that. Innocent, too."

Cade cleared his throat and asked, "You had sex, then?"

"Oh, yeah." Liam's smile vanished when he noticed the looks on Cole and his faces. "Hold up. He wanted it. I didn't force him to do anything. Look, he laid his cards out and I laid out mine. We were in agreement."

"His cards?"

Liam winced, then said, "The guy was abused as a kid. He said he was trying to figure out if he was into guys or not. He didn't want those experiences to color the rest of his life."

Cole was rigid beside him, an air of hostility wafting off of him. His voice was rough when he spoke.

"Understandable. When did you part ways?" Cole asked.

"Around two. Give or take five minutes," Liam said.

"Did you see where he went?"

"Well, I let him out the back door. The one leading into the alley behind Glitter. I don't know where he went after that."

Cade breathed a sigh of relief. Tommy was off the list, then. That meant they could concentrate on catching their killer and Tommy wouldn't have any more cops at his front door.

"Is he alright? Did he do something?" Liam asked.

"He's fine as of right now seeing as you just confirmed his alibi," Cade said.

Liam's jaw tightened, his hands clenching into fists. The guy was pissed. Cade cocked his head to the side, watching Liam try to get himself under control.

"So, this has nothing to do with me? I'm just his alibi?" Liam asked, a bite to his tone.

"Exactly, and I'm gonna need you to write a witness statement, so if you have time, I would like for you to come with us to the station," Cole said.

Cade's gaze darted between Cole and Liam, one more hostile than the other. What the hell was it with those two?

"Sure," Liam said through his teeth.

Cole and Liam stood at the same time, glaring at each other. Liam motioned toward the front door.

"If you wouldn't mind. I'll be just a second," Liam said.

Cade stood and pulled a reluctant Cole with him outside. Cole was shooting glares over his shoulder, much to Cade's amusement.

"Wanna tell me what that was all about?"

Cole shoved his hands into his pockets and rocked back on his heels. His gaze flittered around for a moment before settling on Cade's eyes.

"Sorry. I just… snapped."

"I'm pretty sure that's a first. You alright, babe?"

He reached out, laying a hand on Cole's shoulder. Cole hauled him closer, leaning his forehead against Cade's.

"A hell of a day, huh?" Cole asked.

"You can say that again," Cade said and took a step back, clearing his throat. "Now, let's get out of here before we do something more unprofessional."

Cole's laughter made his heart soar. It was strange how one person's happiness could mean so much to another. Cole had taken it in stride when he'd freaked out earlier. He'd said and done some stupid things, yet Cole hadn't judged him. There were so many parts of his life, parts of himself, he couldn't share with others. Not that he'd particularly wanted to. Not until Cole.

The front door opening brought him back to the present. Cole's laughter faded, but a tiny smile remained. Cade turned to watch Liam close and lock his door. The scowl was gone and it seemed the attitude was as well.

Liam followed them to the station in his own car, then walked with them from the parking garage into the elevator. Once they were on the right floor, Cade strode straight toward Claire's desk.

"Hey, Miss Claire. Liam here is gonna write a statement. Do you mind helping my partner with it?"

"Sure." She turned a smile Liam's way. "Come with me, honey."

Cade turned back to the elevator, pushing the button to make the doors open again. He stepped inside and waited for the elevator to descend.

"Where are you going?" Cole yelled.

He glanced over his shoulder. Cole was looking at him with a puzzled expression. The doors started to slide shut.

"Vice."

Cade

Stepping out of the elevator on the floor of the vice department, he almost collided with the only female detective there. He managed to sidestep her so they were both standing in front of the elevator, Cade with a hand preventing the door from closing.

Vice detective Emma O'Neil grinned at him. "I'm guessing you didn't get out on the wrong floor, huh?"

"Most certainly not."

There were only two people in vice who didn't hate him and the woman in front of him was one of them. Two, plus Stryker who didn't care either way.

"Oh, I'm gonna enjoy watching this," Emma said.

She grinned up at him, her eyes twinkling with mischief. She held her hand out, indicating for him to proceed her and then she followed him into the squad room.

Unlike the homicide department which was divided into cubicles except for the two offices, the vice department was one huge room with a few desks to the right, two couches to the left and the whole back wall lined with shelves that were filled to the brim with case files. Detectives Joseph Chan and Matt Stryker slouched on a couch each, Stryker looking to actually be asleep. Gillies was at his desk—the one furthest from the entrance—typing away at his keyboard. The team leader, Ian Mackintosh, was seated at his desk, his eyes unblinking as he watched something on his screen. None of them noticed Emma and him entering the room.

"Hello, boys," Cade said and wagged his eyebrows at them, smiling like the Cheshire cat when they all let out groans or grunts.

"Fuck off, Lawson," Mackintosh said without looking up from his computer.

"Aw, Mackie, you don't want the intel I've got for you?"

"It's Mackintosh, and I'm not sure your intel is worth it," Mackintosh growled.

"Oh, baby, I'm worth it and you know it," Cade purred.

He planted his ass right on Mackintosh's desk, making sure to put his crotch right in the man's line of sight.

"So, guess what I found at a gay nightclub."

Groans and pleas for mercy went around the room. He really loved teasing these guys. They were so bloody easy.

"STD's?" Mackintosh suggested, rolling his chair back from Cade and his crotch.

Cade wagged a finger at him disapprovingly while clicking his tongue. "It's called Glitter. I'm sure you guys know it."

"Why would we know any gay clubs?"

"Because you're all closet cases?"

Gillies smacked his head down on his table and it sounded like it hurt. Cade bit his cheek to not laugh outright.

"What the hell do you want, Lawson?" Mackintosh asked.

"Besides pulling your leg?"

Mackintosh glared at him. Though he didn't feel threatened, he still put his hands up.

"Alright. Alright."

He grinned at them all before saying, "The Destroyers bought Glitter."

A lot of big eyes turned his way.

"Let's hope none of ya needs to go undercover there. You'd all break within half an hour."

He knew these guys took pride in their undercover work, and the fact none of them protested said quite a lot.

"I'll take your silence as a thank you. See ya, boys," Cade said with a wave.

Emma was standing right next to the doorway, a smug smile on her face as she held up a hand for him to high five as he passed her. He walked toward the elevator, stopping in the hallway between the squad room and the kitchen. There, he leaned against the wall. He didn't need to wait long before his target rounded the corner. Brown eyes met his and widened as the man came to an abrupt halt.

"Cade."

"Hi, Brent."

Cade opened his arms, knowing his former partner wouldn't be able to resist. With a shake of his head and a beginning smile, Brent stepped into his embrace. Cade wrapped his arms around him and squeezed him tightly. He pulled back and planted a loud kiss on Brent's cheek.

"What are you doing down here?" Brent asked and looked over Cade's shoulder into the squad room. He knew Brent was watching for the other detectives. It was bad enough Cade was down here. No one needed to know they were talking.

"I got some intel for you guys." Cade shrugged, a smile playing on his lips.

"Oh. So, you just came down here to yank their chains a bit?"

"That, too."

Brent laughed, likely knowing how that had gone.

"How you been?" Cade asked.

A soft smile graced Brent's face. "Pretty good actually. I like Vice."

"Good. That's good. Listen, I—"

Brent raised a hand, cutting him off.

"Don't, Cade. You've apologized more than enough. I'm fine. I promise." Brent got a gleam in his eyes. "Turns out, I'm quite good at this Vice thing. Oh, and I heard you got a new partner."

Cade couldn't help but snort. "Temporary partner."

"You don't sound so happy about that," Brent said.

Truth be told, he wasn't exactly sure how to feel about it.

"Shut up, probie," Cade said.

He ruffled up Brent's hair. Brent grimaced and batted his hand away, though he didn't put much strength in it.

"How are things with the boys down here?"

"Peachy. Everything is just as it should be," Brent said with a wink.

"I'm glad you like it."

They'd both been hurt, and he'd felt like shit when Brent was forced to transfer to Vice. He missed the guy. He'd been a good partner.

"Lawson?"

They both turned. Cole was standing by the elevator, waiting impatiently. Cade held up two fingers indicating he'd be two minutes more. Cole didn't look happy about it.

"I'm pretty sure that guy's the epitome of dark and dangerous," Brent said, awe evident in his voice.

"Oh yeah, he is."

He knew he sounded and most likely looked like a teenager swooning over some dreamy hunk. He just couldn't help it. The man was hot as hell with the dark stubble covering his jaw and those green eyes of his.

"Oh my god. You're sleeping with him."

He grinned at Brent, who stared at him with his jaw close to the floor.

"Plausible deniability, Brent. Plausible deniability."

"Fuck you," Brent muttered, but a smile still grazed his lips.

"No, thanks. I've got dark, dangerous, and sexy over there for that."

"Ha. I've missed you, asshole," Brent said.

"Who the fuck wouldn't," Cade said as he walked backwards toward Cole. Brent snorted at him. Cade blew him a kiss before turning around and waving over his shoulder. He stepped into the elevator, Cole right behind him. He glanced up, catching Cole looking at him curiously, but Cole quickly averted his eyes. Cade had to bite his lip not to smile.

"You're dying to know, aren't you?"

"No," Cole grumbled.

"Liar."

"Shut up or tell me."

"He's my former partner. The one Slay talked about," Cade said.

"You went to see him?"

He shrugged. "Well, I went to tell vice about Glitter, but essentially, yes, I went to see him."

"Why?"

The elevator doors sliding open made him stall on answering until they were inside the parking garage.

"We were working a case. I was part undercover, working Slay over while having him believe I was crooked. Things went bad and Brent was targeted."

It was only the tip of the iceberg, but it was all he could say.

"So, you're saying that Slay threatened me earlier?"

"Yeah."

"Great."

"Don't worry, I'll protect you from the big, bad biker."

Cole looked him over, scrunching his brows together. "Right."

Cade flipped him off. He may not be that much of a fighter when it came to hand to hand combat, but he was a cop; he knew how to aim and pull the trigger.

"I found out how Torell can afford the house. He and his brother inherited a lot of money when their grandmother died. Old money," Cole said.

"He's legit, then?"

"Looks like it."

He really tried, but he just couldn't keep it in any longer. He stopped walking and when Cole noticed and turned around, he blurted out, "What exactly are we doing?"

Cole looked at him with a serious expression coloring his face. "Solving a murder."

"Not that." He gestured between them. "Us."

"We're partners. Who fuck," Cole said.

Not exactly how he'd put it, but sure, he could go with that.

"So, we're clear on that?"

Cole nodded curtly. "Absolutely."

"Good."

Cole turned and walked toward the car. He followed Cole with his eyes, his gaze dropping to Cole's ass. He bit his lip to hold back a groan. *I'm so fucking screwed.*

Chapter Eight

Cade

"YOU'RE DROOLIN'," Lara said.

"Huh," Cade said before his brain un-clouded. "Oh."

It was way too early for him to even be awake and, least of all, be at the station's gym. Though the sight of Cole training and sparring without a shirt on was well worth it.

"Liar," Cade said after having rubbed a hand over a dry chin. Lara just laughed, undeterred. She bumped his shoulder.

"You were so checking out your partner. Admit it, you think he's hot."

He looked away from her, his eyes instantly landing on Cole. A smile worked at his lips.

"He's so hot, he makes steam look cool," Cade said in a singsong voice, his eyes devouring his partner both at work and in bed. Hell, yeah, he thought Cole was hot.

"Where've I heard that before?" Lara mused with her nose scrunched up and her eyes narrowed in thought.

"Hercules," Cade answered, deciding to put her out of her misery while still doing his best to not crack a smile.

"Morgan," Lara said on a sigh.

"Yep. She's totally got me hooked. I'm a grown man. I can admit it."

"Admit what?" Cole butted in as he joined them, sweat dripping from his forehead and into his eyes as he leaned down to take the towel Cade held out for him.

"I'm addicted to everything Disney," Cade stated with a shrug and a grin.

"It's not the only thing you're addicted to," Cole said with a grin and a chuckle, not seeming to get the same train of thought as Cade did at those words.

When Cole sat down next to him, he leaned in close.

"I'm pretty much addicted to your dick," Cade whispered, his lips almost touching Cole's ear and making a shiver run through his body.

"Tease," Cole said as he swatted him with the towel. Cole stood back up after grabbing a water bottle, which he took a few sips of before putting it down. He crossed his arms over his chest and looked at Cade and Lara with raised eyebrows. "You two just gonna sit there in your workout clothes, doing nothing?"

"Yep. I'm fairly content right here," Cade said while patting the bench he and Lara were sitting on. "We've become good friends, Mr. Bench and I."

"I'm sure you two have a lot in common," Cole said.

Cade mock-gasped and flipped him off.

"Come on, then. I'll give you somethin' to do, brat," Lara said while wagging a finger at Cole as she stood up.

"Uh-oh. Marine versus marine," Cade said and rubbed his palms together. This could turn out to be fun after all.

"You're a marine?" Cole asked with a surprised yet awed look on his face.

"Born 'n' bred, honey," Lara replied with a cheeky smile.

"Daddy was a Recon Marine and Granny was a Raider." She shrugged. "There was no other way for me to go."

"What's a Raider?" Cade asked when he noticed Cole freezing up at the word. Yeah, he was a bitch sometimes. Well. It wasn't like Cole shared much on his own anyway. Cole's whole no-mixing-work-with-personal-stuff thing apparently also extended to the guy he was fucking. Cade wanted to know everything about this man and if he had to play dirty to get it, he would. Lucky for him, he knew all the tricks in the book. Hell, his grandma might as well have written the damned thing.

126

"Forefathers to the Recon Marines. They were the first on ground durin' World War Two," Lara said.

Huh. That didn't shed much light on Cole's reaction. Maybe his grandfather was a Raider too? No matter, he'd get it out of him eventually.

"No breaking bones," Cade yelled after them when they walked to the mat. "The captain is just gonna blame me for it."

It was true. If anything got broken, misplaced, or just about anything else, Morris automatically blamed him. All because of that one time with the tambourine. That guy could hold a grudge like no one else.

As Lara and Cole got into position across from each other, he sorta wished he'd had the foresight to bring popcorn. Or a camera. This was going to be epic. Cole wasn't going to hold back just because Lara was a woman, but she didn't know that. Cole didn't land any hard punches at first, lulling Lara into a false sense of superiority. It was when Lara started to let her guard down that Cole attacked with a series of vicious punches and kicks, not holding anything back. Lara dodged, but he'd caught her off guard and cornered her. Cade was sitting on the edge of his seat, curious to see if Lara could best Cole. Even from here, he could see the sheen of sweat on Lara's skin.

Lara put space between them, her eyes following every movement from Cole as she kept her fists up in front of her. Cole rolled back on his heels, a huge grin splitting his face. If Cade wasn't mistaken, Cole was having a hell of a good time.

Cole circled around Lara, trying to get closer without her noticing, but Lara kept a good three feet between them. Cole kicked out but Lara caught his foot. She twisted it so he didn't have a choice but to roll his body, which would usually take someone down, but Cole kicked off with his other foot, spun in the air and kicked Lara in the chest. She released his other foot as she was pushed backwards, almost falling on her ass. Cole tucked and rolled, coming right up on his feet again.

Lara glared at him as she rubbed her chest. "What the hell was that?"

127

Cole shrugged. "I know a guy."

"You seem to know a lot of guys." She crossed her arms over her chest, an eyebrow raising at Cole.

Cole grinned at her, his eyes gleaming.

"I do, and trust me, you don't want them all in the same room. When we are, even Uncle Sam is shaking in his boots," Cole said.

"I'll make *you* shake in your boots," Lara said. She beckoned him closer with a finger.

They got into position across from each other, Lara watching Cole with scrutinizing eyes. She was prepared when he swung at her and managed to duck away from his fist. Lara landed a blow that made Cole step back and shake his head before he gathered himself again, a dangerous smile creeping onto his lips. It happened so fast the next thing Cade saw was Lara on the ground, Cole crouching over her as he held her down until she tapped out.

Tanner walked into the room and promptly took a detour around Lara and Cole. He was obviously smart enough not to want any part of that action. Cade kept up with his running because he wanted to stay in shape even though he wasn't on the beat anymore, but sparring was a whole other thing. Since neither Tanner, Mike, nor he, could keep up with Lara, they tended to spar with each other, if they absolutely needed to.

Tanner whistled at Cole. "Are those scratch marks? Caught yourself a wild tiger for the night, did ya Banks?"

Cade almost swallowed his tongue when Cole's dark, hungry, and hooded eyes connected with his own for a moment before Cole glanced back at Tanner.

"Something like that," Cole answered with a wry grin.

If only they knew. Cade was the one with bite marks on his ass.

Cole

Cole just got out of the showers when his phone rang. He slung a towel around his hips, grabbed his phone, and placed himself away from the lockers so he'd have some privacy.

"Banks."

"Hiya, Gunner," a chipper voice said.

"Franklin. You find anything?"

He'd called him two days before, asking for his help. Franklin had been out on a call then, but he'd texted the day before, letting Cole know he was back and would start looking into it for him.

"Sure did. Turns out, your boy Henway went to college with some rather fancy people."

"How fancy?"

"Think billionaires and Senators' kids kinda fancy."

"Shit. They helped him bury his record?"

He rubbed the bridge of his nose. God damned it. This whole thing just became ten times more complicated.

"Looks like it."

"I need names," Cole said.

"I'll send you a text with them, alright?"

"Sure. Thank you, brother."

"Aw, you're welcome, sweetie," Franklin said.

Cole hung up while shaking his head. He loved the guy, but he could be flamboyant as shit. It was a good thing their unit hadn't been a part of the Don't Ask Don't Tell policy. They'd have been down half a team if it that was the case.

He jerked his head up when he heard someone entering the locker room. From where he stood, he could see part of the lockers and he soon got a clear view of Cade as he stopped in front of his locker and started to undress. Cade pulled his workout shirt over his head, slowly revealing creamy skin, inch by inch.

He couldn't believe he'd had that man every night the past few days. It didn't matter how exhausting their workday had been, Cade was always up for something, even if it was only a lazy hand job as they kissed messily.

After making sure they were alone, he snuck up on Cade, pressing his front against Cade's back. Cade jumped, then cursed him vividly. Cole ran his hand over the bare skin of Cade's stomach, the muscles contracting beneath his fingers, before leaning down to put his mouth by Cade's ear.

"You need a shower after sitting on the bench?"

Cade turned in his arms and looked up into his eyes.

"Not really. I just caught you watching."

Cade shrugged as a blush rose on his cheeks. Cole's eyes dropped to Cade's lips. After everything in the gym, he really wanted to fucking ravish the man. Lara managed to get him on his toes, adrenalin pumping through him, but Tanner's comment made him remember all the dirty things he'd done and still wanted to do to Cade.

"My guy came up with some names," Cole said instead.

"Alright. Let's get to it, then."

When he didn't release Cade, the other man narrowed his eyes at him before looking around quickly and rising up on his toes to press a kiss to his lips. Cole growled against Cade's lips as adrenalin and desire burned through him. He nibbled at Cade's lips before opening up for Cade's tongue. Cade's back hit the locker with a thud. He slid a hand into Cade's hair, tugging it to move his head and get better access. He rubbed his tongue against Cade's, his other hand sliding down Cade's naked torso. Feeling the burning skin under his hands felt so fucking good. He grasped Cade's hip, his grip bruising. It just made Cade kiss him harder.

When Cade's hands ventured under Cole's towel, he broke the kiss, taking a few steps back to put some space between them. They both stood there, heaving for breath as they watched each other. Cade licked his red and swollen lips, a mischievous expression on his face. Fucking hell. Just the smell of Cade could get him hard. Having him look at him with lust darkening his eyes, made it almost impossible to stay away.

A door slammed open, followed by loud voices.

Fuck. Fucking fuck. Cole turned his back to the men just entering and pulled his clothes out of his gym bag with jerky movements. They both dressed quickly, reality crashing down on them hard. Surprisingly, Cade finished first and was waiting by the door for him when he was ready.

He held the door for Cade to walk out first.

"That was close," Cade said over his shoulder.

"Too close," he said. "We're not gonna be doing that at work again."

"Technically, we aren't at work. Yet."

It didn't matter. They were still surrounded by coworkers.

"Still not happening."

"And *I'm* supposed to be the prude," Cade drawled.

Cole turned to tell Cade off, but the look on his face was somber and understanding. He didn't care if people knew he was gay, but if they were found out, they would be split up as partners. He didn't want that. He liked working with Cade.

He checked his phone for the names. Franklin had supplied him with social security numbers, names, addresses, and phone numbers. He dropped down into his chair and booted up his computer. He printed out what he could find on them.

Cade retrieved the photos of them from the printer and put them up on the whiteboard, writing their names under the pictures. Stepping back and glancing over his shoulder at Cole, he said, "Henway had some powerful friends, huh?"

"He sure did," Cole said.

"We've got a lawyer, two trust fund babies, an engineer, and the owner of a big software development company."

"If they did it themselves, I think we know which one of them hid Henway's record," Cole said.

Cade bobbed his head. "Jeffrey Davies. The owner of Sense Tech."

Cade got out all the papers they had on him. He watched as Cade went through them and then Cade looked up at him with a frown. "How did you get his name?"

"My friend got them digging into Henway's missing record. Why?"

Cade didn't answer straight away, instead, he looked thoughtful as he chewed on the end of his pen, his eyes studying the picture of Davies. Cade took the pen out of his mouth to point it at the picture. "Everyone else went to college with Henway, but not this guy. It doesn't even say which college he went to." He turned to Cole, his head cocked to the side. "Did your guy say when Henway's files were hidden?"

"No. I'll see if he knows."

He sent Franklin a text, knowing he'd answer fast. Sure enough, a few seconds later his phone vibrated with a new message.

"He says about eight months ago."

"Eight months? Isn't that the same time as he met his wife?" Cade asked.

"Yeah, I think so," Cole said.

He got out his notes. It took some time, but he found the one he needed. "Mrs. Henway said they married after two months and the wedding was six months ago."

"I guess the question then is were the papers hidden before or after he met her?" Cade asked, an eyebrow raised at Cole.

"I'll ask my guy if he can get a closer date."

"I'll call Mrs. Henway," Cade said, getting out his phone.

While Cole waited for Franklin to answer, he picked up Cade's and his coffee mugs and headed to the kitchen. He came back with coffee and Franklin's answer. Cade was still speaking with Mrs. Henway when Cole entered the room. He put down Cade's coffee on his desk in front of him. Cade glanced up, a smile spreading on his face when he noticed the coffee.

Cole leaned back against the desk opposite Cade's and watched the man try to hold back a moan after taking a sip of his coffee. Cole had learned pretty quick that the easiest way to get a compliant Cade was to give him coffee. Well, he had other ways too, but as they were at work, coffee was the only way to go.

"She said they met at a speed dating event on the first of August," Cade said the second he hung up.

"His record was hidden two weeks prior to that, so my guess is Henway didn't come here to start over," Cole said.

"Tommy may have been right," Cade said.

Cole nodded, the same thought having struck him. "Makes me glad we're investigating Henway's murder and not Tommy's."

"Agreed."

Cade stood, picked up his coffee mug and walked to the whiteboard. He tapped Davies's photo on the board with a finger. "This guy is the most exposed. The one who has the most to lose."

"You think he could've killed Henway?" Cole asked.

"It's a possibility."

Cole quirked a smile. "Let's find out."

Cade

The building in which Sense Tech was located looked like it cost a fortune. Jeffrey Davies was doing well for himself. Why the hell would he commit fraud? Then again, a lot of rich people did it.

Once they made it through the security and the guy at the front desk directed them to the right place, they took the elevator to the tenth floor. They stepped out and Cade stopped to look around the open space. There was no questioning which office belonged to Davies. His name was on the door in big, white letters. A woman sat behind a grand desk in front of it, conversing with a man in a pristine grey suit.

"Jeffrey Davies?" Cole asked as they neared.

He turned around, greeting them with a smile and held a hand out for them to shake.

"Welcome. What can I do for you, detectives?"

"We're here about the murder of Chris Henway," Cole said.

Davies didn't look all that surprised, just confused. He glanced from Cole to Cade. "Excuse me? Who? And did you say murder?"

"Perhaps we should take this conversation to a more private location," Cole suggested.

"Let's," Davies agreed somberly.

They followed him into an office with a big wooden desk and floor to ceiling windows looking out over the Inner Harbor. It was quite a stunning view.

"Please, have a seat."

Cade sat down, knowing Cole wouldn't. He'd probably do his whole standing in the corner with a scowl on his face routine. Davies sat down in his chair, leaning forward to catch Cade's eyes.

"Who is this man you were talking about?"

"Chris Henway. The man whose record you made disappear," Cole said.

"That's a crime, by the way," Cade added.

Davies' eyes went wide with shock. He shook his head as if to clear it. "Yes, I'm well aware of that, which is why I would never do it."

"You wouldn't help a friend start a new life?" Cade asked.

"Depends on whether they need a new life because of something they did or something that was done to them. Besides, I've never even heard of someone named Chris Henway."

"So, you didn't kill him either?"

He felt Cole's disapproving glare to the back of his head.

"No."

Cade had been around a lot of liars in his life, and he was so certain Jeffrey Davies wasn't lying, he would bet his grandmother's Chelsea Bun recipe on it. Which was saying a lot. It was the only thing he could make from scratch. Anything else was a no-go. Hell, he once managed to set a pot of spaghetti on fire. He still didn't know how that happened.

"Excuse us for a second," Cade said as he stood then motioned for Cole to follow him.

He turned so Cole was the one standing in the corner with a view of Davies and the door. He shoved his hands into his pockets, a bout of nerves hitting him hard as he met Cole's questioning eyes.

"He's not lying," Cade said in a soft voice, just low enough for Davies not to overhear.

"Why are you so sure?"

He drew in a breath. What the hell was he supposed to say? What could he say?

"Just... trust me?"

He watched as emotions flashed in Cole's eyes too fast for him to catch. Cole gave a curt nod of his head. Cade gave Cole a brief smile before turning and going back to sit down in front of Davies.

"Would you look at some papers for us?"

He ignored the deadly look Cole gave him. That he'd actually brought the papers was probably enough to get his ass kicked, but now that he was handing them over to Davies? Hell, who knew.

"Um, sure," Davies said a bit hesitantly.

Davies took the papers Cade held out for him, looking somewhat confused. Davies frowned and then made his way to his chair where he booted up his computer. He clicked around for a few minutes. Cade wasn't sure, but he had a hunch Davies was hacking the Sex Offender Registry. He liked that guy.

"Holy shit," Davies burst out. "Someone left one hell of a trail back to me. A big ass trail. Anyone could've found that."

Was Davies saying what he thought he was?

"Someone set me up. You have to believe me," Davies said, panic seeping into his voice.

"We do. Though I still have to ask you where you were last Wednesday night," Cade said.

"Let me check my calendar." Davies turned back to his computer, clicking around for a few seconds. "I was on a date with my wife. The restaurant can confirm it and I was with my wife the rest of the night."

Well, the guy couldn't have been two places at once, so at least they could cross him off the murder suspect list. Though he still didn't know how Davies and Henway were connected.

"Which college did you go to?" Cade asked.

They hadn't been able to find out. The guy didn't have so much as a Facebook account, so information had been hard to come by. Or maybe that reflected more on Cade's ability with computers.

136

"I didn't go to college. I just had the talent, so I worked my ass off to get where I am now."

From the looks of it, he'd done one hell of a good job of it. Davies had a lot to be proud of. Which meant he also stood to lose a lot.

"Someone hid Chris Henway's record."

"And you still found it? I'm sorry to sound pretentious, but if I'd done this, you most certainly wouldn't have found anything," Davies said.

So, either someone did a piss poor job, or someone deliberately did a piss poor job to lead them straight to Davies. Someone wanted to hang him for their crimes. But why the long game? If Henway hadn't been murdered, the chance of anyone finding out about those records were slim.

"Do you have any enemies or someone who would want to harm you?"

Davies raised an eyebrow. "Besides my father-in-law? No, I don't think so."

He didn't seem too worried about it.

"Your father-in-law? Is that serious?" Cade asked.

"No. He's just pissed I make more than him. He's just a dick." Davies shrugged. "He's a judge, so obviously he thinks he's better than everyone else. He can't even be glad about his only daughter being happy. Prick."

Not a lot of love there, then. It was worth looking into.

"We'll get back to you once we have something more," Cade said. He stood and shook Davies' hand.

"Thank you."

Cole

"I want to check up on the father-in-law," Cade said as they walked to the car.

"You think he'd be jealous enough to do something like this to his son-in-law?"

Cade stopped by the Camaro, turning around and crossing his arms over his chest. With a raised eyebrow, he asked, "When someone is killed, who's the first person you suspect?"

Letting out a sigh, Cole ran a hand through his hair, frustration hitting him. "The significant other."

"A father-in-law isn't too far from that," Cade said.

He was right. To some people, family meant nothing. Love meant nothing. He knew that better than most.

He got into the car, his baby purring as she came to life. The judge and his wife lived on the other side of town, so he settled in for a long ride with Cade insisting on them having a karaoke contest on the way. His ears were bleeding by the time they arrived at the Abbott's, but he was smiling too.

As they stood outside the house he turned to Cade. "How do you want to play this?"

"Just let me do the talking," Cade said.

He was fine with that. Not like he could shut Cade up anyway. Well, not if he wanted to keep his job, that was.

Cade rang the bell, his eyes widening and his face twisting into a grimace at the horrible sound it made. When the door opened, Cade was all poised and professional.

"Hello, Mr. Abbott. I'm Detective Lawson and this is my partner, Detective Banks. May we come in for a moment?"

"Judge. Judge Abbott. But, please, come on in."

They followed him inside, Cole immediately noticing the lack of, well *everything* personal. No family pictures on the white walls. Not as much as a grain of dust anywhere. Nothing was out of place. It was almost like the house wasn't lived in. A vase stood on a table in a corner. It was ugly, so it probably cost a fortune. He shook his head. Rich people.

Abbott led them into a dining room where they all took a seat at the table. They both declined Abbott's offer of coffee. He didn't want to stay there any longer than necessary. The place gave him the creeps.

"Mr. Abbott. I'm afraid we're here because of your son-in-law," Cade said.

At first, it looked like the man was about to correct Cade on his title again, but he swallowed the words and raised his chin. "Did he do something?"

Cole quirked an eyebrow at the man. No *is he alright* or *did something happen*?

"We believe he may have. Do you think he'd be capable of committing fraud?" Cade asked.

"Jeffrey? Committing fraud? Maybe," Abbott said.

It wasn't a clear answer, but the man certainly didn't disagree.

Cade leaned over the table, his head cocked to the side. "How about murder?"

Now *that* surprised Abbott, his eyes growing wide and his mouth dropping open, words escaping him. It was probably a first for him.

"Murder?" Abbott spluttered. "You think he murdered someone?"

"Yes. We believe he committed fraud, and something led him to kill the man he did it for."

"But that's not how it was—" Abbott cut himself off and leaned back in his chair, his arms across his chest.

"How what was?" Cade prodded.

Abbott shook his head. "Nothing. This is all just so confusing. Sure, I never really believed he got that company legally. You know, he never even went to college."

"So, you don't know anything about this?" Cade asked.

"No, I do not know anything about any of this."

Cade stood up, smoothing down his shirt before holding out a hand for Abbott to shake. "Alright then, Mr. Abbott. Thank you for your time."

Abbott couldn't get them out of the house fast enough. Not that either of them wanted to stick around. The place was eerie. When they got in the car, Cade turned to him.

"Notice how he repeated what I said? No contractions? How he kept looking away and rubbing his left hand? That man was lying his trousers right off," Cade said.

"Thanks for putting that image in my head."

Cade flipped him off, a grim expression on his face. "Jeffrey Davies was set up by his father-in-law."

He nodded. "Yeah, but not for murder."

"No," Cade said, pulling a face. "But we have no proof."

"We have something. Which is why I'm handing this over to the feds."

He'd expected Cade to argue then, but he just let out a deep sigh and settled in his seat.

"Hey." He touched Cade's chin, running his fingers over the stubble there. "We'll figure it out." He pressed his lips to Cade's. Cade yielded to him immediately. All it took was a kiss and Cade was pudding in his arms. Unfortunately, it went both ways.

"I feel like the worst cop ever. I suck," Cade said, his lips just touching Cole's.

"I'll give you something to suck," Cole mock-growled.

He felt Cade smile against his lips and stole another kiss before Cade pulled back to glare at him mockingly.

"Asshole."

"That too," Cole said with a wink.

Cade rolled his eyes but as he leaned back in his seat, a smile covered his face. He didn't know why, but every time Cade smiled because of him, this feeling flooded him. Serenity. Peace. Something that made him feel at ease. Feeling at ease wasn't a good thing for a marine, yet with Cade, nothing felt better.

While Cade grumbled about them being at a standstill for the rest of the day, Cole couldn't help but think they did have something. This went higher than just some child molester having rich friends with means to make records disappear. A lot higher.

Chapter Nine

Cade

CADE WAS getting really tired of having no lead. He couldn't even imagine being on this case for two years. He let out an annoyed sigh and rolled his shoulders to get rid of the kinks he'd gotten from sitting at his desk for days on end. They hadn't figured out a fucking thing since debunking Jeffrey Davies.

They were stuck waiting for the crime lab to finish up. It took weeks, sometimes months. It definitely wasn't like in the movies or TV shows; it just took them a few seconds and then they had all the answers. Since when are CSI's cops, anyway? Generally, he liked a good mystery but sometimes things were just too far from reality for him to watch.

Between all the reviewing of old cases and the nonexistent progress on the Executioner, he felt like he'd been run over by a steamroller. Or more likely a horny Cole. Damn, but that guy knew just how to—

"You alright?"

Cade glanced up and caught Cole's questioning eyes, brow cocked and a crooked smile playing on his lips. Cade's lips quirked into a smile all on their own. He'd found that to be his natural reaction to Cole smiling at him. It didn't happen too often, though Cade did try his best to bring it forth. It was an amazing sight.

"Just kinks," he answered.

"Want some help with that?"

"Maybe later," Cade said while wagging his eyebrows and licking his lips. Cole's eyes darkened at the possibility. That look right there—unadulterated lust. It did things to Cade. Just to even believe that this man, this big, stoic, lethal man would ever look at Cade like that was, well, unbelievable. It shook Cade to the core.

"Coffee?" Cade asked with a smirk.

"Tease," Cole muttered before following him.

Cole walked so close behind him his arm brushed Cade. He glanced over his shoulder, then opened the door to the conference room and scanned it quickly.

"Um. I thought you said coffee. The kitchen is that way." Cole pointed over his shoulder.

Ce rolled his eyes. He looked over Cole's shoulder, finding them alone, and pulled the man by his lapels into the room and slammed the door behind them. He pushed Cole against the door and pressed their mouths together in a frantic kiss. Cole opened to him, his hands quickly finding Cade's ass, squeezing and pulling Cade closer.

He kissed down Cole's throat, savoring his taste. He loved the taste and the smell of the man. It was heady as fuck. Cole was breathing hard, his hand gripping Cade's hair, pulling enough for it to sting.

"What's gotten into you?" Cole asked.

"I've got some frustration I need to work out."

He rubbed his half-hard cock against Cole's thigh, hissing at the delicious friction.

"We are not doing this here. We're at work," Cole hissed through his teeth. He may have sounded stern, but he looked divided between duty and lust. Cade could work with that. He kissed Cole down his neck, nipping him gently but hard enough to elicit a reaction from him. It was Cole's weak spot; it got him going every damn time He loved that he knew that. That Cole decided to let him close enough to find out.

"Cade."

When he didn't stop what he was doing, Cole cupped his jaw, raising his head to get him to meet his gaze.

"What's really going on?" Cole asked.

Cade bit his lip, trying to hold back all he was feeling, knowing he'd just scare the man away if he didn't. He turned his head a bit to the side and batted his lashes innocently up at Cole.

"Just kiss me?"

Cole looked like he was about to object but something made him lean down and press his lips against Cade's. He moaned when Cole's tongue slid into his mouth, taking control as he deepened the kiss. Cole pushed Cade against the wall and slid his hands under Cade's shirt. The warmth from them and the calluses on Cole's fingers had him shivering. He grabbed for Cole's belt buckle, managing to get it open despite his fumbling fingers.

Cole wrapped his hand around Cade's fingers, stopping any further motion and pushed away from Cade. They were both breathing heavily, Cole clenching his fists repeatedly and Cade leaning back against the wall. Cole buckled his belt. It didn't look like he was going to finish what they'd started.

"You're seriously gonna leave me hanging?"

"Yep."

"Well, this," Cade gestured toward the tent in his pants. "Is not gonna go away as long as you look at me like that."

"Like what?"

He may seem cool and calm, but Cole's eyes told a whole different story. A sly smile found its way to Cade's lips.

"Like you want to eat me."

Cole leaned close, his breath whispering over the sensitive skin of Cade's neck before he pressed his lips just under Cade's ear, making a shiver run through him and a moan slip past his lips. Whispering against Cade's neck, Cole confessed, "I do."

With a cheeky grin, Cole opened the door and slid out easily, leaving Cade alone with his lusty thoughts and unyielding hard-on. Just fucking great.

Cole

He really did want to fuck Cade. Just not here. He was trying hard to be professional, but Cade took him by surprise, as did the lust he always felt around Cade. He tried to slow his breathing. Despite Cade being in another room with the door closed so he couldn't see him, he was still half hard. There had to be something in the fucking water. Or maybe it was the coffee. Yeah, it was probably the coffee.

He leaned back against the wall, crossing his ankles and stuffing his hands into his pockets. He waited, his eyes not wavering from the door he knew Cade would come out of soon. A moment later, the door opened, revealing a flushed and rumpled Cade. He watched with a poorly hidden smirk as Cade smoothed down his shirt, trying to regain his poise. When it didn't work, Cade threw him a nasty look and a middle finger as he stalked toward the kitchen. Cole shook his head when he found himself smiling like an idiot. Riling up Cade was fun.

He went to Tanner who was sitting behind his desk, looking like he was deep in thought. He'd be good to hide behind when Cade decided to retaliate.

"What're you up to, Tanner?"

"I'm trying to come up with a way to kill my sister-in-law without suspicion falling on either my brother or me. Hypothetically, of course."

"Of course."

Tanner swiveled his chair around to look up at Cole. He cocked his head, a speculative look covering his face. He looked like someone about to ask something stupid.

"You're the kind of guy who'd know how to do something like that, right?"

Bingo.

"Come on, man. Help a brother out," Tanner said.

"I don't have a brother or a sister-in-law." Well, unless you counted his marine brothers. Then he had a lot of brothers and two sisters-in-law. Lots of nieces and nephews too.

"Why are you being so boring? I thought Cade got you all opened up," Tanner said.

That made him freeze up, his muscles tensing as if preparing for a hard hit.

"Why are you even here? Are you hiding from Cade?"

Cole cleared his throat. "Why would I hide from him?"

"Um. Because he's crazy and addictive?"

He got the last part right. Cole had never felt more drawn to another human being than he did Cade. It frankly scared him more than he liked to admit.

"Will you look at *that*." Tanner let out a low whistle.

Cole looked up to find the focus of everyone else's attention to be a young blonde woman walking from the elevator toward the bullpen. Cute freckles sprinkled across her nose, making her look younger than she probably was. She definitely held herself taller than a college-aged girl would, or maybe it was ingrained in her. Either way, there was something disturbingly familiar about her.

"Oh. My. God."

Cole turned his head to see Cade just outside the kitchen, mouth agape and eyes big and round, an incredulous look on his face. Cole—along with everyone else—jerked his head back around to the woman as she whirled around at Cade's outburst and let out a squeal before running down the hall, heading straight for Cade.

As she jumped on Cade, her arms wrapped around his neck which she burrowed her face in, Cole noticed the big smile filling Cade's face, the happiness shining through, something he hadn't seen the likes of on him before.

When the woman leaned back in his arms, she gave Cade enough room to plant a loud kiss on her cheek. Cole noticed Tanner looking up at him as if expecting him to know and explain what just happened. He didn't have a clue.

He hadn't even thought about asking Cade about family or whatever that girl was.

He cautiously made his way toward Cade and the woman. When he reached them with Tanner right on his heels, Cade had put her down and was cradling her chin, squishing her face.

"What the hell are you doing here, baby girl?"

"Seeing you, duh."

They were definitely related.

"Don't be a brat," Cade said. The strict tone of his voice didn't match with the shit-eating grin on his face. It was hard to look away from Cade when he was like that.

"It runs in the family," the woman deadpanned.

"True," Cade mused.

Cole felt Tanner at his back. He glanced over his shoulder to find Tanner looking from the woman to Cade and then back at her again.

"How is this ugly bastard related to you?" Tanner asked, stepping around Cole.

"Flattery will get you nothing," Cade drawled.

Tanner blinked innocently at him. "I wasn't trying to be flattering, I was genuinely curious."

Cade rolled his eyes and placed his hand over Tanner's face to push him away. Tanner chuckled and batted Cade's hand away.

"Banks, Tanner, this is my sister, Grace," Cade gestured toward Tanner. "Grace, this is Detective Shawn Tanner."

They shook hands, Tanner holding on for a bit longer than necessary. Not that Cade's sister seemed to mind. If Cade hadn't told him the ring Tanner wore was his grandfather's, and he wore it because it was one of the only things he had left of him, he would've been slightly disturbed.

"Gracie, this is my partner, Detective Cole Banks."

Cole met Grace's blue eyes which were so much like her brother's, it almost startled him. He smiled as he shook her hand.

"A pleasure to meet you, ma'am."

"Ma'am?" She looked almost giddy as she turned to Cade. "You did good with this one, hon."

Grace held up her hand, Cade meeting it with his in a high five. He had a feeling those two together could only lead to disaster.

"Why don't you go on to my place and we'll meet you there later?"

"Alright. But you have to wine and dine me," Grace said.

"As you wish, milady."

Cade bowed gracefully, his movements looking well-versed. Maybe he'd been forced to take dancing lessons, because, if he was being honest, the only kind of dancing Cade would willingly go to would be pole dancing or something just as atrocious.

"Later," Grace yelled as she made her way to the elevator with a spring in her step. Anyone within distance was watching her. Everyone except for Cade who was looking at Cole with a speculative look in his eyes. Cole turned, cocking an eyebrow at Cade.

Cade crossed his arms over his chest and narrowed his eyes at him. "What?"

"Nothing," Cole said.

"Really?"

"What do you want me to say?"

"Nothing. It just seemed like you wanted to say something."

Cole cleared his throat. "She seems a lot like… you."

A huge grin spread on Cade's face. "Just be glad you haven't been introduced to the rest of the family. They're all much worse."

"No one can be worse than you," Cole said with a smile. Of that, he was certain.

148

"Meh, you haven't met Uncle Melvin. That man knows how to throw a fucking party," Cade said with a chuckle.

He had a feeling there was something Cade wasn't saying, but he let it go. Everyone had their secrets, and they were secrets for a reason. He followed Cade into their office and dropped into his chair, pretending he wasn't watching Cade over the top of his screen and only looking away whenever Cade glanced up.

It was only two hours later when they clocked out and headed to Cade's house. He parked behind Cade's car. When they made it to the front porch, Grace was standing in the open door, waiting for them with a bright smile on her pretty face.

"Hey. I made coffee," she said.

"You're an angel. Thanks, sweetheart."

They followed her into the kitchen where she poured all of them a cup of coffee. Cole took an appreciative sip.

"So. How long have you two been together?" Grace asked, making both Cade and Cole choke on their coffee.

"What?" Cade squeaked, still battling for breath.

Grace raised an expectant brow at him, leaning back against the kitchen counter. Well, hell. With the way she looked at them, there was no way she meant as work partners.

"We aren't," Cole said once he stopped coughing and took another sip while remaining stoic. As stoic as he could with the thoughts now running through his mind. Together? Cade and him? Could they…? Would he…? No. That could never happen.

"Come on now. I'm not stupid," Grace said and crossed her arms over her chest. Between the way she was staring her brother down and her stance, she looked like an angry pit bull. Okay, maybe more of a mad chihuahua. She was kind of cute when she was angry. Like her brother.

"No one's saying that, baby. We're just not together. We have sex, sure. But we aren't together," Cade said.

He actually looked quite calm and indifferent as he said it, like it didn't mean anything to him, which stupidly made Cole angry. He mentally berated himself for his idiotic feelings and thoughts. He was being silly. Foolish. There was no way this was going any further. They had a job to do and once it was done Cole would be heading back to Fairfax. There was no way he wanted this to go any further. Right?

"So, you're putting your career—your job—on the line just to fuck your partner? Not even for a relationship, just for some tail?"

"Temporary partner," Cole felt the urge to point out.

Grace turned to him, fire in her eyes as she stared him down. If eyes could kill… he'd have been obliterated.

"Grace," Cade said on a sigh, running his hands through his already tousled hair. "I promised to take you for dinner, so let's go."

Cade held out his arm to let Grace go first. She glared at him before letting out a huff and stomping to the front door. Cade let out a sigh.

"Sorry," Cade said while putting his arms in the sleeves of his jacket.

"S'okay."

Cade looked uncertain, like he wanted to say something, but deciding not to, he just gave Cole a curt nod and turned to leave.

Cade

Not a word was uttered during the car ride and as Cade sat down across from his sister in the café he'd chosen on a whim to eat at, he felt like he was going to burst from the lack of conversation, mostly because he knew when Gracie wasn't talking, she was scheming. It was sort of a family trait.

"How long?"

He glanced up from the knife he'd been playing with for a while, watching her warily before he answered.

"Have I known him, or have I been fucking him?"

"I'm pretty sure he's the one doing the fucking," she retorted.

She got him there. They'd never really kept anything from each other. It was just how their family worked. He'd been a bit dramatic at his coming out, knowing full well that everyone already knew, but that didn't mean he'd held back on the glitter. He'd practically shouted from the rooftops that he liked dick and especially in his ass. He'd been seventeen and one hell of a drama queen.

Remembering Grace was still waiting for an answer, he snorted, then let out a defeated sigh. "Two weeks."

"Two—Are you fucking kidding me?" she screeched.

"No. How's the family?"

"Dad still cringes when you're mentioned," Grace said. She leaned back in her chair, her arms crossed, and her eyes narrowed on him.

"Nice, Gracie. Real nice."

They sat, staring at each other in silence until their food was put down in front of them. They started to eat in silence but five seconds in, he let out a sigh. He really hated silence. It was different with Cole. They didn't need to talk. He just wanted to be in Cole's vicinity. But with Grace, it was a strange and unusual occurrence.

"How are my nephews and niece?"

Grace looked up, a smile finding its way to her lips.

"Good. They're real good."

"And you? Is there some lucky guy stowed away somewhere I don't know about?" he asked.

"I'm twenty-two."

She said no more as she returned to cutting her steak. Guess she considered that answer enough. They went back to eating their dinner, Cade enjoying a meal that didn't come in a box or from Mrs. Jones. They hadn't been eating much else lately because it meant he got Cole to himself for a bit longer.

Grace laid down her cutlery with enough force for it to clang loudly, catching his attention. He looked up, his eyebrows meeting as he caught the frustrated look on her face.

"You know I love you and support you. But I'm worried. This *affair* you've got going on… I don't know… what if something happens and you lose your job? It's all you have."

"Well, I guess I could always become a thief," he said with a wink and a cheeky smile.

"You'd make a lousy thief," she groused, but unable to hold it back, she let out a sparkling laugh. She sounded so much like their grandmother it made his heart clench painfully in his chest. In eight years, he hadn't seen anyone from their family but Grace. At least not more than once. The only reason he remembered the last time he'd seen their father was because it was when he'd thrown Cade out, telling him to never come back and to stay away from their family. It had broken his heart, but he'd still done it, if not for nothing, then to keep them all safe.

"Why are you even with someone like him?"

He looked up at Gracie, surprise filling him along with dread. He tried to keep his voice even as he asked, "Someone like him?"

"Yeah, someone who's only a cop because he has something to atone for."

Who the hell didn't have something to atone for? Shit, wasn't that why he was a cop himself? Was that all she saw when she looked at him as well? Did she not know the sacrifices he'd made to be where he was? The sacrifices he kept making to keep people safe? To keep her safe? How could she not know that neither he nor Cole did what they did for themselves?

"Is that all you see?"

"What else should I be seeing?"

"Oh, I don't know. How about his determination to do everything to bring people closure? How about his honesty? He doesn't trick people into thinking he's something he's not. Should we talk about his loyalty and dedication? Because he's got that in spades. He's a good man, who's served his country more times than he can even tell you about. He's the kind of man who, no matter what, will protect complete strangers, just because he has a chance to. Oh, and did I mention that he's fucking hot?" He ended his rant and when he looked at his sister, the small smile on her lips and the adoration in her eyes was not what he expected to see.

They shared a long look before Grace leaned back in her chair and gave a curt nod of her head. "You like him."

"Duh."

"No, I mean…" She waved her hand dismissively. "Oh, you know what I mean."

"I plead the Fifth."

He said it with a smile, though he wasn't sure how to feel about it. He knew he was probably way too invested. More than Cole, at least. Grace's hand covered his on the table and he held on as he glanced up, finding her eyes soft as their gazes met.

"Promise me you'll be careful," Grace said.

"Don't worry about me. I'll be fine."

153

She let go of his hand, sitting back in her chair and crossing her arms over her chest. "Uh huh. Just so we're clear, I'll crush him if he hurts you."

That brought a smile to his lips. "I wouldn't expect otherwise."

She cocked her head to the side, a smile forming on her lips. "So. Tell me about this case of yours."

"I'm not at liberty to discuss it with you."

"What the hell just came out of your mouth?"

He grinned. "I know. I'm a disgrace to our family."

Grace shook her head, a laugh bubbling out of her. He watched her with a fond smile, wondering when the hell she grew up to be the beautiful, intelligent, young woman in front of him. Time was fleeting. You never really had enough of it.

Ignoring the lump in his throat, he said, "It's a serial killer. Ten victims so far and the only thing they all have in common is each one has molested children who were close to them."

"Like *family* close?"

He nodded, knowing exactly what was going through Gracie's head right then.

"Why exactly are you trying to catch this guy again?" Grace asked.

"I know. Something about it is just… wrong. But murder is against the law and I've taken an oath to uphold it."

"Well, you *are* good at it."

He glanced down at his hands on the table. "Doesn't feel like it right now."

Grace covered his hands with hers, giving him a reassuring squeeze.

"Start at the beginning," she said.

He did; telling her first what he knew about the first victims, then everything after he'd been added to the case. He told her what he could without revealing confidential information.

"So, let me get this right; the guy's record was hidden - not erased. But the guy who'd seemingly done it would've obviously known to erase all evidence, so someone set him up to take the fall. Why?"

"I'm certain his father-in-law was involved with that. He was surprised about the murder, though. So that wasn't factored into whatever deal he made."

"So, you've practically got three cases in one."

"Three?"

"The serial, the fraud, and the setup," she said.

"I guess you can put it that way. But Cole turned over the fraud case to the feds," Cade said with a one-shouldered shrug.

"You alright with that?"

"Yeah. It's for the best. There's a reason I deal with dead people and not computers."

Cole

He'd only just sat down on the couch when his phone rang. He let out a groan before getting back up and walking to the kitchen where he'd put the phone earlier before going outside to have a look at Cade's car. Cade had complained about his car being weird every time he switched gears, which made sense since the clutch needed to be replaced. He could do it himself, but he was probably just going to convince Cade to keep driving with him. He usually did so anyway.

He stepped into the kitchen and walked over to the counter where his phone was buzzing away. He picked it up, feeling a bit more optimistic when he saw the caller ID.

"Banks."

"Gunner. I've got some news," Dom said.

"What did you find?"

"A connection between the case you gave me and the one you're working now."

He dreaded asking, but he needed an answer. "What the hell are you talking about?"

"Chris Henway."

"Spit it out," Cole said.

"I know you got Franklin to look into his record and the people that buried it. I recognized one of the names, so I looked into Henway's family. Turns out, Thomas Lowe wasn't their first or only foster kid. They had three before him. They were older kids. All close to seventeen or eighteen when they were placed with the Henways and guess what happened after they turned eighteen?"

"They disappeared."

"Exactly. I've found absolutely no trace of them."

"What are you gonna do now?"

"Detective Samuel's case is closed since she found her killer. I'm doing what I can to get in and speak with him. Chris Henway is dead so that only leaves his family and Thomas Lowe. I don't think he knows anything seeing as he wasn't the right age and he was taken away from the Henway's, but I'll give it a shot. I'm gonna have a chat with the Henways, but I'm almost certain it was all Chris Henway's doing. That's why his papers were hidden. So he could keep working for these sons of bitches."

"Seems like you've got it under control," Cole said.

"We're getting close, Gunner."

He rubbed a fist over his chest, feeling his heart clench painfully. "Are we?"

He was surprised his voice didn't sound weaker.

"Look. I know it won't bring him back, but I want to bring down these bastards. When it's time, can I count on you to have my back?"

The silence was earsplitting. There was only one answer he could give.

"That's gonna be hard when I'll be flying the plane. But, yeah. I've got your six, man."

Dom got quiet for a moment before he asked, "Are you telling me you've got Meg hidden away somewhere?"

"You really think I was gonna leave my baby girl with those fuckers?"

Once they'd been discharged, Meg was so busted up that she'd have been used for scrap anyway, so he'd taken her with him. Let those assholes wonder how someone managed to misplace an aircraft with a wingspan of over 132 feet. It took a few years with the small amount of time he'd had outside of work to fix her up, but she was as good as new now.

A rich laugh sounded through his phone. "Man, you're insane. You actually stole a military aircraft?"

"She belongs to the Black Raiders. She belongs to us."

"I hear you, brother," Dom said.

They hung up shortly after, Dom promising to call if something new surfaced. Cole went back inside and, for once, he decided to make himself some real food. The selection of products in Cade's fridge was sparse, but he managed to make a mean spaghetti carbonara. He took his time eating, pretending he wasn't glancing at his watch every ten seconds. When he couldn't take sitting around and waiting anymore, he went upstairs to take a shower. He stepped under the spray and a contented sigh pushed through his lips. Hot, soothing water cascaded down Cole's body and washed away the stress of the day.

He soon found himself humming the Battle Hymn of the Republic. At least it wasn't Disney. He wasn't sure how Cade managed to do it, but Cole now knew the lyrics to at least seven Disney songs. It was making a serious dent in his man card.

He was deep in his thoughts when a hand slid down his back. Lessons beaten into him, hard training, and fundamental instincts made him spin around and nail the fucker to the wall. Startled blue eyes met his.

"Holy shit, Cade," he gasped out, prying his fingers forcibly away from Cade's throat. He placed his hands on either side of Cade who was standing with his back against the shower wall. He dropped his head forward, trying to steady his breathing.

"It's okay. I'm sorry. I shouldn't have—"

Cole jerked his head up. "Don't."

If anyone was to apologize, it sure as shit wasn't Cade. He had no idea how Cade managed to sneak up on him. They stood there for a long time, staring into each other's eyes. Then a thought struck him, and he cleared his throat before asking, "Where's your sister?"

"Downstairs. I gave her the guest room. Didn't think you'd mind," Cade said with a shrug, a small smile playing on his lips.

Cole ran his fingertips down Cade's jaw. He looked up, catching something in Cade's eyes for a second before it disappeared again.

"I'm sorry. Did I hurt you?"

"Yeah, I've got a few places that need kissing." Cade batted his lush eyelashes, the gleam in his blue eyes waking up certain parts of Cole.

"Oh yeah? Here?" He leaned down to press his lips against the pounding vein in Cade's neck.

"Mmm. Further down."

He didn't have to be told twice. He dropped down to his knees. The lustful eyes that met his when he looked up, had him almost combusting on the spot. He leaned in to press a kiss to Cade's hip. He kissed and licked a trail around the part of Cade obviously wanting his attention the most. Cade muscles quivered beneath his hands as he trailed them down his sides and around to grab Cade's ass in both hands.

He placed a wet kiss on the tip of Cade's hard cock, licking his lips and tasting Cade's pre-come on his tongue. He closed his eyes, humming in appreciation. He glanced up at Cade's throaty moan.

"Fuck. That's hot," Cade panted before closing his eyes and dropping his head back against the wall with a loud moan.

He took Cade into his mouth, the taste of him making him moan. Fuck. He took Cade to the back of his throat over and over, then swirled his tongue around the head of Cade's cock, dipping the tip of his tongue into the slit.

"Baby," Cade whimpered.

Fuck. Cade was close.

He got up and started kissing Cade down his neck. He reached down, enveloping them both in his hand, pumping up and down and dragging lots of unintelligible words out of Cade. Cade's gasps, his whimpers and moans, they drove him absolutely crazy. He couldn't get enough. He sealed his mouth over Cade's as he brought them right to the edge, then tipped them over. The pleasure rippling through him was immense. His whole damned body was tingling. Cade leaned on him as they both gasped for breath.

Cole turned up the water pressure and reached for the soap. He lathered and washed them both, taking his time running his fingers through Cade's hair. The contented smile on Cade's lips caused Cole's heart to skip a beat. Brushing it off like it was nothing, he finished up in the shower and when they stepped out, he wrapped Cade in a towel, drying him off. Then he picked him up, Cade wrapping his legs around Cole's waist. A contented sigh escaped Cade before lips grazed over the sensitive skin on Cole's neck. He carried Cade into the bedroom where he put him down gently on the bed before leaning forward to steal a kiss.

He got up to grab a pair of boxers from the dresser. He dropped them onto Cade's stomach, waiting for him to put them on before he crawled back into bed.

"You know I'm just gonna take these off of you again, right?" Cole asked.

Cade didn't answer, he just grinned and wrapped himself around Cole. Cade didn't sleep naked, claiming it was because if someone broke in, he didn't want to have to fight them off in his birthday suit. That was a habit Cole was going to rid him off. He liked having Cade wrapped around him naked. All skin against skin.

"You guys talk it out?" Cole asked.

Cade hummed in confirmation, then ran his fingers lightly over the scar on Cole's hip before trailing them over the ones on his left side. He'd caught him doing that a lot, yet Cade never asked about any of them. He liked that Cade respected his need for some privacy. Not every tale was for all ears.

Most of his scars were from battle, some from a shitty childhood, and one from a crazy ass seagull. Sometimes, being stationed on a ship had you experiencing some fucked-up shit. That bird had set its sights on him and for two weeks straight, whenever he was on deck it chased after him until one day it caught him and took a chunk out of his hair. Protocols and paperwork be damned. He'd pulled his gun and shot it three times. It may have been overkill but that thing was gunning for him. They'd called him the bird whisperer after that. Luckily, the nickname hadn't followed him for long.

"Wanna talk about it?" Cade asked.

"Talk about what?"

"Cole," Cade said with a sigh.

"I don't—" He cut himself off at the stern look Cade was giving him.

"Fine. What do you wanna know?" He asked gruffly, but the way Cade lit up, fuck, that made it worth it.

Cade jumped up on his hands and knees, bouncing a bit in his haste. He was like a pumped-up kid. Cade cocked his head to the side, studying him intensely.

"Did you have a nickname? You guys have nicknames, right?" Cade asked.

Of all the things he could've asked this was what he chose? Cole couldn't help the laugh that burst out of him.

"Yes, I have a nickname," Cole said.

"What is it?"

"Gunner."

Cade wrinkled that cute nose of his. "Gunner? Why?"

"I was a driver on my first tour and my team had a knack for ending in situations we needed to get out of quickly, so a good mission always ended with someone yelling *'gun it'* and well, I guess it just turned into Gunner along the way. In the famous words of my team leader, 'Gunner knows how to fucking gun it.' Never a dull moment on that tour. But I always got us out."

He'd just turned eighteen when he was deployed for that tour. It felt like a whole other life. His second tour was at sea. It was on that tour he'd met Tank and Mad Dog. Mad Dog, also known as Axel Bates, was one crazy fucker. He'd actually been thrown out of Recon and sent to an aircraft carrier as an explosives expert. How the fuck he'd managed that, Cole still didn't know.

It was the same tour someone discovered that Cole could fly and put money on the table, saying he didn't believe Cole could best the number one pilot on board. He'd taken that money from him later that night. Two weeks later, a month before the three of them were to go home, they were recruited for a black-ops team.

"How many tours were you on?" Cade asked.

"Officially? Two."

"Unofficially?"

"Classified."

Their eyes met, understanding flittering through Cade's. He felt locked onto Cade's eyes, lost in those swirling pools of riveting blue. Whenever he looked into those eyes, he felt something stir inside him that he couldn't put words to. It was strange. He hadn't felt anything for so long, and now, he couldn't stop himself from feeling everything.

Cade cocked his head to the side, and Cole braced himself for what was about to come out of his mouth.

"Who died?"

He knew pain was showing in his eyes. He didn't try to hide it from Cade. He couldn't.

"Our medic. Derek. Doctor Death."

"That's his nickname? Doctor Death? Doesn't really inspire confidence."

"Neither did he."

Cole found himself chuckling under his breath as memories of Derek went through his mind. Derek on the battlefield, throwing his arms up in frustration as he declared that Franklin was on his own if he insisted on annoying the squids enough for one of them to shoot him in the ass. Derek telling DJ he was shit out of luck because he wasn't getting anywhere near his dick after DJ'd been attacked by the women of a village they'd passed through. The stupid ass should've kept the thing in his cargo pants. Derek bugging the shit out of the lieutenant and then running away, through the camp and jumping over shit like he was trying to win the Olympics.

"What happened?"

Cole blinked, finding Cade in front of him again. He cleared his throat, trying to will away the memories.

"He gave his life for a brother," he said, closing his eyes and dropping his head forward. He rubbed the back of his neck, too many emotions assaulting him at once.

"It's not your fault," Cade said.

"Cade, don't."

"No. I know it wasn't your fault. I know you'd have done everything in your power to save him," Cade cupped his chin, raising his head so they were at eye level. "I know you did your best, and sometimes our best isn't enough. But you can't go back in time. I wish we could. But we can't. All we can do is live in the present and get as much out of it while we can. For them."

"You're right," Cole choked out, knowing it was the truth but that didn't mean it didn't hurt like hell. It didn't make it easier either.

"Of course, I am," Cade quipped, erasing the dark atmosphere surrounding them. When Cade looked like he was about to say something cocky, Cole shut him up the only way he knew—pulling him into a hot and dirty kiss.

Chapter Ten

IT WAS right there. In the girl's eyes. Right there.

It was always noticeable in the eyes first. You could always find it there. The fear. The doubt. The self-hatred. In those blue eyes were the look of someone abused. There was no doubt.

This time, the girl wouldn't just be avenged; she'd be saved. Saved from the monster that was so clearly still in her life. She would be free from her abuser forever. That was a vow made to her that night, even if she would never know.

Following her was easy. The girl was paranoid, of course. But she wasn't expecting the Executioner. From her lifeless eyes, it was easy to tell the girl didn't expect anyone. She didn't think she'd ever be saved. But she would.

When the girl went straight to a house, a middle-aged man opening the door with a lecherous grin, it was clear that tonight was a night for the Executioner. Tonight might be the last, but it would also be the greatest. It wouldn't be after the fact. It wouldn't be after a mistrial because some slimeball lab technician fucked up a DNA sample or it vanished mysteriously. No. Tonight, a girl would be set free. Free from her prison. Free from the nightmare she lived. Tonight, they'd both be free.

Cade

He opened the fridge and let out a snicker when he found what he was looking for. He stuffed the chocolate into his mouth and went in search of his partner. He couldn't hear him, but that meant nothing. The guy could walk right up behind him without Cade noticing.

When he couldn't find Cole downstairs he shrugged and licked off the melted chocolate on his fingertips, deciding to call Grace to find out if she'd gotten home alright. She'd left the night before, claiming if she had to hear her brother have sex one more time, she would hang herself. Now, all he had to do was find his phone.

"Cole?"

He trudged up the stairs while patting himself down in search of his phone. Damn that thing. It always managed a disappearing act. All on its own, no doubt.

"Cole, have you seen my—"

His words dissipated at the sight that met him when Cole appeared in the bedroom doorway. Naked. With drops of water on his skin. Oh, but what a sight it was. All that bare, delicious skin.

"What were you looking for?" Cole asked, leaning a shoulder against the doorframe and cocking an eyebrow at Cade.

"Don't know. Don't care," Cade answered before licking his lips and biting down on his lower lip.

"Cade."

"Huh?" He jerked his gaze up from Cole's steadily rising cock to find Cole looking at him with pleased amusement. Crooking a finger at him, Cole beckoned him closer. When he got close enough for Cole to wrap a hand around the back of his neck, Cole pulled him so close their bodies were touching from chest to thigh. Cole leaned down, his lips so close Cade could feel the warmth from his breath on his own lips. He let his eyes fall shut.

"What were you looking for?" Cole asked.

Feeling the smile on Cole's lips against his own, he opened his eyes just enough to squint up at Cole, displeased with his teasing.

"I don't remember," Cade said while doing his damnedest to keep still. It was no easy feat.

"Really? Why is that?"

"Well," Cade said as he rubbed against Cole's thigh. "My brain kinda went south along with my blood when I saw you standing there in all your naked glory." He leaned back as much as he could in Cole's embrace to look down at that glory.

"Glory, huh?"

"You're a god. Now, kiss me," Cade said with a tug on Cole's upper arms which he'd grabbed to hold himself upright. Damn. But this man could make him fucking swoon.

"Bossy," Cole said before slamming his mouth over Cade's in a wild, hot kiss. Cole's tongue was demanding, claiming. As were his hands.

"Clothes off," Cole demanded with a tug on Cade's shirt.

He lifted his arms up to let Cole pull his shirt off. The chilly air hit his heated skin. He shivered, almost certain it wasn't because of the cold. He popped open the button on his trousers and pulled them down along with his boxer briefs. He stepped out of the trousers and straightened, reveling in the sharp intake of breath coming from Cole.

"Turn around," Cole said.

"Who's bossy now?" he asked before he turned to put his hands on the wall and spread his legs.

The heat turned up when he felt Cole right behind him, his body so close, yet not touching. The anticipation was driving him nuts. Every time Cole touched him or even just looked at him, his body fired up and he had to bite his cheek not to beg, just as he was right then.

He knew he was being needy. He couldn't help it. But it was just sex. Who was he kidding? It may be just sex for Cole, but it sure as shit wasn't for him. He'd never been able to separate it. He'd been a fool for thinking he could do it with Cole.

He let out a surprised gasp when cold, wet fingers started probing around his hole. When the hell did Cole get the lube?

"Fuck," Cade said, then hissed when a finger entered him.

He was panting heavily by the time Cole pressed a third finger into him. He rocked back on Cole's fingers that were rubbing against his prostate, a needy sound escaping his parted lips. He groaned when teeth bit down gently on his neck. He tilted his head to the side to give Cole better access.

Cole's fingers disappeared and he whimpered at the lost contact. The whimper soon turned into a loud moan as he was filled up by Cole's thick cock, the mix of pleasure and pain making him lean forward, pressing his forehead against the wall as he panted for breath.

"Okay?" Cole asked in a low, husky voice next to his ear.

"Fuck, yeah," Cade finally managed to force out, the pleasure of being stretched, of being this close to Cole, robbing him of his ability to speak. He looked over his shoulder to watch Cole as he started thrusting into him.

His thoughts scrambled until all he could think about, all he could feel, was Cole. Cole pounding into him. Cole's hands, one on his hip and the other on his shoulder. Cole's mouth, his lips, on Cade's neck, behind his ear, down his shoulder.

He wasn't prepared when Cole's hand found his erection, pumping his hand in time with his thrusts. Cade struggled to keep his hands on the wall when he came, everything blurring as pleasure rocked through him. If it wasn't for Cole's strong arms, he'd have been in a heap on the floor.

"Cole," he gasped out.

He was barely breathing when Cole came, his fingers tightening around Cade's hip. Cole's hips lost their rhythm, a cross between a curse and Cade's name flying from his lips. Cole wrapped his arms around Cade, his forehead pressed against Cade's shoulder as his breaths came out in pants. Glory, indeed.

Cole

Cole let out a contented sigh as he fell on the bed, pulling Cade down over his chest. Cade sighed and burrowed closer, his breathing as unsteady as Cole's.

They laid there for a bit, basking in the afterglow until Cade pushed up on one hand to be able to look down at Cole.

Cole squinted up at him. What was he up to now?

"What is it?"

"I'm hungry," Cade said. His lower lip jutted out in a pout and he started excessively batting his long eyelashes.

Cole chuckled. "You're like a damned kid."

"Yeah, well, you get to have sex with this *damned kid,* eat this *damned kid*'s food, sleep in his bed and… I guess that's it. But, you gotta admit, the sex is one hell of a plus."

Cole couldn't help himself when that wicked smile of Cade's quirked up. He smothered it with a kiss. His tongue slid between Cade's lips just as a constipated sort of music sounded, breaking them apart.

"That's *your* phone." He poked at Cade who just rolled away and burrowed his head under his pillow. "Cade."

"I don't care. I'm never moving from here. Feed me, slave," Cade said.

Cole snorted as he got out of bed to find wherever the hell Cade had put his phone this time. He had a bad habit of losing his things. Or putting them down when something more interesting caught his attention.

The phone started ringing again just as he picked it up. Why the hell Cade had put it in the fridge he didn't even—actually, he'd probably done it while searching for food. Crazy bastard. It was a wonder how he kept in shape with all the unhealthy shit he ate.

Looking at the name filling the screen had him snorting out a laugh. *Satan's Boss.* There was only one person that could be.

"Banks."

"I don't care what you have to do, but get Cade's ass out of bed, asap," Lara's sharp voice sounded in his ear.

"Yes, ma'am," Cole said, almost saluting out of old habit and making him shake his head at himself.

He was already halfway up the stairs before she got to the point of her call.

"We've got another one. I'll send you the address, just put some coffee and chocolate in Cade."

"Chocolate?" he asked as he held the phone between his ear and shoulder while trying to pull on his pants.

"Don't ask. I don't know. But that shit works," Lara said.

"Of course, it does," he said with a snicker. "We'll be right there."

He hung up and pulled on his shirt before going to get Cade out of bed.

"Get up, there's a new victim." He pulled the blanket off Cade, making him roll into a fetal position in an attempt to keep his warmth.

"Bad slave. Very bad slave," Cade mumbled as he slapped away Cole's hands. He turned around on his stomach, trying to crawl further up the bed, that perky ass of his in the air as he shimmied up on his knees. It was too much. Cole couldn't stand the temptation. A loud smack sounded, followed quickly by a throaty moan.

"Now I'm just horny," Cade grumbled as he looked over his shoulder with an accusing glare at Cole.

Cole rolled his eyes but leaned down to press a kiss to Cade's lips.

"I'll make it worth your while if you get up right now."

"This is blackmail."

Cade got out of bed, walking stark-ass naked to the bathroom. When he returned a moment later, Cole's head was still tilted from admiring the view through the open door.

Cade narrowed his eyes at him. "Blackmail."

He grinned at Cade. "Coercion. At most."

"You're the worst slave ever," Cade groused.

A smile covered his face as he spent a few seconds watching Cade stumble around, trying to find his clothes. He'd be ready before Cade anyway. Might as well enjoy the show.

Cole

Cade was munching on his chocolate and taking sips of his coffee as Cole put the car in park in front of the crime scene. Surprisingly, Cade was the first one out of the car. The chocolate must've done its deed. He got out of the car and followed Cade to where Lara stood waiting for them on the front lawn.

"Victim's name is Adam Page. Married, and a father of two. No criminal record and nothing to suggest he was a sexual predator," Lara told them as soon as they were within hearing range. She turned and walked with them to the house.

"His wife found him about forty minutes ago," Lara said.

They walked through the house and into the master bedroom. Cade looked around with a frown on his face. He then settled his gaze on Lara.

"Where's Doc?"

"At another crime scene. He'll be here as fast as he can," Lara said.

The victim was spread out on the bed, wrists and ankles tied to the bedframe. He was fully clothed, his white dress shirt covered in blood.

"Copycat?" Cade asked as he studied the crime scene. Cole suspected they were thinking the same thing. Something wasn't right.

"No. Something tells me this is our guy," Cole said anyway; a nagging feeling in his gut telling him as much. "Besides, we haven't let out any important details."

He gestured with a nod of his head toward the victim's bound hands. They were tied with neckties. If they looked in the victim's closet, they'd find four neckties missing.

"What do you think?" Cole asked Cade.

"I think our killer was angry and in a hurry. This wasn't planned."

"I guess we'll have to wait for the ballistics to know if it's the same gun."

He didn't doubt that it was. This was the breakthrough he'd been waiting and hoping for. He turned to Lara. "When were the wife and kids supposed to be home?"

"Let's ask," Lara said and made a beckoning motion.

"They're still here?"

She nodded.

"I thought it was best to keep her around until you had a chance to talk to her. The kids aren't here, so it's just the wife. We'll be taking her in after you talk with her. I had a feeling we'd have to hurry with this one," Lara said.

She was right. Everything seemed hurried. They may not have much time before their killer did something more drastic.

"Good. Thanks."

They followed her into the open kitchen which led into the dining room where the victim's wife was seated at the table.

"Mrs. Page," Cade said.

A blonde woman with tearstained eyes and cheeks looked up at them, confusion and sorrow stark on her pale face. Cade sat down opposite her.

"I'm Detective Lawson. This is my partner, Detective Banks. Can you tell us what happened?"

"I don't know." Her voice broke, worn out by the crying.

"Mrs. Page, where are your kids?" Cole asked.

"At school. They've got some sleepover thing there." She put her head in her hands. "What am I going to do now? How do I tell them… this can't be happening."

He felt for her. He knew what losing someone you loved felt like. He knew it all too well.

"When did you get home, Mrs. Page?" Cade asked.

"A bit past ten. I was out with my girlfriends. We were having a night out. Amber dropped me off. She can tell you."

"Does Amber have a last name and a number?" Cade asked.

She nodded. Cade wrote it down as she told him.

"Mrs. Page, did you touch your husband at any point?"

"I felt his neck for a pulse." She sucked in a breath. "He didn't have one."

She broke down, shaking and crying. They wouldn't be getting more out of her then.

"I'm sorry for your loss, Mrs. Page," Cade said.

Cole felt someone step up behind him and glanced over his shoulder.

"Doc is here," Lara said in a low voice.

"Get a uniform to take her to the station," Cole said, motioning to the woman Cade was talking softly to.

"Will do."

Lara crouched down in front of Mrs. Page, taking her hand as she tried to comfort her enough to get her out of the house. Meanwhile, Cade got up and made his way to him.

"Doc's here."

They left for the main bedroom. When they entered the room, Doc was removing his thermometer from the body. He waited until Doc looked up at them.

"You got a time of death?"

"He's only been dead about two hours. The cause of death looks to be several gunshots to the upper torso." He pointed at the victim's bloodied chest. "There are no signs of him being moved."

Doc stepped back, removing his gloves.

"It seems your murderer knows where to hit, not only to kill someone slowly but fast as well."

Cade went outside as they waited for Doc to finish up and bag Mr. Page. Cole followed him after a few more words with Doc.

Cade stood, leaning back against the wall of the house. He tried to brush his hair away from his eyes, but it kept falling down again. Cole had to stop himself before he reached out to do it for him. He placed himself across from Cade, leaning back against the railing on the front porch.

"What are you thinking?"

Cade pursed his lips. "I'm thinking, why would someone as meticulous as this guy get something like this wrong?"

It didn't make sense to him either. He shrugged. "Maybe he didn't. Let's have a closer look at Mr. Page. Maybe we'll find something."

Cade nodded, stepping away from the wall. "Let's go, then."

They made it to the Camaro just as a news van pulled up. A reporter and a cameraman jumped out of the back, looking like they were about to set up shop. Cole kept an eye on them as he unlocked the car and opened the door. He cursed under his breath when they ducked under the tape and trudged toward the house. What the fuck did they think they were doing? He slammed the door shut, startling Cade who was reaching for the door handle on his side.

"What's wrong?" Cade asked, but Cole was already stomping toward the jackasses, so he didn't bother answering, knowing Cade would follow.

"Hey," Cole yelled, making both of them come to a halt. The reporter, a young, bleach blonde woman with her face covered in makeup, turned to look at him with big eyes, acting surprised.

"Can I help you?" she asked.

Cole snorted. "Yeah. You can go ahead and put your hands behind your head."

"Excuse me?"

"You're both under arrest for trespassing, hindering a police investigation, and contaminating a crime scene," he said while waving over two of the uniforms who should've stopped these dumbasses in the first place. The reporter glared at him, her mouth twisted into a grimace as she crossed her arms over her busty chest.

"You can't do that. Don't you know who I am?" she asked.

He took a step toward her, his lips thinning and his eyes darkening, making her take a step back.

"Honey, you could be the president and I wouldn't give a shit." He turned to the uniforms. "Take them in."

"Yes, sir," one of the cops said and pulled out his handcuffs.

He didn't wait around to watch the show she was most likely to put on. He walked back to the Camaro, Cade following right behind him. He got into the car, and sat there, trying to shake off the annoyance he felt. He glanced fleetingly at Cade when he felt his eyes on him. Cade was smiling at him. A smug smile.

"You really don't know who she is, do you?" Cade asked.

"I don't care who she is."

"Really? So, if she'd actually been the president, you would've arrested her?"

"She committed a crime," he grunted.

"You're cute," Cade said.

"Shut up."

Chapter Eleven

Cole

"NOTHING. WE'VE got nothing on this guy. It doesn't make sense," Cade said, frustration leaking into his voice.

"Tell them to keep digging. There has to be something. Check the wife and kids for ER visits and talk to the kids' teachers, see if they've been quiet or different in any way. The Executioner has a specific type he goes after. He wouldn't have gotten it wrong, and even if he had, why the hell would he take the time to tie the guy up? If he messed up and was afraid he'd be recognized, he would've just shot the guy," Cole said.

"He's a serial killer. He wouldn't want one in his collection who doesn't fit," Lara said.

"So, Page fit the profile, but something obviously went wrong. We need to find out what and why," Cade said.

Cade crossed his arms over his chest and leaned back in his chair. Cole laid his head in his hands.

They sat in silence when Tanner popped his head through the door. "Guys, you should come see this."

The look on Tanner's face didn't bode well. Cade quirked a brow at Cole who shook his head slightly in answer to the unspoken question. They followed Tanner to his desk where he had a video paused on his computer screen. It looked like a newscast. Tanner pressed play and the voice of the one and same reporter who'd been trespassing on their crime scene, filling the room.

"It has been confirmed that the serial killer known as the Executioner has taken yet another life last night," she said.

Cade glanced up at Tanner. "What?"

"Just wait," Tanner said.

"A source within the Police Department has confirmed that the victim, Adam Page, does not fit the profile of the other victims. As many have cheered on the Executioner for his choice of victim—sexual predators—it seems he has now taken the life of an innocent husband and family man. Our hearts go out to the victim's family and friends."

"That's bullshit," Cade exclaimed.

"This isn't good," Cole said, unease filling him.

"I know," Tanner said. "That's why I thought you might want to see it."

Tanner shrugged and walked off, probably headed for the kitchen to get some coffee. They were definitely going to need that now.

"He's not gonna stand for being called a liar. For being told he got it wrong," Cade said.

"We don't have much time before this goes south. Everyone connected to that statement needs to be under protection," Cole said.

"Lara?" Cade asked.

"On it," she called over her shoulder, as she was already on her way to the captain's office to let him know of the breach.

"It's not the first time," Cole said. He didn't word it as a question. The look on Cade's face was all the confirmation he needed.

"No. It isn't."

"That was Miss President on that video. *After* she was supposed to be under arrest."

"No shit," Cade growled. He thrust his hands into his hair, pulling at the ends.

"Are we talking more than leaking to the press?"

Cade gestured for him to follow as he walked toward their office. When they stepped back into it, Cole closed the door behind them. Cade leaned his backside against his desk, putting his hands behind him for support. The dark look on his face didn't exactly bode well.

"Remember what I told you about how something went amiss with the Destroyers?"

"Yeah. Your partner was targeted," Cole said.

"That's not all."

Cole didn't say anything, he just waited patiently for Cade to explain, though Cade looked conflicted about it. Cade sighed, dropping his gaze to the floor.

"They had insider knowledge," Cade said, his voice barely more than a whisper. "That's when we found out."

"Who knows?"

"The chief, the captain, Brent, and me," Cade said.

"That's why he was transferred to vice," Cole guessed.

"Part of it, yeah."

Cade was holding something back, but if it was because it was confidential or something else, he didn't know. He opened his mouth to ask Cade about it, but he was cut off by the door opening and Lara stepping into the office.

"Guess who I found loitering around in the captain's office," Lara said. She gestured behind her where a man with short, dark hair and captivating green eyes stood, a smile on his face.

"Mikey," Cade exclaimed. He hugged the guy tightly then patted him all over like he was looking for something. "I can't believe it. You're alive."

"Fuck you."

The guy turned and smiled at Cole, holding his hand out for him to shake.

"Hi. I'm Michael Hobbs, Lara's partner."

"Cole Banks. I'm the guy they stuck with that one." He gestured toward Cade who made a face at him.

"He adores me," Cade said.

He more than adored Cade. That thought had him freezing to the spot, something clenching hard in his chest. Luckily, no one seemed to notice.

"We need to go back. We must've missed something," Cade said.

"I'll go with. An extra pair of eyes and all," Mike said.

"Thanks, man," Cade said, slapping Mike on the shoulder.

As they all stepped into the elevator, Cade was telling Mike some story that obviously entailed a lot of hand gestures. Just before the doors opened, Lara held out her car keys and Cade snatched them without looking. Then Cade and Mike made toward Lara's car. At no point did words cease to come out of Cade's mouth.

Cole raised an eyebrow at Lara. She just rolled her eyes and started toward his car. He stood dumbfounded for a moment, then he trotted after Lara.

"What just happened?"

"Those two gossip like a pair of schoolgirls and I've already got one I have to listen to at home. Thought I'd spare us both the agony."

He grinned at her. "I appreciate it."

He unlocked the car and they got in just as Lara's car sped past them. He buckled in and turned on the car. It came to life with a roar.

"So, what did you realize back there?" Lara asked.

"What?"

"Don't play daft with me, Hotshot," Lara said, her scrutinizing gaze firmly on him.

He groaned and dropped his head back against the headrest.

"I just realized that I actually like Cade," he said.

He liked Cade a hell of a lot more than he should.

"Yeah. He's like a god damned parasite. Once he's got a hold of you, he ain't letting you go," Lara said and shrugged. "Though, after some time, you don't really want him to."

Cole put the car in reverse and backed out of the parking spot. He tried to relax his hands on the steering wheel as he drove out of the parking garage.

"How did I reach that state already?" he asked, mostly to himself.

Lara patted him on the shoulder and if he hadn't been driving, he'd have glared at her.

"Oh, you poor—"

He cut her off. "If you say, 'unfortunate soul', I will stop this car and kick you."

Lara snorted a laugh, shaking her head at him.

"He's got you wrapped around his finger," Lara said.

Cole rolled his eyes but knew she was right. Making Cade smile was the best feeling and even though it didn't take much, he didn't want to stop. Lara had a knowing smile on her face while he drove and though he fought a brave battle, he couldn't hide his own.

Twenty minutes later, they all stood inside the Page house. Cade and Matt got there first, of course, but they'd waited the two minutes it took before Cole pulled up to the curb, before going inside.

"Check everything," Cole said.

Lara held out a box of gloves for them all to take a pair from. They each started in a corner of the bedroom, working methodically through everything. They'd been at it for at least half an hour when Cade cleared his throat to get everyone's attention.

"I doubt these belong to Mrs. Page," Cade said and held up a black pair of girl's hipsters with a snoring Snoopy on them. Definitely not Mrs. Page's. Also, they were too big to belong to any of their kids.

"Check the size," Lara said.

"Fourteen," Cade said. "Kid's sizes."

Silence engulfed the room for a long moment, the sound of Cole's heart beating so loud he thought the others would hear. He squeezed his eyes closed.

"I'd say we're looking for a girl between fourteen and sixteen," Lara said, breathing a sigh.

"Guys?"

Cole opened his eyes to gaze at a white-faced Cade. His knuckles were white from him clenching the bag he'd just put the panties in. His eyes flashed when they caught Cole's.

"There's dried blood in these," Cade said.

Cole sucked in a harsh breath. It wasn't as if they didn't already know, but fuck, it always hurt so bad. Every. Damn. Time.

"He kept a trophy," Mike said, his voice rough.

Cole nodded his head.

"Let's go ask the wife which young girls are close to the family," Cole said.

"We'll stay. Make sure we get everything," Lara said, motioning between herself and Mike.

With a dip of his chin, Cole turned and followed Cade through the house. When they walked outside, he grabbed Cade's arm, making him come to an abrupt halt.

"Hey," he said gently and cupped Cade's jaw to turn his head toward him. Cade's eyes were shuttered when they met his.

"We're going to find her and we're going to make sure she's safe."

Cade nodded, a glimmer of emotion showing in his eyes. Determination. He didn't comment on Cole saying safe instead of fine, alright, or something just as stupid. That girl was never going to be fucking fine. Adam Page had made sure of that.

He'd tried to stay emotionless around this case. Hell, he hadn't just tried; he'd done it. Then he met Cade. He could feel all his walls starting to crumble and he didn't like it one fucking bit. It was all too fucking close to home.

The ride to the station seemed endless. So many thoughts and scenarios churning around in his brain. Cade must've noticed because he turned down the radio and kept the singing to a bare minimum. They didn't speak as they made their way to the interrogations room Mrs. Page was in. She seemed to be doing a bit better than earlier, though the box of Kleenex in front of her was half empty.

"Mrs. Page," Cade greeted her.

She looked up, her watery eyes focusing in on them as they stood opposite her.

"Are there any girls in the age range of approximately between fourteen and sixteen close to your family?" Cole asked.

"No, the only teenager in the family is my nephew, David. But why is that important?"

"Please, Mrs. Page, just bear with us. Is there anyone you can think of? The age isn't too significant," Cade said.

"Um, well there's Sara, our former au pair, but she's twenty-one now and she lives in Sweden," she said, confusion clear in her voice.

If the guy wasn't already dead, that was something they would've dug deeper into. An au pair was a perfect target for someone like Page.

"Anyone who's maybe around your husband and kids?"

"Like the babysitter?"

He narrowed his eyes at her. "How old is she?"

"I don't see how this has anything to do with my husband's…" she swallowed and looked down at her clenching hands.

"I'm sorry, ma'am, but we can't tell you that, just know that it is really important that we find this young lady." No way was he going to tell her about their suspicion.

"Is she alright? Did something happen to Julie? Where is she? Was she there?" Mrs. Page asked, her voice turning shrill.

"Ma'am, please, slow down. What did you say her name was?" Cole asked.

"Julie. Julie Elton. She lives down the street. She's been our babysitter for two, almost three years."

"How old is she?"

"Sixteen, I think. I don't know. Why are you asking me all these questions? Are you going to find out who did this to my husband?"

He left that question to be answered by Cade as he left the room. When the door closed behind him, he stood there, in the hallway, his hands clenched into fists. He wanted to shake Mrs. Page. Wanted to open her eyes. Instead, he drew in a deep breath and relaxed his hands.

He walked to their office, dropping down in his chair. He hated everything about this case. He hated how people could be so ignorant, so stupid. He tried his best at being indifferent, but people like Mrs. Page made his blood boil red hot.

"You alright there, Hotshot?"

He raised his gaze, finding Lara standing in the doorway looking concerned. Her eyes were assessing as they moved over his face. He knew she saw more than he wanted her to when she stepped closer, her eyes softening as she watched him. He cleared his throat and attempted to get his emotions back under control.

"I'm fine. Cade is still with Mrs. Page. She's oblivious to what her husband was," he said.

"Deliberately?" Lara asked.

He closed his eyes, pulling a face. "I don't think so."

He didn't have to open his eyes to know who trudged into their office next. He could tell it was Cade from the sound of his walk. He could tell it was him by his smell. It was like he was wrapped in a bubble of Cade.

"She gave us a name. Julie Elton. Lives down the street and she's their babysitter," Cade said.

Cole's eyes shot open and he stood, walking around his desk to stand by Cade who looked no better off than he felt.

"I'll get on her file," Lara said and moved behind her desk to fire up her computer.

"Alright," Cole said before turning to Cade. "Let's have a chat with the Eltons."

They were in the car when the information on Julie Elton ticked in on Cade's phone. Cole watched out of the corner of his eye as Cade scrolled through the information.

"Julie Hannah Elton. Sixteen. She's a sophomore at Frederick Douglass High School. Parents are Elisabeth and Patrick Elton. She's got a younger brother, Thomas. Age ten," Cade said.

"Anything stand out?"

"Not one thing," Cade said.

Cade got quiet after that, his lips pursed as he gazed out the window. Cade was the first one out of the car when Cole parked in front of the row house belonging to the Eltons. Cole shook his head and got out of the car to follow Cade up the steps to the front door. Cade rapped his fist against the door and stepped back.

A stocky man with horn-rimmed glasses, brown eyes, and a full beard opened the door. His clothes were out of place, his shirt buttoned wrong. He watched them with bewilderment, blinking his eyes at them.

"Mr. Elton? Patrick Elton?" Cade asked.

"Yes. Can I help you?"

Showing his badge, Cade said, "Detective Lawson, my partner," he gestured at Cole, "Detective Banks. May we come in?"

"Uh, sure. Of course."

He waved them inside and they followed him into the living room. The place seemed bigger than it looked from the outside. Mr. Elton gestured for them to take a seat as he went to get his wife. Cole glanced at Cade who shrugged and made his way to the couch. A woman appeared in the doorway that most likely led to the kitchen, her short, red hair standing on end as she marched toward them.

"Is this about our daughter? Did you find her?" She asked just before they managed to take a seat on the plush couch.

"She's missing?" Cole asked, cold sliding down his spine as he shared a foreboding glance with Cade. Shit just went from bad to worse. He had a tough time believing that The Executioner would harm the girl, but he or she might be deluded enough to take the girl with them.

"Yes. She was supposed to be at a birthday party yesterday, but she never showed, and she hasn't been home since. Shouldn't you know this?" she asked.

"Ma'am, I'm afraid that's not why we're here. You know about the death of Mr. Page?" Cole asked.

She blanched for a moment before narrowing her eyes at him.

"The neighbor? Yes, we heard," she said, looking suspicious.

"What does that have to do with our daughter?" Mr. Elton asked in a subdued voice.

Cade straightened up, visibly pulling himself together as he drew in a breath. "We believe she might know something regarding Mr. Page's murder."

"Why would she know anything about that and I'm sorry, did you just say *murder?*" Mrs. Elton screeched.

Mr. Elton wrapped his arms around his wife, his eyes haunted as he looked at them pleadingly. Cole could feel Cade stumble mentally beside him.

"I'm afraid we can't share that information with you, ma'am," Cole said

"Anywhere you know of that she might've run to? Anyone she would feel safe enough with to go to if she was scared?" Cade asked.

Before they could answer, someone's phone started playing Britney Spears' song *I'm A Slave 4 You.* It took Cole a few seconds to realize it was coming from his phone. Pulling his phone from the inner pocket of his jacket, he stared at it as it spewed its heinous sounds. He answered while sending Cade a suspicious glare.

"Banks."

"Julie Elton just showed up at the station. She's alright and she has something she wants to tell us," Lara said.

"We'll be right there," he said and hung up.

Cade looked expectantly at him, but it was the Eltons Cole turned to. "Julie's at the police station."

Relief was stark on both their faces, tears staining Mrs. Elton's cheeks.

"Is she alright?"

"Yes. You can follow us there if you want," Cole said.

While the Elton's gathered their things, Cade followed him outside and into the car. He pulled away from the curb once he heard the Eltons' car start. When he stopped at the first red light they reached, he turned to Cade.

"When?" he asked.

"I don't know what you're—"

"Why?"

Cade slumped in his seat, his lip jutting out in a pout.

"I was half asleep," Cade mumbled, doing everything to avoid Cole's eyes.

The light changed before he could berate Cade and he reluctantly stepped on the accelerator. He glanced up in the rearview mirror to make sure the Eltons were following along.

"It seemed like a good idea at the time," Cade admitted.

Cole glared at him as much he could while driving.

"As I said, I was half asleep. Look, just… give me your phone, I'll change it back," Cade said.

Cole snorted. Like hell, he would. "No."

"No? Why— oh, my. I think I just discovered your deepest, darkest secret. You're a Britney fan."

"Laugh it up, homeboy. I just don't want you touching my things," Cole said, unable to ignore the triumphant grin splitting Cade's face.

"Oh, I *am* laughing, and I think you're lying," Cade said.

Cole shook his head. He jerked in surprise when a warm hand squeezed his thigh and cursed loudly when his dick sprang to life.

"Lying, baby. You do want me touching your things, you *Britney's Bitch*."

"Cade," he growled.

"I know," Cade sighed. "Inappropriate."

Cade was deflecting. It was Cade's survival mechanism he'd learned. Cade didn't deal very well with these situations. He didn't know exactly why, or if there was something in Cade's past that brought it on. But he did know Cade meant well.

"At least the girl is safe now," Cole said.

"Mhmm."

He glanced over at Cade, the thoughtful expression on his face making him sigh before asking, "What are you thinking?"

Cade turned his deep blue gaze his way, a gleam finding his eyes as a smile stretched on his face.

"Just that I really don't want to share you with Britney."

Lara

"I need to record this, honey," Lara said before she turned on the recorder and stated her name, rank, the cause of the interrogation, and then she let the social worker do the same. Then she turned to Julie.

"Please state your full name for the record."

"Julie Hannah Elton," she said in a soft, low voice, strained from crying.

"Just start from the beginning, sweetheart," Lara said with a friendly smile, trying to ease the discomfort she knew Julie must be feeling.

"I… I've been babysitting Will and Jane since I was fourteen."

Julie drew in a deep breath, trying to get her wits about her and not stammer while she talked.

"I saw him touching Will one day. I freaked out. I didn't know what to do. Not that it mattered. Adam knew I'd seen. He came to me. He said…" she sniffed as tears started running again. "He said he wanted me. He said it was me or them. I couldn't… I couldn't let him touch them. I couldn't let him hurt… They're just kids, you know? Five and eight. Younger, then.

"He paid me, to keep up the charade that I was babysitting. He gave me gifts, too. If I hadn't been too scared he'd find out, I would've gotten rid of them. Burnt them if I could."

Lara didn't doubt that as soon as she could, Julie would be doing just that. She took a deep breath and steeled herself before saying, "Tell us about that night. What happened?"

"I got off work at 8 pm and I was home about nine."

"Why that late?"

"The later I get there the less time he has."

Lara tried to swallow past the lump in her throat. She was glad Page was dead and not only because it meant the end of Julie's abuse, but because she didn't know what she would've done to that pig if she'd gotten the chance.

"What happened when you came home?"

"I went to the Page's house. Adam was there. No one else. I'd been there half an hour when suddenly, she was just there. I don't know how she knew, but she was there. She knew and she came for me. Saved me. She told me to run, so I did. I had no idea she was gonna... that she was..."

Julie hiccupped in her attempt to breathe in air. "I didn't know until I saw it on the news. They said that the Executioner had killed someone who didn't fit the profile. That she'd killed someone who wasn't a—"

Julie looked down at her hands while she fought the tears and swallowed hard a few times before continuing. "When I saw his picture, I knew. I knew I had to tell you. He wasn't innocent. He was a monster, and even though he's gone, he still makes me scream. Now it's just *only* in my dreams."

Lara's vision blurred and she didn't care as she reached across the table to take Julie's hand in hers. Julie glanced up, her teary gaze meeting Lara's.

"She wouldn't have killed someone innocent. She knows right from wrong. She just decided to do something more about it. I wish I'd been as strong as her," Julie said.

"I know, sweetheart. I know. But it's still against the law. We have to take her in. Did she tell you her name?" At the slight shake of Julie's head, Lara continued, "Did you get a good look at her?"

Another headshake.

"She had blonde hair, I think. Dark clothes. The lights were out."

That was strange.

"Why were the lights out?" Lara asked.

"I think the power went out and then she was just there," Julie said with a shrug.

"Alright, sweetie. Your parents are here. I'll go get them for you."

Lara got up, feeling conflicted. It was hard staying in the role of homicide detective when her mind did everything to compare the broken girl in front of her with her own daughter. She didn't know what she would do if something like that ever happened to Morgan.

"Detective?"

Lara turned back around. Julie's eyes were locked on the golden shield sitting in Lara's waistband, only visible because she had a hand in her jacket pocket, holding the fabric away from it.

When Julie's eyes met Lara's, she said in an even voice, "She was wearing a badge just like yours."

Cole

When Lara exited the interrogations room, her eyes seemed haunted as they met Cole's. He waited while she leaned back against the door, her eyes squeezed shut. He watched as she drew in a deep breath, posed herself and straightened. She opened her eyes and turned to him.

"You were right. She's a detective."

It didn't surprise him. He knew how it felt when doing your job just wasn't enough. He wasn't exactly a saint, but he'd always worked inside the law. Well, except for one time. He had no regrets there.

He followed Lara into their office. Cade and Mike were already there, both leaned back against their respective desks.

"So, we've got a police officer, a detective most likely. Female. How does she know 'bout the victims?" Mike asked.

"SVU? Sex Offender Registry?" Lara suggested.

"SVU. Yeah. She's most likely handled some of the victim's cases or found them through her work," Cade said to the room but kept his eyes on the whiteboard filled with pictures and keywords. Filled with everything they had on the case.

"Doesn't explain the last one," Cole grumbled.

"Maybe she got lucky. Maybe somethin' or someone triggered it?" Lara said with a one-shouldered shrug.

"Crosscheck the detectives in BPD's SVU department with all our victims," Cole said to Lara who swiveled in her chair to hastily type on her keyboard.

Something was bothering him. Something obvious he hadn't considered. He just knew he'd missed something. Something vital.

"Nothin'. Well, nothin' that fits. Some of the victims have been 'round Maryland and have encountered quite a few SVU officers. Besides that, we've only had one transfer from FCPD and that was over a year ago."

Cole picked up his work pad and started writing down anything and everything he could think of that was connected to the case.

Eleven victims. One female. Eight Caucasian, two African-American, and one Hispanic. Five from the ages of 19 to 28. Six from the ages of 30 to 44. All having molested a younger family member at some point. All were found in their own bed. Nine in Fairfax and two in Baltimore. Five found on a Tuesday, another five on a Wednesday, and one on a Saturday.

Why change from a weekday to the weekend?

"It was on a weekend," Cole burst out, jumping from his chair and walking to the whiteboard where he put a hand over a picture, his gaze searching the calendar hanging to his left.

"What?" Cade asked.

"The ninth victim was killed during a weekend. She could've gone back to Fairfax. Throwing us off when she moved. When the Executioner moved to Baltimore."

"But, why?" Mike asked.

"Because she would've been on call on the weekdays. She had to wait for a weekend she wasn't on call. Otherwise, she wouldn't be able to explain why it would take her hours to get to the station," Cade said before Cole could even turn to look at Mike.

"Expand the search to before the last victim in Fairfax, and make it transfers from Virginia not just FCPD," Cade said, following the same hunch Cole felt deep in his stomach.

"On it," Lara said, her fingers shooting across the keys.

His stomach was in cramps. His gut feeling told him they didn't have much time. He grasped the back of his chair, leaning on it as his head spun with all the information and clues gathered over the years.

"Alright. What I don't get is that all the other murders have been premeditated, but the last one? Leaving a witness and she just went for the kill. Sure, she tied him to the bed, but no sexual assault, at all. Just a few rounds of bullets. She usually drags it out, but this was done in a hurry. Why?" Cade asked.

"Julie said she knew. That somehow, she knew, and she came for her," Lara said while tapping her fingers on her thighs as she thought.

"She knew. She must've followed Julie. No other way for her to know about the abuse unless they were close somehow and I seriously doubt that. She would've acted far earlier. She wouldn't have found anything in the Sex Offender Registry either. Does Julie have a job?"

"Diner, two streets over from the State's Attorney's office," Lara said with a knowing look in her eyes as she raised an eyebrow and cocked her head to look up at him. If their perp was an SVU detective, then she would be working at Baltimore's Special Victims Unit which was situated at the States Attorney's office.

"What time does she work?"

"She's in high school, so after four? She said she was off work at eight."

"Well, it fits. Our perp could've bought dinner from Julie on her way home from work," Cole said.

"So, she sees Julie at the diner, follows her home, and finds the neighbor abusing her, tells Julie to run and kills the victim. She had time to tie him to the bed and shoot him, but nothing else. So where does she go? Why not ensure Julie's safety?" Lara asked.

They didn't get to ponder on that as Lara's computer made a beeping noise letting them know it'd found a match.

"Callie Thompson. Transferred from Prince William County PD, Special Victims Unit, three weeks before the last victim in Fairfax," Lara told them as her eyes scanned down the text on her screen.

"I've talked to her. She's the one in SVU I talked to about the victims. God dammit! She practically told me…" Cade shook his head and ran a shaking hand through his already tousled hair.

Under other circumstances, Cole would've done something when Cade put his head in his hands, obviously guilt-ridden, but he just didn't have the time. He felt an urgency with this case like he could feel something was about to go down.

Think. Think! Prince William. Thompson. Fairfax… Thompson?

"Thompson? As in former Chief of Police of FCPD?"

Lara went back to her computer and a few seconds later she confirmed his suspicion.

"Where does he live now?" Cole asked with a feeling of worry and dread spreading in his stomach. If it had been his father, if he'd been in Callie's shoes, he knew what he'd do.

"Baltimore. Moved here two months prior to Callie."

"She's here for him. He's her endgame. She knows she messed up with the last victim."

"What? Why?" Cade finally looked up, confusion clear in his voice and on his face.

"All the victims have had personal relations to their own victims. She moved after him. She didn't kill in between when they moved to Baltimore. Her hunting ground was in Fairfax, where he lived. He's the thing connecting her to Fairfax. She lived and worked in Prince William. Now he's the thing connecting her to Baltimore," Cole said while pulling on his jacket after securing his gun.

"He's her trigger," Lara said breathlessly, her eyes big with the sudden comprehension.

"Call for backup. You, stay here," Cade ordered when Lara moved to get up. "Give me the address."

They hurried down to the parking garage. Once in the car, Cole jammed the key in, turned it, and sped out onto the street as Cade turned on the siren.

They were nearing the end. Once they apprehended Callie Thompson the case was practically over, save for the paperwork and court. He couldn't wait to finally close the case, yet he didn't want it to be over. Not when it meant leaving Cade.

"You alright?" Cole asked, taking his eyes off the road to look at Cade for a few seconds.

"I have a feeling I should be asking you that," Cade said, keeping his eyes on the road and his face blank.

"Cade."

Cole swallowed, a lump clogging his throat. Trying to keep the conversation—if you could even call it that—off of himself, he said, "It's not your fault. You couldn't've known."

Finally, Cade looked at him, those big blue eyes watching him with equal amounts of weariness and guilt.

"Don't worry about me." Cade ran a hand through his tousled hair, letting out a deep sigh. "I just wish I could've helped her. I don't blame her for what she's done. Trust me, I know how that sounds. But once in a while you just get that feeling that no matter what or how much you do, it just isn't enough. You know, sometimes, the only one who can stop a criminal is another criminal."

"Cade—"

"Look. Don't worry about me. Yes, I feel like shit for not catching on to what Callie is. I just need some time, because I feel bad for *not* feeling bad about not catching Callie earlier."

Cole didn't know what to say to that, so he kept his mouth shut as he hightailed it to the other end of town with blue and red lights blinking from the front window.

"Did you work for him?" Cade asked after a few uncomfortable minutes of silence.

"Thompson? No. He retired before I transferred to Fairfax."

"You do that often?"

"Do what?"

"Transfer. You don't stay long in the same place, do you? This is, what, the fourth place you've been in five years?"

He kept his face blank, well aware that Cade's eyes scrutinized every movement he made. He couldn't let him see. He couldn't let him in. He wouldn't drag Cade into the mess that was his life. Nothing good would come of that. He'd just lose... he'd lose Cade.

The realization burned through him, making it hard for him to do anything but grip the steering wheel hard and try not to crash the car. He *needed* Cade. Fuck! He fucking needed him, but either way, he'd lose him. Cade wanted in but he couldn't let him, and Cade wouldn't stick around for someone like him. *Cole* wouldn't stick around for someone like himself.

"Yes," Cole said, his tone harder than he meant for it to be, but at least it made Cade just nod and turn his head away without further questions. Not that that was very pleasant, but that's how it had to be for now. He had to leave. He had to leave before he hurt Cade even more. He felt the decision settle with a hard twist in his stomach just as they reached former Chief Thompson's residence.

"Wanna wait for backup?" Cole asked.

Shaking his head, Cade said, "She's never killed anyone who didn't deserve it. Besides, she knows me."

Knowing Cade was right he said, "Alright. Lead the way."

With their guns out and their wits about them, they walked up the driveway and when they reached the front door, Cole let Cade take the lead. Cade reached for the doorknob, turning it and breathing a small sigh of relief as the door opened with a low click. Cade nodded at Cole before taking a few steps back and letting him open the door so Cade could enter first.

Cade

He caught Cole's gaze, emotions flickering in his deep green eyes before Cole seemed to shut them down forcefully and then he flung the door open. Cade leaned on his training, clearing every room with Cole as they steadily moved in the direction of strained voices.

Cade stilled as they reached the living room. A heavily built man with gray temples and a hard look on his face was bound to a kitchen chair in the middle of the room, a small woman standing to his left, gun drawn and pointing at him.

"Callie."

She looked up from her father, seeking Cade's eyes.

"Cade," she said, her eyes lightening up at seeing him. She liked him. She probably trusted him, too, and Cade would be damned if he couldn't at least try to live up to that trust. He had to do something. He had to keep her safe and yet give her what she deserved. Justice. That's when it all fell into place for him.

"Put the gun down, Callie."

"No, not until he admits to what he did to me," she exclaimed in a broken voice.

Cade's heart clenched at how devastated she sounded. He felt his heart breaking at the look in her eyes as she seemed to relive exactly those things; the way her body shook slightly, the way her hands clenched, the way her eyes misted over at the vile things that had been done to her—by her own father.

"I have no idea what she's talking about. Get me the hell out of here," the man had the gall to order even when he was bound to a chair, a gun pointed at the back of his head, acting as if Callie was still the frightened, young kid who'd done everything he'd told her to out of fear. But she didn't fear him anymore.

"Tell them! Tell them, *father*. Tell them what you did to me," she cried out at him, her gun hand shaking in her rage and heartache.

"There's no need to lie or play dumb, Mr. Thompson. We already know," Cade sneered at the man, disgust in his voice.

"Abusing your own daughter," Cade said with a curl of his lip. "Tell me, how does it feel to be on the other end? Are you as terrified as Callie was when she was a little girl, betrayed by the one person who was supposed to always protect and love her but instead gave her scars so deep no one would ever see?"

Cade saw nothing even resembling regret in Thompson's eyes and contempt even greater than he'd already felt for the man filled him to the brink. Cade knew this was only the second man he'd ever truly hated.

"It's over Callie. Put the gun down. You don't need to die because of him too," Cole said from behind Cade as he stepped up next to him.

"No! I will shoot him unless he admits to what he did," Callie said, pressing her gun against her father's temple.

Cade lowered his gun and glanced up at Cole. "I don't know about you but I'm not gonna stop her."

Cole

It took him no less than a second to figure out where Cade was going with that. He was saddened when he realized how in touch he and Cade really were, especially now that he'd made his decision to part with him.

He shrugged, returning his gaze to Thompson as he lowered his own gun. "I've been after her for years. She's never killed anyone who didn't deserve it."

"You can't do that," Thompson spluttered and tried to pull away from Callie.

"Better do as she says, chief. She's highly unstable. She's killed a lot of people. Ain't that right, Callie?" Cade asked.

The proud smile on Callie's face was answer enough. From the frantic pulling against the ropes, Thompson was starting to realize just how serious Callie was. Just how dangerous she was.

"There's only one way you walk out of this alive, Thompson," Cole said. "Did you abuse your own daughter? Did you rape and beat her?"

The bastard took the time to *think* about it.

"Yes. Yes, I abused her. Now get me the hell away from her," he hissed out through clenched teeth.

Cole's smile was almost a match to Callie's satisfied smirk as she handed over her gun to Cade and let him handcuff her. Cole pulled out his own handcuffs, turning his smile on Thompson.

"Mr. Thompson, you are under arrest for the extended abuse and sexual assault of a child," Cole said while swinging his cuffs on a finger in front of the shocked man.

"What the hell? You can't use this. I was under duress," Thompson spluttered, his face turning red with anger.

"You just admitted to abuse of your daughter to an officer of the law. You weren't under duress, *sir*. Detective Lawson had already detained Detective Thompson," Cole said.

Cole knew it was a long shot. This wouldn't hold in court, but it was enough to arrest him and give them time to gather enough evidence to convict him. He just hoped Callie had something more than this up her sleeve.

"This is bullshit!" Thompson screamed as Cole clamped the handcuffs around his wrists.

"Mr. Thompson, you have the right to remain silent. Anything you say can and will be used against you in a court of law. You have the right to an attorney. If you can't afford an attorney, one will be appointed to you. Do you understand these rights?"

"You can't do this!"

"I'll take that as a yes."

Chapter Twelve

Cade

THE BACKUP consisting of mostly uniforms showed up just as Cade was leading Callie out the front door. He held up his badge and yelled for them to stand down.

"It's gonna be okay. I won't let him get away with it," he said, keeping his voice low so only Callie heard.

"I know. Thank you, Cade," Callie said while looking up at him with those expressive green eyes of hers holding so much gratitude he felt his own eyes watering.

Fuck. This girl had been hurt all her life by someone close to her and yet, she seemed to completely trust Cade. It broke his heart, but it also gave him hope. Hope her father hadn't taken away everything. He led her to the nearest car, his hand gentle around her arm.

"I'm not stupid. I know he'll just retract his confession. I just wanted him to admit it out loud. He hasn't been hurting anyone since me. It's the only reason he's still alive," Callie said.

He held a hand on the top of her head as she got into the back of one of the marked cars. He reached in to fasten her seat belt for her.

She wore a smile on her face, though it was small and melancholy. "All he cares about is his reputation. It's ruined now."

"I'm still going to do what I can to get him convicted," Cade said. He was going to take that bastard down, no matter what.

"I know. I want him to go down. Don't worry, I have all the evidence you'll need. I am the daughter of a cop, after all."

"What did you do?"

"He never used a condom. He put me on the pill the second I got my period. So, I saved some of the clothes he ruined. But I didn't want to rely on that, so I went to the electronics store and bought a video camera. I put it up. I have him on video."

"Where do you have these things?" Cade asked.

"In my safety deposit box."

He put his hand on her shoulder, squeezing to let her know he got it. Then he stepped back, closed the door and watched as the car drove off before he made his way to the Camaro. He leaned against the car and watched as Cole and two officers led the screaming and flailing former Chief Thompson toward a marked car. He turned his back on them as he waited. He didn't know how to feel. He didn't know where he stood with Cole. He'd felt something shift between them in the car, but he wasn't sure what. He was looking at the ground when Cole stopped in front of him, his gaze on the black pair of booths in front of him.

"You alright?"

Every time that dark, sensual voice swept over him, he felt helpless.

"Sure."

"Cade."

Cole said his name on a sigh. Like he was an inconvenience. Fucking eh.

"She said she has evidence." He looked up at Cole, trying not to let too much show in his eyes. "I'm gonna hold him for as long as I can."

He was gonna do all he could to ensure Thompson went to jail because he got why Callie hadn't just killed him. It would've been too easy.

"I'm sure you'll find it," Cole said.

When he couldn't read Cole's eyes, he cut his own to the ground, nerves making him fidget. He was clueless as to where they stood. Everything was just one big mess.

"Let's just get back to the station so we can get this over with."

Callie

She sat in the metal chair. By the metal table. The one she was cuffed to. The handcuffs cold against her skin. It was constructed to feel unpleasant, but all it made her feel was comfort. She felt safe. She didn't wait there long before Cade came in through the door and sat down in the chair opposite hers. She was almost done. She had faith in Cade. He would right all the wrongs. She didn't much care about anything else. Though there was one thing nagging at her, she belatedly admitted to herself.

"The girl. How is she?"

Cade looked up from the file in his hands, a small smile finding its way to his lips.

"She's safe. She's with her family."

"Good. Make sure she gets the help she needs. Please. Don't let her end up like me."

Determination settled on Cade's face. He gave a sharp nod of his head and she relaxed back in her chair.

"You know the drill," Cade said.

She did. She waited for him to state his part into the microphone before she started talking.

"My name is Callie Thompson. I'm a detective with the Special Victims Unit in Baltimore. I am guilty of the murders of eleven child molesters. Noah Billings. Jason Fisher. Mason Kennedy. Oliver Cruz. Miles Collins. Matthew Donnelly. Samantha Dunn. Elliot Suez. Ryan Baker. Chris Henway, and Adam Page."

Their names, their faces, was forever seared into her mind. But so were the names and faces of their victims. They were what fueled her.

"You'll find things I took from them—trophies—in my safe deposit box."

They both knew she hadn't taken anything from them. But Cade needed the things in the box to be evidence, otherwise, he couldn't use it against her father.

"I was eight. The first time. You know what he said? He said I had to take my mother's place now that she was gone. I was a kid and I'd just lost my mother. How can anyone do something like that?"

Cade's eyes were filled with so much pain and understanding when she met his gaze.

"I didn't understand it until I was at least fifteen. I had to *learn* that it's not alright. Because it was as natural and normal to me as tying my shoes. It's fairly common, unfortunately. You know, if there's no one to tell you it's wrong, then how else are you supposed to know?

"When I found out what it was he was actually doing to me, I got so angry. I tried to get help. But no one's gonna believe the kid of a police chief. Because he's *such a good man.* Everybody knows him. He protects. He serves. He doesn't hurt," she spat out, disgust coating her words. How many times did she hear it? Hear how fucking great he was? How everyone loved him?

"I told Richie. My dad's best friend. My substitute uncle. Yeah, I was real stupid back then," she said.

"What do you mean?"

"Surely, you don't believe a man's gonna trust a kid over his best friend? Someone he's known since kindergarten?" Callie shook her head, a grim look on her face. Disdain. Disgust. Anger. It was all there, out in the open. She didn't have to hide it anymore. "As I said, I was stupid. I was scared. I didn't tell him my father molested me. I just said, 'Richie, daddy hurts me. He hurts me.' He went to my father and told him. I heard my father say to him 'she's been spinning stories east and west. I don't know what to do. I think she feels neglected because of her mom.' Richie believed him. Of course, my father knows how to manipulate people."

She'd been hiding by the top of the stairs. She'd heard every word they said, and word by word she felt the hope and belief inside her dwindle until there was nothing left but fear.

"That night, when Richie went home…" she trailed off, looking into space, her eyes blank, but filling with tears. "He tied me to the bed."

Tears streamed down her cheeks as she saw and felt that little girl she'd once been. Screaming. Crying. Begging. Nothing worked. How she wanted to save that little girl. But she couldn't turn back time. She couldn't change the past, couldn't keep her from breaking.

"He didn't have any rope, so he used his ties."

Oh, how she'd fought. How she'd pulled and pulled, even after her wrists started aching and bleeding. She could do nothing but feel. Until she stopped feeling anything at all.

"He told me to shut up. To never say anything to anyone again. He pushed his gun into my mouth. I couldn't breathe. I couldn't breathe…"

"Daddy, please. Please." She cried, fear surging through her, tearing her body apart from the inside as he was tearing her apart from the outside.

Pain. So much pain. Why was he doing this?

"Shut the fuck up!" he screamed down at her just before a loud smack sounded through the room.

Adrenaline was pumping through her veins, fear clouding her head, making her unable to feel the side of the pistol slamming into her temple. She couldn't feel a thing. She screamed. She trashed. She tore at her bonds.

Her mouth was forced open. Something cold and hard was shoved down her throat. She couldn't breathe. Her eyes started to fill with water as she choked. She was gonna suffocate in her own vomit. She didn't even care. This would be a good way to go, right? No more pain. No more fear. It could all be over. Just a bit more and she could finally be free. She could die.

He didn't let her.

She blinked her eyes, Cade once again in front of her.

She took a deep breath and straightened, pushing the fear and pain deep down. "He ruined my life. I wanted revenge. I wanted him to pay. But I knew waiting was the only way. I did my homework. I found out what evidence I would need to bring him down."

"I'll get it and I will make sure he rots in jail," Cade said.

"Let's see how long he lasts. A molester and a cop? They're gonna have their fun with him."

In that moment, she truly felt sadistic. She wanted him to pay. She wanted him to hurt, to bleed. She needed it.

"My first kill. Noah Billings. I didn't know what I was doing. I just knew he needed to go. He had to die for what he'd done. He walked. We all knew it was him, but he still walked. We didn't have enough evidence. The girl, Isabel, she was a minor and no one believed her besides me. Her uncle could never have hurt her. Bastard had them all fooled. But not me. I knew. I knew what he was.

"That night, I didn't know what to do at first. Nothing beyond making him hurt. That's how the worst night of my life came to mind. I did to him what was done to me."

She looked Cade in the eyes.

"I liked seeing them so frightened. Hurt. I wasn't born like that. I wasn't born this way. I was made. Made by the cruelty of the one man who was supposed to protect me."

Cole

He'd been watching from behind the two-way mirror as Cade talked with Callie. When Cade stood to leave the interrogation room, Cole stepped out into the hallway to meet him. He was out in time to see Cade close the door behind him and lean his back against it, his chin touching his chest. When he looked up, noticing Cole, his blue eyes couldn't contain the anguish he was feeling.

Cole didn't think about it, he just walked over there and pulled Cade into a hug, wrapping his arms around the smaller man and leaning his cheek on top of Cade's head.

"It's over. It's over now," he said.

The hallway was empty, but right at that moment, he couldn't have cared less if it was filled with people. He put a finger under Cade's chin, lifting his face as he leaned down to press a kiss to his lips. The lips under his trembled but then they softened and pressed against his own. The kiss wasn't about anything but being there for Cade when he needed it. He pulled back and hugged Cade tight, pressing a kiss to the top of his head. He took a deep breath, Cade's unique smell filling his nose. He'd needed that.

"I don't get it," Cade said when they parted.

"You never do."

There was no understanding how a parent could molest their child. None. How many times did he ask himself that question? And every time, he got no answer.

"Thank you," Cade said.

Neither of them noticed Captain Morris until he walked right by them, barking at them. "Banks. Lawson. My office."

They shared a surprised look before they both trotted after Morris. He could feel Cade's apprehension even though the man didn't show it. When they stepped into Morris' office, Cole closed the door behind him. Morris' palms rested on his desk as he leaned on them while he glared at them.

"So, tell me, what bright idea of yours made you think you could just break the damned protocol?"

"Sir, I—"

"No. I don't want your dumbass excuses, Lawson. Banks, start talking."

Cole stepped forward, moving in front of Cade. "Sir. We assessed on the scene that the probability of Thompson turning her gun on us was much less than of her putting a bullet through Mr. Thompson. We acted accordingly to the knowledge we had at the time."

The captain looked between them before settling his gaze on Cade.

"Alright. Piss off Lawson," Morris barked.

Cade didn't need to be told twice. He practically ran out the door, leaving Cole to fight a smile. He turned back to Morris.

"With all due respect, sir, I've been after Thompson for over a year. I know her. I know how she reacts. Besides, I trust Lawson. We worked well together, and I knew he had my back, just as I had his."

Morris didn't say anything for a while and just sat back in his chair, watching Cole with contemplating eyes.

"He's a mouthful, ain't he? How's it been working with him?"

"Frustrating but efficient, sir."

Cole couldn't help the smile that found his lips. Well, it was the truth. Whenever Cade disagreed with him on something, all he needed to do was touch him or kiss him, and Cade would get so distracted, he'd forget what they were arguing about. It didn't matter that Cade usually won the argument later on. He liked working with Cade. He wasn't just comic relief, he was a great cop and an even better detective. He might be goofy and childish, but he was damned good at his job.

"Would you want to continue on?" Morris asked.

The question took him aback. He stared at the captain who raised a brow at him. He blinked and cleared his throat, still unsure what to think of it.

"Sir?"

He stuck his hands into his back pockets so he wouldn't fidget.

"You've put in a request for an open transfer, Banks. Would you consider staying here an option?"

He felt like the air was sucked right out of his lungs.

"Here? With Lawson?"

"Exactly. As you said, you work well together and from what I've seen, you seem like a good counterpart to Lawson."

If only he really knew.

"From what I can tell, you're able to control him. Someone like that is damn hard to find. I would like to keep you."

A chance to be with Cade, for real, but was it worth it? He couldn't give Cade what he wanted. Could he?

Cade

He was grumbling under his breath, his eyes cast down as he walked down the hallway for the umpteenth time. He grunted when he walked straight into someone. He looked up and frowned at the man in front of him.

"Shouldn't you be home in bed?"

Mike made a grimace at him. "But I missed you so," Mike purred.

"Yeah, right. Go home, dumbass. Before I have to scrape you off of the floor."

"Love you too," Mike said.

"You know it, baby," Cade called after him. Mike flipped him off over his shoulder as he walked to the elevator.

Cade turned around to continue his pacing, but Lara was standing in his way.

"Where's your partner, darlin'?"

"I don't know. I haven't seen him since I left him with the captain."

He rubbed his arms. Cole had been in there for quite a while now. He just hoped like hell Cole wasn't in trouble because of him.

"Maybe he's waitin' for ya at home. Maybe wantin' to *celebrate* your victory."

The innuendo in those words made him stare at her. The knowing smile spreading on her lips made his mouth drop open. Then he clamped it shut, looking at Lara with narrowed eyes.

"I'm that transparent?"

That sounded like a whine. Bloody hell. Did he just *whine?*

Lara's smile turned softer.

"No darlin'. He is."

"Oh."

He jerked his head up. "Wait. You're condoning this?"

She shrugged. "If he makes you happy, then I'm all for it."

"Oh, he makes me happy alright." He wagged his eyebrows. He turned to leave, but at the last second, turned around again.

"What's his tell?"

She looked up at him, her smile somber and her voice serious as she said, "He can't help but smile whenever he looks at you, and darlin', that man doesn't smile easily."

The meaning of those words burned through him like wildfire. He needed to find Cole. He headed straight for Morris' office. He knocked on the door but didn't wait for an answer before he walked right on in.

"Captain."

Morris glared up at him from where he sat behind his desk looking through his files.

"Lawson," Morris grunted.

Cade glanced around the room. Huh. No Cole.

"Have you seen my partner?"

Morris lips quirked into a smile. Why did he look like he knew something Cade didn't? Wait. Nope. That was probably just his face.

"I sent him home for the night. After he defended your honor," Morris said.

"I think we both know that it had nothing to do with me."

"He's a straight shooter."

Morris stood up so he could glare down at Cade. He grinned right back up at him.

"Hey. We both know there's nothing straight about me. I like dick too much."

Morris didn't even look surprised. He just looked like he might slap Cade for the hell of it. He knew he was lucky to have a captain who was so accepting. Not that he gave a shit about what anyone else thought of him, but still, it ensured that no one was harassing him so he could do his job right.

"Are you trying to get suspended?"

"It's working, isn't it?"

"Piss off, Lawson."

"Yessir." He threw in a half-assed salute before hightailing it out of there. He didn't actually need to get suspended.

He had another problem, though. Cole's car was gone. Which meant that he didn't have a ride home. He was standing in the middle of the parking garage, considering his options, when Lara stepped out of the elevator.

"Ah. Lara, sugar, would you mind dropping me off at my place?"

She rolled her eyes at him, but she didn't protest when he jogged after her and got into her car.

"Thanks."

She just grunted and started her car.

When Lara stopped the car at the curb in front of his house, she turned to him before he could get out.

"Whatever you two decide, just know that I'll stand behind you no matter what," she said.

He leaned over to press a kiss to her cheek, happiness filling him. If it wasn't for her, he wasn't sure he would've made it this far. She'd shown him what he could be, so he'd held on through all the shit and made it through to the other side.

"You know I love you, right?"

"I love you too, darlin'," Lara said.

He got out of the car, feeling lighter and better than he had the whole day. He was smiling to himself as he walked up the driveway. It had been one hell of a day and all he wanted was to finally get out of his clothes and snuggle up next to Cole. Well, a bit more than just snuggling. Cole promised to make it worth his while. He was looking forward to that.

"Cole? Babe?" He called out as he walked through the door. "Cole?"

His car wasn't in the driveway and the lights were off, but he wasn't at the station either. So where was he?

He was dead on his feet, so he decided to go to bed. Now that their case was closed, he could rest easy for a night or two. He walked through the bedroom door and promptly froze. The room was as they'd left it the night before. Except for Cole's clothes he'd folded neatly and put on the dresser as he'd done every day they'd been together. Neat freak.

Cade took a long look around the room, anguish slowly seeping into his body, chilling him to the bone. He whirled around, walking with fast strides down the stairs and threw the door open to his guest room. He sucked in a harsh breath. The suitcase that had been neatly tucked into the corner was gone.

This couldn't be happening. He couldn't just be gone. Had the man who'd dedicated his life to running toward bullets actually run away from Cade?

He slumped down on the floor and leaned his head back against the wall, closing his eyes when he felt them starting to burn with unshed tears.

"Good going, Cade. Falling for a guy who doesn't want you," he mumbled to himself. He snorted. "No, not a guy who doesn't want you. A guy who wanted you until it wasn't convenient anymore and left without a bloody 'Bye, doll. Thanks for the fuck, see ya never.'"

What the hell. Another person walking away from him was nothing. If he kept telling himself that, maybe someday it wouldn't be a lie.

Chapter Thirteen

Cade

"WHY DON'T you just call him? It's been what, three weeks?" Lara said, looking up at him over her computer screen. He scrunched up his nose, trying to look offended. It was twenty-two days, and no, he certainly wasn't counting.

"I can't just call him," he mumbled, trying to stay focused on the case file he was looking through, in an attempt to dissuade Lara.

"Why not, darlin'?"

Cade sighed. No such luck then.

"Well… he just left. Not a word. He was just gone. Does that sound like someone who wants to keep in touch?"

Hell, no. That screamed of someone who wanted to cut off all communication. Cade hadn't just been flabbergasted but hurt, too, when he'd walked into his house to find it empty, all trace of Cole ever being there as good as gone. Like he'd never been there in the first place.

"Maybe he just needs some time. You know, to turn things 'round in his head and come to terms."

Cade cocked his head to the side and squinted at her. "Why do you sound like you know something I don't?"

"Because I do."

"Rhetorical, Lara. It was rhetorical," he said while shaking his head at her, a ghost of a smile on his lips.

"Aw. But it's true. Just ask Morgan," she said.

"No need. You know she comes to me when she needs to vent about her all-seeing-all-knowing mother."

"You do know that isn't why she's been spendin' the week with you, right?"

"I know. She's worried 'bout me. A sixteen-year-old girl is worried about a twenty-nine-year-old. Shame on me."

"Oh, sweetheart. That's just what family does. We take care of each other, which means we also worry 'bout each other."

"Have I told you recently how much I love and appreciate you?"

"No. You've got some making up to do, darlin'," Lara said.

That made him perk up a bit, a smile spreading on his face. "Want me to sing you a love ballad?"

She looked at him with disbelief. "You actually know one?"

He grinned at her, rubbing his hands together excitedly. This was gonna be fun. "Nope. But I can sing you some Disney?"

"Only if you do it so loud it won't only be me sufferin'."

He stood up, clearing his throat dramatically. Then he belted out 'Les Poissons' from *The Little Mermaid*, laying it on thick with the French accent and using his stapler as a prop; there were fish being chopped up, bones being pulled out, and crabs being stuffed during this scene in the movie.

"Lawson. Shut the fuck up," Booth yelled from the bullpen.

Cade kept singing, ducking when someone threw a stapler at him. He chuckled and as his gaze connected with Lara's, he let out a full-blown laugh. He bloody loved bugging the shit out of his coworkers. He picked up the stapler and threw it back, barely missing Snow's shoulder. She picked it up and flipped him off. He collapsed into his chair, laughter still racking through his body, and moved his mouse to wake up his computer.

"I know what you just did," he told Lara while keeping his eyes on his computer screen as he typed away, filing his latest report with a little more energy and a smile on his face.

"I know you do."

"Thank you." He looked up when Lara's hand covered his, squeezing gently. She was smiling at him, silently offering her support. He loved her for that. He also hated needed it.

Mike walked in clapping his hands. "Heads up, people. We've got one."

Since Cade was without a partner—again—they were working as a team. Which was what they were supposed to be doing, just with four detectives, not three.

"Oh, Lord, somebody actually died during business hours?" Cade said in mock surprise, a hand over his heart and his mouth falling open.

"Well, there's a first for everythin'," Lara said with a wink at Cade.

They all grabbed their things and made their way down to the parking garage, where they piled into Lara's car. Mike cursed out Cade when he made it to the passenger side door first.

"I'm the cripple here. I should get the front seat," Mike said.

"Too bad you're only a cripple 'cause you got yourself shot, ain't it?" Lara said.

Cade was grinning as he tilted his seat back, closed his eyes, and listened to Lara and Mike chattering the whole way. He could almost convince himself that everything was back to normal. If only he could convince his heart, too. He just had to go and fall for a guy like Cole Banks. He should've seen it coming, but stupid as he was, he'd lost himself in the way Cole made him feel. Had lost himself in those stunning eyes.

He was jarred out of his thoughts by the car coming to a stop and the motor being turned off. He opened one eye and glanced over at Lara.

"You alright, darlin'?" she asked him.

He groaned and pushed himself up from the reclined seat. He clicked off his seatbelt and with an unintelligible mumble, he got out of the car. No, he wasn't alright. But he had work to do. *They* had work to do. He slammed the door and walked around the car to Lara and Mike's side.

218

Lara was watching him with concerned eyes, but he knew her pity wouldn't last long. If he didn't get his shit together soon, he was in for an ass-kicking. He straightened up, smoothing down his suit jacket, and drew in a deep breath.

"We'll talk to the LEO's," Lara said. She wrapped a hand around Mike's upper arm and dragged him toward the cops standing around their cruisers.

Cade barely got to acknowledge it before a cop stepped in front of him. She wore a neutral expression, though it wasn't hard to see that the scene affected her.

"Detective? This way," she said.

She turned on her heels and Cade had to run a few steps to catch up with her. He followed her down the alley, ducking under the crime scene tape. He knew what was awaiting him would be gruesome, but he could just barely keep from grinding his teeth in anger as he looked down at their newest murder victim. Black hair was strewn over her face. Her pink nail polish was cracked. Her denim skirt was ripped into pieces. Her jade colored eyes—matching the pair of panties around her neck—were spotted in red from the asphyxiation.

Cade knelt down next to her sprawled body and looked at her beautiful face contorted in pain and horror, bruises starting to show on her cheeks and her fearful eyes open but unseeing.

"Can I take her?" Doc said from behind him, startling him out of his trance. He cleared his dry throat and managed to say, "Sure. Go ahead, Doc."

He was standing in the same place when Mike walked up behind him, making him look over his shoulder at him.

"Her name is Amelia. Amelia Coulson," Mike said in a gravelly voice, his eyes never leaving her body as Doc and his assistant lifted her onto the slab. "Mary's little sister."

"Mary Coulson? As in Elias Tully's victim? That Amelia Coulson?"

"Yes."

Mike's eyes were filled with so much pain, Cade could barely stand to look at him. He didn't doubt this case was going to take a toll on all of them.

Cade

He managed not to trip over himself as he got out of the elevator at shit o'clock in the morning. It was a Sunday, and he was supposed to be snuggling with his pillow right then. He skidded to a halt in front of Lara's desk, throwing his arms up. "I'm here. Whose ass do I have to kiss?"

Lara raised a disapproving eyebrow at him. He stuck his tongue out at her. It was her fault for calling him in on his day off.

She crossed her arms over her chest. "I've just been down to SVU and guess what?" she said with a tone that made him reluctant to ask.

He grimaced as he plopped his ass down into his chair. "What?"

"There was a match on the rape kit DNA from the Coulson case."

That was bloody fast. He sat up straight.

"It's an active case. Same M.O. 'cept for the killing. Guess whose case it was."

He didn't have to think about it. He'd had an inkling and now it was confirmed.

"Callie," he breathed on a heavy sigh. If there was one place Cade dreaded, it was prison. But he would do it. If not for Callie, then for Amelia and the other young girls who were most likely in line to end up like her.

"I suggest you go talk to her, she might know somethin'," Lara said.

"Yeah. Yeah, I'll go. I'll just have to call the detention center," he said, already dreading that particular call.

"Don't worry about it. I'll do that, you just go get something to eat."

Morgan wasn't the only one who'd been mothering him. Granted, he was acting like a whiny little bitch. Being left by someone he'd thought wanted to be in his life didn't exactly bring out the best in him.

He walked into the kitchen to pour himself some coffee and steal Tanner's lunch. He was convinced Tanner still lived with his mother 'cause there was no way that man could cook that good. He was in the middle of devouring Tanner's pasta salad, which was filled with a lot of yummy bacon when Mike walked into the kitchen. When he saw Cade, he halted, staring at him for a moment before blurting out, "You look like shit."

Cade grunted, then stuffed some more bacon into his mouth, chewing loudly to annoy Mike.

"Thanks, Mike. It's nice to see you too. Tell me, is it the norm to be three hours late every day on your first week back?"

"Fuck off," Mike said before dumping himself into the chair across from Cade. Before he got a chance to stop him, Mike reached across the table and dug a fork into the pasta. Rolling his eyes, he begrudgingly pushed the container into the middle of the table.

"Case taking a toll?" Mike asked around a mouthful of pasta.

"You know it."

"You know someone who looks like her or something?"

Cade swallowed hard before he could answer. "Or something."

Shit. Yeah, that was one hell of an *or something*. That night was forever etched into his brain. The look on Michaela's face, the pleading in her eyes when she'd seen him. It was hell remembering it. It was his punishment. He hung his head, unable to close his eyes without seeing too much of his past flash behind his lids.

"How are you doing, Mikey?"

"Me? Oh, you know, between being shot and living with Samuels, I'm just fucking peachy."

Though he said it with a grin, Cade knew that Mike was in some serious pain and not just from the bullet. With how he himself was feeling lately, getting shot would probably hurt less. There was nothing worse than heartbreak. Not even a knife in the gut. He knew. He'd been through both.

He got up, leaving the rest of the pasta to Mike. He walked out of the kitchen, fleetingly glancing to his right when the elevator doors opened. He took a step, then froze. He slowly turned back toward the elevator, his breath caught in his throat at what he saw. Dark brown hair gave way to green eyes cautiously searching the room until they landed on Cade. He watched as recognition sparked and the pupils widened.

"Cole?" he asked, not actually believing his eyes. Was he seeing things now? He wouldn't put it past himself. His mind liked to trick him.

"Cade," Cole said, a smile widening on his face and his eyes lighting up as he walked toward Cade with long strides. That, he did not expect. Holy shit, that look did something fundamental to him. He was barely breathing when Cole stopped a few inches from him, looking down at him with a frown and a raised eyebrow.

"He didn't tell you, did he?" Cole finally asked, making Cade raise his brows and cock his head to the side in confusion. The only thing making sense in his mind right then was that Cole stood in front of him, looking sexy enough to eat.

"Who didn't tell me what?"

Cole didn't answer him. Instead, he tugged on Cade's arm to get him to follow as he made his way to the captain's office.

"Captain," Cole said after knocking twice on the open door.

Morris looked up with a scowl that was quickly replaced by a pleasant smile when he saw Cole. "Banks. Come on in."

Morris never looked at him that way. Morris' eyes cut to Cade for a brief moment. Just long enough for Cade to pout and Morris to glare at him disapprovingly. Then Morris turned back to Cole.

"I didn't expect you until tomorrow."

Before Cole could answer, Cade spat out, "What the hell?"

He looked between them, then settled his gaze on Morris, narrowing his eyes. "You knew he was coming? Wait. Why are you here?" He asked as he turned to Cole. He felt like he was missing a big piece of this puzzle.

"He just transferred here," Morris said.

Cade felt his jaw dropping and his eyes bulging almost to the point where they were in danger of falling out. He cleared his throat, trying to pretend he hadn't just been caught completely off guard. "Say what now?"

"I transferred to Baltimore PD," Cole said.

"So, we're partners? For *real* this time?"

The smile on Cole's face warmed him like nothing else. His heart was beating like crazy. At the moment, he didn't even care if the others could hear it.

"This is yours, Banks." Morris opened a drawer, pulling out a badge and a gun, sliding them across his desk.

"Now piss off, I have work to do," Morris said, waving them off impatiently.

"Yes, sir," Cade said with a mock salute and turned on his heels to practically run out of the office. He kept walking, the sound of Cole's footsteps right behind him, a comfort he hadn't known he needed. He didn't say anything until they were inside the elevator.

"What the hell just happened?"

Cole dangled his new badge in front of Cade, his eyebrows raised and a smirk on his face. "You just got yourself a new partner."

He liked the sound of that.

"You got a place to stay? No? Good, you can stay with me," Cade said without waiting for Cole's answer and then he was out of the elevator and on his way to his car, a snorting but chuckling Cole on his heels. He was taking the man home with him. There was a lot of shit they needed to talk about, though he was much too happy to be angry at Cole.

"You came just at the right time," Cade said over his shoulder.

"Why's that?"

"You get to accompany me to the detention center."

"What've we got in jail?"

Cade turned, walking backwards with a wry smile on his face.

"Callie Thompson."

Cole

Cole felt unsteady as he put his car in park. He stepped out and followed Cade up the driveway and through the front door. Cade's silence was unsettling. He was never quiet. Not unless he was scheming or worse. Cole gulped. They continued into the kitchen where Cade settled back against the counter.

"So?" Cade asked, a brow raised.

Cole swallowed hard, his Adam's apple bobbing.

"I'm sorry. I should've told you. Morris offered me the job before I left. I didn't know if I… if I wanted to take it and I just kinda…"

Why the hell did he have to develop foot-in-mouth syndrome now of all times?

"Freaked?" Cade offered with an understanding smile on his lips.

"Well, yeah. I guess."

He'd done so much more than just freaked. He'd been a fucking mess.

"Being away from you sealed the fucking deal," he said, hoping Cade would hear the honesty in those words.

Waking up to the heat of another person close, waking up with the weight of someone's head on his shoulder, that wasn't something Cole ever imagined he would have and certainly not want. That he craved it—the nearness, the feel of that heartbeat over his own, the way a leg always seemed to pry its way between his, the way an ear was pressed against his chest listening for his heartbeat, the soft puffs of air—that he needed it to sleep, was one hell of a surprise. Well, it might slightly also have to do with the sex that came before and sometimes after. But all in all, it was knowing and feeling Cade in his arms that ensured Cole's sleep and peace of mind.

He'd found it almost impossible to sleep in the three weeks he'd been alone in his own bed, away from Cade. It was absolutely impossible not to think about him. Impossible for his mind not to sort through every last memory of Cade as he lay down to sleep. It'd scared him shitless and he'd considered not taking the job. Good thing he had his best friend to knock some sense into him.

"Cole?"

He must've drifted off into his thoughts. It definitely wasn't the first time Tank had called his name from the look of his crossed arms and the raised brow over expectant eyes.

"Huh?"

"What the hell is wrong with you, man?"

"What?"

"You're just sitting there, looking at nothing. So, what's up, zombie?"

"Nothing. I—"

"Don't give me that shit, Gunner, I know you better than that. Something or someone has you all messed up. My bet is on someone," Tank said with a cheeky grin while wagging his eyebrows up and down.

"Don't you have something better to do? Making some more babies?"

"I've got five, man. It's not like I'm about to run out of 'em."

True that. Their youngest, Trooper, was three. Ranger had just turned seven and the twin girls, Kennedy and Reagan, were eight. Marshal was the oldest, at ten. They'd been busy. Oh, and did he mention Tank had a crazy sense of humor? Well, it might be related to the fact his own parents named him Ford Knox. Tank had carried on the tradition. How the hell he'd gotten Emilia in on it, Cole could only speculate about.

"How the hell can she keep spewing them out anyway?" Cole asked with a grin. That woman was something else.

Tank scowled at him. "You done changing the subject?"

He slouched down in his chair. Fuck.

"So?"

The way Tank was looking at him told him if he didn't come clean, he was going to be in for a world of pain.

"Two things. They kinda go together," Cole started. The next words stuck in his throat. How the hell was he supposed to explain? "I was offered a transfer to Baltimore PD."

"That's great, man. That's what you wanted, right?"

"Yeah," he sighed.

"You don't sound convincing." Tank glared expectantly down at him. "The second thing?"

"Cade Lawson," Cole said, his voice breaking. "My would-be partner in Baltimore."

"What about him? He nasty?"

"You've got a way with words, man."

"I have five kids."

"The only thing wrong with that is what you named them," Cole teased.

Tank snorted and made Cole laugh. It felt right, even as it felt wrong. Cade was the one who should be making him laugh, not his best friend.

"What's with this Cade Lawson, then?" Tank asked.

"Well. We kinda…" He bit his lip and ran his hands through his hair as he leaned forward, doing his best not to look at Tank. Which was damned stupid since the man knew him better than he knew himself.

"What the hell, man? You slept with him?"

"Yeah," he said on a longing sigh. Hell, he hadn't been able to get Cade out of his head. At all. It was so fucking quiet and dull without him.

Tank leaned back in his chair with a calculating look on his face. Cole really hated when he did that. It meant he wasn't going to like the next words out of Tank's mouth.

"It's more than that, isn't it?"

"Yeah. But I don't…I can't…" he ended on a deep sigh. How the hell was he supposed to explain it, when he didn't fully understand it himself?

"Yes. You. Can. Come on, Gunner. If you like this guy so much, you should give it a try."

"A try at what? Come on, you know me."

"You mean the guy you used to be or the closed-off bastard you've been the last few years?"

He didn't even have it in him to curse out the man. He was right, anyway.

"Exactly. What the hell do I have to offer him? I've done my damned best at not feeling anything," Cole said.

"Well. I'd say he's been doing a damned fine job making you feel so far."

"What?"

"Cole. You haven't been this upset in years. He's definitely got those wheels churning," Tank said while gently knocking Cole on top of his head with a closed fist. "It's an easy decision and just a few weeks ago you would've just shut down, put a lid on those feelings, done what you needed to and moved on."

Cole found himself speechless.

"We've been trying to get through to you for a long, damned time, Cole. I'm just glad someone managed it. You know, I kinda like this guy already."

Tank had been right; it *was* an easy decision. Looking at Cade now, his eyes big with unanswered questions and hope, he knew he'd made the right decision.

"Just… tell me what you want."

Catching Cade's eyes, he straightened and swallowed the lump of fear clogging his throat. The man in front of him deserved him pulling up his big boy panties and for once not running from his feelings. He hadn't felt more exposed, more vulnerable, than he did in this moment, and he'd been to war more times than he wanted to count.

"You. I want you," Cole said in a hoarse voice.

Cade's pupils flared, black enveloping the blue. His lips parted and his tongue poked out to wet his lips, drawing Cole's attention to those kissable lips he just wanted to sink his teeth into. He did just that, slamming his mouth over Cade's, sucking his lower lip into his mouth and biting down. Cade whimpered into his mouth.

Cole swept his tongue into Cade's mouth, tasting and exploring everything he could reach. He slid his fingers through Cade's hair, settling his hand possessively at the back of Cade's neck. Cade put his hands on Cole's chest, the heat of his skin burning through Cole's shirt.

He turned Cade around and slammed him against the wall. He wrenched open the button on Cade's pants, ripping down the zipper and then the pants. Cade had his hands against the wall, holding himself up as Cole latched his mouth to his neck.

"Work... babe, we gotta... work. We have to... *ungh!*"

"No more talking about work, got it?" Cole said while caressing the red spot he'd just made on Cade's round, fleshy ass cheek. He watched as red tinted Cade's cheeks and neck. He loved that fucking blush. It was crazy how good it felt to be able to not only make this man blush but be able to render him speechless as well. Cade pushed back against him, making him concentrate on what was in his hands.

"Got it. Now, *please*, fuck me."

Cole brought his fingers to Cade's lips and he greedily sucked them into his mouth. He let Cade play with his fingers for a bit before pulling them out with a groan. He pressed a kiss to the back of Cade's shoulder. He trailed his fingers down Cade's crease, circling and putting light pressure on his hole. He pushed one finger in, twisting it to hit that spot. Cade hissed.

"Hurry. I can't..." Cade's words trailed off into a moan when Cole added another finger. Fuck. This round was gonna end fast if Cade kept making those sounds.

230

"Lube?"

"Drawer."

"Stay," Cole barked.

Cade rolled his eyes at him but didn't move an inch. He pulled out a drawer in the kitchen, a bottle of lube rolling toward him. Apparently, Cade still had lube stored everywhere. He found a condom, opening and rolling it down his length. He grabbed the lube and tried not to see how much was left in it. He couldn't blame Cade if he'd been with someone else, but it still hurt to think about. He looked up, catching Cade watching him over his shoulder.

"Only you, baby."

There was so much emotion in those expressive, dark, blue eyes.

"There's been no one but you. Besides my hand, that is. Well, both my hands. I like to live vicariously sometimes," Cade said with a shrug, a smile playing on his lips.

Fuck, he'd missed this crazy son of a bitch.

Cade had stepped out of his pants and Cole didn't waste any time with Cade's shirt. Buttons went flying when he ripped it open. He pulled his own shirt off and tugged down his pants. They only made it to around his feet before he couldn't wait any longer.

"It's gonna be hard and fast, baby," Cole whispered, his lips at the back of Cade's neck, trailing kisses and licking his way to Cade's ear where he bit down on the lobe, making Cade gasp out a, "Fuck!"

He turned Cade around, pressing his back against the wall and their fronts together. Cade's mouth sought his immediately. He pressed in close, noticing just how aroused Cade was.

"Missed you so fucking much," Cade said between kisses. "I even missed you putting my chocolate in the fridge."

"Don't think I've heard that one before," Cole said with a low laugh.

"I'm one of a kind," Cade replied cheekily.

It was true. And Cole was turning into a fucking sap. He grabbed a hold of the back of Cade's thighs and lifted him up, pressing him into the wall as Cade's legs wrapped around his waist. He didn't waste any time pushing into Cade.

"Okay?" He had his lips on anything of Cade within reach while his palms cupped that marvelous ass and his cock sheathed inside his tight, hot hole.

"Fuck yeah."

He kept still for a while, letting Cade adjust around him. Though they both liked it rough, he didn't want to hurt Cade. Never that. So, he waited until Cade was begging for him to move.

"Please, baby. I need you."

He crushed his mouth over Cade's and started thrusting into him. Cade's nails bit into the skin of his upper arms. Being inside Cade was like coming home. Like it was exactly where he was supposed to be. Cade gasped into his mouth before wrenching away from him and dropping his head back against the wall, panting heavily.

"Right there, baby. Right there," Cade gasped.

Cade slipped his fingers into Cole's hair, gripping it tightly as he moaned with every one of Cole's thrusts inside him. Cole's lips found the skin between Cade's neck and shoulder. When Cade became incoherent, Cole slowed his thrusts and claimed Cade's mouth in a deep kiss.

"Touch yourself, baby," he said against Cade's lips.

Cade whimpered and pulled one of his hands from Cole's hair and reached down between them, taking himself in hand. The sounds falling from Cade's lips, the expression on his face, almost pushed him right off the edge.

Cole slammed in faster, harder, chasing the pleasure he could feel at his core. Cade's eyes fell closed as he dropped his head back against the wall.

"Open your eyes. Look at me," Cole gasped. "I need to see you."

Dark blue eyes flashing with pleasure and something hidden in those depths he couldn't quite recognize, was all he saw as he felt Cade come all over them both. Cade crying out his name over and over was what tipped him over. He tightened his hold on Cade's ass. Pleasure shot through him like a blaze of fire, blinding him for a moment. His legs strained, shaking from the aftershocks, both from the exertion and the pleasure. He leaned his forehead against Cade's, both of them gasping for breath.

"How are you still standing?" Cade asked.

"I'm a Raider, baby. The only way to get us down is with a bullet," Cole said, his voice breathy.

"Which you gladly run toward. I get it. You're a Marine. You're a big, bad, lethal bastard."

Cole rubbed his nose against Cade's, a contented smile on his lips. He'd never smiled so easily before. Or so much.

"But I'm *your* big, bad, lethal bastard," Cole said.

The smile that stretched across Cade's lips was utterly breathtaking. He should've known from the first time Cade really smiled at him; there was no way he could stay away from Cade.

"And you better not forget it," Cade said.

Cade tilted his head back, silently asking for a kiss. Cole was only happy to oblige. He pressed their lips together,

"Now, let me down. We *do* have to get back to work," Cade said, tapping Cole on the shoulder.

He lowered Cade to his feet, moaning when he slipped out of Cade's slick heat. Cade grinned and winked at him before moving around him and walking toward the stairs.

"Shower?" Cole asked.

"That sounds suspiciously like *Round Two*," Cade said with a raised eyebrow as he looked over his shoulder at Cole who was following him. Cade didn't stop him, though.

Cole

He sent the guy a withering glare. The look on his face made Cole feel certain his gun and badge would be untouched when he got them back. Hell, he'd just gotten them. Three hours ago, to be exact, because Cade never said no to a round two. Cade who'd been chatting and singing the whole way to the detention center and Cole was only happy to have his eardrums violated as long as it meant he was with Cade.

A corrections officer led them through the gray halls and into a closed-off room with a table and a few chairs in the middle. On one of those chairs sat a woman wearing a gray jumpsuit, her hair pulled into a ponytail. Her gaze was firmly on the tabletop and she didn't seem to register them walking in. Only when the correctional officer slammed the door behind him on his way out did she look up. A bright smile spread across her face.

"Cade."

"Hey, Callie, how ya doing?" Cade said in greeting as he pulled out one of the steel chairs across from Callie and sat down.

"Just fine, thanks. Actually, it's somewhat freeing. You know, to actually be able to see the walls of your prison."

Even though her tone of voice held a twinge of sarcasm, Cole didn't doubt the sincerity of her joke.

"Well, hon, you look great. I mean, you could be walking 'round in an orange or striped jumpsuit," Cade said with a wink and joined in on Callie's laugh.

"I think I did quite well," she said, gesturing to the gray shirt hanging loosely around her shoulders.

Cade and Callie shared a look Cole couldn't interpret, and he was rather glad he couldn't. He didn't know what to think of their easy banter. Well, except for the fact it made him feel uneasy and he fucking hated feeling uneasy.

"Grey really makes those beautiful eyes of yours pop. You should try letting your hair down too."

"You going gay on me, Cade?"

Cade stuck out his tongue at her before his face split into a big smile.

"Baby, I was born this way," Cade said, grinning.

"So. I take it this isn't a social call what with Detective-silent-and-brooding over there looking like he wants to strangle both of us," Callie said.

Cade looked to be deflating a bit at that, as he sent Cole a questioning glance. Cole ignored him, keeping his eyes on the prisoner in front of him as he pushed the case file across the table. Callie met his eyes, holding his gaze for a moment before she glanced down at the file, opening it and pulling out the pictures and documents. She placed one of the photos right in front of her, trailing her fingers over it before she let out a defeated sigh.

"A dead girl. I told my boss this would happen at some point."

"What do you mean?" Cade asked.

"I mean, that I asked to get investigators on this case because someone was bound to end up dead. I wasn't equipped to handle this sort of case. I deal with rape victims. *After* the fact. But she wouldn't listen to me and now we've got a nineteen-year-old girl with her panties around her neck and an ME cutting her open on a cold slab." The tone of her voice made it clear just what she thought of that.

"Tell us about the first victim," Cole said.

She turned her gaze his way, watching him with scrutinizing eyes for a moment before she started talking. "You got my file on her?"

He nodded. "Sara Woods. Twenty-two. College student."

The file hadn't said a hell of a lot. Just the facts. Where. When. How.

"Have you talked to her?" Callie asked.

"We haven't located her yet," Cade said.

She bobbed her head, not seeming surprised.

"She'll be hiding. Maybe in a women's shelter," Callie said, leaning forward in her chair. "She didn't want to name her rapist. But she did say he was her boyfriend and that he was in a gang. The West B. Jackals. Which is the reason she didn't want to press charges. Even with the DNA, I still didn't have a match for it. He was next on my list, though. But then I met Julie. I saw it. In her eyes. The way she behaved toward other people. Toward men. I had no doubt she was still right in the middle of it all. She was still being abused. That's why I followed her. I didn't count on catching that son of a bitch red-handed. But I did, and Julie needed me, so I took care of it. I didn't have my gear so I knew I'd leave behind evidence. I knew it would be my last one. I don't regret it. I just wish I'd had enough time to find Sara's boyfriend as well."

Cade covered her hand with his. "Me, too, Callie. Me, too."

She nodded her head, though her eyes were unseeing as she stared off at the wall behind Cade and him. Cole pushed his chair back and stood. Callie's eyes jerked toward him.

"Promise me you'll protect her. Please? Keep my promise?"

Cole nodded, watching as Callie's eyes returned to Cade and her lips spread in a sadistic smile.

"Promise me you'll make sure that bastard gets what he deserves," she said.

"I promise," Cade said.

Cole was out the door before Cade could even stand. He was suffocating in there. If they needed to speak with her again, he wouldn't be able to do it and though he didn't want anyone else going with Cade, someone else would have to. He kept his mouth shut through the prison and halfway through the parking lot, but once they were out of earshot and mostly out of sight, he couldn't hold in his question any longer.

"You've been to see her, haven't you?"

"Yes," Cade answered as he walked past Cole and toward the car.

"That's it?"

Cade froze on the spot, his shoulders tense as he twirled around to glare at Cole.

"Yes, that's it," he ground out between clenched teeth.

He wasn't the only one affected by this little lovely visit after all.

"She's a serial killer," Cole said, unable to keep his voice devoid of emotion.

"Yes, I know that, Cole. I know. But she has no one. She's been through hell and she's got no one. You don't know what that does to someone. You don't know what she went through."

At that, Cole winced before he could catch himself. With Cade's wide-eyed stare he knew he'd caught it.

"You know?" Cade whispered and Cole couldn't help but look away at the hurt he detected in the other man's voice. How the hell did he get that from a wince?

Damn it! Damn it all to hell!

"Cole," Cade's hands cupped his jaw, forcing him to turn to Cade and look into those startled, deep blue eyes. He tensed, waiting for the questions to start. He couldn't explain. He didn't know how. He hadn't ever talked about it. Not to anyone. He didn't know the words.

"I'm sorry," Cade said in a soft voice before pressing his lips against Cole's briefly and then pulling him into an embrace that seemed somewhat more intended for Cade himself than for Cole.

Cole let him snuggle in close, keeping an arm around him while his other hand burrowed into Cade's soft hair.

Cole let out a breath he didn't know he'd been holding in and sagged against Cade. Cade sighed as he put his head on Cole's chest and tightened his grip for a few seconds before releasing him and pulling back to look up into his eyes.

"Evil people suck," Cade said with a pout, blinking those doe eyes innocently. Cole let out a laugh and felt—if only marginally, but still—lighter. A little less burden on his shoulders.

"You're so bad," he chuckled before pulling Cade back against his chest and placing a kiss on his forehead.

"Bad boys, bad boys, what'cha gonna do, what'cha gonna do when we come for you," Cade sang.

Cole laughed and smacked Cade's ass, making the other man jump and stick his tongue out at him.

"Get in the car, Bad Boy."

Cole caught himself glancing at Cade whenever he could. They were at a red light when Cade turned and smiled at him. They were actually doing this. Whatever this was. It didn't matter as long as it involved him having Cade.

Cade

Lara swiveled around in her chair so she could look at Cade. He glanced up, catching her troubled gaze.

"The gang Sara's boyfriend is involved with…"

Cade cocked an eyebrow at her. "What about them?"

"They're prospecting in the Destroyers."

Cade leaned back in his chair with a groan. "You've gotta be fucking kidding me."

He stood, stretching his arms over his head before heading toward the captain's office. Claire stared at him with big eyes, shaking her head but this couldn't wait.

"Captain," Cade said after knocking on the open door.

Morris, who was on the phone, looked up and waved him inside while looking like he wanted to kill whoever was on the other end of the line. Poor guy.

"You bastard," Morris growled.

Cade watched with raised eyebrows as Morris proceeded to tear apart the guy on the phone, ending the call with a threat of shoving his gun up the guy's ass. Cade stayed quiet and unmoving, afraid to draw Morris' attention onto himself. Morris rubbed his face, groaning loudly and dropped his hands to his desk. His eyes settled on Cade.

"Well, spit it out, Lawson," Morris barked.

Whatever that guy did to anger Morris, he'd most likely deserved the lecture he'd just gotten. Morris wasn't one to get pissed easily. If he were, Cade would've been without a job years ago.

"Sir. Our case is connected to the Destroyers," Cade said.

Morris groaned. "Again?"

"Technically, it wasn't actually last time. But the rape victim's boyfriend is in a gang, the West B. Jackals, and they're prospecting with the Destroyers. I think there's a connection between that and our current murder investigation."

"Shit. What do you wanna do? Go back under? Is that even an option anymore?" Morris asked.

"I can make it happen," Cade said.

"Are you sure?" Morris asked, his eyebrows hitting his hairline.

"Yes. This isn't something we can do from the outside. This isn't just about a rape and murder victim. There's no way he wasn't ordered to kill her. He might be a thug but he's not stupid enough to do something like that while prospecting. He just raped her as well."

"Alright. I'll put it in motion, then."

To anyone else, the captain might've seemed too quick to send him undercover, but this wasn't some deep undercover mission to bring down the mob. This was different. This was Cade. This was what he did. What he was good at. He dipped his chin, turned on his heels and walked out of Morris' office. He ran into Cole who came from the kitchen, three mugs in hand. Cade cocked his head to the side, watching Cole with a grin.

"My, haven't you become domesticated," Cade said.

Cole's eyebrows went up as he stopped in front of Cade.

"I'd rather make the coffee myself instead of risking you burning down the Nespresso machine. Again," Cole said.

"One time. It happened one time," Cade said, trudging after Cole. "It wasn't even my fault."

Cole sent him an unbelieving glance but didn't say anything. When they entered their office, Cole gave Lara her mug first, then turned around to give Cade his. Cade crossed his arms over his chest and scowled at Cole.

"Seriously? Forget what I said about you being domesticated," Cade said. "I'm your partner. You're supposed to give me my coffee first, not last."

"Well. If you don't want it…" Cole took a step to the side and held one of the mugs over the trashcan. Even though Cade knew Cole wouldn't throw it in and risk breaking the mug, he still jumped forward and pulled the mug out of Cole's hand.

He took a blissful sip before moving behind his desk and dropping into his chair where he cradled the mug against his chest and gave Cole the stink eye.

"Should I be worried?" Cole asked Lara.

The look she sent him clearly stated that he should've figured that out sooner. "He's on his third cup already," she said.

"Third? What do you do? Go to the bathroom and drink it so I won't see?" Cole asked.

Cade shrugged, a slight blush warming his face. Technically, he just went to the kitchen and drank it there whenever he needed a break. He raised the mug to his lips and, watching Cole over the rim, he took a long swallow.

"Did you tell the captain?" Lara asked.

Cade glanced over at her, his eyebrows furrowing before he remembered. "Oh. Yes, I told him."

"Told him what?" Cole asked.

"That our murder case is connected with the Destroyers," Cade said and held his breath. The fiery expression crossing Cole's face was frightening to say the least. It also made Cade's heart skip a beat.

"Come on, then," Cole said, pulling his jacket off the back of his chair.

"But… coffee," Cade whined.

"I think you've reached your quota for the day," Cole said.

Cade groaned and pushed to his feet. He glared at a grinning Lara, put down his mug and walked out of their office with a pout on his lips.

"Where are we going?"

"To see Liam Torell," Cole said over his shoulder.

"To ask about the club?"

They stepped into the elevator, Cole turning around to face him.

"He's the closest we'll get to an inside man right now," Cole said.

Cole was right, of course. Liam may have seen or heard things while he worked, though the Destroyers were a tightknit bunch of assholes. It was worth a try anyhow.

He followed Cole out of the elevator and into his car where he claimed the right to the radio. Cole shook his head but didn't object. The car ride consisted of Cade singing and Cole laughing at him if he wasn't singing along. Cade was mighty proud he'd managed to bring out that side of Cole.

When Cole parked in front of Liam's house he leaned across the console, placing a hand on the back of Cade's neck and pulling him into a quick kiss. Cade didn't care if he looked like a fool with the gigantic smile on his face. They got out of the car and Cade had to bite his cheek as they walked up to Liam's front door.

"Looks like he's got company," Cole said, gesturing toward the other car in the driveway, a smile playing on his lips.

Oh, he had company all right.

Cade was trying to hide his grin when the door opened and Liam stood there, blinking at them.

"Hello, Liam. May we come in?" Cade asked.

"Yeah. Sure."

At least he was wearing a shirt this time. Not that he would mind. The guy was hot and he had eyes. Though he'd wager his boyfriend was hotter. He bit his lip to keep from smiling. Boyfriend. He liked the sound of that.

Liam led them into the living room. Cade sat down next to Cole on the smallest of the couches. Cole squinted at him, which made him bite his lip not to smile as their sides were pressed against each other for them to fit on the couch.

"Detectives. Can I get you anything?" Liam asked.

"Coffee would be great," Cade said, smiling up at Liam.

"Just get him some water, please," Cole said.

"Oh, come on, I need sustenance."

Liam sat down on the other couch, obviously trying not to take sides.

"Try meat," Cole said, then realized his mistake. "Don't you dare say it."

"Say what?"

Cade batted his eyes innocently up at Cole, who grumbled something under his breath and tried to ignore him. Catching Liam's eyes, Cade winked. A smile split the guy's face.

"Stop eavesdropping and get in here, Tommy," Cole yelled.

A brown-haired head popped out from the doorway. It was pretty obvious by the size of the shirt he was wearing that it was Liam's.

"Um. Hi." Tommy did a little awkward wave of his hand, then proceeded to glare at the offending limb before planting his ass on the couch, a blush covering his face. Liam snaked an arm around Tommy's waist and pulled him flush against himself. Tommy's shoulders relaxed and he leaned against Liam.

"What can I help you with?" Liam asked.

"What goes on in the club?" Cole asked.

"You mean besides the drugs and sex?"

Tommy elbowed him in the side. "Be nice."

Liam glanced down at Tommy, the look in his eyes saying much more than he probably thought. He turned his attention back on them with a troubled expression.

"Something's been brewing, that's for sure," Liam said.

"Go on," Cole said.

"They've been jumpy lately. They've even locked down a fair part of the building," Liam said, rubbing his nose and sighing. "I think we all know that they didn't buy Glitter for the profit."

"Location," Cade said, nodding his head.

"That, and the basement," Liam said.

That was weird.

"What's in the basement?" Cole asked.

"A tunnel."

"You have got to be kidding me. A tunnel? Really?" Cade asked.

Liam shrugged. "It's very old, from way back when. Civil War or something."

He met Cole's gaze.

While Liam relayed what he knew about the basement, Cade ushered Tommy into the kitchen under the pretense of wanting coffee. This time, Cole let him, a knowing gleam in his eyes. Cade leaned back against the counter while Tommy flitted around, opening cupboards and turning on the coffee maker.

"Is he treating you right, kid?"

A blush crept up Tommy's neck. "Yeah. I mean, it's tough, but I trust him."

The tiny smile and the way he bit his lip as if he was thinking about something he shouldn't, it was all the conformation Cade needed.

"Good. Otherwise, you've got my number."

Tommy nodded, a smile of thanks on his lips. There hadn't been a lot of people in Tommy's corner his entire life. Cade knew that and he wanted to be one of the exceptions.

"So, um. I heard you caught the person who killed Chris," Tommy said tentatively.

"Yeah."

"Why did she do it?" Tommy asked, wringing his hands nervously.

"She's the only one who can really answer that question, kid."

"But I heard she's a serial killer, is that true?"

"Yeah. She killed pedophiles and sexual predators."

"Oh."

Cade placed a hand on Tommy's shoulder, making the kid look up at him.

"You should try and go see her."

He had a feeling it might bring the kid some closure.

"I'll think about it," Tommy said.

Chapter Fourteen

Cole

COLE WOKE up to Cade burrowing closer, his soft breaths tickling the hair on Cole's chest as he nuzzled his face into Cole and tightened his arms and leg around him. Cole ran his fingers slowly through Cade's blonde strands and rolled some around his fingers. The strands were a mixture of different shades of blonde, some even close to brown, and they were all just a bit curly. Enough to make Cade look adorable when his hair got too long, as it was at the moment.

Cade let out a contented sigh. Even in his sleep, he wore a smile on his face. Cole ran the tips of his fingers down Cade's jaw. How could he ever have been so lucky?

"You guys look so adorable," Morgan said from the doorway.

Yeah, Cade certainly was… *Wait. Morgan?*

Cole jerked his head up to see her standing with one shoulder leaned against the doorframe and a sappy look on her face. He cocked an eyebrow at her before joining her in looking affectionately down at Cade. How had he not heard her? And how the hell did she get in?

"I have a key," she answered one of his unspoken questions, followed by a one-shouldered shrug. He smiled at her, letting her know he was fine with it. He glanced down just as Cade blinked his eyes open, looked up at him and then closed his eyes again with a contented hum.

"Morgan is here," Cole said.

Cade mumbled something that could've been a, "Hi, Morgan," though he wasn't sure. He scooted out from under Cade, who immediately spread out on his stomach, looking like he enjoyed having the bed to himself immensely.

"She just deprived you of morning sex," Cole said casually as he got out of bed. Luckily, he had his boxers on for once. Cade was seriously rubbing off on him.

"Huh?" Cade jerked upright. "Bloody hell."

Getting tangled in the sheets as he shot out of bed, Cade fell in a heap of pillows and duvets on the floor with a loud, "Uhmp."

"Don't hurt yourself," Cole said while trying to suppress a laugh. Morgan didn't suppress anything, though. She was bent over laughing. He could still hear her when he turned on the water. He smiled to himself as he got under the spray. He'd known choosing to be with Cade meant choosing his family, too, and he couldn't have been happier about it if he tried.

When he'd showered and dressed, he walked downstairs to find Morgan on the couch and Cade in the kitchen, finishing his first coffee of the morning. Cade leaned on the kitchen counter to stay upright, obviously not completely awake yet. He could help with that.

Cade looked up over his shoulder and put his coffee mug down on the counter as Cole stepped up behind him. He ran his hands down Cade's side to his ass cheeks, which he grabbed and squeezed.

"The things I want to do to you," he whispered into Cade's ear, causing a shiver to rock through Cade's body. He pressed a kiss to Cade's jaw. Cade turned his head to get a real kiss, but Cole stepped back, letting go of him.

"Morgan," Cole said, shaking his head.

Cade glared at him, murder in his eyes, then he turned on his heels, storming off. Cole followed Cade into the living room with a grin etched on his face. Cade placed himself right in front of Morgan, hands on his hips.

"You bloody devil. Do you know what you just cost me?" Cade screeched at an unresponsive, non-caring Morgan, who just continued twirling a spoon around in her cocoa, thoroughly ignoring Cade's crazy morning rant. For all he knew, she was used to it.

"I don't think I've ever seen him get out of bed that fast before," Cole told Morgan. She glanced up at him over Cade's shoulder, a smile tugging at her lips.

"You're welcome," she deadpanned.

Cade's mouth dropped open and he stared at Morgan with an incredulous expression on his face.

"You cost me sex, young lady. Sex. With Cole. Shame on you." Cade wagged a finger at her before dropping down on the couch as far away from her as he could get, a sullen look on his face and his lip jutted out in a pout.

"You take after your mother. Devil," Cade grumbled.

"Oh, for god's sake, you big baby. Here," Morgan said and dug something out of the pocket in her hoodie. She threw it to Cade who deftly caught it like he'd been expecting it, while still not looking at Morgan. He stuffed the thing into his mouth.

"You're still not forgiven," Cade mumbled around what turned out to be a Ferrero Rocher.

How could he eat that in the morning?

"I think I'll be just fine," Morgan said.

She grinned at Cade before turning her gaze on Cole. Her eyes twinkled before she winked at him.

Cade

He was doing his best not to break any of the bowls he was washing up. Morgan coming by was alright. She knew she was always welcome. It wasn't that. It was the prospect of missing out on anything *Cole* that made him not just cranky but unsure and miserable.

He gave a start when arms wrapped around his waist from behind and a warm body pressed against his back. Guess he'd been that far inside his own head and thoughts he hadn't heard Cole come in, or it could just be Cole's ability to walk around without a sound. If he hadn't grown up with people with the same ability he would've been freaked out.

"I'm sorry, baby. I was just teasing. Don't be mad at Morgan," Cole said, resting his head on Cade's shoulder. Guess he'd picked up on the *being mad* part.

"I'm not mad at Morgan."

"Talk to me, babe."

Cade wiped off his hands in the dishcloth and turned around in Cole's arms. He craned his head back to meet Cole's gaze.

"I just got you back," he said and immediately felt like an ass when he caught the hurt flashing through Cole's eyes.

"I'm not going anywhere," Cole said.

"I know," Cade whispered.

Cole wouldn't have come back only to leave again. That just wasn't how he worked. Cole was a man of his word.

Cole let out a deep sigh. "I'm sorry I left you, especially like that," he said while keeping his eyes cast down.

Instead of telling Cole it was all okay, he opted for a more Cade-like retort.

"I'm sure you can find some way to make it up to me, otherwise there's always karaoke night at Beverly's."

Cole's eyes met his and he was caught in green flames of hope.

"Anything you want," Cole said before claiming Cade's lips in a hot, sweet kiss that made his toes curl. Cade felt it but ignored it to his best ability when something inside of him started to unravel.

Cade was moaning and rubbing against Cole by the time Cole broke off the kiss, only moving a fraction of an inch away to be able to look down into Cade's eyes.

"Better get going," Cole said against Cade's lips.

"Now?"

"Go get ready. I'll take care of that," Cole said with a kiss before moving away and grabbing the dishtowel. Cole was grinning stupidly at Cade when he swore under his breath before walking toward the stairs.

Cole

Once he was done washing the dishes, he dried his hands and made his way into the living room. He sat down in the armchair opposite Morgan who was still on the couch.

"Everything alright?" he asked, watching her intently.

She looked up from her phone. "Sure. Whatever."

"Wanna give that a second try? Maybe make it sound more convincing."

She made a face at him, then put her phone into the front pocket of her hoodie. She shrugged. "I just didn't want to be at home."

Cole arched a brow at her and leaned back in his chair, waiting for her to explain. She turned her blue eyes on him, pain so evident in them.

"My father showed up," she said, her voice so low he almost didn't catch it.

"You wanna talk about it?"

She looked conflicted for a moment, but one look at Cole's firm expression and she let out a deep sigh.

"I don't get how she can just…" She threw her hands up in frustration. "She keeps telling me not to be disrespectful to him. I don't get how she can do that. He cheated on her and he's been a complete asshole to her."

"She's strong-willed and smart."

"I know. She's the best mom ever. I'm just so mad *for* her. I wanna kick his ass for what he did and still does to her. I don't care about me."

"She doesn't care about herself, either. She's just thinking about you," Cole said.

Morgan shook her head, a sigh pushing through her lips. "She should start thinking about herself, too. Maybe we ought to get her a boyfriend." Her lips quirked into a wry smile. "Or a girlfriend."

"I'm not really sure she would be up for that."

Morgan cocked an eyebrow at him. "The woman-on-woman part or a relationship?"

"Both. I think. You probably shouldn't be asking me about relationships," Cole said, holding back a wince. Yeah. He definitely wasn't the person to ask.

"I think you're doing just fine," Morgan said and winked at him. "Uncle Cole."

Cole had to blink back tears. Sap. He was such a sap. Granted, this girl was something else, and if she wanted to call him Uncle Cole, he'd be proud to bear the title.

"Thanks, sweetheart."

He got up when he heard Cade bounding down the stairs. He leaned down to press a kiss to Morgan's forehead. He ruffled her hair, laughing when she squeaked and batted his hands away.

"Be good," he said.

"Yeah. You, too. Break his heart again and I'll break one of your balls," she said, mock scowling at him.

He snorted and raised a brow at her. "Why stop at one?"

"My mom will want to have a go at the other. I'm the sharing type." She shrugged, trying to look innocent but she wasn't fooling him.

"Of course, you are."

Just then, Cade walked into the room, folding his shirt collar down over his tie and then straightening the sleeves of his suit jacket. His shirt was the same blue as his eyes, making them pop. Damn, but Cade looked good in a suit.

"You ready?" Cade asked.

Cole glanced up, the amused smile on Cade's face telling him he just got caught ogling.

"Yeah. Let's go," Cole said, clearing his throat.

Cade wagged his eyebrows at him. He chuckled under his breath as he followed Cade to the front door where he grabbed his jacket and put on his shoes.

"Don't do anything I would do," Cade yelled to Morgan.

She propped herself against the doorframe in the hallway, glaring at Cade with an unimpressed look on her face. "You know that only leaves me with staying here, doing nothing, right?"

"Yup."

"I hate you," Morgan said, the smile on her face betraying her.

"I hate you, too. Cock-block," Cade said over his shoulder as he walked out the door.

Cole rolled his eyes and turned around. Morgan grinned at him. Cole pointed a finger at her, his face set in a stern expression.

"Don't turn into your uncle. One Cade is enough," Cole said, a smile breaking through on his face.

Morgan threw her head back and laughed. He shook his head but couldn't hold back a laugh of his own. Morgan's eyes were gleaming with joy when they met his. She blew him a kiss which he pretended to catch and stuff into his pocket while winking at her. If this was how his life was going to be from now on, he would consider himself the luckiest guy on the planet.

Cole

After another terrifying run-in with Mrs. Jones, who'd threatened them with bodily harm—or as Cade would say; sexual harassment—if they didn't come to dinner soon, they were finally stepping out of the elevator and into the homicide department.

"I swear, that old hag is trying to ruin my sex life," Cade said.

Mike stepped up right behind Cade as he said it, Mike's face splitting into a grin. "What sex life?"

Cole had to hold back a laugh at the offended look on Cade's face. Cade didn't answer Mike. He just glared at him over his shoulder, a sour look covering his face as he walked to their office. When Mike looked at Cole, they were both still grinning, although they did their best to hide it.

"Welcome back." Mike slapped him on the back.

"Thanks, man."

Mike glanced toward Cade for a moment, something passing over his features briefly before he turned back to Cole. The expression on Mike's face was serious when he asked, "You're staying this time, right?"

Cole's lips quirked into a smile. "Definitely."

"Good," Mike said with a nod.

He followed Mike into their office. Now, it was officially his office, too. He liked that a lot. When he dropped into his chair, his eyes were on Cade, who was pretending to be pissed at Mike. It didn't last long, as Mike did his best to make Cade laugh. When Cade's laughter rang out, a shiver ran through Cole's body and he had to swallow against the lump appearing in his throat. He should've known from the beginning. There was no way their relationship could've ever remained at just sex. If he hadn't been so far up his own ass, he would've noticed how he strived to make Cade laugh. He should've realized that making Cade happy, made him happy. He should've known.

A movement to his right made him turn and he was caught in Lara's knowing gaze. Cade and Mike never noticed when Lara moved from her desk to stand in front of Cole.

"Thank you," Lara said.

"What for?" Cole asked, confusion lacing his words.

"For making him happy," Lara said, a wry smile appearing on her lips. "For coming home."

He was struck speechless and Lara was back at her desk before he could manage to form an answer. He shook his head and turned his gaze back on Cade who glanced toward him just then. He met Cade's eyes and instantly, his lips spread into a smile. Cade beamed at him before turning his attention back to Mike. Cole turned on his computer and pretended not to glance up at Cade every other minute.

They'd been buried in paperwork for hours when the captain's booming voice echoed through the whole department, making Cade jump and drop his, luckily, empty coffee cup. "Lawson. Banks. My office."

He was starting to think Morris practiced saying those four words in the mirror every morning. When they entered Morris' office, he was standing behind his desk, leaning down on his hands. The expression on his face was unsettling, to say the least.

"Lawson is going undercover," Morris said.

"What? Why?" Cole sputtered.

He looked from one to the other, apprehension filling him. He settled his gaze on Cade when he looked like he was about to say something.

"Because it's obvious the Destroyers had Amelia Coulson killed, and they may be a biker gang, but they don't go around killing civilians unless they have a bloody good reason," Cade said.

"Lawson is going to find out what that reason is," Morris said.

"I take it we can't do that from here?"

Cade shook his head. "I'm lucky my cover is still intact, otherwise I wouldn't be able to get in. Their clubhouse is a fucking fortress. There's absolutely no way in unless they open the door, and they're too tight-knit to ever let any information slip."

"I want you to go under tonight." Morris gestured toward Cole. "Banks can finish up here. You just go home and do whatever it is you do to get ready."

"Yes, sir," Cade said before turning to Cole. "I'll see you at home."

Cole nodded, unsure of what to say. Cade bounced out the door, closing it after himself. Cole was staring at the door when Morris spoke.

"You still staying with him?"

"Until I can find something of my own," he said.

And he was. He didn't want to be intrusive, though he doubted Cade even knew what the word meant. He thought it was best to have a place of his own, at least for now.

"From tomorrow, stay somewhere else until he's back," Morris said, a concerned frown wrinkling his forehead.

"Yes, sir."

Cade

Cade trudged up his driveway, getting his keys out to open his door and it was only as a result of lifelong training that he didn't hesitate, not even for a second. He let the door fall shut behind him with a thud and walked with relaxed steps into his kitchen, his senses on high alert. He put his keys and phone on the kitchen counter and opened the fridge to take out the plate of chocolate Cole had, without a doubt, put in there. Cole had a habit of putting things in the fridge that shouldn't be in there. He shook his head with a smile on his face. He couldn't help but adore Cole's quirks.

Cade turned around and leaned back against the counter as he popped a piece of chocolate into his mouth. "You know, other people just knock on the damn door."

"That would entail drawing attention," a deep, gravelly voice sounded just as the dark-haired, black-clothed man Cade knew only as Neil, turned the corner and stepped into the kitchen. He watched Cade with a speculative look in his intelligent grey eyes.

"You're doing well," Neil said, not asked. Never asked.

"Obviously. Why are you here?"

"You're going undercover." Another statement. Cade had always thought the guy was made of them.

"Yep," Cade said.

"I'll get you what you need."

That had him raising an eyebrow as he looked at the man suspiciously. "What's in it for you?"

"Confidential."

"Yeah? Well, fuck confidential. I wanna know what I'm going into. I still work for you, jackass."

Despite being a cop the past nine years, he'd still been working for Neil. He was always working for Neil. That was the choice he'd made.

"This has something to do with Slay, doesn't it? That's why you're in on letting me go undercover," Cade said.

He put it out there to get a reaction. Just... something. Neil always had an angle and he wanted to know what it was. Unfortunately, Neil was good at hiding things. Even from himself, if Cade wasn't wrong. Which was highly doubtful.

"It's need-to-know Cade, and yes, Slay and the Destroyers are involved."

That was enough for him. For now. "Alright. What do you need?"

"You have a way in," Neil said with a raised eyebrow.

"No. I'm not fucking Slay. No fucking way."

"Because of your partner."

Cade let out a loud breath and slumped back against the counter. He squeezed his eyes shut and rubbed the bridge of his nose. He should've known. Hell, he did know. He just hadn't wanted to believe it.

"Thought I wasn't keeping tabs on you?"

Cade shook his head, a sigh escaping his lips. "I hate you sometimes."

"I don't need your love, Cade. I need your skill set. Banks, though, seems to need your love."

"It's not like I don't want to give it to him," Cade said, rolling his eyes.

When Neil didn't say anything, Cade turned his eyes on him. The man was watching him with his head cocked to the side, his gaze penetrating like he could see right through Cade. If he wasn't as good at his job as he was, he would've started sweating and fidgeting. But he was.

"Don't hold back because of a technicality," Neil said.

"Did you seriously just call the first twenty years of my life a technicality?" Cade asked.

"You can't change what happened back then, but you sure as hell can shape what will be."

Cade stared at him for a long moment, freaked out more than anything. Neil must've had an epiphany or something. "Ring-ring, it's the church calling, and they want their fucking preacher back. What the hell, mate?"

"As I said. I'll get you what you need. You do your thing and try to stay alive, savvy?" Neil asked.

"Fine. But I'm still not using Slay as my way in."

He was adamant on that account. There was no way he was jeopardizing what he had with Cole, and besides, just the thought of Slay was enough to make him physically ill. The only reason he'd been able to go through with it back then was because Slay was a bottom. There was no way in hell he'd ever have allowed Slay into his body.

"You have another way in if I remember correctly," Neil said, his voice darkening.

He gave a sharp nod of his head. He did, and it was the way he'd already planned on using even if Neil had wanted him to use Slay. Good thing Neil suggested it himself.

"For the record. You're a dick."

"Someone has to be."

Cade snorted. "You're a stupid dick, too."

He turned around, leaning his forearms on the counter as thoughts rambled through his mind. A lot of things were just set in motion and he wasn't sure how to handle all of it.

"You know," Cade said and turned around. "I think you're... Gone. Wow. Not even a goodbye?"

He snorted at himself. Of course, Neil would run off before Cade got time to pick at his brain. Too bad. He broke off another piece of chocolate and made his way into the living room. He pulled out his phone to make a call to Morgan.

"Hey, kiddo. You get home alright?"

"Yeah. Thanks for not ratting me out to mom," she said.

"Anytime," he said.

She was supposed to be in school, but whenever her father showed up, she tended to drop by and stay until she'd cooled down enough to either go to school or go home. It looked like he might have to kick that bastard's ass. Again.

"Let me know if you need anything, alright?"

He could hear the smile in her voice as she said, "I will."

"I love you, kiddo."

"I love you too, Uncle Cade."

When she hung up, Cade wore a smile. It lasted a few seconds before he remembered what he needed to do. He walked over to the couch and pulled off the cushions. He grabbed the bag wedged inside the couch and put the cushions back in place. He walked outside with the bag and put it in the trunk of his car. He was on his way back inside when the Camaro drove up the driveway. He turned and started down the steps of the front porch. Cole was out of the car and pulling him into his arms seconds later. Their mouths met in a slow, burning kiss. He slid his fingers into Cole's hair, grasping it tightly. When he pulled back, Cole ran his fingers down Cade's jaw.

"What did Morris say?" Cade asked.

"Just that I shouldn't be staying here while you're under," Cole said.

Cade nodded. "Yeah, that's probably best."

"How long do you plan on being under?" Cole asked, emotions darkening his eyes.

"Not long."

Cole followed him inside, keeping quiet even through dinner. It was obvious Cole had something to say but was holding it back. Once the dishes were done, Cade sat down next to Cole on the couch.

"What do you think about all this?" Cade asked.

Cole glanced up from the file in his hands. Of course, he'd brought work home. It was probably the coroner's report on Amelia's autopsy. Cole put it down, clearing his throat and rubbing his eyes before glancing at Cade.

"I don't like it," Cole said.

"That's all?"

"What? You want me to throw a fucking fit about it? You want me to rant about how I don't fucking want you anywhere near that sociopath?" Cole asked, a growl in his voice.

"Better?" Cade asked with a smug grin.

Cole glared at him before turning away and reaching for the file on the coffee table. Cade rolled his eyes and pushed up to his knees on the couch. He swung a leg over Cole, straddling his lap and linking his fingers together at the back of Cole's neck.

"Baby?" Cade asked.

Cole huffed, then he grasped Cade's shirt in his fist and pulled him in close. The green in his eyes was almost completely swallowed by the black of his pupils.

"I don't want you to do it. I'd gladly do it myself. But I understand. I know why you have to do it."

Cade swallowed hard, certain he hadn't misinterpreted the emotions clouding Cole's voice. His breath hitched.

"I'll be careful," he whispered.

"I know, and if you do something stupid, I'm gonna fucking kill you."

A grin spread on Cade's face and he cocked his head to the side. "Did you just mention fucking? Because I'm game."

Cole shook his head, his fingers grasping Cade's chin to bring his face closer. "Shut up, Cade."

"Why—"

He was cut short by Cole's lips on his own, that devilish mouth and tongue driving him insane. Cade let out a moan when Cole arched up and their jean-clad cocks met, creating delicious friction. Cole's hands found their way under Cade's shirt sending ripples of anticipation up his spine. He shivered beneath Cole's hands, a throaty moan spilling from his lips. A deep rumble rose from within Cole's chest. The heat emanating from Cole was scorching against his skin. Burning just right.

He was so hard it hurt.

He whimpered when Cole broke the kiss to pull Cade's shirt off. The second it was off, Cade smashed their mouths back together, biting at Cole's lip. He thrust against Cole, wanting the clothes between them gone. He needed to feel Cole, skin on skin.

"Please," Cade gasped.

Cole stood up, taking Cade with him. He wrapped his legs around Cole's waist, holding on as Cole made his way up the stairs. Cade latched his lips to the side of Cole's neck, licking and nipping at Cole's heated skin. Cole's fingers tightened on Cade's ass, making him moan and press closer to Cole's body.

Cole put him down to sit on the edge of the bed, stepping back to run his gaze over Cade, his eyes dark as night. Cade bit his lip as he watched Cole shred his clothes slowly, enjoying the show. All that mouthwatering skin on display. Once all Cole's clothes were on the floor, he ran his searing gaze down Cade's body, stopping at the tent in Cade's pants. Cole crouched down in front of him and glanced up, meeting Cade's eyes as he flicked open the button on his jeans. Cade gulped, fisting the sheets in his hands as he watched the lust, the desire, burn in those dark eyes. The way Cole looked at him, like he was the most important thing in Cole's life, like he was everything Cole had ever wanted, brought him right to the brink.

The sound of his zipper made him squeeze his eyes closed and bite his lip. He lifted his hips to let Cole drag his jeans and boxers down his legs. A shiver ran through his whole body when Cole ran his hands up Cade's legs ever so slowly. One hand settled on Cade's hip, the other wrapped around his dick making him jump and curse.

Wet heat surrounded his dick and he nearly bucked off the bed but Cole's hand on his hip kept him in place. His eyes shot open and when they landed on Cole, he damned near combusted. Cole's lips were stretched over his dick, his head bobbing as he swallowed Cade, over and over.

"Fuck," Cade gasped, grabbing at Cole's hair. "Cole. Baby. I can't…"

Cole's eyes met his and he sucked harder, one of his hands finding Cade's balls and tugging on them. Cade's breathing grew ragged, the sight before him pushing him right off the edge. His fingers tightened in Cole's hair and he shouted as he emptied into Cole's mouth. Cole swallowed greedily, drawing out Cade's orgasm until he whimpered when it became too much. Cole let him slip from his mouth and as Cade gasped for breath, Cole pushed him back on the bed and crawled up his body until he could bury his nose in the juncture between Cade's neck and shoulder.

There were things Cade wanted to say. Things Cole made him feel. But he couldn't. Instead, he pushed at Cole's shoulder, making him turn onto his back so Cade could crawl on top of him. Cole grinned, putting his arms behind his head as he watched Cade with such intensity, so much trust showing in his darkening eyes. He wanted to cherish this man who'd let him in when he'd kept everyone else at bay. This man who'd taken a chance on Cade. On them.

There was nothing hurried about it. He took his time to rediscover Cole's body. He mapped out every dimple, every dip and scar as he kissed and licked his way from Cole's neck to the inside of his thighs. This time, he wanted it slow. He wanted to feel everything, every second of it. The sounds coming from Cole spurred him on.

They were both getting desperate by the time he'd gotten himself ready for Cole. He did it as fast as he could and along with an array of 'fuck's' coming from Cole. Cade withdrew his fingers and grabbed the lube and a condom. He tore open the foil packet and rolled it down Cole's length. He squirted a generous amount of lube into his hand and wrapped it around Cole's cock.

When he sank down on Cole, taking him inside his body, their eyes met and held, their emotions unspoken but ever so present between them. Cade bent down, pressing their lips together. He kept their mouths sealed when he started to rise up and sink down on Cole's cock.

"Fuck," Cole gasped against his lips.

Cole's fingers brushed down Cade's chin, the touch so soft and tender. It was so unexpected from a man like Cole and Cade knew to cherish the moments when Cole bared himself to him. It was fucking beautiful to watch, to experience.

He chuckled when Cole lifted him off of him and pushed him to his back, getting between Cade's legs. Cole's mouth stopped any other sound from leaving Cade. Cole pushed Cade's leg up, hooking his arm underneath it. Cade whimpered against Cole's lips when he pushed in and started thrusting. He scraped his nails across Cole's shoulders, holding on tight as Cole rammed into him with enough force to make the bed slam against the wall. The heat. The burn. It was all suddenly too much, and he couldn't stop himself from tumbling over the edge. He looked into Cole's dark eyes as he came, pleasure shooting through him. Cole followed right after, his body shaking with the force of his orgasm. What Cade saw in those green eyes, the desperation mixed with desire and adoration, made it hard to breathe.

He pressed a tentative kiss to Cole's lips. This time, Cole was the one to wrap around him. To hold him close. For once, he knew he was right where he was supposed to be. Everything was as it should be and walking out of his house that night, walking away from Cole—even knowing he was going to come back—was one of the hardest things he'd ever done.

Chapter Fifteen

Cade

HE PAUSED to look up at the white letters adorning the façade. *Serrano.* He hadn't been inside this restaurant for over two years. He remembered the last time vividly. There'd been a lot of yelling and cursing, and a few flying chairs, as well. It made sense with the news Cade was bringing the owner back then. What most of the restaurant diners probably didn't know, was that the owner, Marco Serrano, was an Italian mobster.

Cade went in when the hostess was too busy to notice him. He knew where the man he was looking for would be. He also knew he would be surrounded by a lot of guys with guns. It made him easy to spot. Cade slipped through the room, nearing his target with steady and calculated steps.

Before the men could stop him, he walked right past them and planted himself on a chair in front of the man they were guarding. The man didn't bat an eye at Cade. He just put down his cutlery, brushed off his pristine blazer and waited.

"Hello, Marco," Cade said.

"Cade. What can I do for you, detective?"

Cade motioned at Marco's men, indicating that he'd only talk without them. They were starting to look uncomfortable, shifting around nervously. One of them even placed his hand on his gun. Marco raised a suspicious eyebrow at Cade, but he turned to the men with a stern expression coloring his face.

"Guys. Go take a break."

"But, boss—"

"That was an order." The tone of Marco's voice was cold. Deadly. They knew to obey him.

They all trudged off, even though none of them looked particularly happy about it. The last one to leave looked like he was trying to burn a path through Cade with his dark eyes. Cade smiled up at the man and waved at him. He watched as the guy worked his jaw and clenched the hand he didn't have on his gun into a fist. He glared at Cade but did as he was told, leaving Marco and Cade alone.

Marco leaned back in his chair, a relaxed expression on his handsome face. His Italian roots were easy to spot with his golden skin and dark coloring. He had that commanding air around him, same as Cole. But it wasn't near as hot as when it came from Cole.

"Now. What can I do for you?"

Playing around with this guy was too dangerous, so he just laid it out there.

"I need to get inside the Destroyers clubhouse," Cade said.

"Why?"

"Why? Oh, you know, because I never really had a problem with them until they started raping and murdering young girls."

Marco narrowed his eyes at him, but Cade didn't budge, letting the man know how fucking serious he was. It was a cheap shot. But it was also the truth. He hated he knew just which buttons to push to get Marco to cooperate. His sister was brutally raped and murdered. It was how they'd met two years ago. Once the victim was identified as a Serrano, no one wanted to get near the case so Cade had taken it. He didn't give a shit who or what Marco was, not as long as he could find the bastards who'd murdered a woman, a sister, and a mother. He did. Marco still owed him for that.

Marco got up, motioning for him to do the same. "Come with me."

Cade followed Marco into what he knew was the man's office. Cade closed the door behind him and only took a few steps into the room. Marco didn't stop until he reached his desk. He pulled out a bottle and two shots glasses from a drawer, pouring vodka into both of them. He turned around, holding one of the glasses out for Cade in an offering gesture. When Cade shook his head, Marco downed the shot himself, slamming the empty glass down on the desk.

"What evidence do you have?" Marco asked.

"DNA."

Marco's face gave nothing away as he leaned back against his desk. "Why haven't you made an arrest, then?"

"Because I don't just want to take down one guy. I want them all."

He also really wanted to know what the hell Neil was after. Especially since he'd pushed Cade toward using Marco.

"You have no idea why you're really doing it, do you?"

Cade shrugged, a sarcastic smile finding his lips. "Most likely not."

"Spooks. They never tell you anything. They just count on you being able to do your shit without any intel." Marco downed another shot of vodka. "Does he know you're here? No, wait. That's a stupid fucking question. Did he send you here?"

"You're still asking a stupid question."

Marco glanced up, his eyes cold as ice. Cade didn't dare move as Marco walked around his desk, stopping in front of him. Marco grabbed him by the chin, his hold tight and bruising as he searched Cade's eyes for something. The eyes Cade were staring into were dark, almost to the point of being black. Even if he looked, he knew he wouldn't find anything but emotionless cold in them. But he knew there was more to the man. He knew Marco was capable of loving someone. He'd loved his sister.

Marco must've found what he was looking for because he let go of Cade, stepping back to lean against his desk, his face a mask of indifference.

"I'll get you in. Even if I don't understand why he needs you to do it when he's got all his fancy spook friends who're actually trained for shit like this."

There was genuine anger in Marco's voice, which really surprised him. Marco was not the kind of man to let emotion show in any way. He couldn't afford to be that kind of man.

"I asked to go under. I knew something more was going on. Neil confirmed it by showing up and getting involved."

Marco flinched when he said Neil's name.

"Whatever happened between you two—"

"Is over. It's done with. He's CIA and I'm a god damned mobster. The family is my life and he lives for taking down people like me. There's nothing more between us and you'd do best to remember that."

Cade knew a threat when he heard one.

"You think you don't deserve to be loved?" Cade asked, unable to look Marco in the eye. They both knew what he was really asking.

"Don't you dare compare either of us with you. You turned your life around. You're a good guy. You always were," Marco said.

When they'd met, Cade had been barging into Marco's house, demanding to know who would want to hurt him so he could start investigating his sister's murder. Marco refused until Cade explained to him exactly why he didn't give a shit about who he was or what he did. All he wanted was to catch a murderer.

"So are you," Cade said.

"No. I am not a good guy, Cade."

"Sure, you are. If you weren't, you wouldn't be doing this. You're putting your life on the line. You're trusting me to either succeed or make sure nothing comes back to you if I don't."

"Trust doesn't come easy for me," Marco said.

"I know. Thank you."

Cole

It was strange, waking up without Cade, especially now when he'd just gotten him back in his bed. Well, Cade's bed. There was no who'd accidentally turn on the TV by sitting on the remote and then jump over the couch for cover because the sound was turned all up. Cole had still been laughing half an hour later when it'd happened. Cade had pretended to be insulted but he couldn't quite stop himself from smiling.

Even without Cade, he still had a job to do, and he reminded himself of that as he stepped into the fourth women's shelter of the day. He showed his badge at the front desk. "I'm looking for Sara Woods."

The woman behind the counter narrowed her eyes at him, giving him a sour look. She'd reacted to the name, though.

"I need to talk to her. It's about a murder. The man who attacked Miss Woods just killed a young girl," he explained.

She still didn't look like she was going to cooperate. He had no desire to arrest her, but she was hindering a murder investigation.

"Look." He glanced down, reading her name tag. "Loretta. I wouldn't be here if I didn't have to."

Loretta pursed her lips, looking thoughtful for a long moment. She bobbed her head and waved him along. "Come with me."

He followed her down a hall until she stopped in front of an open door and turned to him, a stern expression on her face.

"If she shows any signs of stress, please don't try to pressure her."

"You can stay with us if you want."

She shook her head before showing him through the door and into a room with a bed, a wardrobe, and a desk. It was sparse, but the only thing that looked unwelcoming was the woman sitting on the bed, a blank look in her eyes. Her blonde hair was matted, her face pale and her body barely more than skin and bones. The woman in front of him bore little resemblance to the one in the photos he'd seen of her, yet it was without a doubt still her.

"Miss Woods?"

She didn't react at all. He looked over his shoulder, finding Loretta gone. He grabbed the desk chair, rolled it in front of the young woman who was yet to acknowledge him, and sat down. She didn't look at him. She just stared at something that wasn't there.

"Sara? I'm Detective Banks."

That got a reaction out of her. She glanced at him, then frowned. The confusion was stark on her pale face. He was pretty sure the only word she'd heard was detective.

"I know Callie promised to help you. She can't right now, which is why she sent me in her stead."

Anguish and fear stared back at him.

"I need to know what happened and who did this to you," he said, keeping his voice low.

She wouldn't meet his eyes, hanging her head so her hair hid her face.

"Sara. Look at me."

She reluctantly did so, her blue eyes taking him in slowly. He kept still and quiet until she met his eyes.

"He's killed someone. A girl. He strangled and raped a young girl," he said. He hated telling her, but he also knew it was necessary.

Tears welled in Sara's eyes. There was so much despair and pain in her gaze it was almost unbearable to look at. A few months ago, he wouldn't have had a problem with it, but now? The poor girl pulled at his heartstrings and he felt nauseous just being in the shelter.

"I know you've been through hell, and I know it's going to take a while before you can start thinking about anything else. But you're already halfway there. You know why?"

She shook her head.

"Because you're fighting."

He gently placed his hand over hers, prepared to remove it immediately if she showed the smallest sign of discomfort. She didn't, though. She just looked up at him with big watery eyes. What he saw in those eyes gave him hope. Hope she was strong enough to make it through.

"Don't let him get away with this."

"That girl. Who was she?" Sara's voice sounded rough, like sandpaper, as if she hadn't spoken in a while. The thought hurt. She was a singer. He'd stumbled upon an old YouTube video of her when he'd searched for her online. Her voice was beautiful. The kind that made the hair on your arms stand up.

"Her name was Amelia Coulson. She was nineteen years old. She just lost her sister. He took the only child her parents had left."

The silence stretched out between them until Sara started nodding her head, determination filling her eyes.

"His name is Ray. Raymundo Esparza. I know where you can find him."

Cole wrote as she spoke. They got a lead on this case. Fucking finally.

Before he left, he took her hand, squeezing it gently.

"No one can take who you are from you. They can only make you forget it for a moment. I believe in you, Sara. I know... I know you're strong enough." He pulled out one of his business cards and laid it in the palm of her hand, folding her fingers over it. "That has my phone number on it. If there's anything, anything at all, you use it, Sara."

She was crying but also smiling as he left. Loretta was waiting for him when he stepped out of Sara's room. He followed her back to her desk where she turned to him, a gentle smile on her lips.

"You know why I let you in there?" She asked.

He raised an eyebrow in question. Somehow, he wasn't sure he could handle the answer to that, not if the way she was watching him was any indication of what she was about to say.

"We haven't been able to get anywhere with her. She won't talk and she barely listens to anything the counselor says. I'm sure you know how impossible it is to help someone who doesn't want help."

"Why are you telling me this?"

"Because, whatever it is you've been through, I just want you to know you can come back here, anytime. Anything you say in here stays in here," she said.

He gave a curt nod of his head, unable to speak. Loretta's sweet, sympathetic smile turned his stomach into knots. He made it out of the building and halfway down the alley to his car before dizziness overtook him. He leaned on the wall, slouching against it. He drew in a few deep breaths, trying to control his erratic heartbeat. He dug his phone out of his back pocket. He couldn't see the screen because it was shaking in front of him.

He clenched his fist, pressing the back of his head against the wall in an attempt to gather himself enough to press speed dial. On the one hand, he wished to god he could call Cade, on the other, he was fucking glad he couldn't.

When he pressed the phone to his ear, he heard the call go through, but all he got was Tank's answering machine. They were probably all on a job. Panic slid over him, enveloping him like a second skin. Despite his hands shaking, he managed to place another call. It was picked up immediately.

"Franklin," he gasped out.

"Easy, baby. Just breathe. Breathe."

With Franklin's soothing voice in his ear, he got himself under control. His lungs started to take in much-needed air and the trembling in his hands lessened ever so slowly. Tears were staining his cheeks by the time he was able to breathe normally again.

"You alright?" Franklin asked.

"Yeah." He would be. When he got Cade back. "Thank you."

"Anytime, brother," Franklin said, his voice soft and soothing. Just like all those times in the desert, on those filthy mattresses or on the god damned floor, when someone couldn't sleep because whenever they closed their eyes, blood and death were all they saw, and then Franklin started talking. The cadence of his voice alone was enough to soothe and calm down just about anyone. It also helped that the guy was a sarcastic son of a bitch who lived to make everyone laugh.

"I've got your back, man. Always," Franklin said.

"I know. I love you."

Cole dried his wet cheeks with the back of his hand, almost snorting at the absurdity of it all. Cade must be making him mushy. Yeah. That had to be it.

"I love you, too, babe."

He loved all his brothers. No matter what. They may not share the same blood, but they were family. He'd do anything for them, and he knew they'd do the same for him. That's the kind of bond you made when you went to hell and back with the same group of people.

"You took your time, huh?"

"What are you talking about?" Cole asked.

"We've all been waiting for you to have your breakthrough. You've taken longer than everyone else. Welcome back, brother."

Cade

When Cade stepped out of the car Marco sent for him an hour earlier, he was at the Destroyers' clubhouse. He knew the one stop on the way there was to switch out the driver with one of Neil's guys. That's what they'd done the other times. Once parked inside the clubhouse's grounds, the driver didn't step out of the car, but he was still another man inside the building if anything were to happen.

A big ass guy with a scowl rivaling Cole's waved him over. He looked like a huge bear. In leather. With a gun. Usually, he found that hot, but Cole had completely turned him off other men.

"Follow me," the bear grunted. He even sounded like one.

Cade followed the guy, resisting the urge to glance over his shoulder, knowing full well there were three guys behind them. It's what he expected from the Destroyers. They may be a bunch of violent misfits, but they knew how to handle themselves and most importantly, their business.

The bear led him through a big metal door behind which Cade knew was a big square room with floor to ceiling windows on one side. The closest buildings on the side the windows faced were at least a mile away, so they obviously didn't fear a sniper attack enough to not put in windows or at least make them bulletproof. Sloppy.

This was the fourth time he'd been in this room to make a deal. When he'd first gotten involved with the bikers, it'd been solely through Slay. Marco's involvement came later, and his cover was only intact because of him and the fact his cover was that of a crooked cop.

Waiting for him inside the room was the club's vice president, Billy 'Bones' Cooper. He'd never asked how he'd gotten that nickname, and he sure as fuck didn't want to know now. Bones wore a sneer on his ugly face as he sauntered toward Cade.

"So, the Italian sent you again. Didn't he learn anything from the last time?"

The asshole was referring to Brent and the shit that went down, causing Brent's transfer to vice. Which should've put Brent higher on the Destroyers radar because of their business but vice didn't have any evidence apart from what little Cade managed to gather two years before and that had been on a murder case. Or cases, rather. The bikers liked to kill. They liked to make people hurt before they killed them, too.

"He likes having a cop as a middleman. Means he won't have to step foot here and that if you kill me, they won't have to retaliate because you'll have every damned cop in this city gunning for you."

Bones stared at him, his expression emotionless.

"Let's make some business, then," Bones said.

Cade stepped closer but kept out of Bones' reach, just in case. "Do you have the items?"

"That, and something more," Bones said.

The grin on Bones' face made the hair on Cade's arms and neck rise. A chilling sensation whooshed over him. Marco had ordered enough guns to arm every last one of his men to the teeth and Bones had more? Not good.

"What?"

Bones gestured toward the crate to his left. The one to his right must contain Marco's guns then and they weren't exactly small crates. He watched Bones with scrutinizing eyes before walking to the crate. He glanced over his shoulder, not trusting Bones in the slightest. He pushed the lid off.

Holy fuck. Most of the things in there were military grade. There was no way they'd stolen them. That would have a lot of dangerous people looking for them, and the Destroyers certainly didn't need that shit. No, he was sure they'd bought them. This went so much deeper than he'd first thought, and he was sure this was just the fucking tip of the iceberg. This was why Neil was involved. It had to be.

Cade reached into the crate and pulled out an M4 Carbine rifle, running his gaze expertly over it as he weighed it in his hands. He put it down to pick up a Beretta M9 pistol. The crate was filled with C-4 and even a grenade launcher. There was enough firepower in there to level a city or two.

"Do you want it or not?" Bones asked, an impatient sneer in his voice.

"I'm gonna have to make a few calls." When they didn't seem to get his drift, he added, "In private."

Bones didn't look happy about it, but he gestured toward a door at the opposite end of the one Cade entered through. Cade put down the Beretta, turned his back on Bones and the other bikers whose menacing eyes he felt all the way across the room and out the door. It closed behind him with a click and he stood, silent and unmoving for a minute.

When nothing happened and no one followed him, he started down the hallway. Luckily for him, he'd been in the clubhouse enough to know which way to go. He took a left turn and didn't stop until he was in front of the right door. Once there, he glanced from side to side before crouching down and pulling out his tools.

Picking the lock only took a few seconds. He wasn't as rusty as he'd thought. There would be a lot of people from his family turning in their graves if they learned he wasn't upholding the Smith standard.

He stepped inside, closing and locking the door behind him. With a hand on the door, he blew out a breath he hadn't realized he'd been holding. He turned around, his eyes scanning the room before him. It was about the size of the police station's bathrooms. It was tiny, with no windows, a desktop computer and two screens on a desk, with a few other gadgets spread out across it.

"Lots of shiny tech for a biker gang," Cade mumbled to himself.

He searched the room for a few seconds but when he didn't find anything substantial, he booted up the computer and let out a snort at the safety on it. Someone was obviously trying really hard to protect whatever was on this thing. Too bad they didn't know the software they had was possibly the easiest on the market to crack. It was a common mistake, though. The software looked high-tech, but it did nothing to protect from intruders, especially not those with access to the computer. It was, however, tricky to access from afar, but that was due to the computer not being connected to the internet.

He sat down in the desk chair after fishing out his earbud and a shiny black pen from the hidden pocket in his suit jacket. He unscrewed the pen cap, revealing the end of the flash drive embedded in it. Fucking spooks.

He put the earbud in his ear.

"Rebel here. The mission is a go."

If he was doing this shit, he was at least gonna have some fun doing it. Luckily, Neil just went along with it.

"Roger, Rebel," Neil said.

"What do you need me to do?"

"Just put the flash drive in a port and my guy will take it from there."

"Aye, aye, sir."

He plugged in the flash drive and the screen flashed once before the mouse pointer started to move. Neil's guy was controlling the computer from the outside. He was looking through files and copying them onto the flash drive. Cade was absently following what happened on the screen when something caught his eye.

"Whoa, wait. Stop. Go back a bit."

He faintly heard Neil tell his guy to go back. Cade's eyes were glued to the screen, but he still nearly missed it. "Stop. Right there."

He sat staring at the names. It couldn't be. "Is this what I think it is?"

"It's an audio file. I'll have my guy play it through your earbud," Neil said.

A few seconds later, the sound came through. It was a recording of a phone call. He recognized both voices.

"She's got the ledger," Elias Tully said.

"I thought you said she only had the documents? That she wouldn't get anywhere with them."

The voice was smooth. The voice of someone who used it for a living.

"She couldn't. But she went to Janice with them and she must've broken into my office and taken the ledger."

Tully's voice was strained. Panicked. It was clear he was on the edge. Which might, finally, explain why he went on a killing spree. It wasn't without reason.

"Are you saying that you don't actually know if she's got it?"

"It has to be her."

"Then get rid of her."

"But I… I can't. How am I supposed to do that?"

"This is your mess, Tully. Clean it up or I'll be sending someone to make sure you can't make a mess ever again."

"I'll take care of it. Please don't send anyone."

"Get it done."

The recording ended, the room turning eerily silent. Cade was still trying to make sense of it all, but one thing was clear to him. So very clear.

"We just heard the State's Attorney order Elias Tully to murder Mary Coulson. The State's Attorney," Cade said, his voice breaking.

"I believe we did."

"Holy mother of God. What the fuck is going on?"

"A lot of shit above both our pay grades, I believe," Neil said.

Cade played the tape one more time while Neil's guy did his thing on the computer. The Destroyers must've put a wiretap on Tully, which was extremely lucky because otherwise, they may never have found out about the State's

Attorney. It wasn't unthinkable for Cade that someone with that kind of power would use it like this. But it did hurt. A lot.

Clearing his throat, Cade straightened and glanced down at his watch. They were almost on three minutes. He needed to get back before the bikers got suspicious enough to come looking for him.

"Are you done yet?" Cade asked.

"Ten seconds," Neil said, adding shortly after. "You're clear to go."

"Copy that."

He took out the flash drive and put it, along with the earbud, back into the hidden pocket. The earbud was too easy to spot if he wore it and the pocket was padded so when the bikers gave him a pat down when he left, they wouldn't find anything.

He slipped out the door, locking it behind him. He got out his phone and called Marco. The bikers were most likely not smart enough to check his phone to see if he'd actually made the call but he still wanted to be sure and he figured he should tell Marco about the guns.

"Cade," Marco answered on the first ring.

"They offered us more merc. Military grade."

"How the hell did they get a hold of that?"

"My guess is they bought it," Cade said.

"From who?" Marco growled.

"Someone with access to the military's weapons."

Marco cursed up a storm. Cade knew he couldn't be happy about it. The Destroyers somehow got weapons Marco didn't know about through Marco's territory. The bikers obviously didn't know just how territorial Marco was or they wouldn't have offered the shipment to him. If it had been anyone but Cade telling him about it, Cade didn't doubt Marco would've leveled the Destroyers.

"Do you want it or not, boss?" Cade asked.

He leaned back against the wall, listening to Marco cursing out the bikers some more.

"Those little shits think they can just come into my city and do whatever the hell they want? Accept the shipment and get the hell out of there, Cade," Marco said.

"Yes, boss."

Marco hung up and Cade shook his head at the man's tantrum. He put his phone back into his pocket, knowing full well he wasn't alone anymore. He turned slowly, putting up the façade he needed to get through this. Just a few feet from him Slay stood, watching him with hungry eyes.

"What have we here?" Slay asked.

"Obviously, the sexiest man on the planet."

That got him a smile full of white teeth. Slay cocked his head to the side. "I heard you were back. Did the cops fire you?"

"They just suspended me. Thought I'd make some extra cash while I have the free time," Cade said with a shrug.

"Let me know if I can help you fill some of that free time," Slay said, running a finger down Cade's chest. It was what Slay would expect of him, now that he wasn't there with Cole; to be the man he'd made Slay believe he was.

"I need to get this deal running."

"When you're done, come find me," Slay said, licking his lips.

"Oh, I will."

That was a promise. He was locking this asshole up for good. Slay ran the tips of his fingers down Cade's jaw, continuing down his throat.

"We have a lot to talk about. Like that partner you brought last time."

Slay's hand closed around his throat, just hard enough for the man Slay knew him as to get excited. Cade rose up on his toes to avoid getting strangled.

"He's no one. I fucked him, but that's it," Cade said. "You know what it takes to keep my interest."

"I do," Slay growled. He slanted his mouth over Cade's, his lips and tongue demanding access, but Cade didn't let him in. When Slay pulled back, he grabbed Cade's chin in a bruising grip.

"You're a fucking tease, Cade."

The man Cade pretended to be around Slay *was* a tease. It was how he'd managed to keep Slay interested in the first place. That and the fact he'd never bent over for Slay. Lucky for him, as much as Slay liked to throw him around, bruise him, and being dominant, Slay also liked to bottom. There was no way Cade would've ever let Slay fuck him. He didn't let just anyone that close.

"I'll be waiting for you," Slay said, and pushed Cade aside.

Cade stood for a second, watching Slay walk away, then he turned around and started walking. He wanted this over with. He wanted Slay far away from him. He wanted back in Cole's arms. His breath stuttered just at the thought of Cole. It had never been hard for him, what he was doing for Neil. Not until Cole. He could easily slip into any role Neil wanted him to which made it all so much harder because when he was with Cole, he'd never played a role. He'd been himself. As much as he could given the circumstances.

He stopped in front of the door, his hand raised just above the handle. He closed his eyes, seeing Cole's green gaze and the smile that always stole his breath. He drew in a deep breath and settled into the role of corrupt cop Cade Lawson. He was calm and collected when he stepped through the door.

"What took you so long?" Bones asked, a displeased frown on his forehead.

Cade shrugged. "I ran into Slay."

He was glad to actually be able to tell the truth. Not that he was bad at lying. He was good. Really good. Which was why he hated doing it. Bones snorted but didn't question him any further. Guess he didn't want all the gay details. Cade would've found it weird that a biker gang not only had gay members but owned a gay nightclub if he didn't know.

"So?" Bones asked.

Cade grinned. "We're in."

Cole

He felt the eyes on him first. Then a shadow fell over his desk. He clenched his jaw before tilting his head back to glare up at Lara. Her hands were on her hips, a red eyebrow raised as she watched him with those piercing eyes. He didn't bother asking what she was doing.

"Don't you have a case to work?" Lara asked.

He grumbled under his breath. Cuss words mostly. He leaned back in his chair with a groan. He'd only been back half an hour and his trip to the shelter was still quite vivid in his mind. It'd made him miss Cade even more.

"You did manage to work before you met him, right?"

He rolled his eyes and pushed out of his chair. "Of course, I did."

"Then get to it," she said.

He threw a nasty glance at her over his shoulder as he walked out of their office. Of course, she just stood there with her arms crossed and a wide smile on her face. He took the stairs down to the floor below. It was strange. He hated elevators, but whenever Cade stepped into one, he just followed. When he reached the landing, he pushed through the door and stopped for a second to orient himself.

A gut feeling had him heading toward the kitchen. He stopped in the doorway. A guy with brown hair, about the same height as Cade, had one hand on top of the fridge and his head as far inside it as it could possibly go.

"Brent, right?"

The guy glanced over his shoulder, meeting Cole's gaze with his big, brown eyes. A smile touched his lips as he nodded. "Yeah. You must be dark, dangerous, and sexy."

"Excuse me?"

Brent's smile kicked up a notch before he said, "Cade."

"Oh."

Yeah, that was explanation enough. Brent seemed to think so as well. He closed the fridge door and turned around, his eyes assessing as he looked Cole over from top to bottom.

"What can I do for you?" Brent asked.

"I'm working a homicide and my lead suspect is in a gang," Cole said.

Brent raised an eyebrow at him. "Which one?"

"The West B. Jackals."

"Oh, yeah. Those guys are some crazy ass motherfuckers. What's your suspects name?"

"Raymundo Esparza."

"Come with me," Brent said.

He followed Brent out of the kitchen and into the empty squad room where Brent stopped in front of a large bookcase filled to the brim with case files. Brent reached out and pulled out a thick file, opened it and after a quick glance, closed it and held it out to Cole.

"You can read it in here if you want," Brent said.

Cole took the file. "Alright. Thank you."

"No biggie," Brent said, walking backwards a few steps before turning around and, most likely, returning to the kitchen.

Cole sat down on one of the two couches and started looking through Raymundo Esparza's file. The guy had two priors for assault. He'd been affiliated with some sort of gang since he was fourteen. It was a damned shame they hadn't taken a DNA test before. It may have prevented Amelia's death.

When Brent walked back into the room, he didn't look up until Brent put down a plate on the coffee table in front of him. Cole put down the file and glanced at the plate.

"A donut? Really?"

Brent shrugged, an amused gleam in his eyes. "You're Cade's partner. I figured you'd need it."

"You're probably right."

"I'm always right. Or didn't Cade tell you?"

Cole chuckled. "You're just as bad as him, aren't you?"

Brent didn't answer, he just laughed all the way out of the room. Cole shook his head and couldn't stop his gaze from landing on the donut. With a groan, he picked it up. He ate the donut, admitting to himself just how good it was, while he looked through Esparza's file. It was big, but most of it was crimes Esparza was only suspected of doing. All either break-ins, or beatings and murders of members of other gangs. Nothing about rape or murder of women. Though he'd probably raped before, the women were probably too afraid to report it.

Something made Esparza kill Amelia. You don't go from rape to rape *and* murder overnight. One scenario he could believe was Esparza being ordered to kill Amelia, and because he was slime, he raped her because it was easy. A sigh pushed through his lips. He stood up and stretched, popping his back. Some of the tension in his body dissipated. He picked up the file, walking to the bookcase and put it back. The amount of files they had could only mean their workload was just as huge. It sort of made him glad he was working homicide, but only just.

He thanked Brent again when he ran into him on the way to the stairs.

"Seriously. It's no trouble. Any *friend* of Cade's and all," Brent said and winked at him.

Cole narrowed his eyes at Brent when he made a zipping motion over his lips. The man wagged his eyebrows as he walked backwards away from Cole. The grin on his face was downright wicked.

Fuck. He knew. Cade and his big mouth. Fuck. He missed the crazy bastard.

He made his way back upstairs, rolling his eyes when he walked in on Lara with her head on her desk. Her idea of concentrating was something else. He pulled out his desk chair and sat down, turning on his computer before picking up the mug of coffee he'd abandoned at Lara's order. He took a sip, grimacing when he found it a tad colder than lukewarm.

"I got you a new one," Lara said, holding up a mug without lifting her head.

"You creep me out sometimes," he said as he walked over to take the mug from her, raising it to his lips and taking a sip.

"I'll take that as a compliment."

"You should."

He shook his head, a sliver of a smile forming on his lips. He walked back to his desk and sat down, turning on his computer to start searching. He didn't get any hits on rapes or murders matching Esparza's M.O. or his DNA. He rubbed his face, a heavy sigh falling from his lips. Maybe the answers were with Amelia. He didn't believe her death was a simple rape and murder. There had to be something more behind it. Esparza hadn't killed a woman before, and he just so happened to be prospecting with the Destroyers. It had to have been a hit. But why? Why Amelia? What did she know?

He stood, pulling his jacket off his chair and grabbed his gun from the drawer in his desk. He needed to check out her apartment. There might be a clue there. He walked out of the office, noting Lara had left sometime while he'd been occupied. He would've thought he was losing his edge if he hadn't known Lara had been through the same training as him.

He ran into Tanner by the elevator. The guy was carrying enough bags of food to feed the entire department. It smelled amazing, but he needed to go. He could eat some when he got back.

"Hey. Where're you off to in such a hurry?" Tanner asked, his face just visible above the food containers and bags.

"I need to go check my victim's home," he said.

"Alone? Where's Cade?"

"Suspended."

Tanner's eyebrows rose, almost hitting his hairline. "Again?"

"He got suspended before?"

That… wasn't really a surprise if he was being honest.

"Yeah. Pretty often actually now that I think about it. Every time he does something to piss off Morris, he gets suspended or sent home." Tanner shrugged. "You know, I think it's when Cade needs a break. But you've met him. Once he gets going, there isn't much that can stop him. Except for Morris."

Cole shook his head. Tanner was probably right. Cade wasn't a quitter. Not if he'd had coffee, at least. The thought made him smile which led to Tanner chuckling at him.

"Most days without him here are drab and boring, gore and death besides," Tanner said, grinning.

"That they are."

He was still sporting a smile when he stepped out of the elevator and into the parking garage. He got in the car and turned up the radio which was on some eighties channel. The drive to Amelia's apartment took longer than he'd expected but he didn't mind. The music comforted him and made it bearable that he didn't have some crazy ass partner singing along to it. He couldn't wait for Cade to be back. How he'd ever survived those weeks without him, he didn't know.

He found what looked like the last parking spot outside of Amelia's building and stepped out of the car. An older man with a shock of white hair on his head stood by the front door and when he spotted Cole, he made his way toward him. Cole reached him before he made it down the front steps.

"Are you Detective Banks?"

"Yes?"

The man smiled and held out his hand. "I'm Carlos Barrett. Someone from the police station called, a Detective Samuels, I believe. She said you needed access to the Coulson's apartment."

Cole shook the man's hand, keeping his professional façade in place as his mind whirred. How did Lara know? She wasn't there when he left. But Tanner was. He must've told her. That was really sweet of her, considering he'd totally forgotten to call ahead himself, and she'd probably guessed that.

"I do. Thank you for taking the time."

Carlos nodded his head, turning around to lead Cole inside the building and up the flight of stairs.

"Oh, it's no problem. I just hope you catch the killer. Those poor girls and their parents. No parent should ever outlive their children."

"I will do everything I can to catch him," Cole said, meaning every word.

"That's good to hear," Carlos said, stopping in front of a door on the second floor. "This is it."

Carlos unlocked the door, told him to take as much time as he needed and gave him the key. He stepped into the apartment, taking in everything around him. Amelia had shared it with her sister, evidence of that was all over the place. The two sets of everything told him she hadn't touched her sister's stuff. It'd probably been too hard for her. He knew what that was like. His father had gathered all of his mother's things and thrown them out but before he could get it all, Cole had grabbed her favorites and put them in a box he'd kept in the bottom of his closet. He still had that box. Along with his clothes and a few other items, that box was all he'd taken with him from Fairfax.

He walked around the apartment, looking for clues or evidence of any kind.

"What were you up to Amelia?" he asked out loud even though she would never be able to answer him. Not verbally at least.

Pictures of both girls were everywhere. All smiles and happiness radiating from them. It was hard to believe they were both dead. Both murdered. He couldn't imagine their parents' pain.

He'd been there about an hour, finding nothing to help their case when he decided to take a break and go find some coffee. He was walking to the door when the floor made a noise he knew well enough to crouch down and start knocking on the boards. One of them gave a hollow sound.

He ran his fingertips over the edge of the board, trying to get a grip on it. Once he got it, the board was easy to lift off. He laid the piece on the floor and looked into the hole. The room lights couldn't reach it, so he saw nothing but darkness. He dug out his phone and used the built-in flashlight. There was something down there.

With a curse, he put down the phone and took off his jacket. He folded up his right shirt sleeve. He stuck his hand down into the hole which was surprisingly deeper than it looked. His fingers skirted across something smooth. He ran his fingers along it until he found an edge to grab.

He pulled out what turned out to be a ledger. One with names in it. It had cartel and drugs written all over it. The Destroyers, too. He sifted through it, most of the names unfamiliar to him. Though he did come upon a few he recognized as some of the big players. He was about to close the ledger when his eyes caught a familiar name.

Chapter Sixteen

Cole

COLE SLAMMED down the phone, cursing vividly. It would take four hours before he could get a fucking warrant. Well, he didn't have four hours. Cade was out there. Alone. He slammed the receiver down a few more times, like that would change any-damned-thing. He needed to get to Esparza before something bad happened. He didn't have any contacts in Baltimore and everybody and their fucking dog were swamped with work. Even though he had a witness naming Esparza as her attacker, he still needed a warrant to sample his DNA. Sara told him where Esparza could be found, though.

He moved his chair back with a forceful push causing it to bang into the wall behind him. Lara eyed him from behind her desk, but she didn't comment on it. He grabbed a piece of paper and scribbled down the address. He thrust it at Lara who caught it and stared at him with huge eyes.

"If I'm not back in an hour send backup."

"Whatever you say, Hotshot," she said.

He caught her glancing down at her watch, though, so he knew she was taking it seriously. He wasn't sure who to trust, not after seeing that name in the ledger, and he didn't want to get Lara involved more than absolutely necessary.

He got in his car and when he turned it on, the radio sprang to life on some weird-ass station. He couldn't get himself to change it or turn off the radio. It was strange how he'd found once he'd returned to Fairfax, he actually missed having an idiot changing the channels non-stop and singing along like he was auditioning for a Broadway show. But at that moment, he thought he might miss him even more, perhaps because he knew how close Cade really was this time. He tried not to think too much about it as he drove to the address Sara gave him.

He parked across from the house, turned off the car and just sat there for a while. Everything seemed to be happening so fast, yet he didn't want it to slow down. He was losing his mind and he didn't care.

The house was old and looked like it hadn't been kept up. The only vehicle out front was a bike and after a quick call, he knew it belonged to Esparza. He got out of the car, looking around but not finding anyone near. Strange.

He walked to the front door and raised his hand to knock, but instinct made him drop his hand and look the door over. The frame was broken. He pushed at the door. It slid open. That didn't bode well. He pulled out his gun before moving inside the house. He waited a second just inside the door, listening for movements inside. He moved methodically, slowly, and when he reached the kitchen, a foul smell met him. He knew that smell.

He moved further into the kitchen where he found a body in a pool of blood. He kept moving, sweeping the place before he went back to the body. He crouched down, pulling out a glove from his pocket and used it as he turned the head face up. Despite the blood and swelling, there was no doubt he was looking at Raymundo Esparza. It looked like he'd been shot execution-style after having his face beat in. Someone was tying up their loose ends.

Cade was right in the middle of this. Worry and something dark churned around inside him. He dropped the glove down next to Esparza and just as he was about to get up, the sound of someone stepping up behind him, made him freeze up. The hair on the back of his neck stood up.

"He got what he deserved."

That voice. Even though he'd seen the name in the ledger, he hadn't wanted to believe it. He raised his arms, holding his gun out to the side. He got to his feet slowly, then turned around to a gut-dropping sight. The man holding him at gunpoint smiled.

"Mike."

"Cole."

Mike's smile turned sardonic, his eyes going cold. "You shouldn't have come back."

Two guys walked into the room from behind Mike. They didn't stop next to Mike. They continued toward Cole, one of them taking the gun from him when they reached him. Then he was being patted down, his phone and keys removed from his pockets.

"Whatever you think you have to do—"

Hands landed hard on his shoulders, forcing him to his knees. He grunted as pain shot up through his legs.

"What? Like, get that ledger from you? Burn it?" Mike asked.

A gun pressed against the back of his head.

"Do you want to know how she got it in the first place?"

Cole didn't say a word. He didn't have to.

"Her sister stole it. From Elias Tully. Which is why he killed her."

"That's the guy who shot you," Cole said, recalling the name from a conversation with Cade.

"Yeah. When he started killing off people like that, drawing attention to himself and therefore, all of us, I had to do something. Then the bastard decided to just shoot me as well."

A grim expression covered Mike's face.

"I don't have the ledger here," Cole said.

"No, I'm sure it's just lying on your desk at the station," Mike said.

If he thought that, then he couldn't know his name was in it. As it was, the ledger was still in Cole's car. They'd better not fucking touch his baby.

"You don't have to do this."

"Unfortunately. I don't have a choice," Mike said in a dangerous voice. Mike's eyes were cold when they met his. It was the kind of emotionless eyes he'd seen so many times overseas. Detached. Like his own must've looked for so long.

"Take him," Mike said.

He was pulled up roughly.

ANA NIGHT

Cade

Bones took a call half an hour earlier and since then, he'd been stalling the deal. Cade was getting angsty, though he repressed the urge to fidget. There were only two things which could make him fidget; one was if he knew he'd been made and there was nothing he could do about it. The other was Cole.

"Are we doing this deal or not?"

"Depends," Bones said, not looking up from the knife he was twirling around in his hand.

This was about to go to shit. He just knew it. He crossed his arms over his chest, glaring at Bones with a mask of boredom slipping into place over his face.

"On what?"

"On what you're prepared to do to keep this relationship intact," Bones said.

"I'll make sure to ask my boss if he wants to continue using his money on your weapons," Cade drawled.

"I've got better deals on the table than this," Bones said.

Cade narrowed his eyes at the bastard. Like hell he did. He leaned back against the crate. He didn't believe him, the look on his face saying as much.

"Oh, really? What the hell am I doing here then?"

"I'm sure you asked to be here. Cop," Bones sneered.

Asshole.

Before he could answer, one of the bikers cleared his throat. They both turned to him as he returned his phone to his back pocket.

"They're here, Bones."

A sardonic smile stretched across Bones' face, making Cade's blood run cold. His hands clenched into fists, dread pooling in his stomach. Bones turned that smile on him as he talked to the biker.

"Send them in," Bones said.

294

"A better deal?"

"Let's just say something interesting came up."

Cade knew things were going bad when he caught Slay lounging against the wall, his eyes firmly on Cade. Slay's eyes on him made a shudder rock through him. He squeezed his eyes closed and fought off the urge to throw up. There was no other option but getting through this. He could do it. He just had to shut out everything but the mission. He opened his eyes just as the door was pushed open and a biker stepped through, several people trailing behind him.

When Mike walked in, Cade managed to stay calm and keep the surprise off of his face. He wasn't so lucky when Cole was dragged in after him, his hands tied in front of him and a gun to his head.

Cole

The car ride hadn't been too long, making him believe they hadn't driven around to throw him off, and if he'd known the layout of Baltimore he could've probably guessed where he was, but he didn't. Because he'd been swept up in everything Cade. So far, he had no regrets. That might change fast, though.

He was pulled out of the trunk they'd forced him into earlier. Blood ran down his right hand but one of the fuckers had a broken cheekbone and he was quite satisfied with that. He managed to get to his feet but couldn't do much more seeing as at least one gun was pointed at him at all times. He let his eyes scan the enclosed courtyard, a row of bikes in front of a big square building led him to believe they were at the Destroyers' clubhouse. He zeroed in on the back of Mike's head as the guy started toward the building.

"Mike," Cole yelled.

The man froze, his shoulders tensing, but he didn't turn toward him. Cole growled under his breath. He wanted to tear the man apart.

"If something happens to him… You fucking bastard. If something happens to him, I'll fucking kill you."

Mike didn't respond, he just waved a hand over his shoulder and the men holding Cole started pulling him forward. Out of principle, he struggled and earned himself a blow to the head. They dragged him through the building, keeping his head down until they suddenly stopped, and he was forced to his knees.

He lifted his head, his eyes meeting the steely blue ones of Cade's. For a moment, his whole world came to a halt. For one moment, it was just Cade and him. Then Cade's eyes turned dull. Cade looked at him with disinterest. Like Cole was some dirt he just had to brush off his pants. The scariest part, though, the thing that made Cole's heart beat faster and freeze at the same time, was that he saw no sign of the man he knew, the man he'd put everything on the line for. The man in front of him now wasn't Cade Lawson; he was a cold, distant, and hollow shell. Cole recognized the man he'd been before he'd met the pain-in-his-ass-detective in what he now saw in Cade. It made him sick.

"What have we here?"

Cole moved his eyes to the man who'd spoken. He was a big guy, the leather cut he wore had *vice president* written in white letters over his left chest pocket.

"He's Cade's partner. He got to Esparza's place before we could clean up," Mike said.

"His partner?"

"Work partner. Though we've had an occasional romp in the sheets. You know I like my men rough around the edges," Cade said.

Why the fuck was Cade telling them that? They'd just use it against him. Against them.

"What happened at Esparza's place?" Cade asked.

"He was a problem we took care of. Permanently," the guy who was apparently the vice president of the Destroyers said. It worried the hell out of him that the guy didn't seem to care about the things he was sharing with Cade. That couldn't be good.

"So now you kill your prospects?" Cade asked.

The vice president sneered at Cade. "He was killing people left and right."

"Sounds a lot like your M.O. Bones," Cade fired back.

The guy showed his teeth as he let out a frustrated growl. Cade was definitely bugging him, but he seemed somewhat used to it, otherwise, he was sure the guy would've blown up by then.

"Whose side are you really on, huh?"

"My own. Obviously," Cade said with a dismissive wave of his hand.

Bones shook his head, clearly not liking Cade's answer. He motioned something to the guys holding Cole and they pulled him to his feet as the fucker pointed his gun at Cole.

"Are you with us, or are you with him?"

Cade shrugged, looking unaffected by everything that was happening. He'd never seen Cade like this. So unaffected. So uncaring. He felt fear's cold touch run down his spine.

"You brought him here. He's your problem, not mine," Cade said. "You're boring me with this. But to answer your question; I'm not with him, or you. I work for the Serrano family and they're not gonna be fucking pleased with this shit you're pulling."

Cole knew that name. Was Cade involved with the Italian mob? What the hell?

Bones or whatever the hell his name was, growled and turned his gun back on Cole.

"He'll die then."

If it kept Cade alive, he didn't care.

Cade cocked his head to the side, an amused smile curving at his lips. "Hmm. A goodbye, then?"

Cade looked like he was waiting for permission. Cade walked until he stood right in front of Cole. Cade didn't look at him, but rather at someone over Cole's shoulder, and he realized that whoever was there was the one whom Cade had asked permission from. Cade lifted his hand, running his fingers down Cole's jaw, making him swallow hard and fight to keep his posture, to keep upright.

He knew this was some game Cade was playing, but as their lips met, he didn't care. He took everything Cade gave him, knowing he might be seconds away from death. One of Cade's hands settled over his racing heart, his fingers bunching his shirt in a tight grip. They were both breathless when Cade pulled back.

Cade smiled up at him and then kneed him in the stomach hard enough for him to fold over. Mike grabbed him, lowering him to his knees. Something cold was pressed in between his bound hands, Mike's body providing cover. The rope around his wrists loosened as Mike cut through it. He looked up at Mike in surprise but quickly hid it when Mike crouched down in front of him.

"Mike, you don't have to do this," Cole said, coughing as breath escaped him.

Mike closed his hands around Cole's and their eyes met. There was no regret. No sorrow in his eyes.

"But I already did."

Mike got up slowly and raised his gun.

"All this because the fucking bookie was an idiot who couldn't keep his dick in his pants," Mike said.

"He's having fun in prison. I made sure of that," a guy to his right said, a leer on his face. There was no mistaking the meaning of his words. If Cole didn't have more important things to think about, he would've been sick.

He looked up, finding Cade's eyes. Those blue eyes held a lot of secrets and he was certain he was the only one who could see the fear in them. He took a deep breath, hoping like hell that Cade could read in his eyes everything he couldn't say.

As Mike pulled the trigger, Cole threw the knife Mike had given him. He heard the guy behind him get hit just as he saw the guy whose throat was pierced by the knife, gurgle in his own blood. He twisted enough to kick out at one of the guys behind him, hitting him in the knee and sending him crashing to the floor. It was a futile plan, but he wasn't going out without a fight. He heard the sound of a gun firing behind him and could do nothing but watch as bullets ripped through Mike, his body jerking at each hit until he fell to the floor.

"Mike," Cade screamed.

Glass sprayed over them. Cole was on his feet the next second, grabbing Cade and throwing them both down on the floor. He draped himself over Cade as bullets rained over them.

Chapter Seventeen

Cade

MIKE WAS hurt. He had to get to him. He had to get to Mike. He coughed in air, the impact from hitting the floor having pushed out the air in his lungs. His ears were ringing with the sound of bullets ripping through the room. The ground was littered with glass shards and bullet shells.

He rose to his elbows, then tried to get on his knees. Arms tightened around him, pulling him back down. He started to struggle, pulling his arm forward to slam his elbow back into whoever was holding him.

"No. Stay down," Cole barked.

He stilled, relief coursing through him. Cole was alive.

By then, Cole should've noticed they weren't the ones being shot at. The Destroyers were being picked off one by one. Sometimes, he was really fucking glad Neil was on his side. Besides, they really shouldn't have put windows there.

"The sniper is with us. He won't hit you," Cade said. He pulled out his gun and thrust it into Cole's hand. "I'm okay. Go get him."

He kissed Cole quickly, savoring the seconds of connection before breaking away. He watched as Cole got up and expertly made his way through the room, taking down a few of the bikers as he went.

Cade crawled the whole way to Mike, staying low so he wouldn't get hit by accident. Mike was on his back, blood pouring out of him and coloring the floor around him a dark red. When he saw Cade, he reached out with a bloody hand. He dropped down in front of Mike, grabbing his hand in both of his as he leaned over him.

"I'm sorry."

Mike coughed, blood running from his mouth. Cade leaned down, pressing a kiss to Mike's forehead with trembling lips.

"It's alright, love. Everything is going to be alright."

He wasn't even sure which of them he was trying to convince the most.

"Tell Lara. And. Brent. I'm sorry," Mike said between coughs.

"No. You can tell them yourself. You're not gonna fucking die, Mikey. I won't let you."

"Protect him. You have to protect him," Mike said, his voice clear.

"I will. I promise, Mikey. I promise."

Tears clouded his sight. This couldn't be happening. Mike touched his chin with the tips of his fingers, a smile forming on his lips. Then his eyes went glassy and his arm fell, his fingers sliding away from Cade's face.

Cole

He was hunting the bastard who'd shot Mike. Even if he hadn't seen the face of the man who'd done it, he knew who it was. Cole caught up with him just as he rounded a corner. The heat of a bullet whizzing by followed by the sound, had him jumping back, shaking his head to clear it. He crouched down, his gun in front of him.

He fired off a few rounds, but his position made it almost impossible to shoot while being covered. The other guy didn't hold back, though. It was a rookie move, really. He heard the unmistakable sound of the slide rocking back as the magazine and chamber emptied. Not giving the guy a chance to replace the magazine, Cole walked around the corner. The guy was down on one knee, one hand on his empty gun and the other reaching back, presumably for a new magazine.

"Police. Put your hands in the air. Now."

The guy put the gun down before getting up. He looked up into Cole's eyes, a sadistic smile on his face. It was Slay.

"Kick the gun over."

Slay did so, but the expression on his face told Cole he wasn't going to just surrender.

"Well, well. If it isn't the new partner. Thought you left," Slay said.

That meant he'd kept eyes on Cade. Fuck.

"I came back," he sneered.

Slay grinned at him. "For Cade? He's a good lay, isn't he?"

He wanted to strangle the asshole. Just knowing he'd had his hands on Cade made him want to kill him, but the fact he'd been watching Cade meant he was in danger.

"Turn around and put your hands up."

"You know, whatever he's told you, it's probably not true. He's an excellent liar. I should know. He got me good, now didn't he?" Slay cocked his head to the side. His face was split in a sardonic grin. "Do you even know how he got inside?"

"Put your hands up," Cole growled. He couldn't help the emotions filtering through his voice.

"You don't." Slay let out a low laugh. "The Italian called us himself. He set us up with Cade. There's no way he flipped to your side, no matter how dirty Cade is in bed. Which means, Cade must've been on his side all along."

Cole didn't care if he was playing right into Slay's hand because that asshole had no idea what was about to hit him. He put the safety back on his gun before placing it in the holster. He kicked Slay's gun to the side so he couldn't reach it and beckoned Slay closer.

"Come on," Cole growled.

"Oh, it's like that, huh?" Slay asked, his eyebrows rising before a smile found his lips.

"Yeah, it's like that."

From the nonchalant look on his face, Slay thought he had the upper hand. He might be bigger than Cole, but as long as Slay didn't pull a knife on him, he wasn't worried. He hated knives. They weren't for one-on-one fights. You brought a knife, you'd end up with as many cuts as your opponent. People got dirty in fights. No one was waiting around for you to land your punch.

Slay tried to circle him, but there was no way he was letting Slay get anywhere near the gun. He sidestepped, getting in Slay's way and halting him. He dodged the fist coming at his head with ease. Slay kept trying but not once did he land a punch. He wasn't even close.

Slay bared his teeth, a low growling sound pushing through his teeth. He'd probably figured out that Cole wasn't just some detective. He wasn't. He was a marine. A Black Raider. His best friend also happened to be a close quarters combat expert and with the amount of time they'd spent in the sandbox doing nothing, trying to beat each other up was a fun way to pass the time.

He was prepared when Slay charged at him, grabbing him around his middle to try and get enough of a hold on Cole to lift him up. He grabbed two handfuls of Slay's shirt, about to pull the guy back when Slay went for Cole's gun. He pushed Slay back just enough that he could knee him in the groin. Before Slay could do more than buckle over with Cole's gun in his hand, Cole kicked out, hitting Slay's kneecap. A crunch accompanied by a howl of pain filled the room.

The gun fell from Slay's fingers as he grasped his leg. Blood ran from his broken nose down onto the floor. Cole bent down, picking up the gun. He could end it right then. But he wanted more. He wanted the fucking satisfaction of taking down Slay. Safety still on, he threw the gun across the floor, away from them. The sound of the gun skidding over the floor made Slay jerk his gaze up.

Slay tried to push up off the ground, but Cole kicked him in the stomach. Slay went down but he managed to pull Cole with him. Cole landed on the ground, rolled, and threw his arm around Slay's neck, getting him into a choke hold. He could feel Slay trying to swallow against his skin. It may only take seconds to render someone unconscious with a blood choke, but his muscles were already quivering with the exertion. Pain radiated from his side as Slay managed to land a blow. He gasped but didn't let go, instead, he wrapped his legs around Slay's arms to keep him immobile. The big guy went slack in his hold. All he had to do was keep the pressure for a few minutes and Cade would be safe from Slay. Hell, all he had to do was get up and get his gun and put Slay down once and for all. His hold was slackening, though, the thought of Cade taking over his senses.

He let go, gasping for air to fill his lungs. Sweat burned his eyes. He groaned as he pushed away from Slay and rose to his feet. The bastard wouldn't be out for long. As soon as his blood flow returned, he'd be groggy, but awake.

The sound of footsteps had him jerking around, remembering too late he didn't have his gun. The man standing in the middle of the hallway wasn't carrying a gun either, though he didn't seem troubled by that fact. He was wearing a black suit, a black tie, and a white dress shirt. Cole could smell *agent* on the guy.

"Detective," the man said. "Here."

He pulled out a pair of handcuffs and threw them to Cole. He caught them and crouched down to roll Slay over on his stomach to cuff his hands together on his back. When he stood back up, the man was still there, watching him intently, like he was waiting for something.

A groan had Cole jerking his gaze down to Slay who was trying to roll over. Was the guy actually trying to worm his way toward his gun? Dumbass. He kicked Slay in the head, rendering him unconscious yet again and maybe even breaking something. It was a small consolation but at least this time, he'd be out for longer.

Cole jerked his eyes back on the suit. There was something about him. He seemed… familiar.

"Who are you?" Cole asked.

The man's lips twisted as if he was suppressing a smile.

"I'm the man who created you."

Definitely not what he was expecting. But what the hell was one more lunatic? That didn't mean he wasn't slowly moving toward his gun.

"The Black Raiders were mine."

Cole went rigid, staring with big eyes at the man. It couldn't be. There was no way. Yet, it made so much sense. Their team was black ops and truth be told, it did smell of CIA but they'd never complained. They'd gotten to be themselves and do what they did best; save people, blow things up, and run headfirst into fucked-up situations they barely survived. One of them hadn't. All because of some bureaucrat who'd never been a marine, who'd never understood marines don't leave their own behind. Ever. The decision to go directly against orders that day hadn't been hard at all. It was possibly the easiest decision he'd ever made. Derek may be dead but because of that decision, Franklin was still among them to cause havoc.

"This is not how I hoped this would go," the suit said.

Cole jerked his gaze back to him, coming out of his thoughts with a snap of his head. Then the suit's words registered.

"Cade…" Cole trailed off. Something clenched hard in his chest. His heart, he realized. Cade had brought it to life. He rubbed his fist over his chest as if that would help.

"He was supposed to make the deal so they'd just continue selling, and we could follow the trail."

"Selling what?" Cole asked, a growl in his voice.

The man raised a single dark eyebrow at him. "You know what."

Everything came back to that last fucking mission. Every-fucking-thing but Cade. Unless… He narrowed his eyes at the suit. "What did Cade do here?"

"He got us enough information to lock down this part of the business."

Cade worked for him? What. The. Hell?

"Where is he?" Cole hissed.

"In an ambulance. With Michael Hobbs."

Even though he felt like he couldn't breathe, he forced out the words. "Is he hurt?"

"No."

A gasp tore from his lips as his body bent forward, relief coursing through him. Cade was okay. He wasn't hurt. He wouldn't have been able to live with himself if something had happened to Cade even if Cade was the one who told him to go after Slay.

"I sent him to Slay because I knew something was amiss. He was trying too hard to hide that he's the president," the suit said.

"You've gotta be fucking kidding me," Cole spat.

That asshole was the president of the Destroyers?

He nodded. "I'll get the rest of the team working on this."

The suit was still in charge of the Black Raiders? The rest of them were FBI agents except for one who was AWOL. Wait. The rest of the team? He jerked his head up, staring at the man with something resembling hope.

"TL?"

Shaking his head, he said, "Still looking for him."

"It's hard to find someone who doesn't want to be found."

"Oh, I'll find him. Bastard's been hiding long enough," the suit said. "Do me a favor? Take good care of Cade. He deserves it and he's definitely going to need it now."

What the hell was that supposed to mean?

Cade

He hated hospitals. The plastic chair creaked under him as he shifted for god knew what time. Neil must've had an ambulance on stand-by because a minute after Cole had gone after Slay, the paramedics were making their way toward them. They had to have been Neil's men. They stepped over everyone else, making a beeline toward Mike and him.

They'd been able to resuscitate Mike in the ambulance and he was being operated on now, but they couldn't say whether he was going to make it or not. If it hadn't been for Neil talking in his ear, keeping him updated on Cole's whereabouts, he would've gone crazy with worry. Cole was alright, though. Neil had told him Cole had taken down Slay and was on his way to the hospital, so Cade wasn't surprised when he showed up five minutes later.

He was out of his chair and in Cole's arms the next second.

"I'm okay. I'm okay," he kept whispering into Cole's shoulder.

He had his fingers curled into the back of Cole's shirt, his eyes closed, his face pressed against him and even though the bigger man was squashing him, he finally felt like he could breathe again. He glanced up into the eyes of the man who made his heart race, the man who couldn't sleep unless he'd folded his clothes and washed the dishes, the man who just couldn't understand that you do not put Nutella in the fucking fridge, the man who… The man who set him on fucking fire whenever he glanced at him with that smoldering look in his dark eyes. And, he realized, the man he was very much in love with.

With love came pain. He just hoped he could make Cole love him enough that when the time came for pain, it wouldn't matter.

"I thought I was going to lose you," Cole said, his voice breaking on the words.

"Never."

Cole leaned his forehead against Cade's. They stood like that, just holding on to each other, breathing the same air, for a long time.

"I never thought…"

"Thought what?"

Cade glanced down, shaking his head. "Nothing."

"Babe. That wasn't nothing." Cole cupped his chin gently. "What were you saying?"

"I never thought I'd ever feel—"

A throat clearing cut him off.

"Detective?"

They turned to find a doctor standing next to them. The look on her face said it all. Mike was gone.

Cole

He managed to catch Cade as he crumbled, heaving for breath. He got him into a chair and made him put his head down between his knees. He rubbed his hand in circles on Cade's back.

"Easy, baby. Just breathe," Cole said.

He kept talking, doing his best to comfort Cade, knowing nothing he said or did would be enough. He couldn't bring Mike back. He knew exactly what Cade was going through and it wasn't about to get easier any time soon.

Lara showed up shortly after. When she looked at him with questioning eyes, he shook his head. Her face turned grim, but then she noticed Cade. She sat down next to him, taking one of his shaking hands. She must've been going out of her mind when all three of them went missing. He hated having put her through that, but Cade was alive, and he clung to that knowledge as he watched the man who'd come to mean so much to him over such a short period of time.

"I'm so sorry, Lara," Cade whispered.

Cade looked up at Lara with so much despair and hurt in his eyes, Cole found it hard to breathe. He never wanted Cade to hurt. He hated that there was nothing he could've done for Mike.

"I couldn't save him. I didn't save him."

"Don't."

He startled both Lara and Cade with the harsh tone of his voice.

"Don't you dare." He kneeled down in front of Cade and cupped his chin gently. "He chose it. He chose to save us. Don't take that from him."

Cade's lip trembled while he nodded as much as he could with Cole still holding his chin.

"Come here, baby," Cole whispered.

ANA NIGHT

Cade wrapped his arms around him and laid his head against Cole's chest. Cade was shaking and not just from crying. He cradled the back of Cade's head, squeezing his eyes closed for a moment as he gathered the strength he knew he'd need for Cade. He looked up, catching Lara's gaze.

"I'm taking him home. I don't give a shit about the statements," he said.

They could wait. Cade was more important.

"I'll hold Morris off for you," Lara said.

Her voice was strained, her eyes teary, but she held herself with the strength of a marine. Cade wasn't the only one who'd just lost someone close to him.

"Thank you," Cole said.

He stood, pulling Cade with him. Cade whimpered and buried his face in Cole's shirt. The pain and heartache coming off of Cade was choking Cole.

"You want me to go get Morgan? I don't want her to be alone. You guys can come stay with us," Cole said.

Lara nodded, tears filling her eyes.

"Chin up, marine."

She nodded, a solemn smile on her face. He would give anything to ease their pain. If he could, he would bring back Mike. He didn't possess that kind of powers or he would've used them nine years ago, but he could be there for them. He could support and comfort them to the best of his abilities.

He'd tried for so many years to not feel anything and yet, now that he most certainly did feel a hell of a lot, he wouldn't change it. He'd rather have Cade in his life and almost drown in the pain and sorrow than not have Cade at all. Because Cade made it all worth it. All the pain. All the heartache. So did Lara and Morgan. He didn't know what he would do if he lost any of them now. Even during this tragedy, his family was getting bigger.

Chapter Eighteen
Cole

CADE AND Morgan were finally out cold after they'd cried themselves to sleep. He was sitting in the chair, watching them as they lay on the couch, huddled up together, when Lara walked in. She went to press a kiss to Morgan's forehead, then she pulled up the quilt covering them both before turning around. Their eyes met.

Cole stood and walked silently into the kitchen, knowing Lara would follow. He offered her some coffee as he turned on the coffee maker. She nodded her head. He got out the milk from the fridge for her and grabbed two mugs from the shelf.

"When I sent someone to check on the address you gave me and they reported in a DB, I thought it was you," Lara said in a low, pained voice.

The despair was stark on her pale face. Even her eyes looked bruised. He swallowed hard, leaning back against the counter to stay upright. He was dead on his feet. Completely exhausted.

"Raymundo Esparza. He was dead when I got there. Mike—" He cleared his throat as it was suddenly very dry. "He was there, with two of the bikers. They were cleaning house."

Their eyes met. There was so much pain in hers. He didn't realize he'd done it before Lara fell into the arms he held open. Neither of them would ever admit that this moment happened. But right then, he just pulled Lara closer. He hadn't cried since… Fucking hell. Since Derek. But he wasn't crying for Mike. He was crying for everyone Mike had left behind. For Lara. For Cade and Morgan. The ones that meant so much to him.

Lara tightened her arms around him for a second before stepping back. They dried their tears in silence and when the coffee was done, he poured them both a cup. They moved into the living room, standing with their mugs in hand as they watched Morgan and Cade sleeping soundly. He felt Lara's gaze burning as he couldn't pry his eyes away from Cade. He looked so vulnerable.

"What are you thinking about?" Lara asked.

Cade is CIA. He didn't say that, though. A wry grin found its way on his face, though it felt forced. "Morgan thinks you need a girlfriend."

Lara snorted out a laugh, though her eyes were still watery.

"Of course, she does," Lara said and dried off a tear. "Never could keep anything from that girl."

Cole arched an eyebrow at her in question. Did she mean what he thought she meant? The smile spreading on her face made him believe so.

"I met someone. Her name's Marika," Lara said.

That got a real smile tugging at his lips. He wrapped an arm around her shoulders, pulling her close to press a kiss to the top of her head.

"She's gonna be so damned happy for you," he said.

"Thank you," she whispered. "I'm glad you came back."

"Me, too."

Lara leaned back in his arms, a tired smile gracing her lips as she watched him. Her usually serious and observant eyes were crinkling at the corners as they shone with mischief.

"Cade was driving the lot of us bonkers," she said.

"Are you implying I'm Cade's buffer?"

"At least you get something out of it," Lara said, wagging her eyebrows.

"Yeah. I do," he said, all traces of humor gone from his voice. He got so much more than sex out of it. He got Cade.

Lara smiled, her eyes glistening. She turned and walked to the armchair opposite the couch Morgan and Cade was passed out on. She sat down with a groan. Cole's eyes swept over the room, stopping at Cade's face. His features were soft in the light coming from the kitchen. His arm was still wrapped tightly around Morgan in his sleep. His heart skipped a beat then, reminding him Cade had melted the ice around it. He'd torn down every single wall Cole had put around it over the past nine years. He was happy but scared out of his mind. He'd never allowed someone to get that close before. Not like this.

A few hours later, Lara was asleep in the chair. Silence encompassed the house. He didn't know what to do with himself. It wasn't that he didn't feel at home because Cade had *become* his home. No, he was restless. His body was primed and ready for attack. There was nothing and no one to attack. When he'd been a marine, there was always someone they could go after. Some bastard to put deep into the ground.

A softly spoken, "Hey," had him turning around, finding Cade leaning against the doorframe, a hesitant smile on his lips. His hair stood on end. Cole was surprised he hadn't heard him. Usually, when Cade just woke, he either fell over something or walked into a few things.

"Hey," he said.

"Um…" Cade looked nervous, nibbling on his bottom lip and averting his eyes.

Cole froze for a second, then marched right up to Cade who jerked his eyes up to meet his. He wrapped his arms around Cade who sagged against him immediately. He pulled Cade close, taking a deep breath and filling his nose with the smell of Cade like a starved man.

"You're never going undercover again."

Cade looked up at him with startling blue eyes. "I can live with that."

"Good."

Their lips met in a gentle kiss. All he wanted right then was to wrap himself around Cade and never let anyone close enough to hurt him. Never let go. Cade broke the kiss, his arms tight around Cole as he leaned his forehead against Cole's chest.

"I know who's behind Mary and Amelia's murders," Cade murmured into Cole's shirt.

Cole pulled back, holding Cade at arm's length to look at him. "What do you mean?"

"I heard a recording of a phone call between Elias Tully and the State's Attorney. He's the one who ordered Mary's murder. I'm sure he did the same with Amelia," Cade said.

"That doesn't make sense," Cole said.

"Yeah. I know. Who would've thought—"

"No. What I mean is Mike said he went to stop Tully because he started killing and drawing attention to them."

Cade leaned back in his arms, biting his lip. His eyes seemed unseeing for a moment and then he shook his head, his blond curls bouncing. He looked up, meeting Cole's gaze.

"You're right. That does not make sense," Cade said

Cole raised a brow. "Makes even less sense than Slay being the president of the Destroyers."

Cade snorted, shaking his head.

"He may have been the president, but he wasn't the head of the operation," Cade said. "Not even close."

"We'll get them," Cole said and pressed a kiss to Cade's temple. He pulled Cade close, hugging him tightly while he decided he wasn't ever gonna let Cade go.

"I know," Cade said.

They stood there for a few minutes, clinging to each other until Cade startled and pulled away. His eyes were huge when they caught Cole.

"Shit. We didn't even give our statements. Morris is gonna kill me."

Before Cade could run off and fall over himself in the process, Cole grabbed him by the shoulders to keep him in place.

"No worries. I called Morris and explained to him. I told him about Mike being the mole. We'll give our statements." He looked down at his watch. "Later today. We've got eight hours."

Cade's features softened as he relaxed into Cole's arms. Cade rose up on his toes and pressed his lips gently against Cole's. He sighed against Cade's lips.

Cade pulled back, looking up at him skeptically. "Let's go get some sleep, then. You haven't gotten any yet, have you?"

Of course, Cade knew.

"No."

Cade took his hand, guiding him up the stairs and into their bedroom. Into their bed. He didn't even care to pretend he didn't see Cade and his things as his. There was no point. He was as much Cade's as he was Cole's. When Cade wrapped himself around him, he couldn't help but feel at home.

Cade

It'd been three days since hell on earth. He still couldn't wrap his head around Mike's death. There were still things that didn't make sense. Questions with no answers. He needed those answers desperately and it was then he found himself walking into Glitter. It hadn't taken him long to pick the lock on the back door. He actually felt proud of that. He walked into the bar area, stopping just next to the bar. His eyes scanned over the spacious room. The place had potential.

The bar was fully stocked so he helped himself to a drink. He ran his gaze over the bottles, settling on Jack Daniels. Whiskey it was. He picked up the glass and walked to the sitting area. He sat down in one of the booths, twirling the liquid around in the glass while he waited. It didn't take more than five minutes and four sips of whiskey.

"Is it clear?" Cade asked.

Neil scooted into the seat across from him, a serious look on his face. Cade tilted his head a bit to the side, taking in Neil's ragged looks.

"Yes. There's nothing there to tie Marco to us," Neil said.

"Good. Should I tell him or…?"

"I'll handle it," Neil snapped.

Wow, touchy much? Maybe that was why he looked like he'd just been mugged and rolled in shit. Not that he was dirty, it was just the overall vibe he gave off. Neil and Marco. Those two had a hell of a history and even if Cade didn't know the first thing about it, one thing was for certain; they felt strongly for each other. Someday, Cade was going to find out exactly what their story was but not now. He took a big sip of whiskey, knowing this was the part of their conversation where he'd need it.

"What was in the basement?" Cade asked.

He knew without a doubt Neil's guys had gone through every inch of Glitter and the look in Neil's eyes made him prepare for the worst.

"Humans."

Cade blanched. That... didn't make sense. "Humans? As in...?"

"Human trafficking," Neil said.

"Bloody fucking hell."

He'd known for a while the Destroyers were dealing in some fucked up shit, but human trafficking? He'd never expected it to be that. Prostitution, yes. Drugs, yes. Guns, definitely. Human trafficking? Not so much.

He knew Mike's life was a small price to pay compared to putting a dent in a trafficking ring but that didn't mean it hurt any less. But at least those people the Destroyer kept in the basement were safe now.

"Where are we with the State's Attorney?" Cade asked, trying to get his mind focused on something else.

"It'll be taken care of," Neil said.

Yeah. With a bullet, most likely. With things like that, he didn't ask questions. Plausible deniability and all.

He leaned forward, placing his elbows on the table between them. "Chris Henway. I wanna know his role in all this."

Neil watched him with his hard, grey eyes. "Henway provided the Destroyers with merchandise."

"You mean he sold people to the trafficking ring?"

"Yes. Foster kids mostly. The reason it's taken so long to find them is because they almost never take anyone underage, not unless they're people who won't be missed. Junkies. Junkies' kids. Foster kids who are just troubled enough it's wouldn't be a surprise if they ran away."

"And let me guess, they know how to clean up after themselves as well," Cade said.

"Exactly."

Cade shook his head. Hell, this case kept getting more and more complicated. There were so many aspects of it, so many people playing their part, it was almost overwhelming. But he'd get to the bottom of it. No matter what it took.

"I think you should look into Judge Abbott," Cade said.

The asshole set up his son-in-law, there was no doubt about that. But he also knew things they could use. If Abbott talked, he'd get a lesser sentence. He was a judge, so he knew how plea deals worked. Well, that was if Neil went the legal way. With Neil, you never knew.

"I already am," Neil said.

"What about the leak? I don't think that was Mike." Well, mostly he just didn't *want* to believe it.

"That's not my problem."

"Right."

Cade snorted and rolled his eyes at Neil who kept a straight face as he watched Cade. He shook his head and dug out the flash drive from his jean pocket and held it out to Neil. He didn't let go of it when Neil grabbed it, holding it between them as he met Neil's gaze head-on.

"What happened with Cole and Slay? What happened with you?"

Neil narrowed his eyes at him. He let go of the flash drive, sitting back in his seat and cocking his head to the side. His eyes searched Cade's face and though it was impossible to tell what he was thinking, Cade knew something happened and he wanted to know what, even if it took challenging his boss.

"Cole took down Slay and then we had a nice little chat," Neil said.

"Why?"

"That's classified."

"Of course, it is."

Wasn't it always?

Neil held out his hand, palm up. Cade knew he'd already gotten more out of the man than he probably ever would on the subject, so he dropped the flash drive into Neil's hand. Neil stuffed it into an inner pocket of his jacket and stood, evidently deeming their conversation over with. Cade stood as well, grabbing his glass and raising it to his lips. He downed what was left, wincing at the burn but wholly welcoming it. He definitely needed it.

The sound of the door opening made him turn toward it. Neil stopped in the doorway, turning slightly, his eyes meeting Cade's. There was something almost sentimental hidden in those dark eyes.

"You may want to ask your boyfriend about his last mission for the Marine Corps."

Cole

The house was eerily quiet. Lara and Morgan went home earlier that day after they'd decided three days of camping out in the guest bedroom was enough. Cade was grieving. So was Lara, but she still managed to catch onto the fact something was bothering Cole. Those three words still rang in his head. *Cade is CIA.* He could ask him about it but there were things he didn't need to know, and if he was being honest with himself; things he didn't *want* to know.

He shifted on the couch. He didn't really mind Cade being CIA. At least they were on the same side. Cade worked for the people Cole once worked for. He couldn't fault Cade for that. Even if he'd left that job in a blaze of fire and—thanks to Mad Dog—a lot of explosions. No. If anything, he wanted to protect Cade. Wanted to make sure Cade would always have someone covering his six. Unlike how his team was left out in the cold.

"You ever going to tell me what happened?" Cade asked.

He froze. He couldn't tell Cade about the discharge, about the last mission. Cade wouldn't understand why. He turned slowly toward Cade who was looking down at him with a strange expression on his face.

"What happened?" Cole repeated, trying to sound like he didn't understand. He didn't succeed.

"With Slay." Cade sat down next to him on the couch, their knees touching. "He's a manipulative bastard and, you know, I just thought maybe he got to you."

"He did." Cole looked up, gentle eyes meeting his. "Which is why I thoroughly enjoyed kicking him in the face."

Cade stared at him for a second, his mouth hanging open. Then he smiled. A big smile that had his eyes crinkling and his damned dimple showing.

"You did that?"

Cole couldn't help himself. He leaned down, pressing his lips to that dimple, making Cade giggle like a schoolgirl. Making Cade laugh was the best fucking feeling in the world. Cade wound a hand into Cole's hair, keeping him from leaning too far back. He grinned as he pressed a kiss to Cade's lips.

"You're awesome," Cade said against his lips.

"Come here," he said, pulling on Cade's shirt.

Cade slung his leg over him, putting himself in Cole's lap. He cupped Cade's chin in his hands and brought him down for a sweet kiss. Cade leaned his forehead against Cole's, sighing heavily.

"I missed you," Cade whispered.

Air eluded him. His voice was breathy at best when he managed to speak. "It's only been a few days."

"A few days too many," Cade said.

He couldn't get himself to admit it out loud because it would feel too real if he did, but he'd missed Cade like crazy. He wasn't sure he could function right without him anymore. It was a fucking scary thought to have.

"We've got some catching up to do then," Cole said.

Cade's mouth came crashing down over his and he gladly welcomed it. He lost himself in Cade, lost himself in that amazing feeling he got every time he made Cade feel good. He didn't doubt for even a second that he'd made the right choice in being with Cade. No matter what, he was there to stay. Right by Cade's side.

Cade

He felt the loss so deep inside him, he thought he might break. He didn't hear anything they said. It was all more or less a blur. Flowers. People dressed in black. People in uniforms. The flag draped over the casket.

Cole was by his side during the whole ceremony, not saying a word, just offering his silent support. Cole hadn't known Mike, but in the end, had Cade? He hated that. He hated that even now he doubted Mike when he'd sacrificed himself for them.

Cole had convinced Captain Morris to give Mike a funeral with full honors. They hadn't disclosed Mike's involvement with the Destroyers, partly because they didn't know much about it and also because, as Cole said, if it wasn't for Mike, they could've both been dead. He took the bullets meant for them.

A hand squeezing his shoulder brought him back to reality. He blinked, trying to clear his vision. Morgan was speaking. She stood in front of them all and spoke as the family representative.

"Mike wasn't just my mom's partner; he was family. He'll always be family," Morgan said. She took a deep breath before continuing. "Mike stayed with us for a while when he was recovering from a gunshot wound not too long ago. I loved every second of it. Even when he'd take twice as much time in the bathroom than me and mom combined. Even when he tried to do the laundry and turned my favorite sweater pink. I… He was there for me, whenever I needed him. Nothing would stop him from being there for the people in his life. He gave one hundred percent of himself every time. Mike was a gentle soul. He hated his job as much as he loved it because he wanted to make a difference, but it pained him to see the things he did when he was working. But he never gave up. He never quit. Because of Mike, I still have Cade in my life." Her tears started falling then, her voice becoming hoarse. "Though I'd rather have both of them, I'm eternally grateful for Mike's sacrifice and I know, without a doubt, that if Mike got the chance to do it over, he would still have saved Cade no matter what happened to him, because that's the kind of man Mike was. He was a hero. He was my hero."

Morgan stepped back and before she could break down, Cade was right beside her, drawing her into his arms. Soon, Lara's arms surrounded both of them. They stood there for a moment, drawing strength from each other and sharing their pain.

Lara released them and stepped back, raising a hand to run her fingers through Morgan's hair. "He would've loved that, baby girl," she said.

Morgan dried off her nose in the sleeve of her dress.

"He would've hated it," she said, half laughing, half crying.

That brought the tiniest of smiles to Cade's face.

"Yeah, he would have. But he would've been so proud of you," Cade said.

Morgan raised her watery eyes to meet his, a smile gracing her lips. She took his hand as she bobbed her head. Mike would've hated the whole ceremony, but it didn't make it feel wrong to have it. Not at all.

Cade sat back down next to Cole who took his hand, squeezing it gently. Cade turned, meeting Cole's eyes. Green pools of understanding and something soft, something that warmed Cade's heart, was what glanced back at him. He'd leaned on Cole so much the past week he feared he would chase him off, but Cole was still right there. He was still by his side and if the determined look in his eyes were anything to go by, Cole wasn't going anywhere.

The rest of the ceremony passed in a blur. More speeches. The three-volley salute. Bagpipes playing—Mike would've complained loudly about that. The final radio call, and then it was time. He stood, his legs shaking beneath him. He squeezed his eyes shut, unable to pull in the air he needed.

A hand on the small of his back made him draw in a deep breath and open his eyes. He glanced over his shoulder. Cole's gaze was steady, his posture strong as he held up Cade. Cole stood so no one could see his gesture, but Cade didn't care, not when he had Cole by his side.

He carried the casket along with Lara, Brent, Mike's best friend from college, and two cops he'd worked closely with when he'd been on the beat. Tears streamed down Cade's cheeks the whole time and though he hadn't seen Lara cry yet, he knew she was worse off than him. She just hid it better. Once the honor guards folded the flag, it was presented to Morgan by an honor guard kneeling down in front of her. Tears streamed down her face as she took it, pressing it tightly against her chest.

When the whole thing was more or less over and he'd laid the ugliest flowers he could find on the casket because he knew Mike would've loved it, he stood to the side, his eyes firmly on the casket. Mike was in there. Mike was dead. The proof of that was staring right back at him and it was hard to fight evidence like that. His mind still kept trying; making him see Mike everywhere. Making him hear Mike's voice. The hope it formed, however brief it was, hurt so much.

"Cade, right?"

He turned to find a young man there, his blond hair in disarray and his brown eyes looking haunted. He hadn't even noticed the kid. For all he knew, the kid could've been standing there for as long as he had.

"Yeah."

The young man glanced around fleetingly before offering his hand. "I'm Aidan."

Cade didn't recognize him or his name. He didn't look much older than twenty. Why was this kid at Mike's funeral? He didn't really fit in.

"What can I do for you?"

The silence stretched out before the kid finally opened his mouth, his words shocking Cade.

"I'm the reason Mike's dead," Aidan said, his voice breaking over the last word.

"What do you mean?"

"He wouldn't have gotten involved with them if it wasn't for me. I should've known. I should've stopped him." Aidan heaved in a breath before continuing. "When he said he'd taken care of it… I should have known."

"Taken care of what?" Cade asked.

Pain and heartache met him in the disguise of brown eyes.

"Ella and Edward Olivier were my foster parents."

Holy hell. He was the State's Attorney's kid?

"You need to come with me," Cade said. He grabbed Aidan by the arm, pulling him along. The kid didn't struggle against his grip, he just followed quietly.

Morgan's gaze caught his across the line of chairs. Her eyes shot to the kid and then back to Cade, her brows furrowed in confusion. Cade mouthed the words, "Mike. Station. Now," and because he'd taught Morgan to read lips a few years back, she understood him. She bobbed her head and mouthed a word back, "Justice." Cade dipped his chin, pulling Aidan with him while he watched Morgan go to her mother out of the corner of his eye.

Luckily, Cole was talking with the captain just by the road. Once he reached them, he only stopped for a second in front of them to say, "We need to get to the station. Now."

Neither of them said anything or asked questions as Cade walked Aidan to Cole's car and put him in the backseat. When Cole got into the car, his eyes sought out Cade's. He took a deep breath, allowing himself to be lost in the green depths of Cole's eyes if only for a moment. Cole reached over, covering Cade's hand and squeezing it before he started the car and pulled out of the parking space.

Twenty minutes later Cade was seated across from Aidan in the interrogation room. Cade's palms were sweaty, his heart trying to burst through his chest. The only thing keeping him calm and somewhat sane was Cole standing behind him, offering his silent support.

"Tell us what happened, Aidan," Cade said.

The kid was staring at his hands on the table. They were shaking.

"Aidan?"

The kid jerked, his eyes shooting up to meet Cade's. He swallowed and cleared his throat. Cade bit his lip and tried not to, but in the end, he reached across the table and took Aidan's shaking hands in his own. Aidan's eyes watered, but it seemed to do the trick because words started tumbling out of him.

"I got placed in foster care with the Olivier's when I was sixteen. Ella was... she became like a mom to me, but Edward just always seemed cold and distant. Everything was fine though. They even paid for my tuition. If I just hadn't come home that day, Mike might still be alive."

"What happened?"

"I came home two days before I was supposed to. I don't remember why, but we were let go early, and I wanted to surprise Ella. She would've liked that. I carpooled with two other students and they dropped me off at home. There were a few cars in the driveway, so I figured Edward was having some meeting or something. I tried to be quiet because he hated being interrupted and especially when he was working.

"I walked inside, heading for my room upstairs but to get to the staircase I had to walk past the living room. Before I got there, I heard voices. Yelling. Something made me stop. Made me listen. I should've kept walking. I should've..."

"It's okay. You can tell me. I'll keep you safe. I promise," Cade said.

Aidan swallowed and bobbed his head.

"I recognized Edward's voice and there were two others I didn't recognize. I pulled out my phone because it sounded like they were threatening Edward. I never got to use it. I just froze. Their words spinning in my head. Over and over in my head. I couldn't make sense of it at first."

"What did you hear, Aidan?"

"It was Edward. He said… He was angry. He was angry because he'd told them not to take kids, but they had."

"Take kids?" Cade asked, a feeling of dread slithering up his spine. Even though he couldn't see him, he felt Cole freeze behind him.

"Edward told the bikers to take me. To *take care of it*."

"Bikers?"

"Yeah. The one who held me was called Slay," Aidan said, shuddering. "I'll never forget that. Or him."

Cade glanced over his shoulder, catching Cole's gaze. They just got one more thing to charge Slay with. Kidnapping.

He turned back to Aidan. "You don't think Ella has anything to do with it?"

Aidan shook his head vigorously.

"I know she doesn't. Edward said he hated me because he had to go break her heart and tell her I ran away. Besides, she's the kindest woman I've ever met. She wouldn't hurt anyone."

Cade had met Ella once and he leaned toward agreeing with the kid, but he also knew better than most just how much appearances could deceive. They'd look into it but right then their focus was solely on Edward and Mike. How did Mike fit into all this? How did Aidan come to mean so much to Mike that he'd freely given his life for the kid?

"How did you meet Mike?" Cade asked, clearing his throat but unable to chase away the feelings clogging it up.

"I was terrified. I didn't know where they were taking me or what they were going to do with me. If they were going to kill me. Make me dig my own grave. Sell me. Turns out, selling me was exactly what they did.

"We drove to this place. It was loud. Music playing. I think Mike said it was a club. They dragged me from the car and inside. That's where I met Mike. There was something in his eyes… I knew, if I was going to survive, he would be my best shot. Then he bought me."

Cade stared at him with his mouth hanging open for a moment before he got himself under control. He'd figured this part would be hard to hear but those words almost broke him right then. A hand landed on his shoulder and he breathed a sigh of relief. He glanced up, meeting Cole's eyes for a moment, and just knowing Cole was there for him was enough for him to get through the rest of the interview.

"I thought he was going to hurt me," Aidan said, shaking his head. "He took me to an apartment, locked the door and led me into the living room. There wasn't much in there. An old couch, a table, some newspapers, and takeout boxes. He sat me down on the couch, and I was too afraid to even consider moving when he walked into the kitchen. He came back with two mugs. Coffee for him and hot chocolate for me. He just pushed the mug into my hands and told me to drink. I didn't think. I just did it. I burned my tongue. Then Mike wrapped me in a blanket and told me he was a cop. He was undercover at that club. That was almost a year ago. I can't believe he's gone and it's all my fault."

"It's not your fault. He didn't die because of you. He chose to save you," Cade said.

Aidan dropped his head forward, his shoulders sagging, and Cade suspected that was a tear he saw glinting in the corner of Aidan's eye.

"It was more than that. He might've saved me but, in the end, he was all I had left," Aidan whispered.

Cade stood, walked around the table and laid a hand on Aidan's shoulder. Aidan glanced up at him with those vulnerable eyes of his. He looked utterly lost. This young man, this broken kid, was what Mike chose in the end.

"Not anymore, kid. You've got us now."

Cade

He splashed water on his face before leaning on the sink, breathing heavily. Mike's voice rang clear in his mind. *"Protect him. You have to protect him."* Now he knew what Mike meant. *Who* he'd meant. Hell, Mike had practically died for the kid. There was no way in hell he'd let anything happen to Aidan.

Protect him.

"I promise, Mikey," he whispered. "I promise."

He looked up, catching his own eyes in the mirror. He knew what he needed to do. He knew what he had to do. He pushed away from the sink, determination filling him. Cole stood waiting for him in the hallway. He glanced up the second he heard the door open, his eyes catching Cade's. In those eyes were a question. Cade nodded to let Cole know he was okay and tried for a smile.

"Morris is on the phone with the marshals to get the kid into the Witness Protection Program," Cole said.

"Good. We need to keep him safe."

Cole nodded. That kid was pretty much all he had left of Mike and Cole seemed to have realized that as well. His eyes softened as he watched Cade.

"Aidan said Mike was undercover," Cole said.

"But not for us," Cade finished.

"Any ideas? Was he lying to the kid?"

"I don't see any reason for him to lie to Aidan. Not unless he really was there to buy kids. Which doesn't make sense, since he only bought Aidan to save him."

"So, he was undercover, but we don't know for whom," Cole said, frowning.

"I doubt they'll come forward and be like 'Hey, we're the ones who recruited one of your detectives without telling you about it.'"

"If they did, I'd shoot them to bits," Morris said, joining them in the hallway. His face was red and his words clipped. His expression was downright murderous.

"We need to take down the State's Attorney while we still can," Cade said.

Morris shook his head. "All we've got is a shaky eyewitness, Lawson. It won't hold up in court."

"That's not all we've got."

He got out his phone, finding the file he was looking for and pressed play.

"This is your mess, Tully. Clean it up or I'll be sending someone to make sure you can't make a mess ever again."

"I'll take care of it. Please don't send anyone."

"Get it done."

He'd copied everything from the flash drive before returning it to Neil and right then, he was bloody glad he'd learned early on to always have a plan B.

"It's on a computer at the Destroyers' compound. It's legal evidence. We can use it."

"I've got something as well," Cole said, turning on his heels and walking toward the squad room. He followed with Morris right on his heels. Cole didn't stop until he reached his desk. He pulled out one of the drawers and took out a small, leather-bound notebook.

"What's that?" Morris asked.

"It's a ledger Mary Coulson stole from Elias Tully. Mike told me it's why he killed her. I looked through it when I found it hidden in Mary and Amelia's apartment."

Cole opened the book and turned it so they could see. The thing wasn't even in code but then again, Elias Tully wasn't the smartest guy. Cade's eyes scanned the pages, freezing at that one name.

He hated seeing Mike's name there, next to all those scumbag criminals. But there was nothing he could do about it. Mike made his choice, and if Cade was being honest, it seemed as if Mike was content with his choice in the end. With a heavy heart, he took the book and looked through the pages with Morris watching over his shoulder.

"Jackpot," Cade said.

Morris grabbed the ledger out of his hand, a triumphant sound escaping him.

"Let's go nail this sucker," Morris said.

Before they'd even left the building, Morris had a warrant for Edward Olivier's arrest. Cade followed Cole from the elevator to his car. Halfway there, Cole glanced over his shoulder, stopping to wait until Cade caught up. Once he did, he raised an eyebrow at his partner.

"You realize it would be faster to just walk, right?" Cade asked.

Cole rolled his eyes and turned around. He started walking again and Cade followed, lengthening his strides to catch up again.

"It's not even half a mile," Cade said.

Cole was at his door when Cade reached the other side of the car. Cole opened his door but didn't get in. Instead, he leaned his arm on it and ran his gaze over Cade.

"Are you planning on walking him from there to a jail cell?" Cole asked.

Cade opened his mouth but before he could answer, Cole asked, "Are you trying to distract me or yourself?"

Cade cursed under his breath, opened the car door and got in. They remained quiet as Cole drove out of the parking garage. Cade couldn't even get himself to turn on the radio. Music and singing right then just didn't seem right.

"You're afraid it's not real. That it's not enough to sentence him," Cole said, glancing at Cade out of the corner of his eye.

Cade closed his eyes and dropped his head back against the headrest, breathing out heavily. He wasn't afraid. He was fucking terrified. A man like

Olivier had contacts and if they didn't make it in time… There would be no one left to arrest.

Warmth enveloped his hand. Cole squeezed his fingers, making him crack open an eye to look at him. What he saw had him breathless. Cole was smiling. A smile that lit up his whole face and made his eyes spark. Happiness spread through him when Cole raised their joined hands and pressed a kiss to Cade's knuckles.

"We're together in this, okay?" Cole said. "I'll be right by your side all the way."

Cade drew in a deep breath, trying to settle his galloping heart. With Cole looking at him the way he was right then, there was no chance of that happening. Cole squeezed his hand.

"All the way, baby," Cole said.

It took him a second to realize that they weren't moving. He glanced over his shoulder. They were right in front of the SunTrust Building and the entrance to the State's Attorney's office. With a last gaze into Cole's eyes, Cade turned and opened his door. He stepped out just as Morris' car and two cruisers pulled up. His gaze swung from them to Cole, who was biting his lip to hide a smile.

They'd left after Morris. Of that he was sure and none of them used their lights. He hadn't even noticed but Cole must've driven like a maniac to get there first, or maybe he knew of a shortcut Cade hadn't found during the nine years he'd lived in Baltimore. He wagged a finger at Cole.

"Gunner. I get it now," he said. "How you haven't gotten a speeding ticket yet is beyond me."

Cole turned his head to the side, his eyes narrowing on Cade. "You checked?"

He felt his cheeks heat up. "Maybe."

Morris jogged toward them, only halting long enough to yell at them. "Stop talking and start moving, you dimwits."

Cade grinned up at Cole. "I'm starting to think he likes us."

The State's Attorney's office was buzzing with activity, people running all over the place. It was a bloody miracle no one crashed into each other. Cade had called ahead to one of the Assistant State's Attorney's he knew, to make sure Olivier was still there. The same ASA met them a few feet from Olivier's office. His face was set in a stern expression. The man was pissed, to say the least.

"Tony," Cade said, shaking his hand.

The man's hair was starting to become more salt and pepper than brown. It suited him.

"Cade," Tony said. "Olivier was about to leave a minute ago, but Miranda intervened. They're in there."

He motioned toward Olivier's office. Cade laid a hand on Tony's shoulder, squeezing gently. "Thank you, Tony."

Tony dipped his chin in acknowledgment. Cade turned and walked with Morris, Cole, and the uniforms toward the office. His heart was beating wildly in his chest, but he didn't let it show. Morris was first at the door which he burst right through. The uniforms stayed outside the office as Cole and Cade joined Morris inside.

Olivier was seated behind his desk, his eyes jerking toward them from the cleavage of the woman leaned back against his desk. Miranda, Tony's assistant, stood and turned around. Her gaze met Cade's and a grateful smile grazed her lips.

"Thank you, Miranda," Cade said.

She walked around the desk, glaring over her shoulder at Olivier. Then she met Cade's gaze and grinned, offering him a sloppy salute. "Anytime, detective."

Cade winked at her. Tony should give the girl a raise. She must've known what Olivier was getting arrested for but she'd obviously tackled it like a pro. Cade also knew Tony wouldn't have let her anywhere near Olivier so that meant she'd done it all on her own. She was his kind of girl, that was for sure.

"What the hell is this, Morris?" Olivier growled.

Cade swung his gaze back to Olivier who was still seated in his chair, his brows slanted in disapproval.

"One of my detectives was buried today," Morris said, moving closer until he stood in front of Olivier. "I'm sure you know him."

Olivier was catching on to something being wrong.

"I know most of your detectives, captain," Olivier said, glaring at Morris. "It's a part of the job."

"Is it also a part of the job to sanction murders? Selling your foster kid?" Cole asked.

Olivier froze, staring at Cole with wide eyes as his mouth hung open. Morris nodded to Cade and he stepped forward, pulling out his cuffs.

"His name was Michael Hobbs. He died because of you," Cade said. "Edward Olivier. You're under arrest for aiding and abetting in murder, human trafficking, and I'm betting, a whole lot of other fucked-up things we'll soon unearth."

That broke Olivier out of his trance. He rose from his seat, grabbing the edge of his desk as he glared daggers at Morris. His knuckles turned white as waves of anger wafted off of him.

"You can't do this," Olivier raged.

Morris chuckled and held up the warrant, waving it in Olivier's face. "Seems we can."

"Put your hands behind your head and turn around," Cade said.

Olivier was smart enough to not resist arrest. After all, he was a prosecutor. Though Cade would've enjoyed taking Olivier to the ground if he'd tried running, he instead took immense joy in clamping the cuffs onto Olivier's wrists and reading him his rights.

"I hope you like jumpsuits and prepackaged food," Cade said.

He pushed Olivier out of the door and allowed the uniforms to take over. He glanced around the room, reveling in the shrewd looks Olivier was getting. He damned well deserved that. Just as Callie's father had. He understood now more than ever. For a man like Olivier, a man like Callie's father, their honor and integrity meant more to them than anything else and like Callie had done, they'd now stripped Olivier of that as well.

He felt Cole step up behind him, his presence warming Cade from the inside out. He started after Olivier, his eyes searching the room until his gaze connected with Tony's. His eyes were grey pools of fire and gratitude. Tony dipped his chin and Cade's lips twisted into a wry smile as he passed Tony.

As he walked out of the building, trailing after Olivier, his eyes caught the steady blue gaze of a man across the street, leaned against a lamppost with a bag slung over his shoulder. The guy grinned and winked at him. It was a close call. There was no telling when Neil's guy would've 'taken care' of the State's Attorney.

Cade had no idea what the future would bring or what horrors from his past might emerge. He just knew he'd be facing it with Cole by his side, and that was all that mattered to him. It was all he needed.

He turned his head, catching Cole's emerald eyes. Cole's smile warmed him from the inside out. In no other relationship of his did he ever experience anything like that. Just making Cole smile was worth anything they might endure. Any pain. Any anguish.

Yeah.

Cole was all he needed.

ANA NIGHT is a writer of suspenseful gay romance. She's an avid reader who has loved the written word since she discovered it. When she was a kid, she never went anywhere without a notebook. She was always writing, be it in the backseat of the car, between classes in school, or by the pool on vacations. When she's not writing, you can find her with her nose buried in a book, singing and dancing, watching her favorite TV shows, or creating book covers.

Ana lives in Denmark where she spends most of her time running from her ninja kitty—that one goes for the ankles—and getting lost in the woods with her horse.

Website: www.ananight.com
Email: ana.night@outlook.com
Newsletter: www.eepurl.com/dBnBw1
Instagram: www.instagram.com/authorananight
Facebook: www.facebook.com/authorananight
Twitter: @authorananight

Made in the USA
Monee, IL
03 July 2021